DARK BACK OF TIME

 V

JAVIER MARÍAS

Dark Back of Time

Translated by Esther Allen

Chatto & Windus
and
VINTAGE
LONDON

Published by Chatto & Windus 2003

Vintage 2004

2 4 6 8 10 9 7 5 3 1

First published in Great Britain in 2003 by
Chatto & Windus
Eandom House, 20 Vauxhall Bridge Road,
London SW1V 2SA

Random House Australia (Pty) Limited
20 Alfred Street, Milsons Point, Sydney,
New South Wales 2061, Australia

Random House New Zealand Limited
18 Poland Road, Glenfield,
Auckland 10, New Zealand

Random House South Africa (Pty) Limited
Endulini, 5A Jubilee Road, Parktown 2193, South Africa

The Random House Group Limited Reg. No. 954009
www.randomhouse.co.uk

A CIP catalogue record for this book is available from the British Library

ISBN 0701169958 hardback
ISBN 0099287463 paperback

For my mother Lolita
who knew me well,
in memoriam;
and for my brother Julianín
who never knew me,
and therefore *sine memoria*

I believe I've still never mistaken fiction for reality, though I have mixed them together more than once, as everyone does, not only novelists or writers but everyone who has recounted anything since the time we know began, and no one in that known time has done anything but tell and tell, or prepare and ponder a tale, or plot one. Anyone can relate an anecdote about something that happened, and the simple fact of saying it already distorts and twists it, language can't reproduce events and shouldn't attempt to, and that, I imagine, is why during some trials—the trials in movies, anyway, the ones I know best—the implicated parties are asked to perform a material or physical reconstruction of what happened, repeating the gestures, the movements, the envenomed steps they took, the way they thrust the knife to become the accused; they're asked to simulate seizing the weapon once again and delivering the blow to someone who, because of it, ceased to be and is no more, or rather to empty air, because it isn't enough for them to say it, to tell the story impassively and as precisely as possible, it must be seen, and an imitation, a representation or staging of it is required, though now without the knife in hand and without the body—sack of flour, sack of flesh—to drive it into, this time in cool detachment and without racking up another crime or adding another victim to the list, but only as pretense and memory, because what they can never reproduce is the time gone by

7

or lost, nor can they revive the dead who are lost within that time and gone.

This indicates an ultimate mistrust of words, among other reasons because words—even when spoken, even at their crudest—are in and of themselves metaphorical and therefore imprecise, and cannot be imagined without ornament, though it is often involuntary; there is ornament in even the most arid exposition and frequently in interjections and insults as well. All anyone has to do is introduce an "as if" into the story, or not even that, all you need to do is use a simile, comparison or figure of speech ("he was acting like a jerk," "she flew into a rage"—the kind of colloquial expression that belongs to the language more than to the speaker who chooses it, that's all it takes) and fiction creeps into the narration of what happened, altering or falsifying it. The time-honored aspiration of any chronicler or survivor—to tell what happened, give an account of what took place, leave a record of events and crimes and exploits—is, in fact, a mere illusion or chimera, or, rather, the phrase and concept themselves are already metaphorical and partake of fiction. "To tell what happened" is inconceivable and futile, or possible only as invention. The idea of testimony is also futile and there has never been a witness who could truly fulfil his duty. Anyway, you always forget far too many moments and hours and days and months and years, and the scar on a thigh that I saw and kissed every day for years during its known and lost time. You forget whole years, and not necessarily the least important ones.

Yet in these pages I'm going to place myself on the side of those who have sometimes claimed to be telling what really happened or pretended to succeed in doing so, I'm going to tell what happened, or was ascertained, or simply known— what happened in my experience or in my fabulation or to my knowledge—or perhaps all of it is only consciousness that never ceases—as a result of the composition and circulation of a novel, a work of fiction. It certainly isn't anything momentous, nor is it serious yet, or pressing, though it may be entertaining to the curious reader who is willing, on principle, to accompany me; and for me it has the diversion of risk, the risk of narrating something for no reason and in almost no order, without making an outline or trying to be coherent, as if I were telling it in that fickle and unpredictable voice we all know, the voice of time when it has not yet gone by or been lost and perhaps for that reason is not even time; perhaps time is only what has already happened and can be told, or so it appears, and that is why time is the only thing that is ambiguous. That voice we hear is always fictitious, I believe, and perhaps mine will be too, in these pages.

I am not the first writer nor will I be the last whose life has been enriched or poisoned or only changed because of what he imagined or made up and wrote down and published. Unlike those of truly fictional novels, the elements of the story I am now embarking upon are entirely capricious, determined by chance, merely episodic and cumulative—all of them irrelevant by the elementary rule of criticism, none of them requiring any of the others—because in the end no author is guiding them, though I am relating them; they correspond to no blueprint, they are steered by no compass, most of them are external in origin and devoid of intention and therefore have no reason to make any kind of sense or to constitute an argument or plot or answer to some hidden harmony, and no lesson should be extracted from them (nor should any such thing be sought from real novels; above all, the novels themselves should not want it)—not even a story with its beginning and suspense and final silence. I don't believe this is a story, though, not knowing how it ends, I may be mistaken. I do know that the beginning of this tale lies outside it, in a novel I wrote some time ago, or before that (in which case it's even more amorphous), in the two years I spent as an imposter in the city of Oxford, teaching entertaining but on the whole quite useless subjects at its University and observing the passage of a previously agreed-upon period of time. Its ending must also lie outside it, and will surely coincide with my own, some years from now, or so I hope.

Or it may happen that the ending survives me, as almost everything that arises from us or accompanies us or that we bring about survives us; our intentions last longer than we do. We set too many things in motion and then leave them, and their inertia, weak as it is, outlives us: the words that replace us and that someone occasionally remembers or passes on, not always confessing to their provenance; the letters smoothed flat, the bent photographs, the notes written on yellow paper, left for a woman who will sleep alone in the aftermath of wakeful caresses because we leave in the middle of the night like a scoundrel who is just passing through; the objects and furniture that served us and that we allowed into our homes—a red chair, a pen, an image of India, a toy soldier made of lead, a comb—the books we write but also those we buy and read only once or that remain closed on the shelf to the last and then carry on somewhere else with their life of waiting, hoping for other eyes more avid or more placid than ours; the clothes that will go on hanging among mothballs because someone may insist on keeping them, for sentimental reasons—though I don't know if there are mothballs anymore—the fabrics fading and languishing in their airlessness, each day more oblivious to the forms that gave them meaning, the scent of those forms; the songs that will go on being sung when we do not sing or hum or listen to them;

the streets that shelter us as if they were endless hallways and chambers that pay no attention to their ephemeral and inconstant residents; the footsteps that cannot be replicated, that leave no trace on asphalt or are quickly erased on dirt, those footsteps don't stay behind but depart with us or even before us in their harmlessness or their venom; the medicines, our hurried scrawl, the cherished photos we display, which no longer look back at us, the pillow, our jacket hanging from the back of a chair, a pith helmet brought back from Tunisia in the 1930s aboard the ship *Ciudad de Cádiz*, it belongs to my father and still has its chin strap, and the Hindu lieutenant made of painted wood that I've just brought home with some hesitation, that figurine will also outlast me, or may. And the narratives we invent, which will be appropriated by others who, in speaking of our past existence, gone and never known, will render us fictitious. Even our gestures will continue to be made by someone who inherited them or saw them and was unknowingly mimetic or repeated them on purpose to invoke us and create a strange, momentary and vicarious illusion of our life; and perhaps there will remain, isolated in another person, certain of our traits which we will have transmitted involuntarily, as affectation or unconscious curse, because features can bring luck or misfortune, the eyes verging on Oriental and the mouth as if sketched on with a pencil—"beaky lip, beaky lip"—the chin almost cleft, the broad hands, a cigarette in the left one; I'll leave no feature to anyone. We lose everything because everything remains except us. And therefore any form of posterity may be an affront, and perhaps any memory, as well.

I am going to commit a number of affronts here because I will speak, among other things, of several dead men, real ones, whom I did not know, thereby becoming a kind of unexpected and distant posterity for them; I will be the memory of them though I have never seen them and they could not have foreseen me in their time, now gone: I will be their ghost. Most of them never set foot in my country and didn't know my language, though one did, a man of whose death I have no record, Hugh Oloff de Wet, who was in Madrid the year I was born in Madrid, and long before that had been on the point of dying before a firing squad here. He had also killed people here, and in other places, before then and after. And there is someone else who, on the contrary, was born in my own house, in the same bed, I imagine, that I would be born in much later.

It is always said that behind every novel lies an episode, however pallid or tenuous or intermittent, in the life or reality of the author, though it may have been transfigured. This is said as if in distrust of the imagination and the inventive faculties, and also as if readers and critics needed something to hang onto, to keep from falling prey either to the strange vertigo of that which is absolutely invented and without experience or basis—as if they did not want to feel the horror of something that appears to exist as we read it, that breathes and whispers and sometimes even persuades, yet has never been—or to the ultimate absurdity of taking seriously what is only a representation, as if they were struggling against the lurking awareness that reading novels is a childish pastime, or at least inappropriate to the adult life that is always gaining on us.

Among my novels, there is one that granted its readers this consolation or alibi in greater measure than the others, and not only that but also invited them to suspect that whatever was recounted in it had its counterpart in my life, though I don't know if that life, in its turn, is part of reality or not; perhaps it won't be if I tell it and I'm already telling part of it. In any case, this novel, entitled *Todas las almas* or, in English, *All Souls*, lent itself to the almost absolute identification of its nameless narrator with its named author, Javier Marías, also author of the present narrative in which narrator and author do coincide and I no longer know if there is one of us or two, at least while I'm writing.

Todas las almas was first published by a company whose name is best forgotten in March or April of 1989, eight years ago now (March is the month that appears in the book, but Eduardo Mendoza generously presented it in the famous Madrid bar Chicote on April 7th, a very notable day for other reasons as well), and a simple glance at the author's bio on the inside flap of the first edition yielded the information that I had taught at Oxford University for two academic years, between 1983 and 1985, just like the Spanish narrator of the book, though it mentions no dates. And it's true that the narrator held the very position I held in my own life or history, of which I have retained some memory, but like many other elements of this and other novels I've written that was only a loan from author to character. Little of what is recounted in the book coincides with what I experienced or learned in Oxford, or only the most incidental things that

13

have no effect on the course of events: the muffled atmosphere of that reserved and aloof city and its atemporal professors who harbor so many illusions about their occupation
and so few about their lot in life (their perennially usufructu-
ary spirit); the very orderly if dimly-lit antiquarian book
stores that I—every bookseller's dream come true—visited
with gloved hands and eyes on the alert; the baleful and pre-
occupied beggars, great numbers of whom move through the
streets in the evening, seething over some remote or imagined insult, with never a destination or goal or apology; the
frantically pealing bells of the neighboring and perpetually
empty churches of St. Giles and St. Aloysius, still stolidly
calling out to the faithful of other, more credulous centuries,
souls who no longer exist but who, because of those bells,
may not have died; the derelict Didcot train station in its yel-
lowish night of languid streetlamps that seemed ready to bid
a final farewell with every flicker of their resigned, exhausted
insomnia; a young, fair-haired woman there, in a raincoat
and pearl necklace, smoking a cigarette and tapping out with
her English feet in their low heels and buckles the remembered rhythm of a music no one else on that platform of
nocturnal stragglers could hear; the daylight suspended for
hours in the spring, making the wan sky come to a halt or
persevere; a gypsyish flowerseller who stood across from my
house on Sunday mornings in her leather jacket and high
boots and long tresses that looked as if they were made of
black rubber, I called her Jane in my book while her name in
life was Anne, Anne Joseph, and she lived in nearby Reading
with its famous gaol and was married to a Mr. Hyde, Anne
Joseph Hyde at the age of nineteen, whether it rained or
snowed or the wind lashed at her humble, foil-wrapped flow-
ers and she had to pull her zipper all the way up and tuck in
her chin, she was there, and she must be thirty-one years old

now, if she's still there, or in the city of Reading with Hyde; and the very ancient and frail porter with the diaphanous gaze who wished everyone a good day from his lodge at the Taylorian where I worked and taught my classes, I called him Will in the book, in whose pages I often spoke to him though I never did in life, in which he was named Tom, or never beyond an occasional cheerful greeting, and now I've learned that Tom has died and therefore they both have died, Tom and Will; it's strange to have had a closer acquaintance with the porter named Will who never existed, or not in flesh and blood, and to feel greater sadness at his death, merely represented in paper and ink—or not even that, because the end of the novel specifies that "Will, the ancient porter . . . is still alive"—than at the death of the real Tom whose real name wasn't Tom, either, but Walter, as I now see in a letter written by him on June 5, 1984, when I was there and sometimes encountered him, his blue eyes full of wonder and one jovial hand raised, at his post at the Taylorian which by then was only honorific: he was allowed to sit in the lodge sometimes so he would feel useful and not lose the thread of continuity, so he could play at still being a porter; in old age as in childhood we are deceived and we play and things are hidden from us, or perhaps that happens at any age. He signs the letter "Walter Thomas (Tom)," the other name in parentheses in case the professor he was writing the letter to didn't recognize his real given and family names, the masters are often unaware of the family names of those who serve them, or who only stand and wait, as in Milton's line. Tom writes without commas, in a hand that is quite steady and very legible for his age, and says he has spent seventy-three years as an Oxford porter and for that reason has recently participated in three morning radio talk shows broadcast by a local station, and a year before that appeared on a television pro-

gram entitled *Return to Oxford* ("many of the professors were very pleased said I was very good"). "I'm starting to get a little old 93," he adds, and explains how after serving for three years in the Royal Flying Corps during the First World War, he was a porter at Queen's College and then for a long time after that at All Souls—All Souls itself (and I never knew that until now), or *Todas las almas* as the book was called in Spanish in a literal and inexact translation—from where he retired at the age of seventy. He mentions Sir Arthur Bryant, whose manservant he was at Queen's and who was always telling him he should write a book. "He's dead now," he says of the historian who surely never bothered to write the history of Tom, "but he was a man it was a pleasure to work for," he observes with the docility of one who was always a servant and perhaps because of that felt himself to be replaceable and secondary, not even a witness. "Good luck professor," that's how Tom takes his leave, Tom whom the recipient of the letter now made public calls "the most obliging man in Europe." "Good luck professor," is therefore also how the gentle and proud porter Will takes his leave of me, Will whom I invented or made up and who assigned me different names in his continuous travels through time—Dr. Magill and Dr. Myer and Mr. Brome, and Dr. Ashmore-Jones and Mr. Renner and Dr. Nott, and Mr. Trevor and Mr. Branshaw—for none of what I now know about Tom contradicts or refutes my fictional Will, who spent each day believing he was in a different year of his long life and for him, therefore, all of time was present or had returned and nothing was past or lost time that cannot be reproduced. He reproduced it without effort of will and so, to his good fortune, none of it was ambiguous to him. Who knows what living year of his journeyings he was in when death caught up to him, from what youthful or mature or elderly moment of his long existence he thought he was departing, what miserable or happy day. Perhaps his wife was still alive for Will on the day that brought his fragile body to a halt, his wife who had died long before in real time, our time, which he had abandoned, and perhaps he thought he was making a widow of the person whose widower he had been for so many years. I was told about Tom's death by his nephew John, also a porter at the Taylorian who no doubt inherited the post, though the inheritance didn't extend to his looks: John was a tall, corpulent man with his hair parted down the middle and the doughty moustache of an old-fashioned boxer, apparently tolerant of the weaknesses of others but with an excess of questionable humor, as I will describe later. He left his job not long ago: his Uncle Tom was spared the distress.

So only the scenery was real, and not even that: it was a skewed Oxford, a replica seen from my imaginary or false perspective, the fabulizing viewpoint of someone who spends a single night in a legendary hotel that will not record his insignificant, pretentious presence alongside that of the famous people who once slept or lived there, or perhaps killed themselves or were killed, lending the establishment that distinction: the room is closed off, and now tourists will only look in. Just incidental things, I said, when it is so difficult to know what will turn out to be incidental or fundamental once our book or story or life is over and has become known or past time which cannot be reproduced. Or maybe the book can, each time it's read, but no, each reading changes it, though none of them rewrites it.

Real, too, was the aspect of the novel that struck many readers as the most novelistic and fictitious, pure Kiplingesque invention, pure make-believe on my part: the story, told tentatively then, of the ill-fated, calamitous and jovial writer John Gawsworth, the incredible king of Re-

donda who never saw his kingdom but sold it several times and had himself called Juan I, and whose real name was Terence Ian Fytton Armstrong, two photographs of whom I printed and described in that book and print here once again to jog the memories of those who have read that novel and introduce them to those who haven't and so will need to familiarize themselves with his face and his various names if they are going to stay in touch with these pages and go on turning them. For of that man I shall have to speak, and quite a lot, since I now, in a manner of speaking, have him in my home. Or rather, though he's dead—and the second photo isn't of him, exactly, but of the death mask that Hugh Oloff de Wet made immediately in incongruous homage to one who left the world a beggar—he lives on in me a little, if that can be said of someone who died twenty-six years ago without ever having had the faintest notion of my existence.

I have before my eyes a copy of his death certificate, dated 1970, and of his third and final wedding license, dated fifteen years earlier; he married a widow five years older—he was forty-three and she forty-eight at their wedding—and both copies were placed in my hands by the granddaughter of that woman who was widowed and married and widowed again, a blonde Englishwoman named Maria, without the accent, of course, but the same name as my Andalucian grandmother whom I never knew, María Aguilera, who must have laughed when she found herself married to a blithe and reckless widower whose last name was Marías and she became virtually a declension: María de Marías. The first certificate says that Armstrong—in death he was no longer Gawsworth, or not to the doctors, and perhaps by then he hadn't been Gawsworth for some time—died in Brompton Hospital in London's Chelsea district and gives the medical causes for his decease. In the box marked "Profession," a civil servant named Vinten or an informant named Lewis wrote, "A poet," and on the next line, under the heading "Qualification," they added that the body had to be buried, "in consequence," and so it must have been. Nevertheless, my house in Madrid is the place where the strange, unhappy spirit of the poet king of Redonda still draws breath and holds out against disappearance or stillness and refuses to declare the party over, and it is also the place where his handwriting lives on, which is to say, his voice that speaks. Or that will speak later, because it isn't yet the moment for you to hear it, though that time will come as I go along writing these lines and turning these pages myself.

But none of the real human beings I have mentioned were among those who first became aware of my novel because none of them knew Spanish or my name or that I was a writer, and they may not have been people who read much, with the exception of the bibliophile and bibliomaniac Gawsworth or Armstrong, but he had died on September 23, 1970—I had just turned nineteen three days earlier—and could never have foreseen me. And though De Wet did know Spanish, who knows what became of him, his life span is not known to us, his traces have been lost.

As I explained in a 1989 article titled "Who's Writing," the nameless narrator of *All Souls*—who, if memory serves, is called only "our dear Spaniard" or "the Spanish gentleman" by the other characters—on returning to Madrid after his two years of false exile or privileged emigration in Oxford, appears in the novel married to a woman named Luisa and father of her newborn child, which was demonstrably not my situation, my case or anything that has ever happened to me. There has never even been a significant or lasting Luisa in my life. That alone ruled out any absolute identification of narrator with author, and, by extension, of any other character with any real person I might have known or come into contact with during my stay. Still, the rest of what the narrator related could have happened to me or been witnessed by me. I could state and declare, as I've often done and am now doing again, that almost all of it was invented except for the setting and some minor personal experiences that are transformed in the book, that none of the characters had a counterpart in anyone who exists or once existed, and, more specifically, that none of them was the portrait or caricature of any of my British colleagues on the Faculty of Medieval and Modern Languages, of which the Sub-Faculty of Spanish, to which I was attached, was part. Though in fact there's no reason to believe anything I state or declare, even if there does exist a credulous and unjustifiable tendency to believe the statements authors make in regard to their books. (I realize, even as I point this out, that I'm involuntarily putting into question the veracity of whatever I say here, and will go on saying, but I'll have to run that risk and appeal to that credulity in spite of everything: attention will be paid or will not be, I'll be heard out or I won't, and there is no reason to do so: there are no two ways about it, that's all.) What I cannot and will never be able to do is demonstrate that the events of the novel did *not* happen to me in my life, since it is always impossible to demonstrate that you have *not* done something or committed some crime if the opposite is presumed, from the start, to be the case, a thing all dictators know very well. To go no farther than Spain itself, that was the judicial policy of the Franco regime, as soon as the war was over and for the long term. A neighbor, an enemy, a rival, an envious colleague, a friend would accuse someone of various crimes, the direr the better, and on the strength of that alone the person would be arrested and tried, or, rather, made the center of a show trial, and his accusers would tell him, "Go ahead and prove you didn't kill, or inform, or loot, or rape," knowing full well that it is almost impossible to prove anything in the negative. And that is what happened to María Aguilera de Marías's youngest son, my father, of whom it was alleged, among other imaginative things, that during the war he had been a "contributor to the Moscow newspaper *Pravda*," and—to my undying envy—"a voluntary companion to the bandit Dean of Canterbury." I must confess that I would pay a handsome bribe or incur almost any shady obligation in order to see myself brought up, just once in my life, on charges so outlandish and archaic. I haven't yet managed to find out much about the wartime role of this "bandit" who was known as "the Red Dean" or *"el Deán Rojo,"* and whose real name was the Reverend Dr. Hewlett Johnson, as if he were an Oxonian, and in fact he received his doctorate in theology at Oxford in 1904, at Wadham College, which is not entirely unknown to me. Of the little that I know about the Dean, the most striking facts are that he was the first to break through the naval blockade of Bilbao in 1937 and that he was seventy-two years old when the conflict broke out and seventy-five when it ended, a commendable age indeed at which to engage in banditry in a foreign country and risk his neck setting sail from Bermeo in a French torpedo boat, dodging mines and Franco's warships to reach San Juan de Luz without mishap, in addition to whatever other feats or felonies he carried out with his voluntary companion, whoever that was, and of course it was not my father, nor, by any means, the Archbishop of Canterbury, who saw no alternative but to issue a statement in 1947 to let it be known that his Dean was speaking and acting only for himself, far beyond the cathedral's limits, and that the Archbishop had no responsibility for what he might say or do, "nor the power to control it." The Red Dean of Canterbury, an indomitable, impervious Russophile and apologist for the Spanish Republic, must have emerged unscathed from his escapades in and around the Iberian peninsula since he lived to be ninety-two, almost as long as my peaceable porter Will, also a combatant albeit in a different war. But because of the Red Dean and his involuntary companionship, I narrowly risked not being born, given that in 1939 the firing squad was the most common and frequent fate of those denounced by cunning and patriotic friends, and if my father went only to jail and no farther it was due to luck and my mother's tenacity—they didn't know then that they would marry each other—rather than to any lack of ill will on the part of the two men who informed against him. And if I hadn't been born, so what? Too many people are born and it's as if it never happened and they never existed; there are so few whose memory is preserved, and so many who die quickly as if the world didn't have the patience to witness their lives and was hurrying to be rid of them, the effort made in vain and the diminutive footsteps that leave no trace, or only in the sharp-edged memory of the one who taught those feet to take steps and made the mistake and the effort, a costly and superfluous luxury that is expelled from the earth at once like a breath, without even a chance to be put to the test. And so what, if no one were born, ever.

So with respect to the scant degree of autobiography in my book, the only thing that was demonstrable in the negative was that I did not then and do not now have a wife named Luisa, nor, in fact, a wife by any name, and still less a child who was then a newborn, and who, if he had existed and was not in vain, would now—horrors—be seven or eight years old, a little thug or who knows, worse still, maybe a little know-it-all who ought to be run out of the country. (I might not have been a good father.) But even that was attributed to me by people who knew little about me and nothing about my private life.

At the time, I was teaching courses on translation theory at the Universidad Complutense in Madrid, an accidental thing that lasted four years—I never thought seriously of dedicating myself to the long-suffering profession of teaching, plagued with subterfuge and intrigue—following several vagabond years not only in Oxford but also near Boston and in Venice. I was not fond of the Spanish university milieu and its many pettinesses so I took advantage of the evening classes in order to avoid all faculty life and appear only when absolutely necessary at the gloomy university, half-empty, its lights dimmed, already taken over by the cleaning ladies who at those hours feel themselves to be in charge of the day's residue and shoo away or give orders to the professors and students, as they gave orders to the passengers and railway workers in the station of Didcot, or in that other station in Mestre, near Venice, where I spent part of one night cast out and wrapped in mist. I gave my classes, which were improvised in the taxi on the way there, and left as soon as they were over, at nine or ten p.m., depending on the day, so there was hardly any scope for fraternization with the students or networking with my colleagues, and almost no one knew anything about me that wasn't more or less public information. And there, not long after *Todas las almas* came out, I had my first warning—or perhaps it was the second—of how everything my narrator spoke of and said, from start to finish, might be ascribed to me. A group of students—most of them women—was waiting for me one night outside the classroom to consult me on various matters, to which I imagine I must have improvised some response, and as I walked through the hallways with my inappropriate briefcase made of hard black plastic with a blue handle, surrounded like some idiotic politician among his handlers and journalists (I've noticed that professors, real, daytime professors, very much enjoy having their students flock around them as they walk, and it amused me to imitate them for once), one young

27

woman, out of the blue, asked me solicitously, "How's the baby?"

"What baby?" I said, surprised.

The student was very sure of herself. "What other baby would it be? Yours." I think she employed the polite form of address—*el suyo*—but she may have said *el tuyo;* I always addressed the students formally as *usted,* but they would use the intimate *tú* with me at the drop of a hat, though only outside of class; the change could happen in a matter of seconds, as if they were unmasking me. And they weren't all young, some were older than me and all of them had graduated from college; my courses were at the level of the doctorate that I didn't and still don't have. More than once I considered enrolling in my own courses and becoming my own student just to get the credits (I would have played it safe and given myself only B's, and I would always have addressed myself as *usted*).

"Mine?" I said in alarm. I still hadn't caught on. "What baby of mine? I have a baby? Believe me, this is the first I've heard."

At that point the other students worked up the nerve to join in, perhaps feeling defrauded, I mean, as if they were victims of a fraud.

"But you say so in your novel, the one that's just come out," they protested, as if producing an embossed guarantee.

"Ah." And I was silent for a moment, and stopped in that hallway dominated by the world-weary cleaning ladies (hand on hip during a pensive pause) who were drudging away with their misbuttoned housecoats and their stringy mops. I wondered if I should make amends and certify the reality of the baby in the presence of those young women, and therefore the reality of Luisa, my storybook wife, as well. Of course I might have divorced her by then, perhaps because she was jealous, for instance, or because she was short-tempered or nosy or talked too much, or because she was a neglectful and agonized mother, the marriage was a big mistake, perhaps I would have kept the child. (Or she might have left me, because I was overly withdrawn and mysterious.) Finally, as I started walking again, I told the truth. "But that isn't me, it's the novel's narrator, I'm not married and don't have any children, or any I know of. And I think I'd know."

"But you were in Oxford," one of them objected.

A single undeniable coincidence (the book's jacket influencing the book itself) sufficed to ascribe all the rest to me, I thought, and that struck me as far too elementary a reaction from readers who were college graduates, most of them students of literature in various languages.

"Yes, and what does that have to do with it?" I answered.

"So it isn't true?" a student insisted. "Because we were all convinced you had a small baby." I remember she said "*convencidas todas*" in the feminine—"we women were all convinced"—perhaps not so much because of the large number of women in the class, always the case in literature classes, as because the discovery had been discussed only among those of her gender. And on the face of one of those female students I thought I noticed an expression of contentment at hearing that I was not married. Nothing to feel boastful or conceited about, given that all the world's professors, male and female, enjoy what could be called "the podium effect," due to which even the ugliest and most squalid, horrible, tyrannical and despicable among them arouse spurious and delusional passions, as I know all too well. I've seen dazzling women barely out of their teens swooning and melting over some foul-smelling homunculus with a piece of chalk in his hand, and innocent boys degrading themselves (circumstantially) for a scrawny, furrowed bosom stooped over a desk.

Those who take advantage of this podium effect are generally contemptible, and they are legion. What I didn't understand, though, was the contentment of that student whose colors were the same as my briefcase (eyes blue, hair black), because she, in any case, was married. Perhaps it was a purely literary satisfaction, and she was happy to confirm that what she had read as a novel was indeed a novel.

"So they talk about me," I thought, "and they took the trouble to buy and read my book right away." As we walked on, more and more lights went out behind us, as if they were waiting impatiently to see the back of us in order to shut down for the night, and the cleaning ladies didn't count. Or maybe the cleaning ladies could do their jobs in the dark, with their eyes closed, as if they were dreaming the work from somewhere else. Maybe from Mestre or Didcot, it's hard to alter the course of our destinies once they're underway, if we don't know they are our destinies.

Not long before or after that I would receive or had received news of the novel's initial reception in the city of Oxford. My former colleagues on the Sub-Faculty were more or less aware that I was working on a book set there, but had only the sketchiest notion of it and didn't know whether it was a novel, a thinly veiled true account, or some sort of vague memoir. The only person who had grounds to know anything more was my good friend Eric Southworth, of St. Peter's College, with whom I often exchanged letters, then and now. The head of the department, Professor Ian Michael, of Exeter College, who frequently visits Madrid—drawn here by his medieval research, his weakness for bull-fighting, his historical and streetcorner fact-finding errands for the crime novels he writes under an angelical pseudonym, and his rash taste for or curiosity about the underworld and aspiring criminals—was also kept somewhat abreast, and only what those two had managed to convey would have been of general knowledge among the faculty.

But then again, no. On one of my visits subsequent to the expiration of my contract—it must have been in the summer of 1987, after spending nine soporific days at a literary seminar in Cambridge with Ishiguro, the agreeable Vikram Seth, P.D. James, the late Angela Carter, David Lodge, the ante-diluvian Wesker and others, all of us roused from sleep during those cloistered days only by the critic George Steiner—I

complied with my tradition of paying a visit to an elderly retired professor I used to drop in on once a month during my
Oxford years and whom some have wanted to see represented in the character in *All Souls* named Toby Rylands, and
therefore I shall call him Toby Rylands here as well, using his
supposed fictional name to refer to someone who neither was
nor is but may well end up being fictional. I've always had
great admiration and respect for this professor, and beyond
that he was amusing, an intelligent, astute man, guileful and
learned and so suggestive as to be almost enigmatic. By suggestive I mean not only that he sparked the imagination with
his imposing presence, his slow intensity and the studied in-
termittences of his speech, but that he continually suggested
deplorable events in his past, remote, semi-clandestine activities and associations that were improbable and theoreti-
cally improper for a university professor, without ever embarking on a story. According to the publicly available
biographical notes (so I'm not committing any indiscretions),
he went by the last name of Wheeler before he began using
the name he now uses, his mother's maiden name; he was
born in 1913 in Christchurch, New Zealand, which did not
prevent him from becoming more of an Oxonian than any
other member of the congregation (which is the term used
for the entire corpus of professors or dons) I ever met; the
biographical summaries state tersely that he enlisted in 1940
and at the end of that year was assigned to the Intelligence
Corps or Information Service or Secret Service, adding that
between 1942 and 1946 he performed "special duties in the
Caribbean, West Africa and South East Asia." However,
these facts were of no use to me when I sat down to portray
the fictitious Toby Rylands, someone quite different from the
person he was and is, for during the period when I saw the
real man most often I was unaware of them (one does not

think of consulting biographical entries, if they exist, on a person one sees frequently), and the man himself, as I've said, never recounted anything in full about his possible inclement or adventurous days, but only allowed them to be glimpsed.

On one occasion, for example, he murmured, "Once I had to entertain and keep my eye on a crown prince, for weeks."

I would wait for a tale to ensue, sensing that this sentence was the preamble to some strange and diverting story that would be well worth hearing out. And, at the silence that followed—Rylands broke off, as if to ponder whether he had done well in proffering what he had just proffered and whether he wanted to recount the episode or keep it to himself—I tried to cajole it out of him: "Oh really? What was that like? They mustn't be very interesting, princes."

Then he passed his immense, peaceable hand over his wood-hewn cheeks as if it were all suddenly coming back to him at once, and that were enough, and perhaps, as he remembered it all, he came to see the story he had been tempted to confide in me as unnecessary.

"Hmm," he said, like so many people in Oxford, where much mumbling is done. "Hmm." And his eyes glittered with recovered youth.

I persisted. "What sort of prince was he? European, African, Russian?"

"He was indeed a prince. A most delightful prince. He drank a lot and I had to go along on his binges. That's why I can hold my drink. This sherry does not convince me, I'm going to tell Mrs. Berry not to bring me any more of it." And he lifted the glass to his pencil-thin lips, thus putting an end to his precarious incursion into the past, or at least to the spoken and witnessed part of it. I know the English word he used was "binges."

I made the fictional Rylands a former spy with MI5, the most famous of the British secret services, and I mentioned wartime missions he was said to have carried out in Martinique, Haiti, Brazil and the islands of Tristan da Cunha, all of it according to Oxford's indefatigable rumor mills. These were things I made up, that was all; they may have been suggested by his incomplete allusions during our conversations, for I knew nothing at that point about the biographical information in the public domain.

Nevertheless, the identification between the two Rylands was understandable, up to a point, because in order to describe the fictional character I selected and embroidered upon and shifted around certain physical attributes of the real person, which must have been what led superficial readers into confusion. The novel says, "He was a very large man, enormous, really, who still had all his hair, white and undulant—a mound of whipped cream—on a statue's head, always well dressed, with more vanity than elegance (bow ties and yellow sweaters, a rather American look or that of a student from bygone days) . . ." "His almond-shaped eyes made the greatest impression; each was a different color, the right one olive oil and the other pale ashes, so that if you looked at him from the right you saw a sharp expression that was a touch cruel—an eagle's or perhaps a cat's eye—while if you looked at him from the left the expression was contemplative and serious, and straightforward as only a northerner can be straightforward—the eye of a dog or perhaps a horse, the two most straightforward-seeming of animals; and if you looked at him head-on you met two gazes, or rather two colors in a single gaze, which was cruel and straightforward, contemplative and sharp." "As for his laugh, that was the most diabolical thing about Toby Rylands: his mouth barely moved, only just enough—horizontally—so that beneath his fleshy, purplish upper lip a row of small, somewhat pointy but very straight teeth appeared, perhaps a good imitation by a well-paid dentist of the set that age had deprived him of. But what was most demonic about that short, dry laugh was not the sight of it but its sound, for it was nothing like the customary (written) onomatopoeias, all of which rely on the aspiration of the consonant (whether it be ha-ha-ha or heh-heh-heh or hee-hee-hee, or even ah-ah), no, in his case the consonant was distinctly plosive, a very clear alveolar 't,' as the English 't' is. Ta-ta-ta: that was Professor Toby Rylands' chilling laugh. Ta-ta-ta. Ta-ta-ta."

And the unmistakable laugh of the real Rylands was indeed like that, as was he himself more or less, though he didn't have fleshy lips or eyes of different colors, but two eyes of so Nordic a blue they seemed almost yellow under direct sun or electric light, a vigilant gaze or, more precisely, eyes that lay in ambush, that seemed to be forming an opinion even when they looked distracted or sleepy or absent, thinking for themselves without the mind's intervention, judging. He was one of those individuals who never demands or remonstrates but before whom you often feel yourself to be deficient in some way, if you haven't entirely abandoned the reflexes of youth; such people make no reproach and do not manifest their discontent, yet you feel forever on the verge of incurring their silent disapproval. This effect isn't easily achieved; it does not depend on one's bearing or manners or wealth or pretensions, or even on the kind of enraged reprisals that in the course of my life I've seen from certain social-climbing businessmen when they were crossed: contemptible, insecure people who inspire no respect and need to convince themselves of their eminence, crushing anyone they can, anyone who is weak, to ceaselessly renew their always scanty confidence (in my younger days, I once had an editor who was like that, I left him with revulsion and without a second thought, his face would go red and his eyes drifted obtusely, he was unable to pronounce a sensible or complete word, sluggish in thought and speech, bewildered when his exploitative will was thwarted—he started out in the black market, they said; I've also known writers of the same ilk, despotic and full of complexes, any disagreement shakes them to the core or shatters them). In fact there's no need, nor is it possible, to do anything extraordinary to produce in others this intimidation and desire for recognition, or at least acceptance. Toby Rylands achieved it without much effort, though he did seek it: with his occasional terseness, his sharp-edged voice that took advantage of old age to sound an occasional note of affliction and make itself dramatic, his eyes that were interpretative when he listened and also when he spoke, as if there were no give and take in conversations with him and you were exposing yourself at every moment, when you spoke and when you were silent, when you were telling your story and when you were waiting as he was holding forth. He was, moreover, reputed to be quite unscrupulous—ruthless, actually—in punishing enemies or those who simply offended him, and for him these were punishments, not acts of vengeance; enlightened men do not take revenge. It was rumored that on one occasion, upon learning that a university in the United States was about to offer some succulently lucrative position to an ungrateful or insufficiently obsequious disciple of his, the tactic he came up with to keep this from happening was to accuse this disciple, *sotto voce*, of coprophagy, no less, which sufficed to make the moneyed Southern puritans cancel the nauseating contract, apparently without even wondering how Rylands could be in possession of such reliable information on practices and activities which, if they truly exist (and I doubt they do; these are figments and affectations of literature and cinema), would certainly never be spoken of openly by anyone, still less in the city of Oxford where almost nothing is overlooked and what isn't known is created or invented. Had he actually said this, Toby Rylands' shrewdness would have been considerable, even Mephistophelian, since he chose a stigma about which no one would ever dare question the defamed man, thus forestalling all possibility of denial or defense. How dangerous credible voices are, authoritative voices, voices that never lie, as if waiting for the day when the time has come and it is really worth the trouble, and then effortlessly they persuade us of the most far-fetched or poisonous things. It may be that my own voice is becoming one of these, with age and some of what I've written, though most of it is fictional. But still I don't lie.

And so I was only concerned with the possible reactions of three people to the as-yet-untitled book I was writing, which I referred to as "the Oxford novel" in my letters to Eric Southworth or Daniella Pittarello around that time. I made so bold as to guess what my Oxford friend Eric might think when he read the book and it caused me little apprehension, outside of his strictly literary assessment; and I saw no threat, either, in the probable reaction of Ian Michael, with his jocular, carefree outlook and his utter lack of piety, he's the opposite of a stuffed shirt. As for the rest of my colleagues, more severe in appearance and more zealous on behalf of the good name of their profession, the University, and Oxford itself, I imagined that having dedicated a good part of their lives to teaching literature (even if it was Spanish or Latin American literature) they would be able, without doubts or difficulties, to distinguish between a work of fiction and a memoir or an essay, and not be upset by any brash digression or comical exaggeration or fabulation of mine with respect to a literary topos that only partially corresponded to the name of Oxford, which I gave it, and to characters that did not represent or caricature them or, of course, bear their names, even if they did occupy the same posts, just as the narrator occupied mine.

Toby Rylands' reaction was of greater concern to me, because of what I've just said about him and because in no way would I ever want to incur his disapproval, especially not for a personal reason. So when I went to see him that summer of 1987 after my impatient sojourn in Cambridge—it wasn't just the two of us at his house this time; we were invited, along with Eric, to Ian's house for lunch in his garden—it seemed fitting to give him some advance notice, and not a bad idea to do so before two witnesses who could become allies or accomplices, if they weren't already. I remember Toby, in a canvas deck chair that strained mightily beneath his corpulence, taking sidelong glances at the river and at us, his irises yellow under the stationary July sun, launching off quick anecdotes sharp as fencers' thrusts or laughing in slow percussive bursts like pistons backfiring—"Ta, ta, ta"—each time Ian or Eric told him something racy or malicious. During a pause in the conversation when Ian had gone inside to see how his blind mother, with whom he lived, was doing, and to ask the maid to bring out dessert, I remarked (the river looked drowsy and dusty): "I don't know if you know, Toby, that I'm writing a novel set here in Oxford."

Toby Rylands looked surprised, so I was certain he must have heard something about it.

"Oh really? And what sort of novel is it? A *roman à clef* about all of us? Hmm. Should we be worried? Hmm. Should we be racking our memories? No, I knew nothing at all about it. Not a word," he said, obviously exaggerating, and added with false petulance, "No one tells me a thing any more."

That may well be the case these days—even retirement is far behind him now, along with his emeritus travels to the American universities that once reverently contracted his services and advice—he's eighty-three years old now. But at that point ten years ago the opposite held true: everyone ran to tell him anything that stood a chance of amusing or interesting him, there are people to whom others tell things only in order to enter into their good graces and win their esteem or their indulgence, their telephones are forever humming.

"Well, I still don't know exactly what kind of novel it will be, I don't know much about my books until I'm done with them, and even then. But of course it won't be a *roman à clef* about all of you, I don't think my colleagues should worry about that. Though a few may insist on seeing it that way, nevertheless, or believe they recognize descriptions of themselves. You know how it is, the fact that I lived here will be enough to create suspicion, people always think we're less imaginative, less capricious than we are. And the truth is that I wouldn't like it if anyone were upset, I'm thinking especially of Alec, Fred and Pring-Mill, not so much of John or of you three, you're more frivolous and I say that as a compliment. Philip certainly wouldn't have worried me, either."

Alec Dewar, that was the name I gave, in *All Souls*, to a character some people identified as the real person I will now, as with Rylands, call by his alleged fictional name and nicknames—the Ripper, the Inquisitor, the Butcher, the Hammer. Alec Dewar was a solemn man who strove to give the impression that he was severe and unyielding. In fact he seemed to me not to know what to do with himself after the close of the work day when the disappearance of the students (who enlivened him by irritating him) forced him to lay aside his role as ogre, and, cast out until morning, he would gaze nostalgically at the closed gates of the Taylorian; he appeared disconcerted by any foreign element in the stubborn routine of many, many years, and if you took an interest in him or asked him any question that was at all personal, as if he might have an existence beyond the university limits, he looked grateful and uncomfortable and immediately lost all his pomp and circumstance, answering timidly, but with the audacious expression of one who has done some extravagant thing, or as if he had been caught out in a gratifying fault. He liked to cultivate an appearance of ferocity and sarcasm and managed to be convincing to the students and the guests at seminars who underwent his scrutiny, but not to his colleagues who were sometimes the recipients of his creaky, hesitant attempts at being pleasant or even witty, which is one of the forms of cordiality in Oxford. His spoken Spanish was timid too, he preferred to speak English with me. Unaccustomed as he was to speaking of himself or of matters unrelated to work, he would, by the second or third exchange, begin to spout phrases that were part cliché and part enigma and that meant nothing. "So it goes in this day and age," he would say without any particular meaning, after explaining, for example, that he didn't have a house of his own in the city and slept in his rooms at his college, I don't remember if it was Trinity or Christ Church or Corpus Christi. These phrases could bring the conversation to a dead stop, transforming his peevishness into a kind of helplessness that was embarrassing to see.

Fred Hodcroft, a charming man, very tall and slim with a woodpecker profile and a feigned air of professorial absentmindedness, used to set grammatical and syntactic traps for me to test the extent of my knowledge, acting as if he really did not know the answers he was trying to extract from me. He was continually pushing his glasses back into place, as if he knew that a fall from his great height was sure to be fatal to them. He was so congenial that you could never let your guard down with him; his Spanish was excellent. He didn't appear to be a devotee of the institution but he probably was, one of those men who can be offended for their entire life without anyone every learning of it or suspecting it: they are all affability, even with those they find reprehensible or who have done them a bad turn.

Robert Pring-Mill, stubby, clerical, and cagey, a close friend of Ernesto Cardenal, the revolutionary Nicaraguan poet-priest, lacked any sense of humor, or rather, his did not coincide with mine, and wary and severe as he was he used to take everything literally to a tedious degree. I didn't see much of him, I don't think he liked me, I was too indifferent to what he venerated: his trans-oceanic friendship must have been more sacerdotal than insurrectionist. His Spanish was excellent, but he tended to avoid speaking it. He seemed permanently displeased—they said he'd been hoping for the position that went to Ian Michaels, who, to make matters worse, wasn't even from Oxford, and perhaps that alone explained why his figure seemed evasive and halfhearted.

John Rutherford, who was at that time translating the nineteenth-century Spanish novel *La Regenta*, which had yet to be published in English, spoke Spanish with a strong Galician accent acquired from his Galician wife and his unvarying summers in Ribadeo: a quiet, patient and worthy man, a magnificent person, with perhaps a touch of unconfessed resentment that even he himself did not grasp. Seen from outside, his life—the whole family playing musical instruments, daughters he sang with at home—seemed idyllic. It was unlikely that anything would anger him, but there could be a certain danger in him: no one is ever entirely resigned, not even to what he chooses.

Then there was Philip Lloyd-Bostock, who died not long after I left Oxford; during my two years there he was often absent because of his illness, but not enough to keep us from seeing one another and giving a few classes together, shoulder to shoulder, as I had occasion to do, one term or another, with each of my colleagues in turn, classes in practical literary translation, in both directions, Gómez de la Serna and Valle-Inclán into English and Woolf and Hopkins into Spanish. Lloyd-Bostock gave the impression of belonging to another world and only passing through Oxford, quite against his will, in order to earn his salary; this set him apart from the others who were visibly assimilated, more or less, to the city and its life of placid valor, if one can put it that way. Some of them may not have had any other life, not when they went home to their houses or rooms at the end of the day nor even during the long summer vacation, though it surely afforded them sufficient time to become their opposites or Hydes—I'm sure Philip took advantage of the opportunity. Some of them must have waited impatiently for the beginning of each new school year in order to feel centered again, sustained, in harmony with their surroundings, justified. For Philip Lloyd-Bostock, however, this world seemed no more than a nuisance, something out of the past to which a certain amount of attention must still be paid, or to which we can turn without embarrassment in case of need because it will always be on our side—in reserve, like the family we come from, perhaps. But perhaps it's only that I knew him when he was already very sick, to those who are dying, everything may start to appear superfluous and already past or gone. He had a carefully groomed moustache and watery blue eyes and exhibited a no doubt deceptive docility—that of a person so tortured he's beyond arguing, or maybe nothing matters to him. Some people wanted to recognize him in the character I called Cromer-Blake, probably because of the double surname and because that character died at the end of the book. Of course Cromer-Blake was also identified with my living and single-surnamed friend Eric Southworth, so in this case, absurdly, two different men were identified with one character.

Eric Southworth: a person of fanatical nobility, so loyal and upright that most of those around him must find it irritating, there aren't many people like that now, maybe a few women. And at the same time he was an easygoing man of extraordinary wit, one of those rare individuals capable of gravity and jest in the same paragraph, so to speak, and sincerely. I've seen him hooting with laughter like a wayward schoolboy over some piece of tomfoolery—an old-fashioned, grandfatherly word, but the right one—and I've also seen him adopt the grave and fearsome mien of a hero of the lecture hall. His Spanish was good, if a touch Renaissance-sounding because of its bookish origins; he couldn't be bothered to speak it there, in the chambers and dining rooms and hallways of Oxford. He was a few years older than I am and his hair was already grey; he used it to inspire the students with respect, though not always successfully, his readily mirthful side betrayed him. He did panic them sometimes, though, when he donned his clerical cap for their oral exams, playing a malevolent character out of Dickens or imitating the exhortatory demeanor of old-fashioned Spanish ecclesiastics—index finger raised, eyes narrowed, voice muted—which amused him a great deal, Catholicism as folklore. Once he asked me to pick up a bishop's or archbishop's biretta for him on calle de Segovia, so I sent him two, one made of silk with a green tassel and the other of satin with a red tassel (or vice versa, I don't know much about such vestments, perhaps they were meant only for a parish priest). He was very enthusiastic about these gifts, though I didn't ask and don't know why he wanted them, I imagine he'll make some private use of them. He gave me no cause for concern with respect to the novel, nor did Ian Michael; both men were overflowing with sharp wit and devilry and had sound knowledge of fiction. Toby Rylands shared these characteristics, but he was more venerable and less predictable, and when I spoke to him about the book I was really confiding my fears as to his possible reaction.

He gave me another of his sidelong glances and what he then said, with some sarcasm, was enough to calm my fears. "I don't think you need worry about that, Javier. But perhaps about the opposite case. It's more likely that those who may feel upset or offended will be the ones who don't recognize themselves in your novel and think they don't appear in it, not even camouflaged or in disguise, vilified or ridiculed. In the end, it's more humiliating not to be a source of inspiration than to be one, not to be considered worthy of fiction than to be worthy, even at the cost of some indiscretion, or of appearing in a bad light as the inspiration for some depraved or absurd character. The worst thing is not to figure in a book at all, when there was a possibility of doing so." He broke off for a few seconds and gazed at the river as if keeping an eye on it, then added with kindly mockery, tapping his craggy fingers on the arm of his foundering deck chair, "Besides, who knows, you could be writing a future classic. All the work we scholars do is condemned to being outdated, unusable, forgotten. That goes for those of us who write; those who don't, like Eric . . . well, his knowledge is scattered to the winds as soon as he leaves the classroom, or even before then, you know that, Eric, you know, don't you?" Yes, Eric knew perfectly well, he knows it and that's how he wants it. "It may be that the only way we'll reach posterity is in a contemporary novel we have no reason to pay the slightest attention to. Can you imagine? How unjust, how grotesque, what a cruel joke. Remembered for what we disdained. That's how it is, that's how it is. It seems unlikely that any contemporary novel will last. Too many are published and the newspaper critics have almost no discernment, but it's possible, at least. What most assuredly will not endure is our research and our explications, which could only be of interest to our future archeological selves—how should I put it?—to a repeat version of ourselves that isn't going to happen. Not even our increasingly impersonal and superfluous erudition will last, with these computers that steal it and devour and store everything and then release it to the first illiterate who knows how to push a button. Hmm. I don't like it." Rylands plunged a hand into the white meringue of his hair, without mussing it, as if trying to protect his archaic brain from this glimpsed future that was paining him, where there would be no place for anyone like him—and surely he had resigned himself to that—but neither would there be a place for people like Ian, who was younger, or Eric, still younger, and both with many active years ahead of them, and this must have struck him as too violent, an amputation or a sacrifice. "I don't like it. Hmm. Even now, these texts of ours, crammed with laborious notes and exegeses, aren't read much; most of their readers are resentful colleagues who read them with ill will, to object to or belittle them, or plagiarize them if we're lucky. To disparage us while we're alive, once we're dead it's not worth the trouble. So what you must do is try not to leave any of us out of your novel; you could be depriving one or another of us of immortality—unforgivable, don't you agree? It seems to me that all you need fear is the fury of those you'll be leaving without a literary posterity. Ta-ta-ta. Can you imagine? People like us, a century hence, doing research on the people we are now. Ta, ta, ta." Rylands often laughed at his own quips.

Eric and Ian laughed as well, aspirating their consonants as they did so. Ian Michael wrote detective novels featuring an inspector named Bernal, but only to enjoy himself and make money in Japan (apparently the trick is to have five or six books with the same character and then success and addiction arrive automatically, especially in Japan with its fondness for repetition, or so they say), and he did not count on occupying a place in the history of literature. Neither did I, with my non-detective novels. Or maybe I do, it isn't an easy thing to say. No, what I aspire to is something else.

"I don't think there's much danger of that," I answered Toby. "If it depends on me, I'm afraid all of you are going to have to go on being mortal."

I must make a digression—this is a book of digressions, a book that proceeds by digression—to admit that I've occasionally put Toby Rylands' idea to use as a persuasive measure or bargaining tool. Once, while still writing *All Souls*, I convinced Francisco Rico himself of what the eminent gentleman from New Zealand had banteringly formulated in Ian Michael's garden while watching the river. To me, at that time, Paco Rico was "Professor Rico, man of vast knowledge," laboriously disdainful, insolent in his vanity and congenial in spite of himself, a complacent man who liked to surround himself with acolytes (and did so). On one occasion, nevertheless—it may have been in Vitoria—I managed to depress him by pointing out that all his professorial prestige and fanfare, his potential halo as a member of the Real Academia Española de la Lengua—he was pushing his candidacy—and his many acclaimed critical writings were destined to last only as long as he did. After him would come others who were by definition more competent, more informed and more advanced in their methodologies, individuals who might well manage to find out all there was to know about *Lazarillo de Tormes*, for example, or the *Quijote*, and who would render his interpretations and discoveries outdated or even absurd in their naiveté—the past always seems naive— and ignorance of new and fundamental information. On the other hand, it can be stated, I told him, that every contemporary novelist—even the most inept of us, the one from Manzaneda de Torío, or the one from Quicena, among the Spaniards; no, it has to be the one from Las Palmas—is in some way superior to Cervantes, though only because we know Cervantes and have his lessons and can rely on him, and what's more we know what has come along in his wake, which in theory gives us a great advantage; yet none of us are better than him, neither our existence nor our pages erase or annul his, which continue to be studied and read without ever becoming outdated or invalid; this is a field in which the passage of additional time doesn't advance or improve or determine the course of what came before; it may be the only field in which time past is not lost but won, not for individuals—we are always losing time—but for our intentions and the body of work we create, if it does last. No one pays any attention to what we write today, but there is a remote possibility that people like Rico may do so many years from now, or people like Rylands, or Michael, or Southworth, and that will never happen to what Professor Rico himself delivers to the presses today, however great its value and merit.

"It's possible," I told him, "that you may be remembered more for having appeared as a character in a novel so enduring that it will be pored over throughout eternity, than for anything it lies within your power to achieve, with all your assiduity and expository talent and all the knowledge you've amassed."

At first the professor made a show of disdain, as was his practice, and even looked a bit piqued.

"Bah," he said, with a haughty pout. "I've already appeared in a novel, as the one and only protagonist, the central and dominant character, the catalyst of the action and, above all, of the passion. An entire novel written against me by a woman, poor thing, to work through her heartbreak."

"Yes, I've read it," I answered, which appeared to surprise and furthermore to gratify him. ("Really? You've read it?" he couldn't help saying, unable to conceal his delight, and that made me think that Rylands was on to something.) "But you didn't come off very well, which I suppose is natural since it was written to settle a score with you. Nor were you particularly recognizable, physically enhanced to make the ridiculous passion more credible. You were taller, I think. And in general a loathsome and clichéd character, if I recall correctly, professor. Papier maché."

The professor had the audacity to defend his achievement anyway; he's not a man to give in easily, only when he's grown bored with the argument.

"Don't be impertinent, young Marías. I came off terribly, but in any case it was obvious she had suffered a great deal over me and that makes me interesting. Doesn't it?"

"Young Marías": that's what Don Juan Benet and a few other friends have long been in the habit of calling me, to differentiate me from my estimable father, who is also a writer though not of fiction. I can well imagine that forty years from now there will still be someone who, on seeing me walk into a room, will say, "Here comes young Marías," and when the others turn around they'll see an eighty-five-year-old man; I've grown used to the idea and even to the scene, there's no way around it, names can do so much. Nowadays Rico calls me "Javier" and I call him "Paco," but at that point we didn't know each other as well and went by other names, "young Marías" and "Professor Rico, man of vast knowledge."

"Not very," I answered. "Making people suffer is the easiest thing in the world, it lies within anyone's power, the biggest fool or idiot, the most ordinary man and the least mysterious woman. In fact, everyone makes everyone suffer, a little or a great deal but always to some degree, even the people who are good to us and take care of us, contact is all it takes. And then, inevitably, there's the other person's disgust which is sometimes apparent and always makes you suffer, doesn't it? But that's not the point, nor does it matter whether, as a fictional character, you're made to seem more interesting than you are. The point is to be a character in an immortal book, if such a thing can happen today; even if you come off looking like a heartless brute, a rat, a moron. Of course it's best not to come off like that, because you'll appear in that light until the end of literature, but being left out would be even worse. At least that's what a foreign mentor of mine thinks. Tell me, do you think that little novel about you is going to last?"

The professor was pensive a few seconds, not wondering what his answer should be but whether he should give one. He pursed his elastic and continually fluctuating lips.

"Frankly," he said at last, "I'm sure not one reader will ever think of it again after putting it back on the shelf. If they read it to the end. I'm surprised you remember it."

"I don't remember much any more, and only because I know you, professor. And there you have it," I said. "You need a more solid author, one with a better chance of lasting. It's not that I think my chances are all that great, but in the end it wouldn't be a bad idea for you to put your chips on some more promising numbers." The professor is so deliberately vain that you can only feel comfortable with him if you're as tractable as his acolytes or match him with a vanity of your own, be it forced or false: he takes it very well, feels right at home, on solid ground, and sees it as an invitation to give himself free rein, in some respects he has a childish disposition, excessive in its gratitude. "I'd like to propose a deal."

Rico adjusted his glasses with his middle finger and looked me up and down, wrinkling up his nose like the sort of accountant who wears an eyeshade.

"And what sort of deal would that be, young Marías? I'm warning you that by my standards you don't yet have much to offer." What's true of his vanity is also true of his impudence—he doesn't mind anyone else's if the other person allows him his own without stiffening up at the first sally.

"I'm writing a novel and would have no problem putting you in it, if you can demonstrate sufficient merit."

"Oh really, how's that?" he asked with interest, then quickly switched to an air of indifference. "What would someone like me be doing in a novel of yours? Are you writing about scholars? Seducers? Illustrious men? Seems implausible to me."

The professor amused me, he almost always does, with his vast knowledge, except for once over the telephone.

"It's more about scholars than about seducers," I answered. "Look: this novel takes place in Oxford and nothing could be simpler than for me to include an elegant Spanish professor, there on a visit—invited to deliver a lecture, for example."

"You must mean a virtuoso and possibly inaugural lecture. Something extremely erudite and stimulating, on the House of the Prince at El Escorial, for example, or the *Libro del caballero Zifar*," he interjected with great conviction. "An extremely distinguished man and a dazzling speaker, no? His Oxford colleagues will drink in his words as if being granted a revelation, no? And handsome, *ça va sans dire*."

"Let me handle the character and the setting, professor, don't you be clichéd, too. Maybe that romance novel was all you deserved and I'm wasting my time. The Oxford University faculty has never drunk in anyone's words, that would go against their principles. They merely tolerate. And anyway, what would your speech be inaugurating?"

"The school year, of course," answered the professor opening his hands wide at shoulder level to underscore the obviousness of the thing. "The opening of the academic year for the entire university. And none of this limiting me to the department of Spanish and Portuguese, careful there, none of your crumbs, no. Michaelmas is what they call the first quarter there, isn't that right? Well then, for the inauguration of that Michaelmas of yours."

Since we were both being pedantic, I corrected his pronunciation: this particular "Michael" is pronounced Basquefashion. "Míkelmas," I said. "Professor, don't be absurdly ambitious. To do that, you'd have to give your speech in English, in which case it would not be a terribly virtuoso performance, I'm afraid your vast knowledge doesn't extend that far, nor does that of your potential fictional character. In any case, you haven't earned it yet."

Professor Rico reined in his aspirations. It was clear the idea had attracted him and was tempting him, or at least the joke of the idea. Making a couple of remarkable movements with his flexible mouth, he recovered his natural disdain.

"Oh yes, your deal." But he immediately left off with his pretence and his interest returned, he's too impatient a man for hypocrisy or haggling. "Tell me, how much of a role will I have?" he asked, as if he would be acting in a play.

"Not much of one, for the moment, not much, Professor. We could just give it a try this time, and if we're both happy with it who knows what future books may bring? For the moment a small role, a secondary character, incidental, but distinct."

"Me? Incidental? Me?"

"No, not you, the character in the novel. As I'm sure

you'll understand, I'm not going to rewrite the entire book to make you the protagonist. I have no heartbreak to work through, you know."

Professor Rico muttered something unintelligible, as if so enthralled with his hastily imagined portrayal that it pained him badly to renounce any part of it. So he muttered something like "Ertsz."

"What?" I asked.

"Nothing, nothing." He went on muttering a while longer as if tallying up sums in his head. He straightened his glasses, pushed up the sleeves of his jacket and finally began speaking clearly again, resolutely even, like a man accepting a bet in poker, and saying, "I see you" or "I raise you." "Very well, young Marías, let's skip the preliminaries and get down to business. What do you want in return? Let's have it."

I thanked him for his confidence and felt like a trafficker in false immortality.

I won't say what I asked for, only that he thought it was a reasonable enough request for a try-out, agreed to do it, and never did. When the time came, he frivolously claimed that while gratified by certain sartorial details and two or three adjectives, he had been thoroughly displeased by the character's behavior and degree of resemblance to him and the amount of space he was allotted. (Nevertheless, I learned from other sources that he was happy and even proud, particularly because people he knew mentioned the brief appearance or cameo to him in apparent envy: Toby Rylands really was onto something.) I didn't hold it against him, after all he had had the kindness to grant me some credit in a hypothetical posterity, I had enjoyed myself, and the character in question—an incidental character—was only partially inspired by him, though there were many people who wanted to see in my Professor del Diestro a dead-on portrayal of

Don Francisco Rico Manrique, which wasn't the case either (he never visited Oxford during my stay there). I had the character appear in a discotheque and the text describes him as, "the famous Professor del Diestro, the greatest and youngest Cervantes expert in the world, according to himself, invariably known in Madrid as Dexterous Del Diestro or Del Diestro the Sinister (depending on the level of antipathy), who, invited by our department, was to give us a dexterous and virtuoso lecture the next morning. I recognized him from his photographs." Then the text adds some further description: "The professor, a distinguished and disdainful man of forty-odd years, in a shirt by Ferré and with a hairline in advanced retreat ('A distinguished Spanish professor,' I thought in astonishment when I saw him, and immediately understood his success), was already nuzzling and allowing himself to be nuzzled by one of the fattest of the girls." As the reader can verify, I made him distinguished, famous, young, hated, successful, a wearer of Italian designer shirts, erudite and a seducer. The professor shouldn't have had any complaints, even if in the end I did not allow him to inaugurate the academic year, in his bad English, before the entire University of Oxford, at Michaelmas or rather Míkelmas.

A few years later, while I was writing my next novel, which was ultimately titled *Corazón tan blanco* or *A Heart So White*, I spoke to him over the phone one morning and mentioned the new book. He immediately asked, "Am I in it?"

His brazenness was so funny I saw no reason not to make him an immediate offer, this time with no strings attached.

"Do you want to be?" I asked. "There's still time. I'm getting close to the end, but I'm just starting a chapter that includes a character who could easily be transformed into you,

I mean into Professor del Diestro. All things considered, I think you'd be just right for me in this scene."

"I'd be just right for you? I? For you? Don't flatter yourself, I can't be just right for anyone. Why? What kind of malicious scene is it?" He's a wary man.

"Well, let's say I could slip you in without the book's being at all the worse for it; on the contrary, it might gain something."

"But this time I have to show my good side." His request had already become a demand. "What are you going to say about me? Let's have it."

"All right, maybe I can read you something now." The scene was partially written, so I picked up a page and read, "Let's see, here it says: 'Suddenly over dessert he fell silent for a few minutes, as if overwhelmed by fatigue from all the frenzy and exaltation, or as if he were immersed in dark thoughts, perhaps he was unhappy and had suddenly remembered it.'" I paused. "So. Interested?"

Professor Rico didn't answer right away, then conceded, "It's not bad, it doesn't displease me. I liked the part about exaltation. Is this character melancholy? I think he must be, since he's immersed in thought, isn't he?

"Yes, professor; immersed."

"In dark thoughts, right?"

"Yes, professor, very dark thoughts."

"Go on, read more."

Professor Rico is not, shall we say, much inclined toward melancholy, perhaps that was why he was interested in appearing melancholic in a work of fiction.

"All right, but only two sentences more: 'In any case, he must have been a man of some ability in order to go from self-satisfaction to dejection so suddenly, without seeming affected or insincere. It was as if he were saying 'What does anything matter now.'" I broke off. "Well, are you tempted?"

"The part about ability is very perceptive," he answered. "But you could change it to 'genius.' Might as well, don't you think?"

"Genius is harder to recognize, Professor Rico, and the narrator barely knows this guy."

"Don't call him a 'guy,'" he chided. "Go on, read more."

"Professor, I'm not about to read you the whole thing right now. Tell me if you want to be in the book or not. This is the only available role, and I'm warning you I could give it to someone else."

Paco Rico was silent for a few seconds. Then he wanted confirmation. "'As if he were saying, "What does anything matter now."'" That's what you said, isn't it?"

"Yes, professor: 'What does anything matter now.'"

"That part I liked. And I do sometimes think that, in moments of dejection. Yes," he said, in a tone that wasn't the least bit dejected. And he added, as if the idea and interest of including him in the novel were entirely mine, "Go ahead, I'll give it my immediate authorization."

So for a few days I went on writing my scene with Professor del Diestro now in it, his name and characteristics all consistent with the Del Diestro of *All Souls*. The character was more fully developed this time—no longer incidental, but now, at the very least, episodic—speaking at some length over the course of a dinner, which he dominates; I thought Paco Rico would be well pleased. But as I was about to finish the chapter I had another call from him, he was in Barcelona, where he lives.

"Hear me out on this, young Marías," he said without preliminaries. Though a few years had gone by, we still hadn't retreated from our ironic manner of addressing each other. We did so only after the death of the mutual friend through whose eyes we had managed to see each other with some sympathy, Don Juan Benet. "I've decided I don't want to appear in this little novel of yours as Professor del Diestro or what-have-you or anything else. If I'm in it I want to be in it as myself."

At first I didn't understand. "Yourself? What do you mean?"

The professor grew impatient. "Myself, Francisco Rico, under my own name. I want Francisco Rico to appear, not a fictional entity who acts like him or parodies him."

"But Del Diestro doesn't act all that much like you, he's not identical to you and I'd have to change him. Rico might not say or do the things he says and does, not all of them, and the character and his role are already fully drawn. I'm not going to change the story to make him more like you, I suppose you can understand that. Besides, how can a single real person appear among all the fictional entities, as you call them. That wouldn't look right."

The professor clicked his tongue a couple of times in irritation. I heard it very clearly, it almost ruptured my eardrum.

"And why not? That's nonsense. There are real places and institutions in your novel, aren't there? There must be one or two, no?"

"Yes, there's the United Nations and the Prado, and . . ."

"Well, there you have it," he said.

"Have what?"

"There you have it: I want to be like the Prado."

I couldn't help laughing and telling him, "Professor, no one doubts your great merit, you truly are illustrious, but I wonder if that might not be a lot to ask, especially while you're still alive. Maybe once you're dead they'll have a bust made of you."

"Don't play the fool with me, young Marías," he answered in feigned irritation. "You know perfectly well what I mean. You're going to call the Prado Museum the Prado Museum in your novel; I don't suppose you'll be writing that someone went to the Meadow Museum or the Field Museum or the Leap Museum."

Why the Leap? I asked myself.

"No. Why the Leap?" I asked him.

"Who cares, the Leap, the Jump, what does it matter? Therefore, just as the Prado is the Prado and not the Leap or the Jump, I must be Professor Francisco Rico with all of my attributes, distinguished professor at the Universidad de Bellaterra and member of the Real Academia Española de la Lengua"—his candidacy had been successful—"and not Del Diestro or Del Fieltro or any other fabrication or illusion, understand? I want to appear as myself. Otherwise not at all, nothing, take me out, I withdraw."

There was an element of reciprocal ribbing in all his huff and bother, but it was clear that the professor, protected by our friendship, was stipulating futile conditions with which no one could ever comply. In fact, nothing can ever be imposed on a writer of fiction, who doesn't need to ask permission to introduce any real person or sequence of events he happens to know about into his fiction; if he decides to, then nothing and no one can prevent him. We aren't trustworthy people and some of us are heartless, though I don't think I am. The professor was a friend and I wasn't about to go against his express desires. I tried to convince him, mainly for my own comfort and convenience. It's not easy to alter a character in a novel once he's been imagined and described, there's a price to pay, you feel what is called regret in English, or *rimpianto*, in Italian; there's no Spanish word that says it exactly, maybe we're not much given in these lands to lamenting what has or hasn't happened, what we did or failed to do; we know more about rancor. Even changing a character's name isn't easy. (You never forget the first name, the one you took away and no one else ever knew, as a mother never forgets the name she chose for the child who was born dead, before she could ever speak it aloud to him, the child no one else ever knew.) The professor in *A Heart So White* already was who he was, and what was more I would have to retype the whole chapter with the new surname, I love marking up a page but hate having any marks on the final version, and I neither own nor use a computer. Therefore a tedious task.

"Then it will have to be nothing at all, because what you're asking for won't work, Professor, and I'm the first to feel it."

Paco Rico said nothing, exuded silence. Maybe he was hoping I would give in. He was undoubtedly irked, but fortunately everything passes quickly with him—no, not everything, his romantic passions last, as I've seen over the years—he isn't a tenacious man and doesn't brood. He did not mutter.

"Well, in that case, he can't be called Del Diestro either," he ordered, and this second and even more futile demand gave me much to think about. It wasn't simply that he wanted to get back at me. He was not Del Diestro because he was Rico with all Rico's attributes, and he wanted to appear in the novel as such, making the distinction. Yet to his mind the name Del Diestro alluded to him, that character could be understood as Rico without in fact being him, as if the precedent of *All Souls* had impregnated or contaminated him and it would no longer be possible to evade or deny the identification if the character and name were repeated: the proof was that he assumed the authority to prohibit me from using Del Diestro. I had invented Del Diestro, he didn't belong to

Rico, but Rico was taking him over, seizing him. He no longer wanted to be recognized in someone else or to have a replica, he still wanted to figure in a fiction but not as fiction: as an inroad of reality into fiction—an intruder. Perhaps he was now experiencing the fear of being entirely fictitious, of returning to and forever inhabiting a terrain in which all is immutable to the end of time or of literature. In life, you can compensate or fluctuate or rectify, as long as the story hasn't yet ended—either in death, which arrives to bring everything to a close, or, above all, in the telling of life and death. What's attributed to you in a work of fiction, however, has little or no remedy, there's no debate about it, no amendment. Thus it is written and thus it is repeated, identically, without compassion or hope—this is the story and these are its words— telling the same thing in the same way every time it's read or leafed through or consulted, just as the action of a painting, once it's "chosen and frozen," never moves forward or recedes, and we'll never see the face of the person who was painted from behind, or the nape of the neck of the one whose face was portrayed, or the hidden side of the one in profile. Thus it is written: the frightful, immemorial threat. I said that what truly brings closure isn't the end but the recounting of that end, and of what transpired before it, the story of life and death, be they fictional or real, though if the life is fictitious then death isn't necessary: writing takes its place. Telling the story is what kills, what entombs, what secures and delineates and solidifies our face, profile or nape; being told in a story can be the equivalent of seeing oneself immortalized, for those who believe in that, and, in any case, of being dead; I am burying myself by this writing and in these pages, even if no one reads them; I don't know what I'm doing or why. (It doesn't matter if anyone else sees them, it's enough that I narrate myself a little, my own reading is enough.) Maybe that's what Professor Rico was intuiting: what I might be doing to him by entombing him in my book.

The name had to be changed and the chapter retyped, and Professor del Diestro of *A Heart So White* came to be named Professor Villalobos, which was the surname of a grouchy teacher at my school, the Estudio, at number 8 calle de Miguel Angel in Madrid, in the 1970s, just as Del Diestro was chosen because it was the surname of another teacher, this one light-hearted, Carmen García del Diestro, or Señorita Cuqui, as she was known, who wore lots of make-up and smoked incessantly in class, or rather, her cigarettes with their lipstick traces slowly burned down between her fingers as she read the classics to us with theatrical enthusiasm, juggling a heavy bracelet that she would take off, put back on and occasionally throw to the floor, denting them both (bracelet and floor), and attempting a bejeweled balancing act to keep her cigarette's ashes from falling, though in the end they always did, on her jacket or blouse, when the work she was reading drove her to make some violent gesture, for example when she made a vicious stab into the air or the shoulder of some favorite student—sack of flour, sack of flesh. What a delightful woman, she must be a hundred years old now and she writes me from time to time, with affection and a cigarette in her hand, most often to congratulate me when I publish an article in defense of tobacco.

But the character was already composed out of elements of Rico, or rather of Professor del Diestro, from the previous novel. I didn't feel capable of changing or giving up much of him so Rico may still be in there somewhere nonetheless—or prowling around outside—though at the end of the chapter I said, to stave off any notion of a resemblance, that when Professor Villalobos "fell into disheartened silence" he looked a little like the actor George Sanders, one of my favorites, whom I once called "the man who seemed not to want anything." Rico bears no resemblance whatsoever to Sanders. I don't know if that sufficed to liberate him. Now I've spoken of him here, by his name and with his attributes. But this is not a fiction, though it has to be a story.

In the first sentence of this book I said I believed I had still never mistaken—yes, *still never,* deliberately incorrect—fiction for reality, which doesn't mean that some retrospective effort on my part is not sometimes required to succeed in avoiding this type of confusion. I want to believe that I'm not much at fault in this; I am not responsible for the fact that certain real people began to behave in real life as if they were characters in *All Souls,* after it came out, or that a few eminent readers, who can be assumed to have been in full knowledge of the facts, took as valid in reality what was only recounted in a novel full of levity and exaggeration. Particularly notable were the remarks made a few months later by the vice-rector or vice-president or vice-chancellor of Oxford University, who, during a solemn assembly or ceremonious conclave (in which, once again, no ambitious and intrusive professor named Del Diestro or Del Fieltro or Rico had any part), said she was currently reading "a very interesting novel, in order to become better acquainted with and delve into the psychological workings of the Sub-Faculty of Spanish." Apparently there were murmurs of alarm, slight mockery, and deep and sincere astonishment—no one had been at all aware of the lady's secret but now presumptive Spanish-language abilities, for my text had yet to be translated into any other language—until my friend Eric Southworth took the liberty of speaking up to suggest to Madame vice-chancellor or vice-president or vice-rector, that, well, if it was her wish to make a close psychological study of the members of the department to which he belonged, it would perhaps be preferable for her to mingle with them personally or have them visited by a group of certified, licensed and officially approved and contracted psychologists, before entrusting so delicate a task to a reading that would surely be "of necessity oblique,"—all said with the characteristic Oxford ambiguity. ("What did you mean by that?" I asked him when he told me about it. "Oh, I don't know, whatever she decided to take it to mean," he answered.)) "May I, with the utmost respect, remind the distinguished vice-rector," he went on during that same plenary meeting, "that she has employed a word that is entirely apt and that she should at all times bear in mind? I refer to the word 'novel.' And perhaps it would be advisable to bear in mind, as well, that this novel was written by a foreigner," he added in fun, given that Eric is not exactly the sort to make nationalistic distinctions. As I later learned, the vice-chancellor, after a moment's consternation, then responded: "Yes, of course, you're correct, I see your point. A foreigner might wish to malign us, mightn't he? And all the more so if he is a Continental." "This particular foreigner, Madame vice-president, is not only a Continental"—Eric played his ace—"he is a Peninsular." "Yes, I see," the vice-rector hastily concluded in fear, as if she had just heard an obscene word that had to be tiptoed past at top speed and disposed of without delay. Apparently, two or three of the professors in the cloister or congregation who were at that moment entertaining themselves on the sly with my novel rapidly concealed their copies under their gowns.

Peninsular or Continental or both things together to English minds—of which fortunately only a few were ill-disposed in principle towards my oblique and nonsensical vision of the city and University of Oxford. Though I sent Ian Michael, Toby Rylands, the Taylorian Library and of course Eric Southworth their respective inscribed copies of the book right away, a few students who spent the 1989 Easter vacation in Spain (the novel had already been in the bookstores for a few weeks when Eduardo Mendoza—handsomely bribed—officially launched it on April 7) moved more rapidly than my country's wretched mail service, which isn't difficult, and, in Ian Michael's words, showed up in Oxford "with wagonloads" of my books, which they distributed, loaned out, or resold at exorbitant prices with unexpected, inexplicable glee, as a result of which, for several days, my former colleagues noticed certain sarcastic gazes or heard certain enigmatic and, of necessity, oblique allusions from their students, without knowing what to make of them. None of this was, of course, my intention.

The first one to read the book—not in vain is he the most inquisitive, the one who most prides himself on keeping abreast of all that happens in several cities: Oxford, Swansea, Southampton, Madrid and Vigo—was Ian Michael, who wrote me a letter from Exeter College that made me sigh in relief when I began reading it but which I returned to its envelope in horror and mortification once I had finished. He very kindly wrote that *All Souls* struck him as my "best novel yet," and assured me he was not saying this "because I have some small role in it, or because of the morbid fascination everyone here is feeling as a result of the mistaken belief that it is a *roman à clef* (students like John London and Huw Lewis come panting back from Madrid with so many copies that possibly they alone had contributed to its selling out)." (His Spanish is excellent but not perfect.) He said he had read it "in one sitting" until five in the morning, and now he was reading it again, more slowly; he spoke of the "inter-weaving of antithetical themes," among them "the fictional Gawsworth: the real Machen" —taking Gawsworth for a fiction; he made a few more literary observations and, in fine professorial fashion, pointed out to me "only a very few solecisms, of scant importance: are the streets a kind of red?"— arguing with my eyesight—"or are they honey-colored?" He had another reservation, of an architectural or topographical nature, which amused me for its punctilious erudition: "It doesn't seem possible to me that the office of Clare Bayes"— the novel's central female character—"could look directly onto Radcliffe Camera from All Souls, where the only windows facing that direction are those of the Codrington Library (or those of Hertford, perhaps?), since Hawksmoor built a false wall to finish off All Souls on the west side, knowing that Wren or another architect would construct something interesting in the space to oppose or complement his neo-gothic towers. I've also noticed the complete absence of any reference to the Oxonian flora which I do not attribute to the (for me) wretchedness or poverty of almost all Spanish writers in this respect, but to your desire to represent an entirely inhospitable city." Here he was mistaken or was being polite, since, in the matter of the aforementioned "wretchedness or poverty," if in no other (my country's inspectors have so often denied me any syntactic nationality: it's a very literate country, the inspectors write a great deal and are applauded by the customs officials, and vice versa), I engrave my name fully and with laurels in the Spanish tradition: so extravagantly urban and distracted am I that I would be unable to identify so much as a pine tree. (Nor do I believe I depicted Oxford as so unpleasant.) He obligingly pointed out a couple of typos, and then gave me news of himself, the most salient—or most distressing—item being that he had been suffering from a case of eczema brought on by allergies ever since he had moved away from the house on the Cherwell and had been forced to place his blind mother in a private nursing home in the village of Freeland, "where Toby Rylands' mother spent the last thirteen years of her life," he said, as if he couldn't help noting the growing number of parallels between the trajectory of his predecessor's life and his own, or as if he were beginning to see Rylands' present as a portend of his future. (And that's what he called him in the letter, "Toby Rylands," the name he went by in the novel, this time it wasn't me who was doing it.) He wasn't sure if the eczema was a psychosomatic effect of relinquishing his mother and the river, or if it was caused by the rug in his new flat, previously inhabited by a "woman who was a radiologist or cobalt therapist," perhaps insinuating that the lady had wickedly irradiated it by flinging herself about on the carpeted floor during her tenancy.

The disturbing part came last. For, after having stated that my book was not a *roman à clef*, which cheered me enormously and filled me with gratitude (since, in fact, it was not, and no one was in a better position than he to see that), Ian Michael went on to speak to me of my former colleagues in the department, calling each one by the name of a character in the novel, thus forcing me into some arcane speculations as to the referent in each case. And in that vein, he informed me that Rylands was "very pleased with one of those false honors"—he was paraphrasing my text, which said "insincere honors"—"that he received news of in the mail: a prize that brought him four million pesetas and the obligation to give a lecture in Salamanca." I was more worried about the next bit. "Your novel angered him, I've heard, and he flung it to the ground before he was halfway through." And he went on, merrily tossing out fictional names: "I saw Alec Dewar furtively leafing through a copy brought to him by a muscular female student in a rugby shirt; later, in the commons of his college, he was bragging about having appeared in a Continental *roman à clef*. . . . Cromer-Blake"—the live one, not the dead one—"is just back from a lecture tour, perhaps a pleasure tour as well, in Italy . . . Leigh-Peele has yet to register a reaction." Worst and most upsetting of all was the conclusion. If one character in *All Souls* was entirely made up (that is, could not be identified, even slyly or in bad faith, with anyone who was real) it was the central female, Clare Bayes, a married woman, also a professor, with whom the Spanish narrator maintained a clandestine relationship during his stay in what for him was always transient territory. Ian Michael, nevertheless, ended by saying, to my utmost bewilderment: "I see quite a bit of Clare Bayes these days since she's moved as well, to a street near my new one, and I often run into her, she's always carrying a lot of things around with her, as in the novel. She's still fairly appealing, but not as attractive as before. No one knows whether she's taken a new lover."

I think I blushed (I know I did: I saw myself reflected on the television screen, I was watching a video and hadn't stopped the tape to read the letter, I'm not sure if it was *Los tres caballeros* or *Mi amor brasileño* with Ricardo Montalbán, I remember that incongruous sambas were sounding in my ears as I deciphered the letter from my Oxonian former boss, the only boss I've had in my life, and who never acted like one, bless him), and of course I got a little worked up about it. Though I thought I would answer him in writing, too, as is proper, I immediately rang Ian up so that he could confirm Toby's unexpected and to me deplorable fury, and I could rescue him at once from his error with regard to the dangerous conjecture of a real Clare Bayes. But when I had him at the other end of the line—it was evening—I thought it best not to inquire after the identity of the woman who, according to him, had lost some of her former appeal. "Good God," I thought, as I watched either the seductive Montalbán or that green parrot in a straw hat, José Carioca, I'm not sure which, dancing, now soundlessly, "as a result of my novel there is now a professor at Oxford whom everyone believes to be an adulteress, guilty of an extra-marital, Continental and, worst of all, Peninsular liaison, some poor woman who did no such thing, or at least not with me, to the point that she's expected to 'take' a new lover after my now long past departure; she hasn't done so because she's not in the habit of doing so, and, as always happens in these cases, she'll be the only one who doesn't know, or perhaps her husband won't either, her husband who'll be taken for a cuckold—made one by the intervention of a foreigner predisposed to malignment—what a calamity. Who can she be? I wondered, but didn't ask Ian, though I couldn't help but mention to him in passing, in a feeble attempt to save the unknown woman from slander and idle talk, that there had never been a Clare Bayes or Clare Bayes-equivalent of any kind during my stay in Oxford. "No?" was all he answered, and it was clear he didn't believe me. I deeply regretted the fact that this woman, whoever she was, would be the object of gossip in so gossip-mongering a city, and I the indirect cause of it, and thus not only would her reputation be placed in question but her good taste as well. (I have no reputation to lose in this respect, but who knew if my taste wouldn't be questioned, also.) If I may, I will state here that during my years in Oxford I lived very chastely, at least with respect to the native women, who in no way struck me as "rather whorish," as Miriam Gómez once said they could be (she said it in her always inoffensive Cuban way and in the presence of her husband, Guillermo Cabrera Infante, who said nothing, both of

69

them having lived in London for thirty years). To my horror I suddenly realized that the high-mindedness and good sense of the lady professor would also be cast in doubt, for, according to British convention and tradition, being seduced by a Spaniard is third among the most sordid and, at the same time, naive entanglements that a married Englishwoman can become involved in: the second is seduction by an Italian, and the first by an Argentine. The worst of it is that there are a large number of people in Oxford with conventional and traditional British ideas. What a terrible disservice to this poor, unlucky woman to whom I wish no harm, I thought; really, we writers should be more careful about what we write, not only because of situations like this one but also because what we write sometimes comes to pass. And if I must be sincere—there's no reason why I have to be, perhaps I'll need to talk about that later—I also regretted not having known her, because if she was no longer quite as attractive that meant she had been attractive when I was a temporary part of the city and the congregation. Or perhaps I had known her. In any case, the two of us apparently made a plausible furtive couple, which gave rise to a certain vulgar curiosity that I was able to quell. I tried to see myself reflected on the television screen again, which is somewhat difficult when the screen is full of bright colors: entirely impossible to see oneself blush against a backdrop of Carioca and Montalbán, Donald Duck and Lana Turner, and I could only tell I was blushing from the heat of my face and the momentary palpitation of an eyelid.

Where Toby Rylands was concerned, my ex-boss Michael, to my sorrow, confirmed the initial rumors going around the Sub-Faculty. For reasons that were not known with any certainty, he had apparently hurled his copy of my book angrily down onto the grass in his garden, where it probably still moldered at that hour, soaked and warped by the intermittent rain and phlegmatic sun, perhaps chewed by some passing dog—a three-legged dog, perhaps, that had run away from its master. Ian told me he thought Toby must have been annoyed by the mention of his adventures in espionage and other escapades—the Spanish word Ian used was *correrías*, the type of word learned foreigners quickly pick up and enjoy using; I, who owe them so much, have used it here in connection with one of them, the bandit Dean of Canterbury, who almost left me forever in limbo—because it irritated Toby to have it spoken of in public, even more so in print. "But the character isn't him," I protested, "though I may have taken some of his physical characteristics on loan; there's not a word spoken by Toby Rylands that I've ever heard Toby say, and I didn't and still don't know anything about any such activities." "No?" Ian confined himself to answering once again; he wasn't accepting any of my denials despite having seen clearly that this was not a *roman à clef*. "No," I insisted, "it's the first I've heard of it: I only imagined, made things up, that's all." Ian's letter was dated on St. George's Day 1989, and our conversation took place four or five days later. It left me very concerned about Toby. He was the one who had all but asked to appear as a character in the book, even if he was half joking, and now he was angry about a mild resemblance and a few involuntary coincidences. Not only did I greatly regret his wrath, which baffled me, but I also had to prepare myself to live in fear of some long-distance punishment if he deemed my recklessness or offense deserving of one, I didn't even want to think about the vile aberrations he might accuse me of if that were the case, practices that exist only in textbooks. (Although I have no interest whatsoever in teaching, in America or anywhere else, my teaching days are over, and while they weren't over yet then,

I was only looking for the conviction and a suitable pretext to bring them to an end.)

A week later my dismay had largely vanished, again thanks to the skeptical I. D. L. Michael, sometimes called "Ideal M" because of his initials, who took the trouble to phone me from Exeter College, full of excitement, in the sole and benevolent aim of filling me in on the conversation about my book he had just finally had with Toby Rylands in the Senior Common Room of the Taylorian, with its pay-as-you-go electric coffee pot. The cause of Rylands' ire was indeed as Ian Michael had imagined; he certainly did not remember that he had never actually told me anything con-crete about his recruitment by the secret services or his spe-cial missions in exotic places or other escapades, he hadn't even given me a proper account of the witty prince he had gone on binges with. The volume, flung from his colonial rattan chair, had lain on the scraggly lawn for nine or ten nights and days, after which, still somewhat intrigued by what he had read before the wrathful interruption—and hav-ing uneasily caught sight, from his window, of the tempting book, semi-sheltered by a climbing vine next to which it had fallen—he'd plucked it from the foliage, brushed it off, smoothed down its pages, started over from the beginning and devoured it in a few hours. I held my breath. "He liked it," Ian told me after an inopportune pause whose only con-ceivable purpose was to prolong my agitation: "He thinks it's your best novel yet. He still isn't amused by your mentioning the espionage, especially not the bit about Haiti, but he says that in the end he has nothing to complain of, since, in his opinion, he inspired the most attractive character in the book, the most profound and memorable, the strongest, the one who says the most intelligent things. In fact, he's now taken the character for his own; it wouldn't surprise me if he soon started imitating him a little. He even repeated to me, as an original line of his own, a sentence your character says." I let out my breath, gladdened and relieved, among other and more important reasons because I saw myself freed from the specter of being accused of the wide variety of depravities I had been dreading for a week by then, balanism, strangury, satyriasis, nequicia, mictionism, pyromania, enfiteusis, positivism, erotesis, felo-de-se, or perhaps even lardy-dardiness, though I don't know if any of those words, which have cropped up here and there in my translations, correspond to vices (I think not) and I'm not about to go and look them all up right now, but their obscene or sinister sonority alone makes them all, without exception, deserve to be tremendous perversions—irreversible degenerations. It would have pained me to be accused of enfiteusis.

I couldn't help feeling some curiosity, which I didn't consider vulgar this time; "Oh really? What sentence was it?" I asked my ex-boss. "We were talking about my cobaltic eczema or some ailment of his when he suddenly murmured pensively 'To whom does the sick man's will belong? To the sick man or to the disease?' Well, something like that, I don't know if he cited it verbatim. Did he cite it verbatim?" "I don't know, I don't remember; I don't know every word of my book verbatim," I answered, echoing his British Latinism, and then inquiring further: "And what's the problem with Haiti?" "Oh, I don't know, you're the one who knows, you mentioned it in the novel."

I swear I knew absolutely nothing about any role played by Haiti in Toby Rylands' dispersed and shrouded past. I could just as easily have said Honduras or Belize, Antigua or Montserrat or Barbuda, yet what I wrote was Haiti where, it now turned out, he had experienced some vicissitudes or left some trace of his escapades; perhaps the boisterous prince was from that island. I refrained from mentioning to Ian—so that he wouldn't tell Toby about it, there's a certain verbal incontinence in Oxford for which the city's inhabitants should not be held too much to blame, it's in the air there, a tendency to instantly release whatever information is acquired, everyone is at risk but everyone also gains—that some of the fictional Toby Rylands' thoughts were more in the spirit of one of the most kindly and astute old men I've ever known, the poet Vicente Aleixandre, who often spoke laughingly and with derision of his ailments, calling them *"mis lacras,"* "my scourges," to mollify them; and the other reflections were invented. I preferred that Toby take all of them for his own as time went on, if he wanted to and the fog of memory favored it; they're his already if he wants them, no longer mine or my poet friend's, they are much more his now, that's how I see it anyway; Toby was also astute, and kindly in his way, though more caustic and punitive, and not as warm. "He liked the way you describe his laugh," Ian added, "so I think that despite earlier indicators we've won him over to the cause." I was silent, listening to my ex-boss absently hum a melody that seemed to me to be a well-known ballad that speaks or tells the story of the Molly Maguires, the Irish secret society whose members disguised themselves as women to strike their blows and bring terror to the police and the judiciary around 1843, emerging again later, thousands of miles away, among the Irish who immigrated to Pennsylvania, I know all of this, believe it or not, primarily because there was a movie about them with the Scotsman Sean Connery. Ian Michael is Welsh, but the character in the novel who could most closely be compared to him was Irish, Aidan Kavanagh. "The cause," I thought, and immediately there came to mind the famous and mysterious passage, this time indeed verbatim: "It is the cause, it is the cause my soul,—/ Let me not name it

74

to you, you chaste stars!—/ It is the cause.—Yet I'll not shed her blood; / Nor scar that whiter skin of hers than snow. . . ." Othello says this to himself just before killing Desdemona who is sleeping her innocent sleep but will awake to learn of her own death; and four centuries after he spoke those words for the first time we still don't entirely know what cause it is that should not be named to the stars, or what Othello meant by the enigmatic and repeated words, "It is the cause, it is the cause"; he didn't even say "She is the cause." I was still thinking about the unknown woman in Oxford, now believed to be an adulteress, and I was the cause, both her Cassio and her Iago, the false lover and the man who incited suspicion, not with my whisperings but with my writings, though without wanting to or foreseeing it. "I hope it's not an Othello she's with," I thought; "it almost certainly is not, there aren't many left these days, at least not in England. Yet there are still Iagos everywhere." And I'm not sure whether I didn't think the second of these three things only in order to calm my fears. ". . . And smooth as monumental alabaster. / Yet she must die, else she'll betray more men. / Put out the light, and then put out the light. . . ," Othello goes on, and I went on remembering. "Hey, how's the atomic carpet?" I asked Ian then, breaking in on his absentminded ditty and my thoughts and citations. "Is it still giving off radioactivity, or is it just shooting up X-rays to unmask you?"

Yes, it was Ian David Lewis Michael who spoke of "the cause," in the least probable—but not impossible—sense in which Othello may have been using the word. And that was how my former, humorously-inclined boss lived the life of *All Souls*, as a small cause of his own, which was rather touching to me and for which I will always be grateful to him (he was more concerned about the book than its own boorish and disbelieving publisher who was making a profit from it: quite a contrast). Not only did he become an ardent defender of the novel, but he followed each of the unexpected phases of its still unfinished career with enthusiasm and delight, gathering opinions and reactions wherever he could, he and Eric Southworth; I never thought that in a city like Oxford, about which so much literature, good and bad, has been written for centuries, my own book could create the slightest stir; on the contrary, I expected indifference, even if it were feigned. Perhaps I wasn't taking sufficient account of the fact that it's a very cloistered place, feeding entirely on itself, at once learned, lordly, and provincial, like Venice, the other city I lived in during those years, to which I flew in terror whenever I could, in a state of febrile expectation and permanent anxiety, it's where perhaps the best and worst things in my life have happened to me—leaving aside, among the worst, the deaths of those I loved who died in other places. It isn't necessary to be as specific as I've just been, but sometimes one has to guard against jokes, in an area where one doesn't allow them, and one always knows where that is. Sometimes one must take precautions, so as not to to be forced, later, to kill with words.

Indifference was indeed feigned by some, as I was to learn, but the dissemblers, such as Alec Dewar, should have been more careful and kept more fully in mind that in Oxford everything and everyone is found out and tattled on. Not only did Ian see Dewar leafing through the copy that the well-built student clad in a shirt imprudently light for that time of year had brought him, but other people also came upon him, carefully and furtively reading when he thought he was alone in the Senior Common Room or invisible in a corner of the library. Nevertheless, around his colleagues in the department he continued to insist on playing the man without a clue ("Oh really? A novel by Javier, set in Oxford? Oh yes, I vaguely recall someone telling me something about it. No, I haven't read it, I'm spending all my time on the Inca Garcilaso de la Vega these days"), probably to avoid having to express an opinion, or in order to let everyone see that no contemporary work, whatever it might be, could possibly interest him. A colleague at his college—whose knowledge was absolutely first-hand—informed me that he did indeed boast to whoever happened to sit next to him in the refectory or at the high tables of having become a novelistic character in Europe—what he said was not "in a novel," but "novelistic," my mole emphasized. Deliberately severe and involuntarily shy, the good Alec Dewar was at last in possession of a topic that was original and his alone: now he was the one to announce the news, answer the questions that courtesy obliged, enlighten his interlocutors and set the course of the conversation, rather than waiting for his dinner companions to take an interest in him and throw a word or two in his direction, which, fearful of his apparently severe and even blustering character, they did not always do. "If you must know, my friend," he said with undisguised self-importance to my informant from Trinity or Christ Church or Corpus Christi, "I have been the subject and central motif of a *roman à clef*, which, as you know, is a French expression meaning 'novel with a key,' one of those books in which the astonished reader never stops wondering whether, or to what incredible degree, it can all be true—all that the author writes about characters who aren't really characters, you understand, but recognizable or somewhat recognizable representations of real persons: recognizable to those who know them, it must be said. There is a very good Spanish word for this, of course you won't know it and it isn't easy to translate or explain, like all the best terms. A very interesting word: *tra-sun-to*," he concluded after taking a breath, bending forward and even changing expression to pronounce it, solemnly spacing out the syllables and speaking in a much higher—evidently even strident—tone of voice that almost caused a cataclysm at the table and of course did cause half a dozen startled jumps (spoons let fly through the air) and another half dozen bouts of choking. My mole was a chemist, and at Oxford there is a not entirely unfounded tendency to believe that every professor or don is an eminent luminary in his own field but lives in the most absolute ignorance of anything beyond it, lacking even the most elementary notions that are well within the grasp of any child. The chemist was fully aware of the meaning of *roman à clef*, and rather irritated at having it explained to him, but not of *trasunto*, and I had to improvise the definition Dewar was at great pains to keep from providing. It is my suspicion that he had probably just rediscovered this deeply interesting word in the work of the Inca Garcilaso or in the dictionary. "Yes? And what does this foreign novel have to say about you, Doctor Dewar? Something we mustn't know? Some compromising piece of information? Some roguery?" my chemist asked him. And Dewar answered complacently, or rather with triumphal delectation—the skin of his pate stretched tighter than usual, his glasses slipping down, "The most fantastic things, I assure you, the most fantastic things. And the funny thing is that some of them are true, no one would ever think it. Well, well, so it goes in this day and age." It's a pity he didn't say exactly which things he would admit to the truth of, because I would have liked, as with Rylands, to know what I had hit on without wanting or trying to. But it is possible—or at least to be hoped, and this alone would justify my book—that the real replica or *trasunto* of the fictional Butcher or Hammer subsequently awoke greater interest among his colleagues and dinner companions, or, better still, greater appreciation, at least until the appearance of the novel in French, the first language into which it was translated, and which all curious dons know, even chemists.

Neither Fred Hodcroft nor John Rutherford had much to say about *All Souls*, and perhaps in their cases the indifference was authentic; anyway, no one was ever tempted to recognize either of them in any of the characters or to see them replicated on any page, which may serve to reinforce the preceding conjecture. I trust that one of Toby Rylands' predictions was, nevertheless, not entirely correct and that neither Hodcroft nor Rutherford, for whom I have great respect and greater liking, were ever bothered or offended because, in their regard, the mistake was not made which was made with regard to Ian, Toby, Eric, Philip Lloyd-Bostock, Alec Dewar, Leigh-Peele, the boozing Lord Rymer, Tom the porter, and even the *belle inconnue* adulteress, or perhaps *connue*, or perhaps not even *belle*, and certainly not an adulteress, or, then again, who knows. And with regard not only to these people, who are all related to the University, but also to certain other Oxonians who had last set foot in a classroom in their extreme youth, decades ago, and who certainly had only been there as impatient students. But I'll speak of them later. I don't imagine that either Fred or John considers himself harmed or deprived of a literary immortality that seems a bit ephemeral and perhaps already sepulchral.

So at least I wasn't punished with the indifference I had expected (there was very little of that), and the novel gave rise, I believe, to more joking and diversion than anger or strife in those who were able to read it immediately in Spanish, and to passive curiosity in those who had to wait for it to be translated into their language or some other language they knew; among those who had to wait was Sir Ralf Dahrendorf, the celebrated essayist and current warden of St. Antony's College, who is of German origin and to whom I was able to send, some time later, and at the request of his secretary (I'm not acquainted with him personally but did so with pleasure, I was attached to St. Antony's under another ruling), a copy in his native tongue, which also preceded the English version and came out just when he took the trouble to request it, more for his domestic than his literary satisfaction, I believe. Perhaps only to flatter me, both Eric and Ian sent word that certain stirrings of envy and even threats of reprisal arose from the members of other faculties and the other departments of our own Faculty of Medieval and Modern Languages or Institutio Tayloriana, who did not have a similar foreign novel to presumably portray or reflect them, however problematically, about which they could crow to their tablemates at the interminable and competitive high tables or dinners that take place on a raised platform (apparently the Slavic high tables were the most torturous, and the

French ones the most tedious). If this were true, I imagine their envy arose not so much from the existence of the book itself as from the muffled but hearty laughter they spotted my former colleagues giving in to each time the book furnished them with some additional piece of news or gleeful rumor.

There was also the occasional megalomaniac professor who staked his claim to a place in those pages, individuals who were unknown to me or with whom I had never exchanged a word, and yet who asserted—swore—that they had served nevertheless as the unmistakable model for this or that character, however incidental or vague. Once open season on identifications was declared, a number were made that, like the identification of the fictional lover Clare Bayes with Ian Michael's mysterious current neighbor, were entirely groundless; it was suspected, for example, that behind the tippling warden named Lord Rymer in the novel was hidden poor Raymond Carr, the illustrious and now emeritus professor, because he had been warden of St Antony's in my time and had concerned himself extensively with Spain in his prize-winning writings, and because of the unintentional equivalence between the consonants of the character's surname and those of the historian's Christian name ("Christian" is a figure of speech): Rymer, Raymond, completely absurd (there are so many customs officials and glib, twisted inspectors), particularly because there was indeed a slight source of inspiration for Lord Rymer, a genuine lord, ruddy, salacious, heavyset and with a real weakness for wine (not that Carr doesn't enjoy a glass now and then, but not enough for any confusion: Carr is thin, and whenever I saw the lord he was staggering; they tell me he's dead now). It was also believed—well, this was Ian again, who alerted the others with his inquiries and reconstructions—that the antiquarian book dealers who appear in *All Souls* as Mr. and Mrs. Alabaster had to correspond to the owners of the Turl Street bookshop Titles, whose name was Stone, in which case I would have ennobled them by transforming them from the vulgar Stone of reality to the monumental Alabaster of fiction ("Nor scar that whiter skin of hers than snow, and smooth . . .").

This sort of megalomania or eagerness for literary protagonism occurs, in any case, with strange frequency, even when the situation in no way lends itself to confusion or alibi, as *All Souls* may have done because of the aforementioned coincidences between narrator and author. I remember that one evening a lady phoned me from one of the eastern regions of my country, a lady I had only seen twice, and briefly, once after a lecture or simulacrum of such that I had travelled to her region to deliver, and once in a Madrid café where I went, at her incomprehensible insistence, to sign a book for her, and on neither occasion had there been time to talk about anything personal, or, in fact, about almost anything at all, so I knew almost nothing about her. Well, she called to tell me she had read my first anthology of stories, published in 1990, and had liked it a great deal, including the final story, which struck her as "exquisite"—an odd adjective to use in respect to that monstrous story but undoubtedly a favorite of hers, I'd heard it from her at other times— "though I did understand that it refers to me and is about me and, in fact, is very hard on me." I'd been dancing the hucklebuck with a friend of mine when the phone rang, and my friend refused to stop or lower the music (she really loves to dance, once she's off there's no slowing her down, it was Anna, or Julia), so I thought I wasn't hearing right and only managed to gape in amazement and ask for confirmation of her bewildering words: "About you? You said the story is about you? What do you mean, about you?" Up to that point she had behaved sensibly and politely, even if everything always struck her as exquisite. "You deny it, then?" the reader from the east answered, verging on fury, and added imperiously (addressing me casually or intimately as "*tú*"): "Do me a favor and turn down that racket, I can't hear a thing." People often address me as *tú* and give me orders, I think I make too many jokes and fail to command respect. "You're not going to deny that the story is out to get me, are you? You're not denying that to me, Javier Marías." I'm afraid I did deny it, nevertheless, and perhaps not in the most polite fashion, it was only natural for me to deny it, or so I believe, and I certainly never wanted to investigate the matter any further. The story in question is one of the things that most affected me as I wrote it. It was about a vengeful butler with whom I spent a rather long period of time trapped in an elevator that broke down between two floors of a New York skyscraper. The butler worked for the local cosmetics king and his new wife, who was Spanish; there was also a newborn baby girl who was sick. It was the first time that I made narrator and author coincide in an apparently fictional piece, the narrator was me. There were no other characters, so I chose not to find out which one my interlocutor from the east identified with: the Spanish wife, the butler, the newborn baby, I myself, or the elevator. At least she saved me from an exhausting and breakneck living-room hucklebuck. Shortly thereafter she sent me a completely incomprehensible telegram; the text was long and poetical and lacked all punctuation, I suppose it must have struck her as overly prosaic to interrupt the great flow of metaphorical surrealism with one or another "stop." The only part that was clear was her remarkable way of signing off: she didn't sign as "your slave," or "your servant," or even "your scullery maid," or "your hired hand"—

all of which would have been embarrassing while yet retaining at least some relationship to traditional epistolary rhetoric—but rather, sounding a much more contemporary note, she took her leave as "your cleaning lady." Which made me quite certain that she had identified with the butler.

Of all the quite random and irresponsible misidentifications that were made in Oxford, the most ominous and objectionable, though not the most serious, was the one endured by my friend Eric Southworth, and in print, as well, two years after the novel first came out. On April 16, 1991, he wrote me a letter in response to a letter of mine in which I had included, for his Hispanistic information, an obituary of the well-known Spanish critic and scholar Ricardo Gullón, who had just died. As I've already mentioned, attempts were made to identify Eric with the character in the novel named Cromer-Blake, who was on the most excellent terms with the narrator, was ill, and in the end died. By some fluke Cromer-Blake's diaries found their way into the hands of the Spanish narrator, who cited them very briefly a couple of times—I dislike the overreliance on this sort of expedient in fiction. But, as I also mentioned, the funereal and afflicted aspect of the character was, instead, attributed to Philip Lloyd-Bostock, whom I saw far less of but who did indeed die not long after my departure, after a long, indecisive and veiled illness. This should have meant that Eric would thus be free of bad omens and unpleasant speculations, but even he was not spared: in his letter to me he enclosed a photocopy of the *Boletín de la Asociación Internacional de Galdosistas*, or *Bulletin of the International Association of Benito Pérez Galdós Scholars*, headquartered in Canada, in Kingston, Ontario—undoubtedly a most stimulating publication, it seems impossible that anything like it could exist and in its "Año XI," or Year XI, no less, or so it stated—with its table of contents and correspon-

"Romanticism, Realism and the Presence of the Word," <u>Media, Consciousness and Culture</u>. Ed. Bruce Gronbeck <u>et al</u>. New York: Sage. (Versión completa "<u>Fortunata y Jacinta, Madame Bovary</u> and Oral Trace," <u>Letras Peninsulares</u>.

"On Monstrous Birth: Leopoldo Alas and the Inchoate," <u>Naturalism in the European Novel</u>. Ed. Brian Nelson. Oxford: Berg, 1991.

Linda M. Willem

"A Dickensian Interlude in Galdós's <u>Rosalía</u>," <u>Bulletin of Hispanic Studies</u>.

"The Narrative Premise of Galdós's <u>Lo prohibido</u>," <u>Romance Quarterly</u>, 38 (1991).

"The Narrative Voice Presentation of Rosalía de Bringas in Two Galdosian Novels," <u>Crítica Hispánica</u>, 12 (1990).

[6] OTRAS NOTICIAS

Stella Moreno (Central Washington University) prepara actualmente su disertación doctoral sobre el tema "Love, Marriage and Desire in the <u>Novelas Contemporáneas</u> of Galdós."

A Diane Urey (Illinois State University) le ha sido otorgada una N.E.H. Fellowship para que prepare un libro sobre los primeros <u>Episodios Nacionales</u>.

[7] NECROLOGÍA

~~Eric Southworth, St. Peter's College, Oxford University.~~
Ricardo Gullón, Madrid.

[8] PRÓXIMO NÚMERO DEL <u>BOLETÍN</u> DE LA AIG

Se incluirán en él:

a) comunicaciones sobre las entidades y publicaciones siguientes:

La Asociación Cultural Benito Pérez Galdós. (John W. Kronik)

El Centro de Investigación "Pérez Galdós" de la Facultad de Ciencias de la Información, Universidad Complutense, Madrid. (Mª del Pilar Palomo y Julián Avila Arrellano)

<u>El Omnibus Galdosiano</u>. (Pedro Ortiz Armengol)

El Grupo de Amigos de Galdós. (Pedro Ortiz Armengol)

"Galdós en Madrid, Madrid en Galdós." (Julio Rodríguez Puértolas)

b) resúmenes del contenido de las <u>Actas</u> siguientes:

<u>Actas del Tercer Congreso Internacional de Estudios Galdosianos</u>. Las Palmas: Cabildo Insular de Gran Canaria, 1989. I, 316; II, 569.

<u>Galdós. Centenario de 'Fortunata y Jacinta' (1887-1987). Actas (Congreso Internacional, 23-28 de noviembre)</u>. Madrid: Universidad Complutense, 1989. Pp. 669.

<u>Galdós, en el centenario de 'Fortunata y Jacinta'</u>. Ed. Julio Rodríguez Puértolas. Palma de Mallorca: Prensa Universitaria, 1989. Pp. 110.

ding sections, the seventh of which was titled "Necrología," beneath which heading appeared the following: ~~Eric Southworth, St Peter's College, Oxford University.~~ And below: "Ricardo Gullón, Madrid." Despite the official correction, Eric's name was as clearly visible there as here, a horrifying sight that I would never wish to encounter again without the line through it, and in any case a thing of extremely ill omen. Fortunately, Eric is a Londoner, not a native of Seville or Cadiz, or a man of Madrid with a Cuban grandmother, like me, so he took no drastic measures, neither plotting revenge nor hatching conspiracies (perhaps he donned his two archbishop's caps for a while and didn't tell me, green tassel and red tassel, silk and satin). Nor, in keeping with Anglo-Saxon tradition, did he decide to file suit against Canada, or Ontario or Kingston or the *Boletín* or even the Galdosistas, who would have deserved it for more than one reason; no, he took his ephemeral demise in stride, as his accompanying letter shows: "The obituary of Ricardo Gullón you sent me can serve to introduce the curious death notice I'm enclosing for you in return, in which, as you'll see, I share the 'Deaths' column with none other than Gullón, for which reason it could be said that not only am I already aware of his death, but, according to some impatient or scatterbrained pen, I've shaken his hand on the road to the great beyond and we may even have walked together a while, inevitably chatting about my favorite of Galdos's novels, *El amigo Manso*, until he took the road towards Paradise and I, let us say, the one towards a long stretch in Purgatory, where I fear Pérez Galdós himself must still be tormented for his many sins. The chair of the Spanish department at Strathclyde called my friend Maurice Hemingway to say how awful it was that I had died, he had just read the news in the *Boletín Internacional de Galdosistas*. Maurice was astonished, took the precaution of ringing me up to be sure I was still alive, then got in touch with Rye, the man in charge of the *Boletín*, to inform him of the mistake. So, when I came back from Italy, a copy of the *Boletín* was waiting for me with my death properly suppressed—post publication, perhaps only postponed—and a letter of abject apology from the editor. *Lo que no se saca en limpio*"—Eric wrote that phrase, meaning "what has yet to be cleared up," in Spanish—"however, is what the devil put the notion that I had died in their heads to begin with. My first thought was that Rye was taking revenge for a review I wrote of his most recent book on Galdós by killing me in his *Boletín*, and internationally, too, but now I'm wondering if it isn't another case of life imitating art, and if the death of Cromer-Blake in your novel hasn't been taken as evidence of my own death. Currently, one of the ways North American university professors demonstrate their own standing consists of counting the number of times their names appear in the publications of other university professors (the 'citation count,' you can imagine the scandalous mutual favors and the inflated rate of unjustified citations which make everything even more unreadable). I'm delighted at the idea of using a death notice to increase my standing and my salary. After all, it's one more mention of my infrequently cited name . . ."

I imagine that, his nonchalance notwithstanding, Eric must at least have crossed his fingers as I've seen him do many times, however much of a Londoner he may be, and of course I crossed mine, just in case, knocked on various types of wood, and got all tangled up in a string of garlic—I can never remember what exactly it's for or how you're supposed to put it on or use it or what you're supposed to pass through it—and though it wasn't exactly relevant nor was I having lunch when I read the letter, I threw salt over the shoulders of my polo shirt which for no apparent reason shrank like mad at the next washing. Perhaps all of it was not in vain, however ignorant and clumsy I was in the execution of my false superstitions. Eric Southworth is still alive (though his friend Hemingway, who called him six years ago to make sure of that fact, is not) and his health is as good as can be expected in someone who works a great deal and does not give up the more pleasurable of his minor vices. Still, in the years since this happened, every time he has travelled abroad he's met with some mishap or accident. He fainted in Orly airport, apparently as a result of a very bad case of food poisoning contracted at a lunch given by the director of the Paris branch of the Instituto Cervantes, and once home in Oxford he had to keep to his bed for far too many alarming days; at Madrid's Barajas airport he missed a plane to Santiago de Compostela (the airport's fault) and, unable to go back to the house where he'd been staying—he'd already returned the keys—he had to drag his suitcases loaded with books around Madrid for an entire day since there was no luggage check where he could leave them (our airport, warm and obliging as ever), placing a severe strain on his back, the consequences of which afflicted him to such an extent that he had to cancel part of a planned car trip through Galicia; later, crossing the southern United States, also by car, he and his travelling companion Nick Clapton fell, for twelve hours, into the hands of an absurd sect hidden away in a valley or on a mountain near Tuscaloosa, Alabama, who called themselves God's Trappers, and all, regardless of gender, wore anachronistic coonskin caps complete with fake tails, like Davy Crockett and Daniel Boone; needless to say, these cultists went hunting for the Englishmen and trapped them, but fortunately they were neither violent nor particularly tenacious, and let them go as soon as they saw they couldn't convert them, though they could just as easily have sacrificed the two like a pair of beavers to their trapper deity. Then, in Tuscany, Eric fell down an embankment one insufficiently starry night and received multiple fractures that confined him for weeks to an open ward in an Italian hospital, like the other Hemingway, who wrote *A Farewell to Arms*. According to his doctors, with a little less luck and from a different spot this fall could have sent him straight to Purgatory (*subito, addirittura,* they scared him in Italian), and one of his ears was permanently damaged by the impact.

Superstitious or not, in the end I don't believe that all this is nearly enough to counteract the curse of the Galdosistas, who, evidently, are every bit as international as their *Boletín*. And though I've watched Eric emerge more or less intact from these tribulations and think he's out of danger now, if not invulnerable or immortal, I beg him at every opportunity to cultivate a greater knowledge of his own country and do his best to leave Great Britain as infrequently as possible. But he's an inveterate traveller and pays me no heed. As far as the "citation count" goes, it's a pity I'm no longer a professor of anything, not even a phony professor (I never really was a professor, not in spirit; if it was up to me I never gave exams and I never walked the halls with students flocking around me), for in that case the many mentions I'm making and will go on making of Eric in this book would surely place him, deservedly and to my great joy, in the highest ranks of the wholly unscrupulous and increasingly idiotic university hierarchy.

Antiquarian or used bookstores abound in Oxford; few places are better suited to their proliferation and prosperity than this immobile city where half of those who die possess magnificent libraries and very often lack heirs, all those unmarried men and women, but still primarily men, who spend their borrowed days surrounded by books, with no care whatsoever for what might come or happen after them—truly it doesn't concern them—when their students, now grown up or old, never look back from their scattered remoteness; no one remembers them and everything goes back to the way it was, as if they had never been born. At those bookstores I have bought copies of books that once belonged to eminent figures in various fields, their pages sometimes bearing the inky trace of an homage, commentary, or difference of opinion with the text those men ran their eyes over so many years ago, when it was apparent that they had been born and were walking through the same streets that now offer not the least evidence of their hurried daily passage, no doubt wearing cap and gown and with these books in their briefcases, no doubt meeting with respect and cheerful greetings from those whose paths they crossed during the time that was lost as soon as it transpired, or was already lost when it was still present and transpiring.

Alfred Leslie Rowse, who devoted himself to Shakespeare without attaining great prestige, made some notes in the margins of a little known and very weighty tome by Henry James, *William Wetmore Story and His Friends*, which few other people can possibly have read; the marvelous Hellenist Gilbert Murray, "Regius Professor of Greek at Oxford University" (the regal Professor Murray), corrected with his own hand the typographical errors in one of his best works, *Five Stages of Greek Religion*; the novelist Angus Wilson gave one of his novels to the filmmaker George Cukor, perhaps while Cukor was shooting *My Fair Lady*, "in the copy of my friend George Cukor," was what he rapidly scrawled; and someone who had been in Spain and may have been at the front, brought back to Oxford the first edition of the book of poems and photographs by Miguel Hernández titled *Viento del pueblo* (*Wind of the People*), which was banned and is almost nonexistent ("*Este libro se acabó de imprimir en Valencia en la Litografía Durá en septiembre de 1937*"; "This book was printed in Valencia by Durá Lithographers in September of 1937"; the publisher was Ediciones "Socorro Rojo" or "Red Aid" Editions). Almost all copies of it were destroyed by *la mano dura de piedra*, the stone-hard hand; I understand that only six are known to exist in the entire world, making mine the seventh, and all of them begin with the same line, "*Atraviesa la muerte con herrumbrosas lanzas . . .*" ("Death passes through with rusting lances . . ."), and all of them contain the other seven good ones of the "First Elegy" which I'll paraphrase here; and another, more revered, Shakespeare expert, John Dover Wilson, must have mailed off a copy of his *Fortunes of Falstaff* from Edinburgh, for I have it in my hand right now and in its day it was addressed to one Arthur Melville Clark of Herriotshall and Oxton, according to his *ex libris*, which no one has removed over the course of the volume's unknown journeyings and I won't be the one to do so, his motto is "Blaw for Blaw," a northern or Scottish way of saying something every language knows and sometimes applies, "Blow for blow," I know it, too, and my father knew it even better, and Miguel Hernández best of all (". . . *y llueve sal, y esparce calaveras,*" ". . . and rains salt, and scatters skulls"), the blows he was dealt were not metaphorical, nor were the jails, and those his lines could deliver were only verbal (*"El sol pudre la sangre, la cubre de asechanzas y hace brotar la sombra más sombría,"* "The sun rots the blood, covers it in snares and makes somberest shadow flow"); and the poet John Gawsworth gave a copy of his *Collected Poems* to another poet, the Scotsman George Sutherland Fraser, on June 29, 1949, still a desolate day in what would become my home once I was born, inscribing on a flyleaf, "For George, *almost* the most traitorous and *undoubtedly* the *dearest* of my Dukes, Neruda," which was the extravagant title the king of Redonda bestowed that year in Cairo on his friend and former comrade-in-arms, the useless Sergeant Major Fraser, thus making him a member of the "intellectual aristocracy" of his both real and fantastical kingdom, with and without territory, another literary island, one, however, that can be located and does figure on certain maps, minuscule and upright and uninhabited, but not on others.

If it weren't for books, it would be almost as if none of these names had ever existed, and if it weren't for the booksellers who time and again rescue and put back into circulation and resell the silent, patient voices which in spite of everything refuse to fall silent entirely and forever, voices that are inexhaustible because they make no effort to emit sounds and be heard, written voices, mute, persistent voices like the one now filling these pages day by day over the course of many hours when no one knows anything about me or sees me or spies on me, and so it can seem as if I had never been born.

Among those Oxford booksellers were Mr. and Mrs. Stone, of the pleasant and seemingly infinite bookstore Titles, in Turl Street, and thanks to the deductive logic of Ian Michael and to his habitual verbal incontinence, which was more festive than busybodyish, they learned—not long after *Todas las almas* had appeared in English as *All Souls*, which allowed them to read it if they chose—that they, too, had been portrayed in a novel, at least according to my ex-boss, whose authority among his townsmen must have been much greater than any I ever saw him exert: Mr. and Mrs. Alabaster, she with a pink wool wrap around her shoulder, seated at her table in front of a gigantic book of accounts, he, well though casually dressed, perched on a rung of the ladder which the narrator always borrowed to climb up and inspect the heights—these were characters for whom I was more indebted to Dickens or Conan Doyle than to any contemporary, living being.

The Stones remembered me well, or so Ian said; he had gone to tell them the story, a copy of the English edition in hand to tempt them with (he may have read a few paragraphs aloud), and though the year was 1992 it wasn't entirely surprising that they hadn't forgotten me, for during my years at Oxford I often visited their shop and had gone over it from top to bottom—there was a basement—with my magnetic fingers, gloved to keep my hands from being impregnated with dust, that particular, thick dust that collects on bookbindings. I was a little worried to learn that the Stones had been frivolously informed of the existence of their presumptive replicas, since the novel said about Mrs. Alabaster, among other things: "she was smiling and authoritarian, with one of those English smiles often seen in films, beaming from famous English stranglers as they choose their next victim." And about Mr. Alabaster the book said, among other

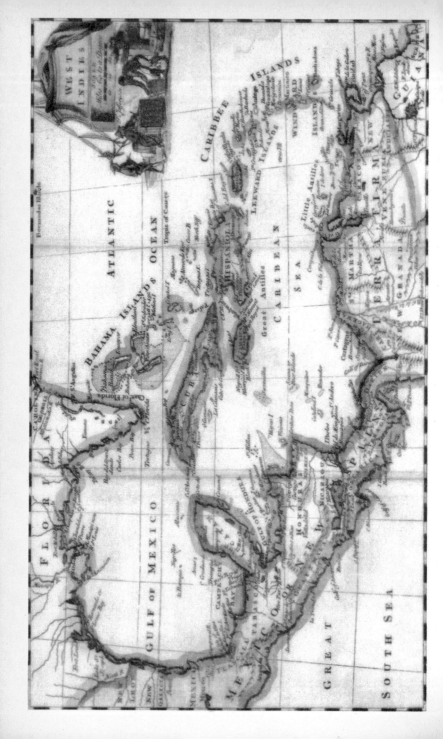

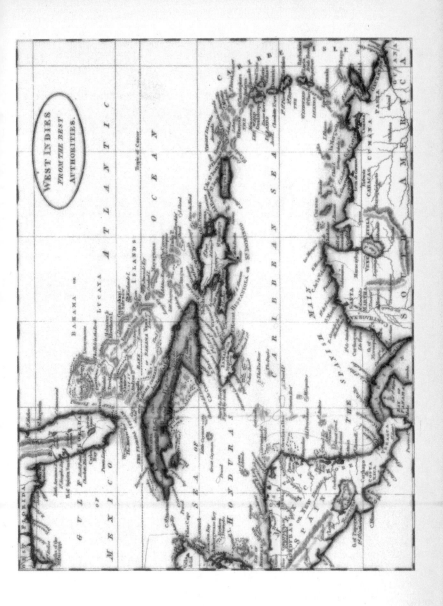

WEST INDIES
FROM THE BEST
AUTHORITIES.

things: "he was also a smiler, but his smile was more like that of the strangler's anonymous victim, just before learning of his fate." It occurred to me that these observations might not strike them as funny, if they had indeed decided to see how they looked represented in monumental alabaster, though, for the most part, both characters were treated with humor and sympathy, or so I think anyway, though what I think about my own texts is of almost no importance, or is important only to me, and sporadically.

So the second time I revisited Oxford—definitely in the summer of 1993, coinciding with my friend Mercedes López-Ballesteros' visit there—I hesitated a good while before mustering up the courage to go into the Stones' store, fearful that if they were to recognize me they might hold my description of those other beings against me, if they had taken it for their own, and perhaps, with pained, accusatory looks on their faces, keep me from coming in at all. I was sure they would recognize me. I brought along a copy of *All Souls* to give them, a friendly gesture even if they'd already bought and read it, as was entirely possible after Ian's blithe instigations. I remember I wandered around for a bit, killing time in the neighboring marketplace, and happened to buy a bunch of grapes, I suddenly felt like having some grapes. Leaning against the counter of a repellent butcher's stall, I leafed through the book one last time in search of positive elements: Mr. Alabaster was presented as having a "certain air about him of an aging and theoretical lady's man (one whose social milieu or early, iron-clad marriage prevented him from putting his charms to the test), who hasn't entirely relinquished the coquetry or the cologne of his less hypothetical years," and was said, furthermore, to be "handsome." As for Mrs. Alabaster, her "vehement gaze" stood out, but also—oh, no—her "capped teeth," which Mrs. Stone—oh no—might turn out actually to have, I'd never once looked at her teeth but promised myself I would this time. The fact that they were booksellers was no guarantee of any familiarity with or understanding of the minglings and fabulations and juxtapositions of literature, some booksellers are inquiring and sagacious like Mr. Bernard Kaye of York or Antonio Méndez and his Albertos of calle Mayor in Madrid, but I'm acquainted with at least one who spends his entire life thrusting aside the things he sells, not to speak of a certain distributor who doesn't even know how to open the products known as "books" which he carries, and is unaware that they contain pages, and among publishers some, such as Gilles Barbedette or Laurens van Krevelen or MacLehose or the elderly Einaudi, are extremely cultured and even erudite, but I've also dealt with others who, if not illiterate, had only an elementary grasp of five languages and chit-chatted in a kind of international pidgin lingo, which was all their vocabulary would permit. Few people are better qualified than the professors of Oxford University to understand what a novel is and not impose responsibilities on it, and yet two or three of them had had rather primitive reactions to mine; there are never any guarantees. I thought about leaning against the counter of an eggseller's stall to write an affectionate inscription to the Stones and, in passing, accidentally break a couple of eggs, getting myself covered in white and yolk and thus inspiring them with pity when I walked into their bookstore a sorry sight, dripping with languid liquid, but I quickly gave up the idea, they'd worry about my dirtying their floor or their books and would greet me with even more forbidding countenances; Mercedes L.-B., whom I'd arranged to meet a little later at Titles, would laugh at me wholeheartedly, and furthermore I was carrying my grapes wrapped in a paper cone and the possible mixture of liquids would be too unpalatable an ooze. I wrote out their inscription, which was sincere but quite smarmy, at a less risky counter (a disgusting fishmonger's stall) and made with slow footsteps for the store and my ordeal.

I walked in, concealing my face a little behind my high paper cone, and there, as ever, was Mrs. Stone, her glasses slipping halfway down her nose, scrutinizing the screen of the closed-circuit (black and white) television by which they kept watch on the suspicious characters who went down to rummage in the basement; in my day I'd been one of the most persistent. In their possession of this modern device the Stones did coincide with the Alabasters, and this was undoubtedly the principal fact that guided Ian Michael in his meddling inquiries and daring conjectures. I didn't see Mr. Stone for the moment and regretted it, since, in my final, terrified inspection of the book, I had found more favorable comments on his false Alabaster twin than on hers. Mrs. Stone raised her eyes when she heard the bell, but said nothing, no doubt she thought it was up to me to make the first move. I did so immediately, calling her by her name, "How are you, Mrs. Stone? I don't know whether you remember me." She looked hesitant for a moment, as if she were trying to recall my name, and then with the contrived stutter that is characteristic of many Oxford residents, said "Oh yes, yes, the Spanish gentleman." And she pointed her hand towards me, palm up. "Mr. Márias" (accent on the first syllable), "Márias, isn't it?" When she smiled, without malice, I took advantage of the opportunity to note the condition of her teeth; they appeared to be the genuine article, which was a source of some relief.

After we had exchanged another phrase or two, I asked after her husband. "Is Mr. Stone not here? I've brought something for both of you."

"You're most kind; tell me, what is it?" she asked, or ordered, almost, unable to contain herself. But she immediately rectified her tone and added, "Yes, Ralph is downstairs, I'll call him. Ralph, love! Would you be so kind as to come up here a moment!" she shouted, her firm voice projecting down the stairs. "The Spanish gentleman is here, Mr. Márias! He's brought a gift for us from Spain!"

If Ralph Stone—I'd never known his first name before—was in the basement then it was he his wife was watching on the screen, or perhaps only contemplating or admiring; they seemed fond of each other and the most difficult and desirable thing in a marriage is managing sometimes to see the other person as new and unknown, the television screen may have helped. At least they didn't communicate between floors with an intercom or walkie-talkie, out and over, or the other way, over and out.

Mr. Stone appeared immediately, bounding athletically up the steps, almost too quickly, as if he'd been posted at the foot of the stairway listening to whatever was said up above. He held out his right hand to me with a smile that was also athletic and open and seemed to promise that he bore me no rancor. After a minimal exchange of superfluous information (everything just the same, in his regard), I handed them my novel in the English edition published by the Harvill Press, with a studied gesture of hesitation. "Well, my present is not from Spain, exactly," I felt obliged to apologize. "In any case, I don't know if you've heard about it. I've brought you a copy, and took the liberty of inscribing it for you."

"Oh yes, of course, we're selling it, and none too badly," answered Mr. Stone, just ahead of Mrs. Stone who was left with her mouth open for a second, I stole another look at her lovely teeth. "But we don't have our own copy, this is marvelous, it's so extremely kind of you to have thought of us.

Thank you, thank you. Look, Gillian, love," he said, passing the book to his wife after having read the inscription or flattery.

I hadn't known, either, that she was named Gillian. I couldn't conceal my surprise; the Stones didn't sell new books, there was never anything there that could be acquired easily in an ordinary bookstore.

"Selling it?" I said, "How's that? It only came out a few months ago and as far as I know you only accept books of the dusty genre, I mean, books that have been ennobled by the slow and majestuous dust of time."

Mrs. Stone laughed, which gave Mr. Stone the chance to break in ahead of her. "Yes, of course, that's true, true. But this is a very special case, isn't it? There's a basis, a certain attraction to our selling it here, don't you think? So I bought a few copies at Blackwell's (publishers don't generally fill orders for us, naturally, since we've nothing to do with them) and there we have them, didn't you see them in the window? We've sold at least four or five."

I hadn't paid any attention to the window before I came in. Four or five copies must have seemed like a lot to people used to dealing in rare or out of print books that appear only one at time, with luck, and who almost never had more than one copy of any given title in stock, or not in the same edition, anyway. And there was no doubt about it, Mr. Stone had to be alluding to the Alabasters. "Dear God," I thought, "the Stones assume they are the Alabasters, therefore they think it's funny to sell in their store a novel that, according to them, speaks of them and of their store, in which they are now selling this novel that speaks of them. But the Alabasters would never have been able to sell my book, which creates and contains them." Still, if the Stones didn't have a copy of their own, perhaps they hadn't yet read it and their references were only to what Ian or someone else had told them.

"Listen, could I put these grapes down in a safe place? I'm afraid they're beginning to drip and I don't want to get anything wet," I said. Perhaps they were past their prime, the grapes they'd sold me at that squalid fruit stand.

Mr. and Mrs. Stone lifted their hands to their faces, both together (it may have been a gesture they'd picked up from each other), whether in consternation or fright or because they were abashed by the lack of an adequate place in the shop to leave a seeping cluster of grapes, I don't know. They looked around, with their hands on their faces.

"Oh, here," said Mrs. Stone finally, pointing to the umbrella stand. The weather that day was fine and the stand was empty, so I deposited my paper cone there with great care to make it stay upright.

"I'm glad indeed," I said, nodding my head towards the window and referring to the spectacular sales figures, "it's very nice to know." And since I didn't dare mention the Alabasters but could think only of them, I changed the subject: "Well, I'll just go and have a look at your latest acquisitions and heavenly treasures, if that's no trouble. I'm waiting for a friend."

"Quite the contrary," Mr. Stone answered, opening his arms wide in a theatrical gesture as if surrendering to an enemy. "The shop is entirely yours, just like old times."

"Ah yes, just like old times."

And they were pretty old by now, those times, I thought as, without much conviction, I clambered up the rungs of the ladder to the highest level, the greatest finds often wait in the most out-of-the-way places, they never reward the lazy. Those times were old by now, 1983 and '84 and '85, I'd arrived in Oxford during the first of those years and had left

during the last, and if they weren't so old for me it was because I had later written that book and through it and its still
unfinished life had maintained my link with the city and with
those times that felt and still feel very much present or not
yet brought to a close, but neither the Stones nor almost anyone else in Oxford had maintained a link with me, or with
the Spanish gentleman I was to them, with my increasingly
amorphous and dissolving face which in any case, hasn't
stayed the same, it's become older and perhaps sadder, as if
the traces one does not leave in any place or any life or any
person are all embodied and accumulate in one's own features, which may be the only thing that registers them visibly. I had maintained my link to the city and its inhabitants
through my book, as if by doing so I could refuse to become
haze and shadow that no one sees distinctly any longer, remembered only barely or with great effort ("Oh yes, he used
to visit us, hunting for rarities, I wonder what's become of
him, that was so long ago"), two years of my life had gone by
here and normally, eight or ten years later, there would no
longer have remained the slightest evidence of my upright
form, with gown or without, or of my voice which apparently
is different in English than in my own language, or of my
hurried daily passage, book-crammed briefcase in hand,
through the distracted streets that tolerate us for a time without growing impatient because they know none of us will
pass through them forever, none of us. Two years is a long
time, and take a long time to go by, yet two years can sometimes be erased as if we had never lived through them, no
one knows them or remembers us during them, no one from
that time or that place seeks us out or misses us, and even we
ourselves can come to forget the people we were then, neither looking for ourselves nor missing ourselves. I forgot the
enormous and unjust scar I saw and kissed every day not for

two but for three years, in days that were even older and in a distant city that wasn't my city either, a scar on a thigh. And when a friend who knew of its existence reminded me of it not long ago in speaking of the woman who bore it on her thigh, it took me such an effort to reconstruct the memory and the image that I even came to see a scar on her breast that never existed before I managed to focus and see again at last, twenty years later, the smooth, scorched crater that formed a conspicuous, indissoluble part of the person I loved. How can I possibly have lost that, I thought, when my friend inadvertently forced me to recover it, how can it be that for years this scar disappeared from my treasured visions, this scar that was familiar to me and that I made my own, and whose bearer, before I saw it for the first time in a cheap hotel room in Vienna, warned me of it with such consideration and tact, as if to say, "Listen, come here, look, there's this thing on me and perhaps you'd rather not see it. You still have time not to, and if you don't then you won't ever have to." But there are things one can't fail to see once told of their existence, still less if what you want is to see everything, all of the person who tells you, and waits. I saw it, and then I saw it every day, until undoubtedly I ceased to see it and my eyes ran over it but overlooked it, though it was still there, smooth and scorched, and although I kissed it, I kissed it without awareness and without merit—if kissing can ever be said to have that—and perhaps I came, so incredibly, to forget it not only because there was a time of mourning or sorrow when the memory was very painful to me, but because on her side the link was broken from the start of the good-bye, or from my loss, and when at last it broke on my side, as well, after long years of concentrated and sterile effort and soliloquies and superfluous farewells that no one answered—as if I were still caught in the spiderweb she was no longer weaving—then all that had happened and had been suddenly became remote and alien, as the past becomes when it does not languish or idle and is not allowed to peer out even once into the present, not even in its most softened and inoffensive and comforting forms. "Oh yes," she may think from time to time, "a young man once lived here with me, he was from Madrid, I wonder what's become of him, it was so long ago."

I climbed to the top of the ladder and stood there a moment, looking down at Mr. and Mrs. Stone from above, as if they were my subjects; they, for their part, had not returned to their duties but were observing me in great expectation, as if they thought a failure to hang on to my every movement and step would be a slight or insult to me during my visit in these new times and therefore had decided to observe or accompany me with their gaze in my quests. I ran my eyes and swift fingers over the top shelf and immediately found a volume I'd been seeking for some time to give to my friend Manolo Rodríguez Rivero, who, for his many escapades, is in no way deserving of such a gift, but who had envied my own copy more than once on seeing it in my house; I often have it out because it's the kind of book you read bit by bit and in episodes: *A General History of the Pyrates*, by Daniel Defoe, in its infrequent complete version, an immense tome, more than seven hundred pages long. I was casually hefting the *General History of the Pyrates* when Mrs. Stone began to talk about the film of my novel that was then being planned by the imposing businessman Elías Querejeta, to be directed by his daughter, whose name, naturally, was Querejeta as well, but not Elías.

"Mr. Roger Dobson told us there's going to be a film based on *All Souls*" she said, to my great surprise, this time beating her husband to it. "Is it true? Will it be filmed on location here in Oxford? Have they picked the locations yet? Have they chosen the cast?"

I had been given little information about the project, still very incipient at that point, though I couldn't have imagined then that Querejeta and Querejeta's discourtesy and inconsiderateness would be so extreme that they would inform me of almost nothing—despite what the contract set forth—even when the film was well underway, and would endeavour not to show me the footage once it was finished, hiding it from me as long as they could while it was being seen at private screenings by all their pet critics and friends and acolytes, as I learned from other people. I had had my doubts about giving my permission to their project and granting them the film rights, among other reasons because I didn't see how a film could easily or successfully be derived from that novel or any other I've written, except the first, which I wrote when I was nineteen and may still be my best. It also made me a little wary when, in a lunch prior to the agreement, Querejeta and Querejeta cheerfully expressed the pathetic idea that the characters of Toby Rylands and Cromer-Blake had been lovers, merely because the book said Cromer-Blake was homosexual and didn't make clear what Rylands was, sexually speaking. "What?" I had answered. "There's not the least hint or suggestion of that. It's a relationship of master to disciple, elder to younger, a father-son relationship, in no way are they lovers or ex-lovers, what nonsense." The fact that they had arrived at this banal idea suggested a failure to understand a word of the book, perhaps even the obtuse reading of a purely commercial mind which, to make matters worse, doesn't believe itself to be any such thing. The imperious businessman persisted, asking a question that was outstanding in its genre and gave an idea of his immeasurable respect for writers and his equally impressive acuity. "Are you sure?" he said, gazing at me intensely as if by that means to convince me of my error. Given that he was going to write the screenplay with the other Querejeta, I should have thought it over a little more. I could have been sarcastic but refrained, after all they were being kind then to take an interest in my novel and very blandishing in their attempts to persuade me to accept their offer. So I limited myself to the obvious answer: "How could I not be sure? After all, this is a novel and I wrote it, and I'm not the sort of writer who leaves everything to the reader's intuition." Naively, I heaved a sigh of relief, believing I had nipped a serious misunderstanding in the bud. I need hardly say that in the film that was finally made and premiered four years later in 1996, Rylands and Cromer-Blake, poor men, had been transformed into two unlikely and rather unlikable and shrill ex-lovers, supposedly impassioned ex-lovers according to what we were continually being told but never saw in the images, who had nothing at all to do with the characters in the novel apart from their family names and Cromer-Blake's illness: in fact, "Robert Rylands"—he no longer bore his very proper upper-class British name because, as Querejeta the director confessed in writing, she had once had a dog named Toby, a weighty artistic scruple indeed—struck me as an unbearable and odious individual, what you might call a drip, the mere sight of whom was enough to make anyone flee the room. There had never been any misunderstanding, it was something else, and if there was an initial misunderstanding it mattered very little to the father-daughter duo that the author had rejected it from the first moment: the author is insignificant. But when Mrs. Stone asked me about it in the summer of 1993, there wasn't yet any screenplay, there was barely even a project, and I still had my naive good faith in both Querejetas, though always more in one particular

Querejeta, to whom I believe I listened quite a bit when asked to do so and in whom I then felt very disappointed, for that reason.

"No, I don't think they've chosen the locations or thought about the cast yet," I answered from my high vantage point, the *General History of the Pyrates* casually in hand. I was looking at the price, £40, a little expensive, I wondered if I liked Manolo R. R. that much. "But yes, it's true that a film is going to be made, and I know they plan to shoot it in Oxford."

Mr. Stone put a single hand to his cheek and I saw his eyes light up with a suggestive gleam as he raised them towards the ceiling.

"And will it be quite faithful to the novel?" Mrs. Stone went on, "or will it only use the parts that are more, more sentimental?"

"Do you mean more sexual?" I answered: speaking from on high confers daring and a sense of impunity, as despots, bankers, businessmen, judges and tyrants have always known. The Stones had read the novel, then, someone else's copy, perhaps even Roger Dobson's. "No, I hope not, I don't think so, but I doubt they'll be very faithful, and of course parts of the book will be left out completely. As you know, the cinema is very rich in some ways, very limited in others."

Mr. Stone broke in then, in a tone both eager and apologetic. "Gillian was asking, Mr. Márias"—both of them pronounced my surname wrong, making it rhyme with "arias"— "because if they happen to need actors to play the booksellers in the novel, you know, that couple, the Alabasters, well, we'd be able to do it with great pleasure, I think we'd be right for the part, don't you agree?" He paused for a moment, he was speaking timidly yet vehemently, as if it truly mattered a great deal to him. "Did you know? In my younger days I had considerable experience on the stage, and recently I've gone back to it, I played a small part in an independent dramatic production, that's what they call them, at the last Edinburgh Festival, my son was involved in putting it on and asked me to lend a hand. Great fun. We are also members of the OSCA"—"the O.S.C.A.," he said each letter separately—"and we've appeared in a few films that were shot here, *The Madness of King George*—ahem—was the most recent. Roger Dobson and Rupert Cook are also members. Acting is marvelous. So, if they consult you on the casting, don't forget us, we'd be delighted to participate. Though we've already written to the Spanish producer, something like Elijah . . . Er, well, I'm incapable of pronouncing it, something with Q and the word 'reject' in it, isn't that right, love?"—he asked his wife, who nodded—"which certainly isn't very promising, for our hope that they won't reject us, I mean, by offering us the parts that are so perfect for us. But we've had no answer at all, and we even wrote on stationery with the OSCA logo, if I remember aright. Is it normal in Spain not to answer letters?"

That acronym again. "The OSCA?"

"The Oxford Society of Crowd Artistes," explained Mrs. Stone; in English, the word "artiste," *à la française*, has a more modest and jocose ring to it than "artist," and is reserved for singers, cooks, dancers, fashion designers, actors and milliners. Mrs. Stone handed a sheet of the stationery with the logo on it up to me, I came down a rung to take it. "The Oxford Society of Crowd Artistes (OSCA)," it said, "is an Oxford-based cooperative of extras for film and television with over one hundred members whose experience covers period dramas, thrillers, the Inspector Morse series and numerous important films, working both on location and in the studio." I kept that piece of paper; in England there are all kinds of societies and organizations like this one.

"You wrote to the Querejetas? How did you know their address?"

"Oh, that was easy, we found them in the annual world guide to movie production companies. Mr. Dobson gave us the name. Do you think there's any chance? Do you think they'll answer us? Or that they'll keep us in mind for the Alabasters?"

I went back up to the top rung and looked at the volume which I already had at home but was now going to buy for Manolo R. R., and a very instructive and amusing volume it is, because you don't have to deal with the pirates, only read about them. There was expectation and agitation in Ralph Stone's eyes, and a little sadness in Gillian Stone's, she was waiting with her hands crossed in her lap.

"I don't know"; I was expressing pessimism rather than doubt. "I'm afraid they may not be very attentive to the wishes and offers of people they don't know." I was going to say "people of no influence" but fortunately stopped myself.

It was hard to believe. The Stones not only assumed themselves to be the model of the Alabasters, but wanted to incarnate them, lend them their presence and their physiques if the fictional characters emerged from the book and acquired corporeality and physiognomies in a film; a strange round trip it would have been had their belief and their appropriation or identification been correct, which it was not. And if such an incarnation were to occur, then the fictional Alabasters would become, in turn, a model for the real Stones, who would study and imitate them, though only while they played the Alabasters before a camera, or who knows if the thing might not have gone even further. Pity that this whole dimension or zone of the novel, like so many others, and, in fact, in the end, all of them, held, from the start, no interest whatsoever for either Elijah or his daughter; I still don't know what they saw in *Todas las almas* to pursue it so ardently at first and then run from it like the devil as soon as they thought it was theirs alone.

It struck me that Mrs. Stone was growing sad, as mothers grow sad when their children are rejected or fail at something, they usually love them all the more for it, in vain; sorrow engenders love, I don't know why it bothers so many people to inspire it. Perhaps the marriage—and maybe it was early and iron-clad—had cut short a vocation for acting that Ralph, the husband, was now trying to return to before the onset of old age or its foreshadowings, and she must have been the most enthusiastic proponent of any project related to this difficult, late, chimerical compensation, perhaps she felt she owed it to him; many women easily feel themselves to be indebted, few men. It must have been she who wrote and sent the letter to the Querejetas, the idea must have been hers. That letter undoubtedly went straight into the wastebasket, Crowd Artistes logo and all; the filmmakers weren't even receptive to the wishes of their avowed source of inspiration, whom, though he is a person of no influence, they did know, or one of them at least wanted to know. I refer to the person who invented the story and the atmosphere and the characters.

At that moment, Mercedes López-Ballesteros arrived with her customary punctuality, "Freud's granddaughter," it was already time for lunch. I'd hardly had a chance to look around the shop at all, my only booty, *The General History of the Pyrates*, was scant in comparison to old times, and not even for my own library. Mercedes was in a cheery and very decisive mood; she was carrying an umbrella because she had no confidence in the British sun and she plunged it joyously into the umbrella stand; we all heard it puncturing the packet deposited there—the nauseating sound of many soft grapes being squashed. I'd eaten only one, just after I bought them. Fortunately the Stones took a sportsmanlike view of the whole thing, they didn't make faces or scold. No book had been stained.

We were about to leave, with Rodríguez Rivero's Defoe wrapped in rough paper, when they asked me to sign a copy of *All Souls* for Rupert Cook, their fellow crowd artiste who had loaned it to them quite a while before so they could read it. "That's how we'll make up for the delay, we'll return it to him with value added," Mrs. Stone said generously after taking it out of her drawer. They occasionally sold books that were signed or inscribed by their authors, the greatest and most costly treasures of any antiquarian book dealer, but an inscription of mine can't be worth much, I'm still contemporary, not even dead yet. They also, with some hesitation, gave me a photocopy.

"It's an interview with us that came out recently. You may enjoy seeing it, we tell a number of anecdotes. And we speak of you and your novel."

"Really?" I took it with curiosity. "Thank you, I'll read it later, it's sure to be of great interest to me."

It was illustrated with a photograph of the two of them, hard to make out on the photocopy, he, smiling with a double-columned folio volume between his outstretched hands, she, more serious, giving him a sidelong glance or perhaps watching out for the valuable folio, and wearing eye-catching earrings and a necklace, perhaps they had dressed up for the occasion, though he wasn't wearing a tie, sporty as ever. It was from a specialized publication, probably for those in the second-hand bookselling trade, not quite as restricted an audience as that of the *Boletín* of the jinxed Galdosistas, but almost. It was called *The Bookseller* and was dated August 12, 1993, very recent indeed; strange that they had already made a photocopy when they couldn't have known I was in Oxford and was going to visit them, entering their store as a distinguished author and leaving it some time later as a literal *pinchaúvas* or "puncturer of grapes," which is a way of saying ne'er-do-well or good-for-nothing in Spanish, even if the act was committed through an intermediary who couldn't stop laughing at her tremendous feat. The photocopy must not have been originally intended for me.

In the interview, the Stones told the story of their business, distributing the speaking parts equitably between them. They had had stores in Devon and in Shipton-under-Wychwood (that name, Wychwood Forest, a place between the Windrush and Evenlode rivers, "a wood that no longer exists, only its name remains, the wood was cut down and razed during the past century, but it's very difficult to renounce your name, names say a great deal") before setting up shop in Oxford. One title they always kept in stock, they said, was *Seven Pillars of Wisdom* by T.E. Lawrence or Lawrence of Arabia, in some valuable edition. Speaking of the back pains that are inevitable in the trade, because of the constant moving of books, Mrs. Stone suggested that the PBFA (which must be a Federation of some sort, in this case no one explained the acronym) should contract the services of a chiropractor, who might have made a good match for the lady cobalt therapist of Professor Ian Michael's eczemic mishap. But the most jolting part of it, to me, was their mention of me in their comments on notable clients. "We even appear in a Spanish novel by Xavier Marias" (as Ralph Stone clearly referred to me, without the accent on the surname but also, stranger still, with my original and almost forgotten name, I renounced that name but remember it, it's mine), "a nice

Gillian and Ralph Stone

the experience we gained and to the customers through them. It was all a hectic programme and we didn't have the first five years but the entire family was dressed from charity shops.

Very early on Gillian started doing catalogues. Our first catalogue was of horse books and we methodically mailed it out to every stud and every hunt secretary in the South West. Somehow we did not get one single order. Then she catalogued some of the books we had bought at Pulborough, including a Paris *Ulysses* and quite a lot of topography. This did much better. We did catalogues of Books on the Environment years before the subject caught on. And as a result of an American customer who farmed in North Devon David Low specialising in Agriculture became friendly and was extremely helpful to us. We always did a Christmas catalogue too because trade went dead before Christmas in Devon. Years later when we moved to Shipton-under-Wychwood we still had a lot of the horse books and they all sold within six months.

Shipton was lovely with the shop on the village green — The Old Post Office Bookshop — the oldest Post Office in England according to the *Guinness Book of Records*. But in 1981 we got the lease of our present shop in Oxford, and though we ran the two shops for a couple of years it was all getting a bit much so we decided to concentrate on Turl Street. It is in such a wonderful position — just round the corner from the Bodleian and so many of the colleges.

I very much enjoy working in the shop and dealing with the customers although there are some we can happily do without. Over the years we have collected quite a few sayings for *Bookworm Droppings*, that marvellous anthology of bookshops. The other day someone came in and asked Sheila Fairfield, our colleague in the shop, 'Can you direct me to a secondhand bookshop?'

We always try to keep certain books in stock. For example *Seven Pillars of Wisdom* is always in demand. When Gillian first started bookselling the first trade edition sold for £5 or £6 and nowadays it goes for anything between £25 and, in a dust-jacket, £100 — or £400

in Japan! *The Rubaiyat of Omar Khayyam* always sells, and secondhand Galsworthy never does. Our all time best seller in the Turl is a slim pamphlet by Professor Mayr-Harting, one of the few new books we stock, called *What to do in the Penuish Peninsula in less than Clement Weather*. It sells at 99p.

One thing about running a general secondhand bookshop is that you're going to make 90% of your sales from 10% of your stock and you're never quite sure which 10% it is going to be. Bankers and accountants rarely grasp the importance of 'mix'. They tend to interpret the appreciation on certain items as an indication of huge profits. Then they say 'By God, that's a return. Can't we get in on this?' They don't realise the matrix behind all the special items. They also don't realise you can be a long time waiting for the right customer.

As regards running a shop in Oxford — there is a huge diversity of customers from dons to tourists, people from all the counties around us. Then there are the presents (Christmas is good in Oxford), summer students, members of the conferences held in the colleges in vacations or even in term time, so we try to have something for everyone. Far flung members of the university come back for Gaudy Nights, and you never know what will come to Oxford and 'do' the bookshops. We even appear in a Spanish novel by Xavier Marías, a nice young man who was at All Souls a few years ago and came into the shop regularly. He picked up on a habit some dons have of not seeing women, so that one might dash up a question, and I might refer to Gillian who might supply the answer. The *supplementary* question then comes back to me. This may go on two or three times. The book is called *All Souls* and we feature as Mr and Mrs Alabaster.

stock. As it is we tend to concentrate on the £50–£500 bracket for stock, though we do attend major auctions and deal in multi-figure books on commission. In the last few years we did have the pleasure of buying books for a tycoon who wanted to recreate a marvellous country house library. We bought some superb books mainly in the field of natural history. It was a very exciting time. Checking and buying so much of such quality over the period we were bound to gain greatly in knowledge and experience. So much concentrated hands-on experience certainly helped when I was writing the natural history article in the new Scolar *Antiquarian Bookseller's Guide.*

We haven't done so many catalogues in recent years as in the Devon days, but we do use occasional lists. At the moment we have stock banked up waiting for time to get at the computer. I've got the books for another history of science list – our last one was very successful. I and an assistant catalogue, one of our books on, or about women, and I want to do one on the history of environmental thought. Nowadays the best books tend to go very quickly in the shop, so catalogues are secondary to shop trade. We also do quite a lot of buying in the shop. In general there is a lot of competition for buying in Oxford. Academic libraries do come up, but we haven't really got into the habit of don-watching. Anyway there's a lot of playing one bookseller against another. In some ways I prefer to buy at fairs or from other booksellers and at auction. In theory we are both approaching retirement, but I expect we shall go on working till we drop. One thing I have said to Ralph, let's put by *small* books. They'll be easier to handle in our old age! Over the years Ralph, and to some extent I, must have shifted many many tons of books.

The shop is open Monday to Saturday, but Ralph and I always try to give ourselves Monday off. In practice this doesn't work, and although we may not actually come in, I still think we may work about twenty Mondays a year. There is so much to be done and we always seem to have substituted hard work for capital. Looking back I think we might have made a mistake in not borrowing more than we did. That might have been just the right time to raise the level of our

Actually I hurt my back playing rugger and I've often thought it wouldn't be a bad idea for the PBFA to engage a resident chiropractor. But that would be private health and many members would be absolutely against that. There was a terrible outcry some years ago when someone suggested a group subscription to BUPA. I suppose you have to remember that the PBFA is an incorporated company of all shades of point of view. Basically you've got 600 mavericks — and some are vociferous. I was Chair-

young man who was at All Souls a few years ago and came into the shop regularly. He picked up on a habit some dons have of not seeing women, so that one might ask me a question, and I might refer to Gillian who might supply the answer. The *supplementary* question then comes back to me. This may go on two or three times. The book is called *All Souls* and we feature as Mr and Mrs Alabaster."

The paragraph is somewhat confusing, especially to someone who has no idea what it could be referring to, and I, initially, had no idea. What in God's name are they saying? I asked myself as I read it, while Mercedes L-B went on laughing and gazing in satisfaction at the viticultural tip of her umbrella. What did they mean, "a habit of not seeing women"? That's about the only thing I really have seen and still look at, always, both in and out of doors, and what's more I know at a glance whether I admire them or not: I didn't understand a word of it. I read and reread it, there in the restaurant, and showed it to Mercedes to see if she understood it any better and would leave off with her smugness, but she shook her head; until I suddenly figured it out. In describing the Alabasters, the narrator of the novel said, "But though he was invariably there as well, I don't recall a single occasion when he answered my questions or inquiries. He would smile and say hello like a lively and energetic man (his whole bearing was intrepid), but he delegated every business matter or response, however trivial, to the greater knowledge and authority of his spouse. He would turn to her and vivaciously repeat the question that had just been asked of him, word for word, appropriating it, as if he were the one who wanted to know ('Have we had anything in by Vernon Lee, darling?'), adding only the word 'darling' at the end." And a little farther along the narrator returned to this: "The cheerful urbanity with which Mr. Alabaster greeted any customer who came in indicated that, in his subaltern passivity, the mere appearance of someone in the door of the shop had to be the great event of his day, and the effusive greeting he addressed to that someone its most glorious and sociable moment. For after that, as I've said already, he was incapable of answering a simple question or pointing a finger ('Do we have a travel section, darling?') towards the shelf that held what the buyer sought."

All of this, it was clear, had not struck Mr. Stone as terribly funny—the "subaltern passivity" part wasn't particularly flattering, I admit—though he had made me aware of this by the most delicate and discreet means possible, providing me, through his wife, by the way, with the photocopy in which he defended himself, or defended Alabaster, whom it was now certain he had taken possession of or adopted. The extraordinary thing was that in this interview the Stones were indirectly arguing with a novel, or rather they were refuting what a fictitious narrator had observed about two booksellers who were also fictitious, however much they had borrowed certain details or traits from the Mr. and Mrs. Stone of reality. And in order to deny that he, Stone, never answered questions and always transmitted them in their entirety to his wife as soon as he received them—but I had said that of Mr. Alabaster—they had found no better explanation than to claim that I—not the nameless narrator, but Xavier Marias, with a name—had acquired an extravagant, depraved habit from the Oxford dons, a habit I had never heard of before, which consisted of not seeing women, not registering them, erasing them, passing the gaze over them as if they were invisible or did not exist: this habit, then, would have led me—and hence my narrator—to address myself invariably to Stone and, we must suppose, to Alabaster, two or three times in succession, on every occasion and on numerous occasions, even though I knew very well that Mrs. Stone and, we must suppose, Mrs. Alabaster—whom, for that matter, I did not see, who were, for me, transparent—were the ones who could supply the answers. Perhaps this explained why, during my grape-bearing visit, Ralph, the husband, especially at the beginning, had tried to speak up before Gillian, the wife, whenever an answer or some information was required, so that I could register with my own eyes and ears that he was capable of supplying any information, requested or not, without having to consult her first. The idea was so appealing to me that I only regretted it wasn't true: according to this, I would have come into the shop regularly without ever seeing Mrs. Stone because of this damnable habit picked up from the dons, so misogynous and cruel, those colleagues of mine; I would thus have asked Mr. Stone—who else?—if he had had in anything by Vernon Lee, for example; and then Mr. Stone, like a madman, would have turned toward no one and would, in turn, have asked this no one, "Have we had in anything by Vernon Lee, darling?"; this highly eccentric reaction—from my point of view, since I saw only air—wouldn't have made me bat an eye, as if I were another madman, nor would I have made any inquiry with respect to his ethereal interlocutor, I would simply have waited out the obligatory seconds and then, not having heard any sort of response because I saw no one who could have supplied it, listened, very phlegmatic and natural, and on a regular basis, to the final reply of Mr. Stone after his consultation with someone who, for me, would have been, at most and with luck, a ghost who appeared only to him: "No we haven't had anything by Vernon Lee in lately, Mr. Márias."

Furthermore, and despite the belief the Stones unhesitatingly expressed in the interview, I was not attached to All Souls during my years at Oxford, and not only that but had never set foot in that strict and exclusive college, and did not do so, in fact, until last summer, 1996, when I was invited there by the kind musicologist Meg Bent after she read my novel. I imagine that the title had forestalled or imposed itself on their knowledge of me, I mean Mr. and Mrs. Stone's. But at least they had said I was a nice young man, which is something to be very grateful for, even if retrospectively. As I passed by the bookstore later that day and saw them through the window in their habitual places at ladder and desk, I waved to them without stopping and hoped that neither Mr. nor Mrs. Stone ever runs the risk of having in reality to consult with a ghost or the air in the silence of their shop; that is, I hoped that when the time comes for one of them to die, they both die together.

And it is something to be very grateful for, even if retrospectively. I said that without intending much by it, only now do I notice it. Though I can be agreeable (I know I can but don't always want to be, and never am with my many compatriots who are disagreeable and venomous and always think the worst: too many slanderers for too many years in this domain of brutality which death passes through with rusting tongues, making somberest shadow flow, and relentlessly); I'm no longer young and may not have been young then either in those distant days when I was thirty-two or thirty-three, long past the age of twenty-one, which, fortunately, was the age of legal adulthood in my time, and also past the age of twenty-seven, so decisive that Joseph Conrad called it "the shadow line" (perhaps it was decisive only in his day); the age of thirty had also been attained and left behind by the time I went to Oxford, the symbolic age beyond which, for instance, dying young, in the traditional sense, is almost impossible, though the modern view is more indulgent, one dies young at seventy-five: people say, "There was still so much left for him to do," as if what we do were what justified our lives or what we miss about our dead, and not their presence and their gestures and their unbiased account of events or, even more, their listening attentiveness to our own account. The times become old times all too easily and are cast off, and what went before them becomes antediluvian, and yet they all gradually and

deceptively overlap, we sometimes think there are no borders
or abrupt stops or brutal cuts, that endings and beginnings are
never marked out with the dividing line that, at other times,
however, we think we see in retrospect; and that belief is deceptive, too, because neither the one nor the other exists, or
only as an enormous exception: not the sure, clean slice—
splinters always go flying—nor the juxtaposition or welter of
confused and indistinguishable days—there are always forgotten patches and blotted out periods, I know them, to help us
see the illusory limits. It's all more mysterious than that, more
like an artificial prolongation, attenuating and inert, of what
has already ceased, a ceremonial resistance to yielding or to
marking the beginning of what is to come, like the streetlamps
that stay lit for a while when day has already dawned in the
great cities and towns and train stations and empty village de-
pots; they stand there still, blinking and upright, in the face of
the natural light that advances to make them superfluous. At
that hour, which is only witnessed by very early risers or the
very nocturnal or very insomniac, there occurs, for brief moments, the visible manifestation—the metaphor—of how
time, respectful time, behaves and what it consists of, for in
time there is always civility and courtesy and even dissemble-
ment, and at that hour, more than during the threadbare moment of twilight, time can be seen for what it is. These electric
lights pretend that it's still night, that their assistance is still
necessary, they make as if not to perceive the conclusion of
their reign, and the daylight, in turn, pretends not to see them
and tolerates them, knowing that these waning lights are no
longer a threat, and even appears to slow its own unfurling
a bit as if to concede them time to grow accustomed to the
arrival of their own futility and the idea of their cessation
("Put out the light, and then put out the light," Othello had to
say it to himself twice to take it in, even if he had already

decided to do it), not forcing them to flee as soon as day-break looms white on the horizon, but only to withdraw, without being routed and in an orderly fashion, as armies once agreed on a cease-fire to allow the enemy to collect and count the dead and, in that way, begin to grow accustomed to the strange idea of their cessation.

I see them sometimes from my house, the streetlamps that hang from the noble building across the way, with its slate roof which this winter's snow slipped off even while it began to build up on the neighboring tiles; the slate forced it to keep trying and make an effort and the snow—which is whiter than skin—kept slipping off and melting onto the plaza until finally it stayed. I see the streetlamps, and other things, too, from my balcony on insomniac mornings or when I've been treacherously awakened or in the aftermath of reckless revelries, nineteenth-century streetlamps hanging from the wall, their bulbs useless now, and the men and women who walk past them on hurried feet left their beds a while ago and may have travelled in trains from the city's outskirts to its center, and in those glowing lamps they can see a reminder of the sheets or perhaps the body they left without wanting to, a reminder that for many other people the night still goes on, though dawn has already broken and the light is expanding around them as they walk or wait for a bus, lifting one foot and then the other in place, like tired wading birds—dark night still painted in their eyes—thinking dimly about what they left behind at home and what awaits them over the course of the unending workday, and by the the time the workday ends and they go back, their home will no longer be the same, and perhaps the beloved body from which they parted will have betrayed them. The woman looks at the streetlamps and remembers the man whose scent she still carries on her, who stayed behind in her bed, egotistically asleep. She's an elegant woman who is almost no longer young, though she still is with a little effort and care on special occasions, she certainly was last night, her low neckline held deep shadows, that dress was bunched up and tossed over a chair, already forgotten this morning, a ghost, she's dressed soberly now and warmly, she won't see the young man again, the man who madly ripped that dress off her, more because he was young than from the desire to take it off, he'll go when he wakes up, without leaving a note, he may even steal something, she's quite certain he will, it doesn't matter, the sharp smell of him will be left between the sheets, and the bus doesn't come. The man looks at the streetlamps and thinks of the woman who gets up later than he does, she goes on sleeping or impatiently pretending to sleep as he prepares to go out into the world, making coffee in the weak light of dawn, she's not thinking about him right now. He's a middle-aged man, well-groomed, his hairline receding, it is not within his power to keep her, or only through economics, through his liberal hand, and money is transmutable, substi-tutable, many people have it, he's not the only one, and it's hard to earn, lugging his briefcase around early and late, he's got nothing that anyone else doesn't have, and she could find another, future means of support during the day, the days, too many days in which to go knocking, under some pretext, at other doors, and the mystery of this today, her today, which hasn't yet begun, will await him at his return, added and alien to the sum of too many unknown yesterdays and no tomor-row, the bus isn't coming and both of them, woman and man, who don't see or know each other, look at the incongruous lights still lit beneath the sun that advances and makes them pathetic and insignificant, though they are the respectful and benign testament to what has already ceased but once existed: until the sleepy hand of some civil servant takes note of the waste and puts out the light, and then puts it out.

Not everyone or everything that comes to an end receives this testament, though most do, in fact there are only a very few who receive no warning and don't have the slightest chance to think about or foresee their end: people who ride in cars or boats or airplanes are not among them because even if they don't dwell on it they know they are at risk, and neither are soldiers or doctors or bricklayers or politicians or those who live alone, almost all of us more or less expect our possible ending when it is about to occur, rare are the cases in which time does not conduct itself in civilized fashion but slices down cleanly with no splinters or forewarning. But they do exist, and I enumerated a few of them in speaking of ridiculous deaths at the beginning of another novel, *Tomorrow in the Battle Think On Me*. In one case I mentioned, I was thinking of a real person who existed; I refrained from mentioning another one I learned of through *All Souls* and John Gawsworth, because in a fictional novel it would have seemed too improbable and recherché, even as an example, more so even than the death of the Austrian writer of Hungarian origin, Ödön van Horváth, to which I did allude ("a bolt of lightning that splits apart a tree on a wide avenue, and the tree, in falling, crushes or severs the head of a passer-by, perhaps a foreigner"): he was killed by a tree blown down by a storm on the Champs Elysées in Paris in front of the Theatre Marigny, where he was waiting for a friend, the

German filmmaker Robert Siodmak, with whom he was planning to escape to the United States, both of them having fled from Nazi Germany. His light was put out suddenly, in the most unexpected place—without an afterward, without testament—on January 1, 1938, when he was only thirty-six years old; Horvath was a foreigner, not in his own country, he had no warning, and he must have been doubly and super-stitiously wept over by his girlfriend, a German actress whose father had died under the same exceptional circumstances—struck down by another tree that was singled out by another bolt of lightning—and who belonged to the family of Mer-cedes López-Ballesteros, not for nothing is she herself "Freud's granddaughter." Even so, it wasn't my *pinchaúvas* friend who first told me about the circumstances of Horváth's death, which I learned of a very long time before meeting her, though she did tell me about the unfortunate girlfriend, who saw this improbable story repeated twice within a single lifetime, her lifetime. I have only one book by Horváth, a play titled *Don Juan Comes Back from the War*. Robert Siodmak, on whom the tree might have fallen as well if he had arrived on time (or maybe they would both have been comfortably in their seats and it wouldn't have fallen on Horváth either), did go back to America, which he had left after the crash of '29, and directed a number of films there until he had to leave again during the 1950s, harassed by the anti-artistic Senator Joseph McCarthy's House Un-American Activities Committee. Among those films is one entitled *The Killers* (in Spain, *Forajidos*), inspired by the famous Heming-way story on which films by Siegel and Tarantino were also later based, which specifically depicts the opposite case, the case of a man who is not only warned of his imminent mur-der or only possible future, but who waits for the moment to come, reminiscing on a motel cot, without wanting to flee any longer or look for a way out. I'm especially grateful to Siodmak for *El temible burlón* or *The Crimson Pirate*, which had nothing at all to do with Defoe's *General History of the Pyrates* and which I watched countless times with great enjoyment during my childhood, so that out of retrospective self-interest I'm glad his was not the head severed by the Parisian tree that was singled out by the storm of New Year's Day 1938.

More mysterious and with even less testament or warning was the death of the English writer Wilfrid Ewart, fifteen years and one day earlier, on New Year's Eve 1922, "in the sultry darkness of Mexico City," when he was only thirty. But before speaking of Ewart it may be wise or useful to speak of the person who led me to him through the aforementioned citation and others, and it's probably best to reproduce here what I knew about John Gawsworth when I wrote *All Souls*, even if it is a few pages long. Now that I know so much more and he lives in me to some extent, and his ghost lives in my house, and I know his handwriting or his voice that speaks, I wouldn't be capable of telling the story in the same way, and the way I told it then is what counted then, and that alone. Those who have already read these pages in that novel can skip them—I believe—without feeling cheated (it's always a pleasure to skip a few pages and it's almost never possible), and those who have no prior acquaintance with them can read them now without having to spend a cent more to acquire them, though undoubtedly the reproduction will not be verbatim and may include a few marginal notes or scattered comments, so in the end I don't know if those who are already happily and frivolously preparing to skip them would be wise to do so. Of course they can also skip all the pages, all these pages, without very serious consequences. The nameless narrator of that novel said:

"After Alan Marriott's first visit, a year or more previously, I had included among the rare authors whose books I was seeking this John Gawsworth, unknown to me until then, whose name he had mentioned and noted down for me before saying goodbye, and for whom Machen had written a prologue. His work, as Alan Marriott himself had said, was very difficult to find." I must point out here that this is the part of the novel that most closely coincides with my (and even with the only) reality and where I loaned my experiences and voice to the Spanish gentleman narrator; that is, I can vouch for almost everything he says and speaks of. Machen is Arthur Machen, the famous author of horror stories and novels of whose work Borges was so fond; like Ian Michael, Machen was Welsh. As for Alan Marriott, he never existed as he is described, but the person who first spoke to me of Gawsworth was Roger Dobson, or Roger Alan Dobson, which, he told me after having read the book, is his full name. He also noticed—a man attentive to coincidences, I hadn't paid any attention—that Alan Marriott's initials were the same as those of his idolized Arthur Machen. The narrator went on to say: "None of the scant body of work he produced is currently in print in England, but little by little, with patience and luck and the progressive sharpening of my predatory eye, I found one or another opuscule of his in my used book stores in Oxford and London, until, a few months later, I came upon a copy of his book *Backwaters*, from 1932, signed, moreover, by the author himself: 'John Gawsworth, written aged 19 1/2' it said in pen as soon as it was opened. There was also a correction in his own hand on the first page of the text (he had added, after the name 'Frankenstein,' the word 'monster,' to make it clear that he was referring to the creature and not the creator). My curiosity was deepened by the sense of temporal vertigo or time negated that occurs when your hands are holding an object that doesn't entirely silence its past, and after that moment I began a course of research that was quite fruitless for many months, so elusive and unknown was and is the figure of Terence Ian Fytton Armstrong, the real name of the person who was in the habit of signing his name as Gawsworth." Soon he will no longer be as elusive, now that the *Dictionary of National Biography* has commissioned an article on the poet-king of Redonda from his reluctant successor and literary executor (the two offices always go together in this legend) Jon Wynne-Tyson, or King Juan II.

"Nevertheless," the text continued, "although his work was no more than conventional and rare, which made its total neglect and the lack of any reprint quite understandable, as I went on ascertaining various facts (no book existed on Gawsworth, not even, it seemed, an article, and he barely received a mention in the most voluminous and exhaustive literary dictionaries and encyclopedias) my interest went on growing, not so much because of the rather average work as because of the far from average man. I first found out the dates of his birth and death—1912 and 1970—and then, on a page of mute bibliography, that several of his works had been published (sometimes under other pseudonyms, each more absurd than others) in places as extravagant and improbable for a London writer as Tunis, Cairo, Sétif (Algeria), Calcutta and Vasto (Italy). His poetical works were collected between 1943 and 1945 in six volumes—most of them printed in India—but, peculiarly, the fourth volume appears never to have been published, though it has a title (*Farewell to Youth*). It simply does not exist. His prose work, mostly short literary essays and tales of horror, is scattered across obscure, strange anthologies of the 1930s, or saw the light—a figure of speech—in private or limited editions.

"Yet Gawsworth had been quite a personality and promising literary figure in the 1930s. A tireless promoter of neo-Elizabethan poetic movements in reaction against Eliot, Auden and other innovators, he had, while still little more than a teenager, frequented and become friends with many of the most notable writers of the decade: he wrote about the work of the famous avant-gardist and painter Wyndham Lewis, and of the hugely famous T.E. Lawrence or Lawrence of Arabia; he was awarded literary honors and in his day was the youngest elected member of the Royal Society of Literature; he met Yeats as an old man and Hardy while he was dying; he was the protegé and later the protector of Machen, as well as of the famous sexologist Havelock Ellis, the three Powys brothers, and the then (and now again somewhat) famous novelist and short-story writer M. P. Shiel. I couldn't dig up much more than that, until finally, in a dictionary specializing in the literature of horror and fantasy, I did: in 1947, at the death of his mentor Shiel, Gawsworth was named not only his literary executor but also heir to the kingdom of Redonda, a minuscule island in the Antilles of which, at the age of fifteen, Shiel himself (a native of the neighboring and much larger island of Montserrat) had been crowned king in a festive naval ceremony in 1880, at the express desire of the previous monarch, his father, a local Methodist preacher who was also a shipowner and had bought the island years before, though no one knows from whom, given that its only inhabitants at the time were the boobies that populated it and a dozen men who gathered the birds' excrement to make guano." I fear that at present only the boobies are left; and I later learned that the elder Shiel or Shiell, the preacher and shipowner, was not a monarch as I said: he only had his firstborn son crowned. "Gawsworth was never able to take possession of his kingdom because the

British government—with whose Colonial Office both the two Shiels and he were eternally in dispute—attracted by the phosphate of alumina on the island, had decided to annex it in order to keep the United States from doing so. Nevertheless, Gawsworth signed some of his writings as Juan I, King of Redonda (king in exile, evidently), and made dukes or admirals of various writers who were his friends or whom he admired, among them his mentor Machen (whose title he simply confirmed), Dylan Thomas (Duke of Gweno), Henry Miller (Duke of Thuana), Rebecca West and Lawrence Durrell (Duke of Cervantes Pequeña). The entry in that dictionary, after *not* explaining any of this—I discovered it some time later—concluded: 'Despite his wide circle of friends, Gawsworth became something of an anachronism. He lived his last years in Italy, returning to London to live on charity, sleeping on park benches and dying forgotten and penniless in a hospital." I also later learned that there were a number of detective novelists among the peers of Redonda, such as Dorothy L. Sayers, Julian Symons and "Ellery Queen," as well as some editors such as Gollancz, Knopf and Secker, and perhaps even a few artistes such as Dirk Bogarde and the exuberantly platinumesque Diana Dors.

"That this exalted man who could be king and who, one day in 1932, with unmistakable enthusiasm and juvenile pride had signed the copy of *Backwaters* now in my possession should have ended his life in this way inevitably made quite an impression on me—even more of an impression than the stories of the violinist Mollineux and the papal theologist Mew—though so many other writers and better men than he have met the same fate." The violinist and theologian had both ended up, against all expectation, as beggars, and in Oxford you see a great many of those, the city is full of them, they make you think and make you fear, for yourself, too. "I couldn't help wondering what must have happened *in between*, between his precocious and frenetic literary and social initiation and his anachronistic and tattered ending; what must have happened to him, perhaps *during* those residences and travels of his across half the world, always publishing, always writing, wherever he happened to find himself. Why Tunis, Cairo, Algeria, Calcutta, Italy? Was it because of the war? Because of some obscure and unrecorded diplomatic activity? And why did he publish nothing more after 1954—sixteen years before his wretched death—having previously managed to do so in places and at times when getting hold of a printing press must have been a heroic or suicidal feat? What had become of the—at least—two women to whom he had been married? Why, at the age of 58, this outcome as a useless old man, this death as an Oxford beggar?

"The Alabasters, with their boundless but prudent knowledge, hadn't managed to do much to help me find texts by him and didn't know any more about him, but they did know of the existence of an individual in Nashville, Tennessee, who, thousands of miles away, knew almost all there was to know about Gawsworth. This individual, whom I held off writing to for a long time because of a strange and unreasoning fear, referred me (when I finally did write) to a brief text by Lawrence Durrell about the man who turned out to have been his literary initiator and the great friend of his youth, and also gave me some other facts: Gawsworth had had three wives, at least two of whom were dead; his problem was alcohol; his great love—I read with apprehension and a flinch of horror—was the morbid quest for and collection of books. 'Morbid,' was how the individual from Nashville unhesitatingly qualified it." The man is named Steve Eng and in the spring of 1988 he published an article titled "A Profile of John Gawsworth," in a recondite periodical with a minimal print run. Though I finished *All Souls* in December of that same year, I didn't learn of that article until much later. The narrator goes on to say:

"Durrell's text presents Gawsworth or Armstrong as an expert and highly gifted hunter of unattainable gems with a magnificent bibliophile's eye and an even better bibliographic memory, who, early in his career, would often start the day by buying for three pence some rare and valuable edition that his eye had lit on and recognized among the dross in the threepenny boxes set out in Charing Cross Road, and reselling it immediately for several pounds, a few yards from where he had found it, to Rota of Covent Garden or some other swank bookseller in Cecil Court. In addition to his exquisite volumes (he kept and treasured many of them), he possessed manuscripts and autograph letters by admired or renowned authors and all sorts of objects that had belonged to illustrious figures, purchased (with what money no one knew) at the auctions he frequented: a skull-cap worn by Dickens, a pen of Thackeray's, a ring that once belonged to Lady Hamilton, and the ashes of Shiel himself. A large part of his energy was expended on attempts to persuade the Royal Society of Literature and other institutions, whose maturer members he tormented with persistent, discomfiting literary and monetary comparisons, to give pensions and financial assistance to elderly writers who, their successful days long over, were insolvent or simply destitute: his mentors Machen and Shiel were two of his beneficiaries. But Durrell also says that the last time he saw Gawsworth, about six years earlier (the text dates from 1962, when Gawsworth was fifty and still alive, so Durrell had seen him at the age of forty-four; but curiously, Durrell, who was the same age, speaks of him as one speaks of those who are already gone, or who are on their way out), he was walking down Shaftesbury Avenue,

JOHN GAWSWORTH AND ARTHUR MACHEN (CENTRE)
BY FREDERICK CARTER

wheeling a pram. A Victorian pram of enormous dimensions, Durrell adds. Seeing it, he concluded that life had finally closed in on and shackled down the mad bohemian, the Real Writer who once bedazzled Durrell, freshly arrived from Bournemouth, with his knowledge and introduced him to London's literary scene and nocturnal haunts, and that he now had children, three sets of twins at the very least, to judge by the extraordinary vehicle ('life has caught up with you as well,' is what Durrell writes). But as he approached to have a look at the little Gawsworth or Armstrong or young prince of Redonda, he discovered to his relief that the pram contained only a mountain of empty beer bottles which Gawsworth was on his way to return, collect the deposit on, and replace with full ones. The Duke of Cervantes Pequeña (this was Durrell's title) accompanied his exiled king, who never once saw his kingdom, watched him fill the pram with new bottles and, after drinking one of them with him to the shade of Browne or Marlowe or some other classic whose birthday it was that day, watched him disappear, placidly pushing his alcoholic pram into the darkness, perhaps as I now push mine while evening falls over the Retiro, except mine has my child inside—this new child—and I don't yet know him very well, and he will survive us." No reminder is needed that this final comment of the narrator's is one I cannot share in. Durrell's article is titled "Some Notes on My Friend John Gawsworth" and was published in 1969 as part of his book of "Mediterranean texts," *Spirit of Place*; it was written as a contribution to a volume in homage to Gawsworth on his fiftieth birthday, but that celebratory volume, so solidly fixed to its date, had yet to see the light in 1969, that is, when the honoree had already passed the age of fifty-seven, a year before his death. One more frustrated project, the friend unhonored. At the age of forty-four, when the encounter in Shaftesbury Avenue took place, Gawsworth had been married for a year to his third and final wife, Doreen Emily Ada Downie, known as "Anna," a widow who was four years his senior and already had a grown-up daughter named Josephine and was the grandmother of the blonde Englishwoman named Maria who, not long ago, gave me copies of the marriage and death certificates of Terence Ian Fytton Armstrong, pseudonyms are futile on such occasions. What follows, in *All Souls*, is a commentary on the two photographs I reproduced earlier, which in the novel appear among the pages I'll now cite:

"Later, I saw a photograph of Gawsworth that more or less—as far as can be told—coincides with the physical description of him given by Durrell: '. . . of medium height and somewhat pale and lean; he had a broken nose that gave his face a touch of Villonesque foxiness. His eyes were brown and bright, his sense of humour unimpaired by his literary privations.' In the one photo I've seen, he wears the RAF uniform and has a cigarette, still unlit, between his lips. His collar is a little loose and the knot of his tie seems too tight, though it was an era of tightly knotted ties. He sports a medal. There are neat, horizontal furrows on his forehead and small folds, rather than circles, beneath his eyes, which gaze with a mixture of roguishness and amusement, dreaminess and nostalgia. It's a generous face. The gaze is clear. The ear is striking; he may be listening. He must be in Cairo, undoubtedly in the Middle East, or perhaps not there but in North Africa, in French Barbary, and the year is 1941 or 1942 or 1943, perhaps not long before he was transferred from the Spitfire Squadron to the Eighth Army's Desert Air Force. That cigarette can't have lasted much longer. He must be about thirty, though he looks older, a bit older. Because I know he is dead, I see the face of a dead man in this picture.

He reminds me a little of Cromer-Blake, though Cromer-Blake's hair was prematurely white and the moustache he would allow to grow in for several weeks only to shave it off and not wear it for the next several weeks was also greying or at least had threads of silver, while Gawsworth's hair and moustache are dark. Their gazes are similarly ironic, but Gawsworth's is more affable, not a trace of sarcasm or anger in it, no forewarning or even possibility of such a thing. The uniform needs pressing." Now that I'm the one talking and not the narrator, I can say that he reminds me a little of Juan Benet, and a little of Eduardo Mendoza, too, to name only writers, though the first could be irascible and sarcastic as well as very affable, while the second seems to be all affability, with a touch of irony. Two people he doesn't at all remind me of are Eric Southworth and Philip Lloyd-Bostock, the supposed real models, living and dead, for Cromer-Blake.

"I've also seen a photo of his death mask. He had just taken leave of age and the passage of time itself when the mask was made, but immediately before that he had been a man of fifty-eight. It was made by Hugh Olaff de Wet on September 23, 1970, the day of or the day after Gawsworth's death in London, in the Borough of Kensington where he was born. His old friend from Cairo, Sir John Waller, donated it to the Poetry Society, but these kind attentions came posthumously and too late. The man who was John Gawsworth and Terence Ian Fytton Armstrong and Orpheus Scrannel and Juan I, King of Redonda, and also, at times, just Fytton Armstrong or J.G. or even simply G. now has his eyes closed and no kind of gaze at all. The folds are definite bags now, the wrinkles in the forehead aren't as distinct (the skull has bulged) and the eyelashes look thicker, which could be a side-effect of the sealed eyelids. The hair would appear to be white—but maybe because the mask is made of plaster—and the hairline has receded since the 1940s, the outer limit of his youth, the war against the Afrika Korps. The moustache seems thicker but also limper, it both bristles and droops, the moustache of an old soldier who's grown weary of combing it. The nose is longer and broader, the cheeks are very flaccid, the whole face is swollen as if with false fleshiness and despair. He's grown jowly. There can be no doubt that he is dead." I now suspect that they shaved him while he was in the hospital or when he was already a corpse, because I've seen a photograph of him in his final days that shows him with an ugly, long , scraggly beard as befitted the beggar he then was. I also know that the correct name of the mask maker, about whom I knew nothing else when I wrote those pages, was Hugh Oloff de Wet; I also know that De Wet was in Madrid the year I was born in Madrid, and that twice long before then he almost faced a firing squad, once in Valencia and the second time in Berlin. And that in Spain he had lost an eye (or said he had) and had killed, there and in other places, before and after Spain. The novel's gentleman narrator went on:

"But with this final face he must have wandered the London streets, wearing the kind of raincoat or jacket that tramps always manage to get hold of. He brandished bottles and pointed out to his incredulous cohorts his own books, lying in the bargain boxes in Charing Cross Road, which he was unable to buy. He must have told them about Tunis and Algeria, Italy, Egypt, and India. In the face of their laughter, he would declare himself the King of Redonda. With this face, he must have slept on park benches and entered the hospital, as the dictionary specializing in the literature of horror and the fantastic said, and with this face he may have been incapable of reaching out the hand that had once held a pen and piloted airplanes. Perhaps he was proud and ferocious, as British beggars often are, brutal and aloof, threatening and haughty; he may not have known how to beg for himself. He was undoubtedly drunk, and at the end of his life he didn't spend years in Italy, only a few weeks in the Abruzzi, in Vasto, for a final binge about which I know nothing. 'A final binge,' was what the individual from Nashville, with whom I have had no further contact, said in his letter. There was no Gawsworth to save Gawsworth, no promising and enthusiastic writer to try to make him see reason and force him to write again (perhaps because his work is not admirable and no one wanted him to go on), or to request and obtain a pension for him from the Royal Society of Literature, of which he was once an elected Fellow, the youngest. Neither was there any woman, among the numerous women he had had, to check his drift or accompany him in it. Or so I believe. Where are they now, where do they lie, those women, British and colonial? Where are his books, the books he could pick out at a glance amid labyrinths of chaotic, dusty shelves, as I could from the Alabasters' shelves and those of many other booksellers in Oxford and London? (I, too, with my gloved and agile fingers that barely graze the spines which they skip across more quickly than my eyes, like a pianist playing a *glissando*, I, too, can always pick out what I'm looking for, to the point that I've often felt it was the books that were looking for me, and found me. They've probably gone back to the world where all or most of them always return, the patient, hushed world of old books, which they leave only temporarily. Perhaps other books that I own, in addition to *Backwaters*, also passed through Gawsworth's hands, bought and sold immediately to pay for breakfast or a bottle, or remained, perhaps for years, among the select volumes of his library, or went with him to Algeria and Egypt, Tunis and Italy and even India, and saw combat. Perhaps one or another of the baleful beggars had owned books, those beggars I walked past every day in Oxford, again and again, and was afraid of and identified with and in whom a slight, passing delirium made me see myself in anticipatory (or not so anticipatory) reflection. Perhaps one of them had *written* books, or taught at Oxford, or had a mistress-mother who clung to him at first but then became evasive and unscrupulous (when she was more of a mother); or perhaps he had come from a country to the south—with a hand organ that was lost upon arrival and that determined his destiny, perhaps when he disembarked at the port of Liverpool—a country to which, he still had not forgotten, it isn't always possible to return." (Death does not know how to walk slowly there.)

Thus closed that chapter of *All Souls* which, in the end, I've reprinted in its entirety here except for the first paragraph—and, as feared, with additional notes and comments. Three lines from those pages gave rise to the short story "An Oath of Fealty" that same year, 1989, a few months after the novel came out, with Gawsworth in his final phase as the main character. But the first time I spoke of him in writing was in a piece of non-fiction, an article I published in the newspaper *El País* on May 23, 1985, twelve years ago now, when I was still living in Oxford and feeling something quite similar to what the narrator called his "slight, passing delirium," with respect to the beggars of that city and the writer who ended up as one in London. The article was entitled *"El hombre que pudo ser rey"* or "The Man Who Could Be King," in obvious allusion to the famous story by Rudyard Kipling, "The Man Who Would Be King," also known in my language as *"El hombre que pudo reinar"* or "The Man Who Could Reign," since that was the Spanish title of the John Huston film based on that fantastical story—the favorite of both Faulkner and Proust—which featured the British actors

Sean Connery and Michael Caine. Both pieces were later reprinted, the story in my collection *Mientras ellas duermen* (*While the Women Sleep*) and the article in *Pasiones pasadas* (*Past Passions*), a collection of my non-fiction. The final sentences cited above refer to two circumstances or facts related only to the narrator; two others that are shared by narrator and author (teaching at Oxford and the possession of books), or perhaps three; and one which, improperly, belongs only to the author, since at no moment in the novel is it stated or hinted that the Spanish gentleman who's telling the story and digressing from it has ever *written* books, even if, in fact he is writing one now as he digresses and tells. It wasn't a mistake or an oversight, a thoughtless intrusion or moment of forgetfulness, it was deliberate, for, as I said before, these are the most autobiographical pages in the novel and it seemed honorable to tacitly confess that by means of this apparent slip which, as was to be hoped and expected, passed unnoticed by those who read it. (I also did it for the risk, one is always tempted to throw in some blots and smudges, for love of transgression and to betray oneself, and to see if they can pass for unblemished text.)

And I still must reproduce the first paragraph of the following chapter, which, perhaps, I could have espoused more than any other and which gives a clear and complete idea of the nature of that slight, passing delirium loaned by the author who breathes and speaks, Javier Marías—or Xavier Márias, he was then—to the nameless narrator who saves his breath and only writes, but for that reason has the more persuasive voice. The paragraph says:

"I asked and still ask myself all these questions not out of pity for Gawsworth, who is, after all, only the false name of a man I never met, whose books—which are the only part of him I can still see, besides the photographs of him alive and dead—don't say much to me, but out of a curiosity tinged with superstition, convinced as I came to be, on certain interminable afternoons of that spring or Trinity term, that in the end I would meet the same fate."

Now that Gawsworth has been introduced to those not previously acquainted with him and recalled to those who met him already in *All Souls*, I shall return to young Wilfrid Ewart of whose light put out suddenly and without forewarning or testament in Mexico City I was preparing to speak earlier.

In his practice of frequently looking after ill-fated writers whom he tried with scant or ephemeral success to salvage from oblivion, John Gawsworth seems to have been assimilating his life to theirs, or foreseeing or perhaps defining himself. In the thirties he collected and edited several anthologies of tales of mystery and terror, I know of at least seven or eight, whose respective titles were *Strange Assembly*; *Full Score*; *New Tales of Horror by Eminent Authors*; *Thrills* (just *Thrills*); *Thrills, Crimes and Mysteries*; *Crimes, Creeps and Thrills*; *Masterpiece of Thrills*; and perhaps *Path and Pavement*—the first published in 1932, the last in 1937, which is to say that all of them were published when the hyperactive and extremely precocious Gawsworth was between twenty and twenty-five years of age. They almost always include stories by the elderly and eminent masters Shiel and Machen—respectively King Felipe I and Archduke of Redonda—as well as by their disciple and crown prince, under his various names. There is one by his pal Lawrence Durrell and many by other future members of the kingdom's "intellectual aristocracy." But there are also many stories by writers who could never receive any dukedom or office or title from King Felipe or King Juan because they were truly, completely ill-fated, like the young suicides Richard Middleton and Hubert Crackanthorpe. Middleton was a man of great and recalcitrant talent who killed himself with chloroform in 1911 at the age of twenty-nine, at number 10, rue de Joncker, Brussels, without yet having published a single book (that began in 1912). Archduke Machen wrote of him: "He was impatient, he would not wait. He could not relax . . . I don't remember hearing him laugh; not openly and largely, with a relish in the deed. His humour was usually tinged with bitterness." And according to a contemporary who saw quite a bit of him, Middleton put an end to his days out of mere "hatred of life", which he used to call "the woe." Next to the chloroform bottle he left a card with this sentence written across it: "A broken and a contrite spirit Thou wilt not despise." Crackanthorpe, who had a lesser and more realistic talent and a more peaceable temperament, nevertheless threw himself into the Seine in 1896 at the age of twenty-six, for reasons of circumstance rather than of principle, after his wife ran away with another man. It took months to find his corpse, which was apparently so disfigured that his brother was able to identify it only by the cufflinks. Both men were Francophiles: Middleton a strict follower of Baudelaire, Crackanthorpe of Maupassant. An English magazine went so far as to claim that Crackanthorpe's Parisian death was "God's punishment for the worship of French idols."

Also appearing in these anthologies of the 1930s were a number of stories by Wilfrid Ewart, under that name or under the name Herbert Gore, which was no less his own, and I included one of them, "The Flats," in the anthology of rare tales of fear titled *Cuentos únicos* or *Singular Stories* that I collected and published in 1989, the same year as *All Souls*, and for which I rescued a few texts Gawsworth had included in the *Thrills* series, texts that have been completely forgotten today. In my anthology I also included a macabre tale by Gawsworth himself (the first work of his ever translated into any language and, for now, I fear, the last); the only story of the kind written by Durrell, the only one written by Sir Winston Churchill, an excellent story by the bilious Middleton, and also a story of my own—the temptation was irresistible—under the pseudonym of James Denham, whom, in the corresponding biographical notice, I described as having been born in London in 1911 and having died in 1943, fallen in combat in North Africa at the age of thirty-two, yet another ill-fated writer, even if this one was apocryphal. (Incidentally, little could I have imagined then that in 1996, when at last the film made by Querejeta Sr. and Querejeta Jr. and not based on *All Souls* was made, one of the character actors would be the very man whose last name I took for my occasional *nom de plume*, the Englishman Maurice Denham, today a venerable octogenarian whose performance is undoubtedly the best thing in the film. Small wonder that I sometimes have the feeling I draw things and events and even people to myself, but I try not to concede much importance to these coincidences—the perpetual activity of chance—or take them for exceptional occurrences unique to the "elect"; in the hands of a certain North American colleague they would have been good for a great deal of unconcealed fascination with one's own life and several books, or at least notebooks.)

Almost all the authors of the *Cuentos únicos* were and continue to be so obscure, to Spanish readers especially, that it seemed appropriate to preface each story with a brief biographical note, which is why I had to invent one in the case of poor James Ryan Denham . . . But about certain very vagabond or obscure authors, I could learn almost nothing; I remember, for example, that in one case, that of Nugent Barker, I was unable to find even the date of his almost certain death, given that he was born in 1888, though who knows if he isn't still alive; everything is possible. Another mysterious case, which was also striking and invited further inquiry, was that of Wilfrid Ewart, in whose note I could write no more than:

"Wilfrid Herbert Gore Ewart (1892-1922) died, as his dates show, at the age of thirty, and Arthur Conan Doyle, the creator of Sherlock Holmes, opined sadly on learning of his death, 'He would have gone right to the top.' For his part, T.E. Lawrence, better known as Lawrence of Arabia, said of him on one occasion, 'He needs no introduction to the reading public.' And the inevitable John Gawsworth, who seems to have been friend to the entire world, wrote, at the beginning of his introductory note to Ewart's posthumous book *When Armaggedon Came* (1933): 'Wilfrid Ewart died a fraction over ten years ago; upon Old Year's Night, 1922, to be precise, in the sultry darkness of Mexico City. The story is too widely known to require further amplification here and too tragic to allow casual comment to dwell upon it. Another of England's great novelists lay dead and Literature was the poorer for his loss. Beside the Tree of Dreadful Night . . . they buried him.'

"The odd thing about the case," I continued, "is that currently there is no way (or I haven't found a way) of learning anything more about this thirty-year-old man who would have gone right to the top, who needed no introduction and whose death was too well known to require further amplification. Ewart's name does not appear in any dictionary or history of English literature or in any contemporary anthology. However, MacMillan Publishers have announced a new edition of his most famous novel, *Way of Revelation*

(1921), about the First World War, in which the author was a combatant, so perhaps we will soon know how and why Ewart died in Mexico City.

"For the moment I can say only that before dying he also published *A Journey in Ireland* (1921), and that after his death, in addition to the aforementioned title of 1933, *Scots Guard* (1934), *Love and Strive* (1936) and *Aspects of England* (1937) were published. Under his own name or under the pseudonym of Herbert Gore, several of his stories appeared in the *Thrills* series and other anthologies of the 1930s. The present tale, 'The Flats,' written in a prose so pure that we may well decide Conan Doyle was right, comes from John Rowland's 1937 anthology *Path and Pavement.*"

It's not at all strange, given the far-fetched, novelistic sound of this and other biographical notes in the anthology, that the one dedicated to the nonexistent Denham failed to arouse any suspicion or attract undue attention; either none of them was believed and doubt was cast on the authenticity of all the stories, or each and every one was accepted without a quibble. Some readers were inclined towards the first stance and surmised that the nineteen stories were, without exception, all mine under different names. Would that it were true, because at least eighteen of them were well worth laying claim to. (Though really, it would have been quite foolhardy and naive of me to attribute apocryphal stories to the famous and much studied author of *The Alexandria Quartet* or to a very well known former Prime Minister of Her Majesty the Queen.) Other more prudent readers thought that "only" three or four were mine, among them no doubt the one by Gawsworth, whom not a few of my readers still took for a fictional character. And I recall that some friends, whom I let in on the game and challenged to unmask me, failed shamefully and didn't hit on my story even at the fifth guess; my estimable father, who has known me for some time but not as well as he thinks, hesitated between crediting me for the story by Middleton, the suicide—which was a little disturbing, though more to me or to him I don't know—or the one by Denham; Don Juan Benet didn't waver for an instant and tore off my mask at the first try.

Getting back to Ewart and his mysterious death, I was indeed unable to find out anything about it before the anthology's publication, and though I am lazy and passive, I don't think I'm all that bad at researching obscure figures and dates. But after my first efforts I didn't persist, or I postponed further investigation. A few months later, however, I received two letters, almost in succession, from Mexico: apparently there is great curiosity (and hence exhaustive documentation) about the foreign writers who have passed through. Of Wilfrid Ewart, forever buried in its violent soil, there was, nevertheless, no information on record, which had made an investigation of the matter a challenge, according to my two correspondents, who each undertook to alleviate the ignorance I had confessed to in the biographical notice that set the whole thing off.

The first letter was from a writer, Sergio González Rodríguez, an essayist, and was accompanied by a lengthy article of his, already published in the magazine *Nexos* in December 1989, under the title, *"El misterio de Wilfrid Ewart."* The second, dated in March of 1990, came from a young man named Rafael Muñoz Saldaña, who, with fewer journalistic resources and bibliographical means at his disposal, told me he proposed to "solve the enigma" that I "had left open." He announced that the "fieldwork" he had carried out had led him "down unexpected paths," but in the end had "born fruit in concrete results." "Though I now have a general idea," he said, "of the circumstances under which Ewart died, there remain many unresolved issues to which I must still respond." The young man in question—he owned up to being twenty-three, which makes him thirty now—took the news that his older compatriot, Sergio G.R., had scooped him like a good sport. I sent him a copy of S.G.R.'s article, and he answered regretfully, and with a note of pride, that the information the article provided was "exactly the same as that I had obtained." But he added with fine resignation: "What I did to explain this mystery to myself is perhaps more interesting than the mystery itself; I met many unusual people, among them an elderly woman who has been racked by nausea for fifteen years, and a priest who restricts access to the church where he officiates, for fear of attacks. Someday I'll tell you all about my adventures in full detail." And, clearly disappointed nonetheless, he added, "If, in the beginning, my intention—which was not without a certain theatricality— was to make a spectacular revelation of the circumstances of Ewart's demise, now I have a more sensible project," which project, incidentally, was not the least bit sensible and I immediately dissuaded him from wasting his time on something that wasn't even theatrical or spectacular. He also had a few comments for me about *All Souls*, which he had just read: "On page 89," he wrote, "he begins speaking about visiting some used book stores; at that moment I stopped reading and thought, 'What would I look for if I were there? Books by Arthur Machen,' I answered myself, and on turning the page I was quite surprised that the protagonist of the novel did the same . . . For some time now I've been a devotee of Arthur Machen, though unfortunately I know very few of his books . . ." It came as no surprise when, a few lines further down, the young man asked me about the "Machen Company," a supposed association of enthusiasts of the work of the Welsh writer and Archduke of Redonda that was mentioned several times in *All Souls* and of which the narrator became a member at the prompting of the character named Alan Marriott. Muñoz Saldaña wished "to contact it" if it actually existed. Given that this "Company" was invented, and I didn't want to disappoint the youthful Mexican Machenian even more, I sidestepped this disillusionment by writing back, "I fear that for the moment I'm not authorized to answer you on that point. Perhaps later," as if it were a secret and mysterious sect that one couldn't simply contact just like that, with oceans in between, without first having evinced a certain merit or passed certain tests. Finally, and after I had let him in on the joke about Denham, he answered, very generously, that "your charade amused me quite a bit . . . I adore these kinds of games, above all when they are carried out well, as in the case of John Bendham,' falsifying—involuntarily, I believe—even more, and so quickly, my third false name, since previously I had used two others for very minor or shady writings. I liked the part about the "charade."

Though we've gone on writing each other from time to time over the years, I'm still hoping Muñoz Saldaña will someday tell me about the woman who'd been nauseous for fifteen years, and who was, in fact, the thing that most interested me in his early letters. "What do you mean, nauseous?" I remember asking him. "What's wrong with her? How can she know that she's nauseous? If she's been that way for so long, you'd think by now it would have become her natural state. The phrase you used was enigmatic indeed."

What comes next has already partially been told in an article called "Remember You Are Mortal," included in my 1993 book *Literatura y fantasma* or *Literature and Ghosts* (I have to admire my own honorable conduct, duly notifying the reader of every antecedent), and a lot of material both there and here is owed, with thanks, to my two Mexican correspondents, who in any case pointed me on my way to finding out more about the short life and sudden death, without testament, of Wilfrid Ewart. Sergio González Rodríguez, in fact, went beyond the facts reported in his article, "The Mystery of Wilfrid Ewart," and ventured certain hypotheses which, though improbable, were amusing and, of necessity, Borgesian, in order to further clarify the mystery, and he generously called on me to develop them ("Only a writer like Javier Marías could indulge without stigma in this type of lucubration . . .": I'm afraid I'm going to disappoint him, and not only because of my tendency to throw in blots and smudges). To him I owe the profusion of citations from the Mexican newspapers that in the early days of 1923 reported the news of a foreigner's death on New Year's Eve, and, as gratuitous and absurd as the story was (and it was that in the extreme), made it even more sarcastic towards the dead man and distressing to those closest to him.

Ewart was born on May 19, 1892, the son of Herbert Brisbane Ewart and Lady Mary Ewart, known as "Molly," who resided at number 8, West Eaton Place, in Belgravia, one of the most distinguished areas of London. His father, who was neither poor nor at all rich, came from a very notable family of military men, a type that wasn't lacking in his mother's family, either: Wilfrid's maternal great-grandfather was General Sir William Napier, author of the monumental *History of the War in the Peninsula*, which we know in Spain as the War of Independence, and in which, of course, he had a conspicuous role; the six hefty volumes of this work were one of several items Don Juan Benet asked me to find for him during my stay in Oxford, with an eye to taking some inspiration from that Peninsular War—when salt rained and skulls scattered—for the bellicose maneuverings of the third and fourth volumes of his novel *Herrumbrosas lanzas*. (I managed to find them for him, but his novel remained unfinished. As if there has ever been anything that doesn't remain unfinished.) Wilfrid's paternal grandfather was General Charles Ewart, a hero of the Crimean War, though a dubious one, I imagine, like all the heroes of that war; a great-uncle of his, Sir Henry Ewart, led the famous charge of Kassassin; another great-uncle, Sir John Alexander Ewart, participated in Balaclava, Inkerman and Sebastopol; and that great-uncle's son, Sir John Spencer Ewart, was at the taking of Khartoum with Lord Kitchener in 1898, and then in the Boer War in South Africa, again accompanied by the legendary Kitchener. Despite all these warlike relatives and his distant kinship with William Ewart Gladstone, Queen Victoria's celebrated Prime Minister, Wilfrid's father worked peacefully and modestly—though under the rather showy rubric of "comptroller"—as secretary to Princess Dolgorouki, the exiled widow of a Russian nobleman who lived in an unusual white neoclassical mansion built by Lutyens and later duly Russified, in a forested spot near Taplow, Windsor.

Ewart's mother belonged to a family that was crawling with titles, both original and absorbed through a series of marriages. According to Hugh Cecil's book *The Flower of Battle*, on the British novelists of the First World War, which dedicates a chapter to Ewart with abundant information that I'm gratefully making use of here, Lady Mary or Molly was the youngest daughter of the fourth Earl of Arran; her sister Caroline married the eighth Lord Ruthven; her older brother, Arthur, became the fifth Earl of Arran in 1884; one of his daughters married the heir of the Marquis of Salisbury, another the Viscount Hambleden and a third the Earl of Airlie. Nothing very healthy could come of all this and Ewart's mother seems to have oscillated between eccentric grace and hopeless imbalance. Cecil tells us that she once received visitors while sitting on the carpet, unheard of at the time but not excessively disturbing except for the explanation she gave of her unwonted position: "Forgive my sitting on the floor," she said, "I always do it now, I find it less far to fall." In the worst of her fits, she ordered the butler to throw a respectable pair of newlyweds—the Viscount and Viscountess Hambleden, no less—out of the house, claiming that they were living "in open sin," and on occasion she would also violently attack her husband; it was therefore deemed that Wilfrid and his younger sisters Angela and Betty could, without detriment and even to their benefit, spend long periods away from the paternal home.

Little is known about Betty, except that as an adult she took to drugs and drink and—as is canonically ordained for the female black sheep of fragile families that suffer any unforeseen event as a setback or drama—married the chauffeur. Angela, however, was always very much attached to her brother, whom she resembled both physically and emotionally. In the First World War, which Wilfrid Ewart survived, she lost her husband, Jack Farmer, two months after the birth of their daughter, whom Farmer never saw. A few years later, Angela married a Mr. Waddington, and unlike her brother had a long life which continued past the age of ninety. Her brother accompanied her to Longueval, near the Bois de Delville, after the war was over, in 1919, to try to locate the hasty, belated grave of Farmer, an officer in the King's Royal Rifle Corps. On the battlefield, still strewn with helmets, muddy boots, shaving brushes and other gear from the year 1916, night fell and it started to rain, and they still hadn't found the grave. Angela had brought a cross made of laurel leaves and she left it at the foot of an apple tree near where Jack fell.

It was unthinkable, it was a crime, that Wilfrid Ewart

should have spent almost four years engaged in trench warfare, with only the brief respites won by his wounds and his nerves. Like his mother, with whom he had much in common, he had a left eye—a direct inheritance—that was blind; and his myopic right eye had great difficulties with distance, though up close it was infallible, or, as Stephen Graham, his friend and impromptu biographer of 1924, wrote, "microscopic in quality." The visionless eye was physically perfect but was not connected to the brain and registered no images. All in all, he was not a tremendously healthy young man, and it must be concluded that either the requirements for participating in that conflict were not strict or Ewart enjoyed some sort of favoritism—those of his class and time having an eccentric concept of privilege. Apparently, his relative Ruthven, then commander of the First Battalion, the Scots Guards, invited him to join his regiment after learning that he intended to enlist. "Why, he must come to us," he told Ewart's father, who had gone to consult him with an inadequate degree of apprehension. "But his eyesight?" Ewart's father objected. "That will be all right. Ask him to come along." He took the physical exam, and the doctor did what was expected: found him fit for service and thereby gave him every lottery number but one so that he would be sure to win himself a futile and unheroic death in the Continental quagmires.

And the number that was drawn was the only one blind Ewart didn't have. He fought in the Second Scots Guards, a corps of great distinction, class, and hauteur, at Sailly-Saillisel and against the Moulin du Piètre and at Neuve Chapelle, where a bullet lodged in his leg, at Gouzeaucourt and in the Somme offensive and the second battle of Ypres, at the Bois de Bourlon and the Yser Canal and the frightful third battle of Ypres, and near Cambrai and at Arras, and in all those places of muck, shrapnel, and bayonets he saw, with his one eye, hundreds of more qualified and able men than he falling around him, his best friends and most warlike relatives. It is entirely implausible that this nearsighted, one-eyed man failed to perish in what was perhaps the cruelest war of the century on our continent. Yet he not only came out alive but attained the rank of captain which obliged him to give orders and look after many people, including, in the war's final months, Stephen Graham, who became his orderly though Graham was eight years older and had published a dozen books as a travel writer and an expert on Russia.

Very early on, however, Ewart was sickened by the war, as most people were; during his years as a combatant or convalescent he implored Ruthven and Sir John Spencer Ewart, persistently and without shame, to get him out of the trenches and post him to some staff duty, his notion of privilege having been transformed by the first bloodbath, but this time his pleas fell on deaf ears. Despite these requests, he did his duty on the battlefield and, as his colonel testified, though not precisely brave, he was unacquainted with fear, and so could be sent anywhere. (Perhaps fear is unknown to someone who gives himself up for dead from the start.) On the front he wrote numerous letters, thus unintentionally laying the groundwork for the battle and landscape descriptions of his first novel, the only one published during his lifetime, *Way of Revelation* (1921), which drew great acclaim from Lawrence of Arabia and Conan Doyle and quickly sold fifty thousand copies.

The most devastating experience, however, may have been the brief truce of Christmas Day, 1915, a spontaneous, non-negotiated ceasefire between his Second Batallion of the Scots Guard and the 95th Bavarian Reserve Infantry Regiment. At dawn—say Cecil and Graham and Ewart himself—

those on both sides began watching each other from under cover in their foxholes, and even calling out greetings. At ten minutes to eight in the morning, a German stuck his head out over his parapet and another stood up and waved his arms. Two more followed in their caps and long field-grey overcoats, without knowing for a few moments whether they would be greeted with handshakes or shots. Then "as by simultaneous infection," all the British troops and the rest of the Germans began coming out into the open, despite the two High Commands' great dislike of these unexpected truces not negotiated by headquarters. Even taking prisoners was frowned upon, and according to their superiors, "killing Huns" was the lone cheerful task of the British soldiers. The enemies began laughing, cracking jokes and shaking hands. They met at the willow-lined stream that separated them, and only the sentries and officers, Ewart among them, stayed back in the trenches. The troops communicated by signs, slapped each other's backs, exchanged cigarettes, cookies, tinned beef, and tobacco, for sausages, sauerkraut, concentrated coffee, and cigars. In the midst of all this confraternization a Bavarian sniper brought down an Englishman, Sergeant Oliver, apparently a very popular man, who no sooner stuck his head out than he fell back into the trench where his corpse lay for the rest of the day, the face covered with half a sandbag or a blanket. But that wasn't enough to dissuade his comrades-in-arms and his adversaries, who paid scant attention to the misfortune. "It makes no difference, it must be an accident," wrote Ewart, as if one man's decision to do his duty and shoot the sergeant lacked the force to invalidate the decision of so many men to neglect theirs and not open fire that day. From where he was, Ewart could hear very clearly the shouts and bursts of laughter from the intermingling grey and khaki uniforms. They were delighted to say hello to each other, meet each other, and see faces at last: faces are not feared, only distant figures are feared, or those that advance ferociously with their imagined features. The episode lasted no longer than ten minutes according to some sources, twenty, according to others, after which time, however long it was, says Cecil, two German officers with shiny boots, who had been denied permission to take photographs of the "Tommies," or privates, warned the Englishmen to go back to their trenches immediately: their artillery would open fire in five minutes. Some sources say that a few Scots Guardsmen were hit as they were heading back towards their own lines, but that even so not a single shot rang out from those lines over the next twenty-four hours. Other sources, closer in time, say that all the weapons immediately began churning up the mud again and "the war took control once more." It makes no difference, it doesn't matter, as Ewart wrote: even if only for the space of ten minutes, the war lost its control and was disobeyed, and he was there and saw it. To say that it was vanquished would be false and pretentious, but it was sidestepped and even mocked for a moment, and the mockery was maintained even after the harsh reminder—or revenge—of all-out warfare (whose primary aim is to exclude and negate whatever it does not enclose or taint) against the poor, trusting figure of a sergeant named Oliver whose fate it was to stop a stray bullet sent by that malevolent war into the untimely, unauthorized truce between a batallion and a regiment on Christmas morning of the year 1915, seven years and seven days before Ewart's own turn would come in Mexico City. "Blaw for Blaw" or "blow for blow," it happens everywhere.

He was a tall, slender man, more than six feet in height, with a calm, dignified look about him, grey eyes, a fair complexion and brown hair. Despite his frail health, he looked vigorous and athletic, and there was usually color in his cheeks. He walked with a very upright carriage, and the uniform suited him, he instinctively wore it with the proper degree of ceremony. His character was quite restrained, as was his demeanor. He recoiled from any excessive familiarity, and was averse to any hint of bad manners. In society he could sometimes appear supercilious or even stupid. Among friends, with champagne or wine at hand, he lost his poker face and showed his jollier side. He never swore; according to Graham, "blasphemies and obscenities passed him by, and he had no interest in them." His handshake was both stiff and limp, and the people he met in America couldn't believe that his haughty exactitude was natural and of long standing; they looked at his face and attributed his abstraction to shellshock. Like most of his generation, he wore a precisely trimmed moustache, and he was always well dressed even when, after the war, he took up with a bohemian crowd and began frequenting the most nefarious Soho dives, fascinated by criminality, drug-taking and the murky places of the soul, as well as by the masses, which, at the same time, he could barely stomach. He spent hours studying their infinite variety while trying to keep a certain distance, in night clubs or the select

Café Royal or the more plebeian café-salon of the Regent Palace Hotel, where he enjoyed listening to the band and was ashamed of the pleasure he took in the place's vulgarity. Mornings, he frequented the motley sessions of the criminal courts, passing himself off as a law student and taking conscientious notes on all the cases. His short life did not allow him the time to lose this penchant, and during his stay in New York, before going to Mexico, he spent part of his evenings watching the night courts deal out their summary justice. He was allowed to visit Sing-Sing, where he was given a demonstration of the electric chair. He wanted to give a message to a certain Jim Larkin, imprisoned there and likely to be sitting in that chair shortly, but the prison authorities forbade it. He took notes everywhere, and went on doing so during his brief time in Mexico: he even took them at a bullfight in Juárez ("The bull kneels to die"; "The crowd burns their programs as a sign of their displeasure"), where he may have seen Rodolfo Gaón, known as "El Califa," fight, and the Spaniard Marcial Lalanda. He had always liked boxing and horse races; he never missed Ascot. All of this is recounted by Hugh Cecil, who never saw him, and Stephen Graham, who saw all too much of him right up to his last day.

He had been writing since he was very young, but not fiction. He made his debut at sixteen in some journals devoted to poultry farming, a science in which he was already, at that age, an expert: the best methods of fattening chickens were no mystery to him, nor were the fowl races of Central Europe, a rather astonishing area of specialized knowledge. In fact, at the age of eighteen, he was considered one of his country's leading authorities on hens. Since childhood he had attracted birds with a strange magnetism, and perhaps that fact contributes (if only slightly) to an understanding of this original facet of his character. His passion for the countryside

and life in the open air was so boundless and constant that it came to exert an influence on his literary development, to dubious or even detrimental effect on the lasting interest of his work, though who can tell anything about ill-fated writers who leave very little work behind. We do know that Thomas Hardy was almost his only model, more for his rural-descriptive dimension than for his undeniable poetic and narrative virtues; meanwhile, Ewart never read Milton or Shakespeare which, particularly in an English writer, does not bode well at all. He met Hardy after the war, in 1920, and though both of them were shy and the conversation was not brilliant or free-flowing, they did hit it off; one of the last things Ewart did before leaving for America was to return to the Dorset countryside and say farewell to the old master. On his first visit there, as he told it, he became so nervous upon finding himself in the presence of his idol that he didn't manage to ask a single question about his novels, though he wanted to know everything about them. Had I been in his place, I would have consulted Hardy about certain doubts of my own, as one of his books—of excellent, cruel stories, *The Withered Arm*—was the first I ever translated, with great rural-descriptive difficulties, at the age of twenty-two, the age when Ewart was already at the front, witnessing the killing, as well as that unconsented and castigated and marred truce of 1915.

It was not, of course, his gallinaceous publications— though they did earn him good money in his earliest youth— that aroused the enthusiasm of readers, critics and illustrious colleagues, but his novel, *Way of Revelation*, in the conception and planning of which Stephen Graham had his part, according to Graham himself, and which Ewart humbly intended as the English *War and Peace* of his time, a feat attempted by so many novelists in so many different countries since Tolstoy.

This novel of five-hundred-odd pages, which generated glowing praise and considerable sales, especially for a debut, is a little hard to take today, and even then its story was a clichéd, sensationalistic melodrama (close, we must suppose, to autobiography), about a young man and his circle of friends between war and peace. In the end it remains unclear which of the two (for in peace there are love affairs, and corruptors) brings him greater sorrow. The characters are flat, none too credible and even less clever, as often happens when figures are taken too directly from reality, without sleeping a while in the imagination; the best parts aren't the war scenes, bogged down by their irrelevant characters, but, predictably, the rural-descriptive ones, in which the human element is lacking. This is Cecil's opinion anyway, and he's not wrong. The story that gave rise to my interest in Ewart, 'The Flats," which I published in *Cuentos únicos*, in an excellent Spanish version by Alejandro García Reyes, is a good and misleading example of his artistic talent: there we can see a writer of poetic prose with considerable technical skill and a good eye for the inanimate world, but in *Way of Revelation* we can also perceive the author's rather run-of-the-mill vision of life and death and his scanty imagination for telling a story, even the story of what has really happened and need not be invented (but to tell what has happened you have to have imagined it as well). It's not so strange, then, that despite the enthusiasm of his contemporaries and his tragic, much-lamented death, Ewart's name has disappeared from almost all the unjust tomes that register not people or their lives and deaths but only the titles and dates of texts that are more or less worthy of being remembered, though almost no one ever remembers them. Still, his book contained a high enough dosage of wartime horrors, morbid civilian dread, disillusioned sentimental hindsight and the ultimate optimism of compensated losses to attract the public of its time, which it did.

Wilfrid Ewart didn't manage to hold out very long against success. At the age of twenty-nine, with combat and one or two amorous embitterments behind him, he enjoyed it without reservations or precautions and with touching innocence: he carried a sheaf of clippings (his reviews) everywhere, showing them to everyone without being asked, until there were too many to fit in his pockets and he had to make do with a selection. Suddenly transformed into a "literary lion," as they say in England, he was surprised—with pleasure rather than vengeful triumph—that anyone he had ever been introduced to even once now claimed to be a friend of his, and that anyone who had ever gotten a good look at him bragged of having predicted that he would do great things. He went to parties and gatherings, teas and coffees and dances, enlightening the ladies and one or another gullible gentleman about his writing process, rubbing elbows with editors who were far more lion-like and saw him only as raw meat, and with veteran writers who tolerated him, no doubt for reasons of autobiographical curiosity and nostalgia, and as a way of fuelling their own resentment, for they knew that, as the historian Froude once said, if anyone does anything noteworthy in London, London will make sure he never does anything noteworthy again. He answered all his letters, dined out every night, wrote all the short stories and articles that the newspapers and magazines commissioned. He expressed many opinions, on literary and non-literary matters; he never missed a soccer match, a horse race or an important boxing match. He lived a charmed life, and he broke down.

Suffering from a bad cold, he went to Liverpool by train, during a storm, to attend the 1922 Grand National, the last time he would ever watch or learn the outcome of that race.

As usual, he picked the winning horse, which should only have heightened his charmed state. But when Stephen Graham went to visit him the next afternoon, Ewart told him that he couldn't write, his hand did not obey him, it wouldn't work. He said it slowly and with difficulty because his breakdown had also affected his speech, and he couldn't be sure that the words ordained by his brain would emerge from his mouth rather than some treacherous, spectral diction. He was frightened, but took it calmly and quietly. He saw a doctor, spent several days in a clinic, and was then sent to the country. He lost weight and grew pale and scrawny, his clothes hung loosely. He spent his time watching birds (his former passion), as a form of therapy.

By June he was somewhat better and able to write to Graham, who had left for America with his wife, whose maiden name, I believe, was Rose Savory. The handwriting was a scrawl, but a more or less legible one that indicated some degree of recovery, as did his mention of medium-term literary projects, once he had been cured, among them the history of the Scots Guards, which he had very willingly promised to write in the ever-modest aim of emulating his maternal great-grandfather Napier and describing the campaigns of the War of '14 just as, a century earlier, his ancestor had described those of the Peninsular War, our War of Independence against Napoleon. Graham answered, encouraging Ewart to travel to Santa Fe, New Mexico, where he and his wife were staying, and there set forth the daring deeds of his beloved regiment: he offered him a house, a horse and absolute freedom, confident that Ewart wouldn't be well enough to accept them. However, one day he received a cable naming the ship, the *Berengaria*, and the date in September when the presumed invalid would disembark.

During the crossing, with New York already close at

hand, a man, a third-class steward, fell into the water and could not be saved. The worst part was realizing that the ship, despite its shudderings and grindings, had moved away from the place where the loss had occurred within only a few seconds, enveloped in the wail of its siren which already sounded more like a first lament than a cry of alarm. By the time the ship reversed it was too late, there wasn't even a place to go back to. That was the worst, for the living, the ship's unstoppable wake, "like a white scar," voracious upon the ocean, the all-too-visible manifestation of time that never waits and goes more quickly than any human will—for truce or salvation or hope—and so forces everything to remain unfinished; that, and the unceasing awareness that the only way to disrupt time is to die and emerge from it.

Ewart spent a few days in New York with Graham, who had come to pick him up, and the American poet Vachel Lindsay, who was the oldest of the three and was always fearful that the younger and less-travelled of the two Englishmen would be mugged or run over by a car or get into some sort of trouble with his exaggeratedly British mannerisms, his vacillating speech (transformed by illness into a real defect), his way, when paying for anything, of holding his money in his hand and laboriously counting it out, his inordinate capacity for surprise, which he couldn't conceal, and his stiffness. Though he had known the suffering of the trenches, Ewart still felt his world to be intact and consequently was amazed that no change took place when he left his boots outside the door of his room at night. "How do men get their boots blacked in this country?" he asked Graham, seriously intrigued. "In the country, I mean, where there are no shoeshine parlours." "Clean them themselves," Graham answered, and Ewart is known to have been unable to do more than mutter, "Extraordinary thing!"

On the long train trip to Santa Fe they stopped in Chicago and Kansas City, and Ewart the whole way lugged along a large iron box he had brought with him from England which contained all the papers and documents he would need to write his regimental history. His travel attire consisted of a pair of army jodhpurs and khaki puttees topped with a vaguely military cap, and he carried a rucksack, more or less as if he had indeed undertaken a colonial adventure (the only thing missing was my pith helmet, but that wasn't purchased until 1933, by my father, during a stopover of the ship *Ciudad de Cádiz* in Tunis). In Santa Fe his spirits improved a great deal as did his nearly paralyzed hands, and he was able to write around two thousand words a day, which—dear God—was not a particularly large output for him; he stayed at the home of the Cassidys, neighbors of Stephen and Rose; he bought a horse to go riding and took various excursions of a pre-eminently folkloric nature, during which he saw Navajo and Apache Indians (among the better-known tribes); the climate relaxed him and suited him well, his anguish was dissipating or perhaps was only deferred; there was greater coordination between his brain and his tongue. Then the Grahams announced that they were departing for Mexico, where they wanted to spend Christmas as the prologue to a stay of two or three months; their plan was to "follow in the footsteps of Hernán Cortés," in preparation for a book Graham was working on about Spain (where he had spent time before embarking from Cádiz for America, and where he had been in contact with Jacobo FitzJames Stuart, undoubtedly a forerunner of the Jacobo FitzJames Stuart I know, one of my more well-bred editors), the West Indies and Mexico, which he entitled *In Quest of El Dorado*, and dedicated "To the literary memory of my friend Wilfrid Ewart" in 1924.

It appears that the Grahams were (understandably enough)

not desirous of Ewart's company in Mexico, or Mr. Graham, at least, was not. As he tells it in his halfhearted biographical volume *The Life and Last Words of Wilfrid Ewart*, also dating from 1924, Graham tried to convince Ewart to take advantage of their absence from Santa Fe to finish his loyal history of the Scots Guards, because it was weighing too heavily on his mind, preventing him from starting on a new novel or, in general, making other plans. At first Ewart seemed to go along with this, but his restless spirit and the unusually cold winter that struck New Mexico that year made him change his mind a few days later and insist on accompanying the couple to Mexico. Still Graham tried to dissuade his former captain (clearly he didn't want even to have to think of him during his time in Mexico), assuring him that the country was far too colorful and seditious for writing and that he wouldn't progress by one line while there. So Ewart decided on New Orleans, and set out on December 15, sending his luggage ahead. Three days later, the Grahams left for Mexico City, secure in the illusion that they would not cross paths with Ewart again until the month of March, when they would pick him up in New Orleans on their way back from their Cortés-bound pilgrimage. This was not to be. In El Paso, Ewart changed his mind once more and had his ticket validated for ten more days, resolving to "take a turn" through Mexico (no more than about four thousand additional miles, after all) before continuing on to Louisiana. Graham says that when a journalist from El Paso told them of this detour, he and his wife couldn't help feeling some apprehension over the fate of their friend, travelling alone through a country still in the final throes of its Revolution and whose language, customs and grievances were unknown to him. The cloak room and safe deposit boxes of the El Paso train station were famous, apparently, for containing numerous items—jewels, money, suitcases, clothing—belonging to travellers who had paused there before making a brief excursion to Mexico and never returned to reclaim them. At least we can be sure that in those days there were mothballs.

In Chihuahua (a very wild city), Graham saw Ewart's signature in a hotel register, made inquiries about his passage through the place and learned that he had left safe and sound. This gesture seems odd, more appropriate to a lone pursuer than a man going along his way, accompanied by his wife, with a slight, distant concern about another man's irresponsible meanderings: no one goes around randomly flipping through hotel registers, just in case; you do that only when you're looking to find someone whose tracks you are following. It was as if the Grahams were now on a Wilfrid-bound pilgrimage, once they learned that Wilfrid was to be found in Mexico. They were most upset to realize, the husband wrote, that if Ewart wanted to abide by his ticket's new period of validity, he would have to leave Mexico City before they got there; they even took the trouble to calculate, railway timetable in hand, which train he would have to take in order to be in Laredo in time to make the Southern-Pacific connection that would take him to New Orleans, his original destination. On discovering that there was a station at which their train to Mexico City and the train coming from there on its way to Laredo would arrive at the same hour, they struggled to glimpse the friend they might have been coinciding with there among the nocturnal mass of thirsty passengers, Chinese stewards, Indians hawking German costume jewelry and raucous vendors of strawberries, melons and mangos. But Ewart wasn't there; in fact, he hadn't left Mexico City.

And the disproportionate and somewhat incomprehensible eagerness to locate him continued; first thing, the morning after their arrival, the Grahams passed by the Hotel Regis, much frequented by North Americans, where they imagined that Ewart, who always needed a room with a bath, might have stayed. He hadn't set foot in the place, so they headed for the British Consulate in search of news, but he hadn't made an appearance there either, nor had he been at the Hotel Cosmos or the Princesa. They conjectured that, pressed for time, he had departed for Laredo without delay. They were staying at the Hotel Iturbide, a place less frequented by tourists than by Mexicans, though they were tourists and busied themselves fulfilling that role during the following days.

On December 30, during one of their outings, they saw Wilfrid Ewart in the distance. At the corner of San Juan de Letrán and 16 de Septiembre, completely unmistakable in his eye-catching jodhpurs and puttees, he was standing on tiptoe peering up at the sky through his tortoise-shell spectacles. In his book, Stephen Graham underscores all too heavily the joy that "surged up in our bosoms," as he puts it, on seeing him. Anything is possible. They all went off to have lunch in a restaurant and the former orderly immediately scolded his former captain for his "willfulness," oddly enough, and not for his uncertain, vacillating nature, as would have seemed more appropriate. Ewart explained that he was captivated by Mexico and had decided to stay. The ticket would expire and his baggage was in New Orleans, but "I've been looking for a place like this all my life," he said to Graham, who didn't pay much attention but tried to make him uneasy with the idea that he was almost sure to lose the box of the Scots Guards' regimental papers. Perhaps the matrimonial pair were simply overprotective, but they seem to have searched desperately for Ewart only to try and get rid of him as soon as they found him, to drive him out of Mexico for the duration of their

Cortés-istical stay. Wilfrid wasn't terribly concerned, he would have the box sent from New Orleans along with his clothing, he had only his rucksack and a cane with him, and he was a bit uncomfortable because he didn't have so much as a change of clothes in Mexico City. But he had opened a bank account and calculated that he could spend the winter inexpensively in Chapultepec or San Angel, where this time without a doubt he would finish his regimental history. Then he would go to Veracruz, return to New York, and spend the summer travelling along the Canadian border, writing a series of articles on relations between that country (Canada) and the United States, truly a gripping subject if ever one existed, and no one knows why an interest in it suddenly seized him, so far in advance and so many miles away.

As he tells it in his *In Quest of El Dorado*, Graham went back with him to the Hotel Isabel, at the corner of República del Salvador and Isabel la Católica, where Ewart was lodging on the recommendation of "a Spaniard" who had given him the address on the train. It was kept by an English-speaking German who, still according to Graham, tried to be ingratiating. He visited his friend's fifth-floor room and admired its view of the mountains. Still, it didn't strike him as a good place to write and "I meditated getting him to change over to the Iturbide." In *The Life and Last Words of Wilfrid Ewart*, however, Graham says the hotel had been suggested by "a Mexican lady" whose card he found with its name written in pencil on the back. He also says that they first went to the Iturbide so Ewart could see the fountain and the "banana palms" that the conjugal couple could contemplate from their suite, and that Ewart, charmed, "had half a mind" to move there that very afternoon, at which point they made for the Isabel to ask for and immediately settle the bill. But the owner took so long drawing it up and made so many mistakes

169

that Wilfrid left it for the next morning. I imagine that these small or not so small contradictions don't mean much and may have arisen from the sheer boredom of having to re-count the same thing twice in the same way. We all try to avoid that (to the annoyance of children), if only so that the same thing will never be quite the same. Nevertheless, the contradictions certainly fertilized the ingenious and entirely baseless speculations as to a possible crime made in the afore-mentioned 1989 article by Sergio González Rodríguez, who fantasized about the possibility that Graham had murdered Ewart out of jealousy related to his wife, literary jealousy, envy of his overnight success, or some brooding military rancor. In any case, Graham's two books both date from 1924, so the hypothesis of lapses or treacheries of memory can be discarded, particularly for a man who turned forty that year, and would go on to live fifty years more.

Ewart's sudden fascination with Mexico City—a surly, quarrelsome place of no culture and no comfort, without one tolerable theatre—was odd. But he was much taken with the climate and the parks, especially Chapultepec, or so he said. He also liked the numerous booths or sidewalk stands run by young female manicurists who were sometimes curtained off and sometimes visible. During that lunch on the 30th he exhibited his gleaming nails to the Grahams with great satisfaction.

Graham's detailed account of the 31st day of December, 1922, in Mexico City, offers excellent proof that, however hard one tries, the events immediately prior to the final event, the catastrophe, have no reason to be perforce significant or even of any interest whatsoever. When someone dies unexpectedly, we try to reconstruct what they said the last time we saw them, as if this could somehow save them; we try to remember the final day, once we know it was final, with an effort we would never make had it been only the penultimate, or just any ordinary day of the many forgotten days of lost time, and so we deceive ourselves, shining on the occasion a light that did not belong to it, not its own light but that of the ending; death, with its suspended brilliance, illuminates whatever came before it ("Put out the light, and then put out the light"), even what was shadowy or grey, in and of itself, and unimportant, never intended or hoped or planned to leave a trace of any kind and was already fading away. Unforeseen or premature death contaminates what preceded it, shooting out its retrospective flames which change everything; what was no more than the day before yesterday is suddenly transformed into "the final years," in the standard phrase of articles and biographies, which often speak of the deceased "during his final years," as if anyone could have anticipated that; and some anodyne yesterday is stylized by the blade of repetition that chisels and idealizes and fixes it forever in our minds, because all at once it has acquired the ominous status of the day before the end, which in its own moment it did not have. We try to confer solemnity on what *turned out* to be the last thing, in most cases a charlatan, fictitious, inculcated, borrowed solemnity, as if it tormented us to think that we might, in our ignorance, lose some word or gaze or gesture of farewell, or to accept that the other person's death caught us off guard, preventing us from seizing the final stretch of his life and being its attentive witnesses, before the metamorphosis. Our awareness of not having intuited this farewell—of not knowing that it was one—weighs on us, if we were convinced we'd see the other person at least once more, though he was already ill and we were afraid he wouldn't last much longer. And we struggle to remember signals, signs, cruel ironies, unnoticed omens of what happened next, and that calms us, like seeing a film a second time or rereading a book and then taking note of the premonitions or forewarnings of its denouement, now that we know what it is and there is no one who can change it.

Speaking for myself, it's difficult to evoke the last time I saw Aliocha Coll or even to know with any certainty when it was; he was a friend who committed suicide quite a while after that last time and not long before our next meeting, which did not take place, and how could I know of his approaching end when perhaps even he didn't know—but of course he did, he knew, he decided on the date—and so I let a couple of days go by in his city (Paris) without calling him, in the optimistic plan of doing it a little later, when I would have wrapped up my stupid activities (but those two adjectives, optimistic and stupid, belong above all to his death, the cessation of his light, which made my perfectly natural thought seem ridiculous and belittled my activities, which were probably only superfluous, and has now entirely erased them: I have no knowledge at all of what I did during those days; my date book says I travelled to Poitiers and returned to Paris, but my memory contains no trace of Poitiers). And given my difficulties with reconstructing that time, I attempted it in a semi-fiction or story entitled "Todo mal vuelve" or "Everything Bad Comes Back," after one of the last phrases he wrote to me, in a telegram. But that story isn't enough, because I believe I have still never confused fiction with reality—yes, I do believe that—and I know that my memory of his final words and gestures and his final state of mind and his final countenance is only amorphous, I think it was over lunch in the Brasserie Balzar on rue des Ecoles, but I'm not sure and don't want to go paging through my date books right now—from which he will have disappeared after that final day, whenever it was—and in any case that lunch which may have been our last meeting is mingled with others that took place in the anodyne indifference of the time that went before and was lost. He was forty-two when he killed himself in 1990 with his unerring doctor's hand, after re-reading a last story—Nerval's "Sylvie"—listening to a last piece of music—I don't know what it was—and finishing his last glass of wine. In fact I wouldn't have seen him again even if I had called him as soon as I arrived in Paris on November 20, because although I learned of his death on the 23rd, he had committed suicide on the 15th. He left two letters, neither was for me, he had already written me many.

And sometimes it's very hard for me to bear the fact that I was unaware of my mother's serious illness, Lolita was her name. It was kept from me and I wasn't living in Madrid and didn't see her often and was too immersed in the passing problems—or perhaps misfortunes, or only chagrins—of my twenty-sixth year to perceive the concealment and try to find out a thing you believe cannot happen and which is therefore the explanation you first rule out. A still juvenile, or superstitious, or complacent belief. And when I came to my belated realization of what was coming to her, I quickly returned from the pointless travels of those months of turmoil and she lasted only a few hours longer after my arrival; sometimes I've thought that she lived those hours and then no more because with me there we were all at her side, at home, the four sons—and the fifth or first still closer, soon to be in her care, the child—and at last she could let herself go, knowing that all four of us were, for the moment, safe and with her and at home. Yes, it's possible. A little more than a year ago I found what must have been her penultimate letter to me, the fourth son she gave birth to, third among those still living, dated November 3, 1977, less than two months before her death; in it she discreetly offered to help me, because during a recent brief visit of mine at home she had seen me looking sad, without knowing why ("The capacity for respect that leads me to forget the secrets people tell me, for I never reveal them, and I try to make peace, has been useful to other people more than once . . . and to you boys? Can't I help you?"), and went on to say, "I slept better while you were here, as I alway do when I know you're here, sleeping; but now I can't sleep and I turn it over and over in my head, I know that there is something I don't know, and that always makes me give free rein to my imagination when it has to do with you boys . . . There are so many problems around all of you!" And perhaps, once she knew that the only one who was missing was now nearby, at home, and that he had said goodbye to her, she could sleep once and for all. I sometimes wonder whether she didn't hold out against that sleep until my arrival, more than she should have and beyond exhaustion, it would have been unlike her not to wait for me before saying goodbye. Not long before she had said to my father,

"I'm a doctor's daughter and I know what I have," because they had hidden the seriousness of her condition from her, as well, and she went on to describe precisely the nature of her illness and what it was going to do to her. In the final hours during which we coincided something ordinary happened that ceased to be ordinary because it was among the last things, and so it is what I remember most. I had recently been in Paris and seen a very large Rubens exhibit there and bought a number of postcards. She was in bed and I sat down on the edge, she had stopped dying her hair—but for me it is always black—and it was a very clean grey, surrounding her face that was so much like mine and that never became wrinkled, or hardly, her skin full and smooth. She looked drowsy and dazed, and I showed her postcards of Rubens paintings to distract her, she enjoyed museums very much. She looked at each one in turn, having to force herself a little to focus her attention and her gaze, I made a comment here or there. She stopped at the portrait of a woman, Helen Fourment, less brightly colored and more sharply etched than the large compositions. "Look at that hand," she said, pointing to the young woman's right hand, then smiling at the extravagant hat. "If I'd worn that I would have looked taller," she said playfully. Every time I see a Rubens now I remember that moment, Helen Fourment's hand, and the hat, and her. It goes without saying that I hadn't allowed her to help me, almost two months earlier; I rarely told my parents about my personal affairs, which generally upset them; like most children, or those of my generation at least, I said nothing. Well, I must have told her something, just enough to keep her imagination from mistakenly wandering toward worse things than those actually happening to me and to calm her apprehensions a little, because in her last letter, which I lost in one of my moves, I remember that she responded tactfully,

saying, "No, I don't understand, but I also understand that I don't understand." In the car that took me to her burial the next day I saw my face in the rear view mirror, and I rode along, drowsy and dazed, thinking: "I'm what's left that's most like her. I'm what's left that's most like her." It was December 24; I don't have many other memories of her final hour, I arrived on the 23rd, a little late.

And I didn't know it was the last time when I last saw Juan Benet, my literary teacher and friend for twenty-two years or more. We did know he was gravely ill and we wouldn't have him with us much longer, but I was sure I would still see him a few more times, and the last visit I made to his house with Mercedes López-Ballesteros wasn't felt to be the farewell by either of us, we weren't somber, we didn't think the time had come yet to say goodbye, in our minds. I had recently come back not from Paris this time but from London, and was spouting funny and semi-apocryphal anecdotes I had heard from Guillermo Cabrera Infante and his wife Miriam Gómez, both stupendous storytellers—imitating their Cuban accents for good measure—and Don Juan, who held them in great affection, always enjoyed their stories. Some of the anecdotes were so ludicrous that they made him laugh very hard, so hard that at one point he started to protest and told me with little conviction, amid gales of laughter, "Ouch, don't make me laugh so much, it hurts me here," pointing to his chest or his side, I don't remember. But I was merciless and went on raving and recounting and exaggerating, I no longer know if it was the incredible story of Borges in Sitges ("a very savage place") with the slice of *pa amb tomàquet* that got stuck, or the one about the erect "homosexualistic" kangaroo in Australia, or the one about the actor Richard Gere and the amatory device that got stuck, or the one about Dr. Dally, half of whose body (longitudinally) was immobile but of varying colors and who sold books that he shouldn't have, the Cabreras are inexhaustible. And thanks to them I made Don Juan laugh endlessly that night and how glad I am now that I did, and that I didn't stop when he said the laughter was hurting him, because it turned out to be the last night, and so my penultimate vision of him is of a Juan in great hilarity. I didn't see him again after that, I only spoke to him over the phone to tell him I had re-read *Volverás a Región*—his first novel, published nearly twenty-five years before—for an article I was writing and that now it had become truly good. "Yes? You think so?" he asked with unfeigned ingenuousness. In fact, I did see him again, but it was a few minutes after he had died, in the first hour of January 5, 1993, almost five years ago now. Vicente Molina Foix was with me and he went home to get some cufflinks for Juan to be buried in, because neither his wife nor his children could find his own that night (no one could have identified Don Juan from his cufflinks). The night Mercedes and I paid our visit was the night of the 12th to the 13th of December, a Saturday. He came to the door to say goodbye, it was late, and the final glimpse was of his tall figure at the top of the stairs to the door of his house in El Viso, with a smile still lingering from the recent laughter like a slight, somnolent trace on the face of someone who's falling asleep, the long shape veiled in penumbra and outlined against the light from inside, saying goodbye with a waving hand, but not in his mind. As soon as he closed the door and we'd gone around the corner, Mercedes burst into tears and buried her face in my shoulder, getting my coat wet. She had worked for him every day for three years, and she, I think, had said goodbye, in her mind.

After Ewart died, many hours passed during which it never occurred to anyone to imagine that he wasn't alive, and many more hours went by before his family and friends learned that some time ago by then he had said his final farewell to the world beyond the ocean, perhaps without realizing it or even saying it to himself, not even in his mind. I don't know why the 31st of December and 1922 are given as the date and year of his death, when there were no witnesses—not even the person who killed him was a witness, and had no certainty of having killed—and he could well have died during the first hour or first minute of January 1, who knows, and therefore in 1923. It's frightening to think of the hours—soon distant and forgotten, yet so slow and negligible while they're going by—during which our friends and relatives think we're alive when in fact we are dead, and they sleep peacefully, dreaming their primitive dreams, or watch television or laugh or curse or fuck instead of dropping everything and running belatedly to meet us and make phone calls and attend to formalities and not believe it, and grieve and despair, to whatever degree. This fear isn't for the dead, for their imagined solitude and abandonment, but for the living who will later have to reconstruct those hours—the actual passage of which is now unusable and annulled, and which are even slower and more negligible in memory—that they lived through unaware their world had changed, easy and indifferent or with a happiness now improper, or maybe even speaking ill of the one now dead. "Put out the light, and then put out the light," perhaps that's why—to make it entirely certain—it has to be said twice, once for the event, once for the telling. And, too, as I said at the beginning, remembering and telling can become not only homage but affront.

Wilfrid Ewart's dead body was not found until nearly noon on New Year's Day, so almost twelve hours had passed without anyone realizing that this was what he was now, a dead body, and no longer one of us, if saying "us" makes any sense. According to the Mexican newspaper *Excelsior*, of Wednesday January 3, 1923, which both González Rodríguez and Muñoz Saldaña consulted and cited for me verbatim, respecting both its incorrect punctuation and its typographical errors:

> *Quien primero tuvo conocimiento del suceso fue la señora Angelina Trejo de Estrevelt, quien presta sus servicios en calidad de camarera en el Hotel Isabel. La señora de Estrevelt, como de costumbre se dirigió ayer en la mañana, ya cerca del medio día a las habitaciones superiores con el fin de hacer el aseo de las mismas. Al llegar al cuarto número 53 miró por la cerradura y le extrañó ver que la luz artificial estaba encendida. Llamó a la puerta varias veces y no obtuvo contestación alguna. Temerosa de que algo hubiera occurrido al pasajero, penetró a la habitación, encontrando las ropas de la cama en perfecto orden. Poco después y dirigiendo la vista al balcón con vista a la calle, que se encontraba abierto, vio el cadáver del señor Etwart, en medio de un charco de sangre ya coagulada.*

(The first to take cognizance of the event was Señora Angelina Trejo de Estrevelt, who lends her

services to the Hotel Isabel in the capacity of cham-
bermaid. Señora de Estrevelt, as is her custom made
her way yesterday morning, already close to noon to
the upper rooms in the aim of ensuring the hygiene of
same. On reaching room number 53, she looked
through the keyhole and found it strange that the
electric light was on. ["Put out the light, and then put
out the light," that again.] She knocked several times,
and obtained no response whatsoever. Fearful that
something might have happened to the transient oc-
cupant, she went into the room, finding the bed-
clothes in perfect order. Shortly after that, directing
her gaze to the balcony overlooking the street, which
was open, she saw the corpse of Señor Etwart, in a
puddle of already coagulated blood.)

At this point, we might well ask ourselves why the cham-
bermaid looked through the keyhole first, before taking
any other step, and the corresponding news article from the
English-language section of the same newspaper does not
clear up this mystery, though it does call Ewart Ewart and
not Etwart, and specifies that

> . . . a chambermaid coming to clean his room *found
> the door locked* [my italics] and peering through the
> keyhole saw that the light was still burning. After call-
> ing several times she became alarmed, and entering
> the room noticed that the bed had not been slept in.
> Proceeding toward the balcony of the window she
> discovered the body lying in a puddle of clotted
> blood. . . .

The fact that the door was locked seems in no way surprising
and is not sufficient reason to peep through the keyhole and

only then knock several times on the door, rather than knocking first, before doing anything else. Perhaps it was the waste of electricity that alarmed Doña Angelina Trejo de Estrevelt and her desire to put out the superfluous light and make the night cease entirely that prompted her to decide to use her key.

Immediately [the article written in Spanish goes on] she gave notice of this funereal discovery to the boy in charge of the elevator, so that he in his turn, could give notice to the administrator of the hotel, Señor Manuel Olvera. He went precipitately up to the fifth floor and, upon reaching room 53, did indeed find the inanimate body of Señor Etwart. [It would have been quite miraculous if that had not been the case, or perhaps the article was hinting that chambermaids can be fatalistic and prone to absurd fancies and you can never tell what they'll come up with.] Immediately he gave notice to the police, the personnel of the fifth precinct presenting themselves moments later, proceeding to raise the corpse. It was in a dorsally prone position and bore signs of a death that was not recent. When the body was examined, it was seen to have a wound from a firearm in the left eye, without exit orifice. It was ordered that the corpse be taken to the Hospital Juárez for the legally mandated autopsy.

The police commissioner, Señor Mellado, made an inspection of the clothing of the deceased finding documents and papers, cash money, a check that had yet to be cashed and a book of blank checks. He also found a receipt from the Banco Montreal where Señor Etwart had deposited on the day of his arrival a goodly sum of money. Señor Mellado drew up an orderly inventory of all this so that the judicial authorities could take cognizance of the case.

Before going on, we need to go back to the beginning of the article, which was published under the following headlines and subheads: "English Subject Dies of a Gunshot," "Barbaric Habit of Firing into the Air, Had an Outcome," "Fatal Curiosity," "Killed When Listening to Popular Rejoicing from Hotel Balcony." The article begins like this:

> From within room number 53 of the Hotel Isabel yesterday, police personnel of the fifth precinct retrieved the corpse of Señor Wilfrid Herbert Gore Etwart, of English nationality and which presented a wound caused by a projectile from a firearm, with an entry orifice in the left eye, the bullet remaining lodged in the skull.
>
> Señor Gore Etwart had arrived the previous night in this capital city proceeding from the United States and on a business trip. From the investigations of the police it is presumed that Señor Etwart died as a consequence of a stray bullet among the many that were fired on New Year's Eve by one of the numerous troglodytes who cannot express enthusiasm without shooting off firearms.

(It's been eons since I've read or heard the word "troglodyte," which has become antediluvian, but perhaps in 1923 it was a novelty and struck the anonymous reporter as precise and perfect for this none-too-objective paragraph remonstrating with his compatriots.)

> The corpse of the English subject was found on the balcony of room number 53, located on the fifth floor

of the Hotel Isabel on Avenida República del Salvador and could be identified owing to the passport contained in one of the pockets of the jacket.

Then, after the narrative previously cited, the article concludes with some repetition and a renewed bout of scolding, but it's worth reproducing here in its entirety:

> The Consul of Great Britain in Mexico, on taking cognizance of the event, presented himself at the precinct house requesting the corpse of Señor Etwart which will be surrendered to him of course.

(The "of course" is rather touching, as if in vehement denial of some offensive insinuation about the honor of the Mexican people, or of their police, who would never withhold the body of a gunshot victim.)

> From the declarations of the hotel employees, it is deduced that Señor Etwart, at midnight on the last day of the year, on hearing the whistles and firecrackers announcing the advent of the new year, went to the balcony out of mere curiosity, that being the moment when a shot fired into the air by one of so many careless individuals was to cause him the lesion that must have deprived him of life almost instantaneously.

(Given that no hotel employee noticed the tragedy until noon of the following day, it's not entirely clear why anything whatsoever "is deduced" from their declarations, which could only have been hypotheses, and the excessive or superfluous explanation that Ewart or Etwart looked out from the balcony "out of mere curiosity" is also surprising, as if he could have done so for some other reason.)

The English section of the newspaper *Excélsior* didn't offer any additional information on the discovery of the body, but did relate the death to an accident that had happened to another guest of the ill-starred Hotel Isabel not far away and about an hour earlier: "A strange coincidence in the death of Mr. Ewart is the accident that befell Carlos Duems, representative of the Duems News Agency, who is a resident of the same hotel of the tragic death of the Englishman."

In its implausible and macaronic English the article goes on to say that towards 11:00 p.m. on the night of December 31, the newspaper's chief wire service editor, Salvador Pozos, found Mr. Duems seriously injured at the corner of Nuevo México and Revillagigedo, where he had been struck by "one of the many crazed Fords jam-packed with New Years' revellers," who had dragged him five yards along the road for greater revelry. Señor Pozos, who was personally acquainted with the victim, a representative of the news agency that bore his name, picked him up and carried him to his room in the Hotel Isabel, located on the same floor as the room occupied by Ewart. Clearly that fifth floor meant trouble, though all in all, Mr. Duems came out of it very well by simply managing to stay alive through those days in that place, for on January 3, just as the newspapers were collecting themselves and beginning to recover from these dreadful events, another British subject named George W. Steabben perished—accidentally, once again, we may suppose—in the crossfire of a fierce brawl that, according to Stephen Graham, erupted between two bands of Mexicans, both riding in cars and firing at each other with no qualms and in broad daylight, though most of them were government officials or congressmen, or perhaps for that very reason, which put all of them "above the law." Sergio G.R. found the details in a collection of periodicals and, with my gratitude, has permitted me to reproduce them:

> On January 3, General Leovigildo Avila and Lieutenant Colonel Constantino Lazcano came out to settle a dispute at the entrance to the Salón Phalerno on calle 16 de Septiembre; surrounded by their friends, they insulted one another and drew their weapons. The outcome of the fray was as follows: the policeman Zavala, wounded in the hand; General Avila, wounded in the arm; Colonel Lazcano, wounded in the shoulderblade and left cheek; Congressman Trillo, wounded in the hand; Pepete the bullfighter, who happened to be passing by, wounded in the right arm; the agent Sotero Reza, wounded in the leg. George W Steabben, who was proceeding to his offices, located across the street from that den of ill repute, received a gunshot direct to the forehead at 17:21 hours.

It does not appear that these celebrated gunslingers were motorized, which again casts suspicion on Graham, according to whose version the unfortunate subject of His Majesty was an honorable merchant walking down the street with his family when he was fired upon. It is a strikingly novelistic injustice that the only person to lose his life in this illustrious free-for-all was the complete outsider to it all, who got a hole in his forehead (that is, had no chance of survival), while the others came away with wounds in their limbs, including poor right-handed Pepete, who may have had to stay out of the bullring for a while, and the dignitaries themselves, the defiant Constantino and the injurious Leovigildo, though the former was left with a scar on his cheek. Sure shots indeed, that carried away, within three days, George Steabben and

Wilfred Ewart. And the bullet that killed Ewart is so implausible that if it had occurred in a novel and not in life no one could give the slightest credence to the incredible fact that death entered him directly through his sightless eye, the eye no image had ever passed through, the eye that was never connected to the brain and was therefore independent of its control for thirty years, to become, at the end of all that time, the fatal conduit through which the bullet that lodged in the skull entered and finally connected them, eye and brain, but only in the moment of their cessation. As the Mexican newspapers of January 4 made it their business to trumpet, once they had learned the dead man's story from Graham who issued a statement and identified the body, it was already "a cruel irony of fatal destiny" that the man who had lived through "more than a hundred battles" and had been "respected by the enemy bullets" and had "defied death on innumerable occasions" had been brought down unarmed in Mexico by some fool's shot fired off at random when, out of mere curiosity, he went out onto the balcony of his room on a night of revelry ("Fate Brought Him to Mexico," read one of the subtitles, with a certain punitive satisfaction). Yes, it was a strange fate or chance or whatever it is that we call it, and we speak of it less and less, this thing which generally occurs only in life, bad novels and good stories, in the first of these to an extreme degree. But to make fate or chance or destiny a little less strange, Ewart's bullet could at least have gone into his forehead, as Steabben's did, or his heart or his jugular or his mouth, or the other eye with which he did see and whose light had not yet been put out, not even for the first time. But it went straight into the blind eye, just beneath the eyebrow, shattering the lens of Ewart's glasses without damaging the frame, I don't know if he was still wearing the glasses when they found him. These chance events and coincidences don't really matter; we might imagine that if the bullet (which couldn't be seen by the unfortunate eye it found in the darkness) had gone toward the other eye it might have been eluded—but bullets are never seen, and only in old books are they heard to whistle, or so Jünger says—and we might also imagine that there was an element of mercy in the direction taken by the stray bullet among the infinity of possible courses, if the eye was thus spared the sight of what was coming to it. What does it matter, nothing is really that strange, and who would be interested, there are no hidden forces guiding anything or leading anyone to the place of his death, all possibilities are contained in the passage of time, that is, in the past and the future. There's little sense in lament or astonishment, Graham's, expressed in his books, or Gawsworth's, or Conan Doyle's, in far-off Mother England, or that of the Mexican journalists who aspired to a solemnity they didn't know how to attain, as they brought their sentences to a close: "Sad was the end of this British officer, who after having risked his life many times in the most terrible combats history records, came to die in such a way." What a pity to want to soar without knowing how, it happens to most of us.

But there were still greater perplexities in store for those readers who were following this story that the world very quickly forgot and that probably no longer matters to anyone. Another daily paper, *El Universal*, gave, on January 3, an all-too-different version of the discovery of the body of a man who, for this article's writer, had borne the name "Herbert Gore," as if he had guessed the pseudonym used by Ewart for his fantastic tales and had decided to use it in describing his death, which seemed fictitious. The disturbingly contradictory paragraph was this one: "Since the police found no pistol, the hypothesis of Señor Mellado was accepted as certain, that is, that Señor Gore had received the wound that caused his death when he was on the balcony of his room, sitting in an armchair, because on said article of furniture a large blood stain was found, which demonstrates that he was there when he received the mortal wound." This is truly an unresolvable contradiction, and not only because the other paper, *Excélsior*, made absolutely no mention of any such armchair or stain. If Ewart stepped onto the balcony out of simple curiosity when he heard the shots ("Mr. Graham believes," said *Excelsior* on the following day, "that his friend, on hearing shots fired, went out onto the balcony to see what it was all about and that his curiosity was explicable given that he was a soldier who for many months had continually heard the rat-a-tat of artillery and the booming of cannon"), it makes no sense that he would take the trouble to lug an armchair out there beforehand, nor that he would do so after hearing the shots, as if preparing to spend a long time watching a spectacle that he can't have seen much of in the distance with his one blind eye. If, on the contrary, the armchair was not on the balcony, but showed the blood, then Ewart couldn't have died "instantaneously"; he would have had to take a few steps before collapsing into its softness and leaving that stain on the upholstery, but in that case the body couldn't have been found stretched out on the balcony, as its discoverer stated and the hotel administrator reconfirmed, unless, after having soiled the chair, Ewart had dragged himself back to the balcony to call out for help from there, a rather futile thing when the street was full of the rousing "rat-a-tat" of firecrackers and pistol shots. Nor does it seem probable that, even if death was not instantaneous, he would have had time to do much strolling about. Señor Mellado, it has to be said in passing, must have been a disastrously bad detective if the fact of not finding any weapon in the room struck him as conclusive proof that the bullet had come from outside, as if murderers were in the habit of leaving their firearms next to their victims in order to make the police's work that much easier. And Stephen Graham's explanation of Ewart's curiosity is entirely unnecessary: a man does not need to have heard the famous rat-a-tat for months during a war in order to take a look out at the street, whether or not shots are being fired there.

There was something excessive in the statement by Graham that was reprinted by the newspapers on January 4 in unusually complete form: not only were the principal and secondary facts of the life and personality of Ewart given— his origins, his books—but also all the random circumstances that had brought him to Mexico which I related earlier, including his great distress at the lack of a change of clothes. *Excélsior* noted: "Señora Graham explains that he stayed in the city waiting for his luggage, since he was known in London social circles as an exemplarily well dressed person, and the fact of not receiving his short pants (trunks) was greatly irritating to him. 'It was just an accident that he travelled to Mexico.'" The first sentence is so absurd—making elegance depend on a pair of shorts, and if they were underwear the thing is even more demented, it wouldn't have ruined him to buy himself a pair of local *zaragüelles*—that we may suspect an erroneous translation of the word "trunks" here. In any case, the Mexican reporters had the undeniable merit of extracting a few words from the silent and mysterious Mrs. Graham, who does not generally appear, by mention or description, in a speaking or active role, and hardly even as a passive presence, in her husband's travel books, even when she accompanied him from the first day of the expedition to the last (Rose Savory was her maiden name, it would seem). According to *Excélsior*, she added yet another line about

Ewart, perhaps superfluous if it wasn't in answer to a specific question: "He had a very pleasant personality, in the opinion of all those who knew him, and he had no enemies, Señora Graham stated." She was being rather audacious here, no doubt, for the second of her claims is a difficult one to make about the winner of a great victory, though perhaps by 1923 he had ceased to have enemies.

But even stranger than the declarations made *in situ* by the matrimonial pair was the mise-en-scène of the death that Graham offered at the end of his aforementioned book, *The Life and Last Words of Wilfrid Ewart*, after painstakingly re-calling and recounting all that the two men of the trio said and did on that 31st of December which for one of them would become the final day of all years. They separated at about 11:30 p.m., strange that they didn't stay together only half an hour longer to celebrate the arrival of 1923 and raise a glass to the future. "Then he went to his hotel and we went to ours," says Graham in his book, "and the pandemonium increased till midnight, when it burst into hell let loose." And he adds with total certainty, as if he had been peering through the keyhole at Ewart's room or there inside it, nei-ther supposing nor conjecturing but simply stating, "Wilfrid went straight to his hotel, undressed, washed, got into his pyjamas, put a blade into his safety razor, and evidently had intended to have a shave before going to bed, when he had been attracted by some new happening down in the street below. He went to the window, and at the same moment a spent bullet went right through his eye and he fell back into the room a dead man." One more stroke of bad luck, or chance or fate or destiny if you like: a "spent bullet" or a cold bullet or a dead bullet is a bullet that has begun to lose angle and velocity in its trajectory. I won't be the one to explain how it's possible that a bullet that didn't leave an exit wound but did remain lodged at the back of a skull had managed to "spend' itself or "grow cold" in its flight, for I know nothing about ballistics or obliqueness and less still about the science of postmortem examination. But that is what Graham wrote, "a spent bullet," and what another writer, Hugh Cecil picked up and repeated, seventy-one years later.

True, the detail doesn't much matter; in the end almost nothing about this death is explicable, including, for example, the fact that the Mexican newspapers, in all their great attention to detail, didn't mention the corpse's pyjamas. And it seems a major narrative licence on Graham's part—if that was what it was, a licence—to decide that Ewart washed first and only then put a new blade in his safety razor, and did so, what's more, in the absurd intention of going to bed freshly shaven, an impractical measure if ever there was, since the beard will grow back during the night and the interested party will arise in the morning needing, in all likelihood, another shave; it makes very little sense to shave at the end of the day if no nocturnal appointment awaits and there will be no one to appreciate the smoothness of your cheeks. It is no less strange that, according to Graham, Ewart fell "back into the room a dead man," for as this phrase depicts the scene, there was no longer either balcony or armchair to receive the plummeting body. And though this could be understood merely as an attempt to dramatize what is already dramatic, it is equally impossible for Graham to have known that the bullet passed through his friend's eye "at the very moment" he went out to the balcony, and not, for example, after he had lingered there for some time, admiring the pandemonium. In any case, Graham doesn't do much dramatizing of his narrative, far less, of course, than its impromptu Mexican chroniclers.

Perhaps that's why he didn't manage to instill much of a

current of predestination into his account of that last day, or maybe that was simple literary ineptitude. Anyway, in his story, he does not explain why Ewart had yet to move out of the hotel by the night of the 31st although on the previous day, the 30th of December, that had been his intention, frustrated only by a long delay in getting the bill. He does, on the other hand, comment that Ewart had twice changed rooms at the Hotel Isabel, and therefore had never actually managed to sleep in the third room, which housed his death (the bed still made up—that detail did not escape Señora Trejo de Estrevelt or the journalists who overlooked the pyjamas, if there were indeed pyjamas). It would have been so easy for this death never to have happened, and Graham did not resist the temptation to enumerate—though concisely and without getting carried away—the linked factors contributing to the misadventure: "It was almost as if some hidden force were guiding him into position for death. He was in Mexico City with an unused out-of-date ticket to New Orleans. Thus in the first place he had been led nearer fate; a stranger had sent him to an unlikely hotel, and he went nearer still. And in the hotel he shifted about till he found the fatal attic where he died. Had we seen the year out in the Square of the great pyramid, perhaps all had been well. Who can tell?"

Yes, who can tell, and what does it matter, all these ifs, all these conditionals with which we pepper our whole lives to explain them to ourselves, to justify and confirm them, and so imagine that they could have been different, or that they couldn't have been; lamenting adversity all the more and rejoicing all the more in good fortune, yet both are only consolations or accolades or regrets or rhetorical vexations, serving only to keep us from entirely and immediately losing sight of what time has discarded, and time does nothing but discard. It would have been so easy for this death not to have happened, but in reality it would have been so easy for nothing to have happened, nothing that takes place and occurs, absolutely nothing, beginning with our birth. And so what if I hadn't been born, I said that earlier. There are too many who are born and it's as if they'd never arrived in or passed through the world; memory or some record remains of so few and there are so many who quickly say good-bye and fade away as if the earth lacked the time to witness their eagerness and their failures or achievements, or as if there were some urgent need to be rid of their breath and their still incipient wills, the effort made in vain, the diminutive footsteps that leave no trace or only in the sharp-edged memory of someone who taught those feet to take steps and made the mistake or had the audacity to go to the effort of gestating and imagining a face, and hoping: as if they were a costly and superfluous luxury that life expels at once like a breath, not even allowed to be put to the test because neither history nor time claims or seeks them. And so what, if no one had ever been born. No one would ever have died then, either, and there would be none of these stories incessantly told, full of horror, random chance and affronts, and temporary salvation and final doom.

It would also have been so easy for George W. Steabban not to have died in that hail of bullets, from a shot to the forehead, only two days later in the very same place, and all the more so since he had already had one brush with his fate and escaped it, according to Sergio G.R.: after his accidental death in Mexico at the hands of Constantino or Leovigildo, someone remembered that this merchant in the meat and sausage industry had fought in the Boer War and had subsequently been a food inspector during the war of '14, Ewart's war. "Not long before that war, in Buenos Aires on a business trip," says my Mexican correspondent in his article, "he was 'confused' with someone else and shot at and beaten, but his strong body managed to survive the attack." And he adds, speaking of his actual death or final doom: "Steabben must have had enormous strength: his death throes lasted twenty-four hours." It would have been so easy for nothing to have happened.

Nothing in Wilfrid Ewart's final day was particularly ominous or worthy of mention, though Graham took care to mention everything. The soon-to-be-dead man joined his married friends around noon, wearing a new shirt he had bought in honor of the day (let's hope he had also bought a complete change of clothes and was able to move about feeling clean and comfortable during his final hours). As a special treat, he read the Grahams a few lines he had jotted down in his notebook, and was particularly proud of what he had written about the dogs known as Chihuahuas, Graham informs us, without any displeasure in his tone. In the streetcar on the way to San Angel Ewart informed them that he had sent a cable to New Orleans to claim his baggage and, at the telegraph office, had become friendly with an English employee named Hollands, who lived with his wife in Chapultepec and had promised to find him a pleasant place to live there. He was going to have lunch with them the next day and it would have been so easy for him to have been present at that New Year's Day lunch. They ate in the celebrated courtyard of an inn where he had eaten before, and Graham noticed that his friend had lost most of his appetite; he refused the turkey and the more solid dishes and ate only strawberries and cream, an interminable serving, or rather one serving after another, cream and strawberries and strawberries and cream the entire time. Ewart told them a number of things over the course of the meal. He had decided that he did not like America, that is, the United States. Nevertheless he would go back and spend two or three years there before reestablishing himself in London, after which he would never return to the former colonies. He had discovered that his political bent was conservative, after having had liberal and even radical leanings. He doubted he would go on writing novels, at that moment he was more attracted by the idea of involving himself in foreign politics, he thought of interviewing President Obregón and General Enríquez and publishing articles on the current Mexican situation, and then writing a book on relations between the United States and Canada, a subject, as I said, every bit as incandescent then as it is now. He couldn't understand why the United States hadn't yet annexed Mexico (it's probably for the best that he didn't write his articles; they might have been misunderstood), and his only argument in favor of an independent Mexico was that it was different and perhaps worth preserving in its difference (he doesn't seem to have had a very brilliant day, he certainly couldn't have imagined that it would be the day of his final farewell to the world, and I don't know if Graham acted as a friend by relating it all in detail).

He again lamented his lack of clothes. "There's nothing to fit me in Mexico City," he said emphatically. He told them he had called at the British Club and asked permission to have his letters addressed there. But they had given him some funny looks and the secretary's behavior had been offensive, "Yes, if—er—your war record's all right," he had said. Ewart was tempted to tell him that he had had the honor of—er—commanding a company of His Majesty's Foot Guards for a while, but forebore. "However, I'll not darken their threshold again," he added pompously, referring to the British Club, so suspicious and discourteous. Ewart must have been the sort of man who expects to be recognized at first glance for what he is or feels himself to be, that is, a gentleman, and who thinks his life story is visible on his face. The club's members later regretted not having given him a warmer welcome.

They spoke of literature a while then, he and the Grahams, but the author under discussion did not lend himself to disquistions worthy of the day that it was or turned out to be, said author being none other than my exuberant compatriot Blasco Ibáñez, who had made a great impression on Ewart with the vast scope of his narratives. Ewart summarized the plots of two of Blasco Ibáñez's novels—and Graham doesn't seem retrospectively recriminatory over this new form of abuse, either—in which the world or half the world was the scene of the drama. Even more than the novels, Ewart had liked the movies based on *The Four Horsemen of the Apocalypse* and *Blood and Sand*, having recently seen the latter film in Santa Fe, with "the elegant Rudolf" (Valentino, that is) in the role of the matador. This memory made him express the desire to go to a hundred bullfights in order to master all the subtleties of that art, though at the same time he didn't see how he could ever go to another one, he had had such a bad time of it at his baptism in butchery.

He was delighted with his life as a writer. He could go where he liked in the world and live off his work, and there were a thousand places he wanted to go. He was to make only one more journey, as we know, an internal journey. That afternoon as they were returning to the center of the city they heard the crackle of rifle and revolver fire, the revelry was commencing.

They spent the evening at the Teatro Lírico, where they saw a revue of the year 1922, the year that was ending. They didn't understand much, since the vignettes were full of local references, but they enjoyed the dancing and liked the scene in which a killer tried to seduce the widow of a hero until suddenly the coffin's lid lifted and the dead man arose from the open grave to protest and forestall the crime.

Leaving the theatre they found the streets almost impenetrably crowded, overflowing with cars and trucks crammed with wide sombreros, dizzy with blaring horns and exploding fireworks and those arching, quavering, yipping cries. People carried paper flags in red, white and green, most of the men were festively brandishing shotguns or pistols—the sound of weapons going off had grown louder—and with cartridge belts slung across their chests they fired into the air from the streets and rooftops. The cafés were packed, orchestras were playing to further add to the pandemonium, the effect of pulque and other cactus-based liquors was making itself felt everywhere. The three English people felt rather tired, but still wanted supper, and they found a table in a place with music, the restaurant of the Hotel Cosmos. There they stayed for quite some time—more strawberries and cream—"and would no doubt have seen the Old Year out, the New Year in," says Graham, "but an unkind Fate prompted otherwise." He does not, however, explain exactly how this Fate—which doesn't seem to have been particularly grim-faced or determined—operated, or why they were all in the street again around 11:30. He had half a mind to leave his wife at the hotel—she must have been the most exhausted of the three, having spent the whole day listening to Ewart hold forth on Blasco Ibáñez and Chihuahua dogs—and then go back to the Zócalo to contemplate the joyous midnight fusillade. But they were all done in and decided to retire to their respective hotels. Of their final discussion in the Hotel Cosmos, Graham notes only a ridiculous conversation about eggs, truly not an elevated subject for anyone's final words, still less those of a writer who would have gone right to the top. It all started when a waiter asked the simple, innocent question, "How will you have your eggs?" which was all Ewart needed to summon forth his former expertise on poultry, perorate at length on the different classes of yolks and whites and sizes and shells, their virtues and defects, and brag of being able to state, within a 24-hour margin of error, the age of any egg—British or foreign, European or American or even African or Asiatic. "One thing I do pride myself on," he said senselessly, "I could tell you almost to a day the age of an egg." These can be said to have been his penultimate words. If he'd lived a day longer, he could have told whether a given egg dated from 1922 or 1923.

It seems unlikely that they spoke of nothing else throughout the entire dinner, for Ewart seems never to have been at a loss for a topic of conversation—he was a feckless chatterbox, at least on his final day, and he could always fall back on his notebook and read aloud—but strangely enough Graham does not record any other aspect of their talk. (Maybe he was dazed.) He only says that once out in the street, "we shook hands; we wished one another a happy New Year; we said good-bye. 'A happy New Year, and may you soon get back that iron box,' were my last words to him, referring to that box of regimental records whose safety must, I knew, be causing him anxiety." And Ewart answered, "Happy New Year," and they parted. Once again Stephen Graham's wife gives the impression of not being present, not even for the goodbye that really was goodbye. At their hotel, the Iturbide, a certain degree of chaos had set in, Graham says, with the staff "in that menacing drunken state which comes after drinking much pulque." At midnight the clamor burst out and "hundreds of thousands of revolvers and guns must have been discharged and discharged repeatedly." It sounded like a great general outbreak of war. Graham leaned out the window and looked at the dark sky, "which told nothing of the myriads of bullets flying into it." Perhaps Rose Savory Graham had gone to bed with unease and foreboding, and looked at his back in silence while he gazed outside, the invisible bullets.

One of them flew a little lower or was spent or grew cold too quickly and embedded itself in the blind left eye of another man, also standing on a balcony, either wearing pyjamas or still dressed in his brand-new Mexican shirt, either standing up or sitting in an armchair, still wearing his glasses and intending to shave before going to bed in a bed that was never unmade or even turned down, a man who had changed rooms twice until he ended up in that fifth-floor room and who had not moved from one hotel to another, as had been his intention since the previous afternoon, in order to be closer to his friends, who sometimes seemed to flee from him and at other times pursued him as if they were hot on the trail of a lover or an enemy. Nothing makes sense, nothing fits, and the thing that makes the least sense of all is that Ewart and the Grahams retired to get some rest in a city and at a time in which absolutely no one was going to be able to rest or sleep until dawn or thereafter. Perhaps his death was a belated intrusion of the all-out warfare that was sidestepped before his eyes one Christmas morning in a remote Flemish quagmire. Perhaps it was the counterpart of that truce of ten or twenty joyous and unified minutes out of the prolonged destruction of months; now it was his turn to be annihilated amid a great, peacetime revelry, as it had been the turn, seven years earlier, of a sergeant named Oliver to be struck down as a reminder of war—or was it war's revenge—during the brief duration of the truce and not before or after, his poor, trusting figure much loved by his comrades-in-arms. "It makes no difference. It must be an accident," wrote Ewart, and the ceasefire was not interrupted for that reason just as the boisterous festivities in Mexico City were not interrupted because he lay the whole night on the balcony or the floor of the room with a hole in his eye, his face not even covered by half a sandbag or a blanket, while Stephen Graham turned back to his wife and, after closing the window to mute the uproar of the general outbreak of war, walked to the bed, perhaps toward her arms reaching out to him, begging for protection, demanding love.

Laurence Sterne may have been right in *Tristram Shandy* which I translated into my language twenty years ago, when he had one of the characters recall that King William was of the opinion that everything was predestined for us in this world, and the King would often say to his soldiers that "every ball had its billet." (Diderot later copied the phrase.) Perhaps that spent or cold bullet was predestined to be billeted in Wilfrid Ewart, and yet the idea is hard to accept, it's so hard to succeed in making something happen, even what's been decided on and planned out, not even the will of a god seems forceful enough to manage it, if our own will is made in its semblance. It may be, rather, that nothing is ever unmixed and the thirst for totality is never quenched, perhaps because it is a false yearning. Nothing is whole or of a single piece, everything is fractured and envenomed, veins of peace run through the body of war and hatred insinuates itself into love and compassion, there is truce amid the quagmire of bullets and a bullet amid the revelries, nothing can bear to be unique or to prevail or be dominant and everything needs fissures and cracks, needs its negation at the same time as its existence. And nothing is known with certainty, and everything is told figuratively.

They buried him two days later, on January 3. Graham and Hollands, the postal employee, identified the body at the desolate Hospital Juárez, which was also a prison; according to Graham, the expression on the dead face was "puzzled and annoyed." An autopsy was performed, and Ewart was found, in hindsight, to have been in perfect health. Twenty-four people attended his burial in the British Cemetery, not far from the weeping cypress known as the Tree of the Sad Night—which was the night of July 1, 1520, and it was sad for Hernán Cortés—near the Tlacopán Causeway: the president and some members of the British Club, R.J. Fowler, the vice-consul, the Reverend Dean H. Dobson Peacock who officiated over the liturgy, the presidents of the Ex-Service Men's Association and the British Society, Hollands, Graham and his wife. She was carrying white roses and dropped them onto the long coffin as it began its descent, this is almost the only time her husband mentions her in the entire book. Lilies grow in that place, or used to grow, because the cemetery "no longer exists," as Rafael M.S. tells me in a recent letter. "It was razed almost twenty years ago to make way for a highway called the Circuito Interior. A very small chapel was put up, in memory of those who were buried there. Called the Capilla Británica, it stands at the corner of San Cosme and Melchor Ocampo and still has an inscription in English. When the bodies were exhumed, they were moved to the Nuevo Cementerio Británico on Calzada México Tacuba, which was built in 1926. A few were buried in individual, clearly marked graves (when it was still possible to locate their kinsmen). The others were buried in a common grave surrounding a chapel with stained glass windows. If his remains weren't taken to England it's very likely that Ewart's bones are there (but it's impossible to know for sure because the names have worn away). Both cemeteries are quite close to the Tree of the Sad Night, but neither can be said to be beside it. Not much is left of the Tree, and around it are only houses."

Muñoz Saldaña also sent me a few other curious pieces of information, such as the list of belongings that Ewart "had with him": "a gold watch and a chain of that same metal, eighty pesos in cash, a Bank of Montreal checkbook that showed a deposit of six hundred-odd pesos, and a few other objects." There is no mention of any clothing or luggage, which seems to indicate that the list refers only to what he had on his person when his corpse was discovered, and not to the things that were scattered around the room. There's no need to note that he couldn't have been carrying all this in his pyjamas.

Ewart was not the only person in Mexico City to die that New Year's Eve: nineteen other people also lost their lives violently over the course of those wild revels.

Neither Muñoz Saldaña nor González Rodríguez has been able to locate the photograph of Ewart's corpse that some sources say was published by a Mexican newspaper (Hugh Cecil mentions it repeatedly in *The Flower of Battle*). Perhaps some mistake was made, by the sources or the newspapers. Muñoz Saldaña comments that in the first couple of weeks of 1923 the Mexican press did publish a photograph of a British subject killed by a bullet wound to the head. "The man is seen lying down, with a bandaged head, *but it is not Ewart since the caption lists another name.*" I wonder if the name might not be George W. Steabben, or that of a third party. Or perhaps the caption was mistaken, since it appears that there was indeed a photograph: on seeing it posted in the English Club, a member realized that the supposed "businessman" whom the press initially referred to as "Mr. Gore" was in fact none other than the famous and promising novelist Wilfrid Herbert Gore Ewart. In so incoherent a matter, it's perfectly coherent that this photograph should be phantasmal.

In London, Ewart's father learned of the death in the worst possible way, that is, from a journalist's tactless phone call. The family had a requiem mass celebrated for him at St. Mary's Bourne Street, and later put up an altar with a memorial by Goodhard-Rendel. What the family does not appear to have done, however, was move his remains from the British Cemetary on Calzada de la Verónica, and so it is possible that they now lie in a common grave whose names have worn off on Calzada México Tacuba.

The trail of tumbling foam he left in his wake was short-lived, though it churned a while longer in the thirties thanks to the efforts of John Gawsworth under one of his signatures, "G," the tersest one; but I'll speak of that later, perhaps.

In a 1989 letter Sergio G. R. pointed out that Stephen Graham, in his autobiography, apparently his last book, titled *Part of the Wonderful Scene* and published in 1964 when he was eighty years old, again devotes an entire chapter to Ewart's death, which varied little from what he had written in the heat of the moment, four decades earlier. Nevertheless, he does add "some disconcerting lines"—in the words of my first Mexican correspondent: "He tells how, after the burial of his friend Wilfrid, he goes to his room at the Hotel Iturbide and feels Wilfrid's spirit all around him. In his unsettled state, Graham speaks to the spirit and begs his pardon 'for all that has happened,' opens the window, and lets the spirit fly away home."

In his article published the same year, González Rodríguez also described the way Ewart's tragedy was, for a period, used as an enticement to tourists, so much so that other Mexico City hotels claimed it for their own. He cites Ronald G. Walker, author of *Infernal Paradise, Mexico and the Modern English Novel*, who relates the following episode: "[The Canadian poet Witter] Bynner and his friend [Willard] John-

son followed the Lawrences" (the David Herbert Lawrences, that is: the famous author of *Lady Chatterley's Lover* and his wife) " to Mexico City in March 1923 to find that Lawrence had secured lodging for them in the Hotel Monte Carlo. They were shocked to discover that by a strange coincidence their room had previously been tenanted by a friend of the foursome, an Englishman named Wilfred Ewart; shocked, because it was on that same balcony to which the bellboy pointed with the pride of an eyewitness, that Ewart had been killed by a stray bullet during a wild fiesta in the street below. News of Ewart's fortuitous death a few months before had, in fact, elicited from Lawrence—before he had set foot in Mexico—the conviction that 'it's an evil country down there.'" "The bellboy," the article adds, "was indulging in the Mexican pastime of frightening and deceiving foreigners: the Hotel Monte Carlo is around the corner from the Hotel Isabel, to one side of the Convento de San Agustín on calle de Uruguay, and in his tall tale he was mixing up Ewart's case with that of George W. Steabben." It was certainly neither risky nor implausible to lay claim to tragedies caused by firearms in the Mexican capital at that time: the article also recounts that in a newspaper dated that same New Year's Day, a company named Balines Americanos (American Ball Bearings) placed an advertisement with the following jaunty slogan: "With gunfire, we salute you all with gunfire." Pity Ewart's family and friends didn't get to see it.

Stephen Graham lived to the age of ninety or ninety-one: he died in 1975, fifty-two or fifty-three years later than his unfortunate friend and former captain on the front lines, depending on how one dates Ewart's borderline death. Given that he was eight years older than Ewart, he enjoyed a total of seventy or seventy-one years more in the world. He didn't waste it, made good use of it, and over the course of his very prolonged life wrote and published more than fifty books, all between 1911 and 1964, of which twelve were novels and the majority travel accounts or studies of Russian subjects, including ambitious biographies of Peter the Great, Ivan the Terrible, Alexander II, Boris Godunof and Stalin. None of them, however, have enabled the old man he finally become to be any less mortal or forgotten today than the young man of thirty whose life and work were cut short one murderous Saint Sylvester's night in Mexico City. Graham's first wife, the silent or perhaps invisible Rose Savory, truly and definitively became both silent and invisible in 1956, and her husband remarried.

The Hotel Isabel still exists at the same spot, that is, the corner of República del Salvador and Isabel la Católica. Apparently the lay-out and decor of the rooms has not changed over the years. I'll have to go and see it when I finally travel to Mexico some day, though my curiosity will not extend to taking a room there, still less room 53 on the fifth floor. Both Sergio González Rodríguez and Rafael Muñoz Saldaña, who went to so much trouble and enjoyed it all so much, and to whom I owe many leads and much guidance, told me something extremely disturbing, but which, by this point, may not come as a surprise: the fateful Hotel Isabel has balconies only on the second and third floors; there are none on the fifth. Perhaps they existed at some point and were later torn down, or perhaps there never were any.

The feeling that books seek me out has stayed with me, and all that has emerged into real life from *All Souls'* fictional pages has finally materialized in that form, as well: in the form of a book, a document, a photo, a letter, a title. So much has sprung from that novel into my life that I no longer know how many volumes I'll need to tell it all, this book won't be enough and its planned sequel may not be either, because eight years have passed since I published the novel and all of it continues to invade my days, stealing into them, and my nights, too, now more than ever, when I have become what Shiel and Gawsworth once were, or so it appears, and it seems incredible that I wasn't afraid of this and accepted it, after having felt and written what I've cited before: "I asked and still ask myself all these questions not out of pity for Gawsworth but out of a curiosity tinged with superstition, convinced as I came to be that, in the end, I would meet the same fate he did." It's hard to resist the chance to perpetuate a legend, all the more so if you've contributed to extending it. And it would be mean-spirited to refuse to play along.

Several books that are directly or indirectly related to Wilfrid Ewart have sought me out, the first one right away, I had it already in 1989 and must have mentioned something about it to my Mexican correspondents, since in a letter dated in November of that year, Sergio G. R. congratulates me and envies it. It is a translation from Russian to English

THREE PAIRS OF SILK STOCKINGS

A NOVEL OF THE LIFE OF THE EDUCATED CLASS
UNDER THE SOVIET

PANTELEIMON ROMANOF

Translated by LEONIDE ZARINE
Edited by STEPHEN GRAHAM

Comrades conserve your energy
USE THE LIFT

—

Notice : The Lift is out of Order

Stephen Graham

1931
LONDON ERNEST BENN LIMITED

Arundel Danders'
copy of my second
anonymous edition

John Gawsworth

Now it is properly befouled and
blasted by the two unholy editors.

£22.50

titled *Three Pairs of Silk Stockings*, published by Ernest Benn Limited of London in 1931, and bearing the subtitle, *A Novel of the Life of the Educated Class Under the Soviet;* the author is listed as Panteleimon Romanof and though that name appears to be an obvious pseudonym, he did indeed exist (1884–1938); Leonide Zarine is credited as translator and Stephen Graham, author of the slipshod prologue, as editor. The extraordinary thing about my copy is that the title page is signed by Graham himself, who, in addition, has written, "Comrades conserve your energy USE THE LIFT," and, lower down, "Notice: The Lift is Out of Order." But before this, on one of the book's endpapers, also appears, implausibly, the signature of John Gawsworth, beneath the phrase "Arnold Ovenden's copy of my second anonymous edition." And below his name, another note, "Now it is properly befouled and blasted by the unholy editors," all of which indicates not only that Graham and Gawsworth—Ewart's witness and posthumous champion, respectively—knew and were in touch with each other (not a very strange thing given Gawsworth's perpetual, frenetic personal and literary activity before he gave himself over in earnest to drink and withdrew from many things) but that they collaborated on the capricious publication of this Russian novel, also known as *Comrade Kisliakof,* when Graham was forty-seven and Gawsworth, with his proverbial precocity, was only nineteen. "What strikes me as the pinnacle of literary fortune," González Rodríguez exclaimed in his letter, "is the fact that you possess a book signed by both Gawsworth and Graham. Immediately I looked in Graham's autobiography for some reference to Gawsworth, but there is nothing in the index of proper names, though Graham makes mention of a wide variety of figures." And that absence is indeed curious, since I now also know that according to certain not entirely trust-

worthy sources Graham formed part of the "intellectual aristocracy" of Redonda. I've grown quite accustomed to these
strokes of luck, literary or not, which for some time now have
formed part of my daily life and even of my habits, but it's
nothing to wonder at that the coincidence struck my correspondent in far-off Mexico as astonishing, since he had concluded his article by saying: "For now, let's agree to admit
that the person to be blamed—if anyone is to be blamed—for
this entire web of ambiguities, misinterpretations and conjectures, is Gawsworth himself, who launches the legend of
the unfinished work and tragic death of Wilfrid Ewart with a
paragraph written in 1933 which Marías includes in his
Cuentos únicos. It's worth re-reading."

Much later, in 1996, I acquired another book that does
not silence its past, a first edition of *Way of Revelation*, the
novel that was wept over in its day and whose author is now
no longer remembered, published in November of 1921,
barely thirteen months before the murderous, weary trajectory of the spent bullet, and barely five before its author's
breakdown—and his hand and tongue began to disobey
him—after having travelled to Liverpool in a storm to see
Music Hall, out of Clifton Hall, ridden by Bilbie Rees, win
the Grand National against thirty-one other horses, a triumph on which Ewart had placed a bet that paid off handsomely at odds of 100 to 9, as I'm informed by that authority
on all matters related to the turf, Fernando Savater. What
makes this copy truly singular is the dedication penned in it
by an author who couldn't have written very many since he
published so little and died so soon. It says: "Angela M.C.
Waddington, from her brother (the author) in friendship and
mutual recollections—Nov. 15th, 1921." It isn't signed, but
this is Ewart's hand, before his breakdown, or rather at the
moment of his highest hopes (it's a nervous hand, and par-

Angela M. C. Ballantyne /
from her brother (the author)
in friendship & mutual
recollections —

Nov. 15/15. 1921.

Holy Trinity, Sloane Street.

+

Wilfrid Herbert Gore Ewart.

ticularly striking is the *e* of the word *recollections*, which looks Greek, as does the *d*, always, like a delta). By 1921, we may therefore deduce, she was already remarried to Waddington, whoever he was. Stephen Graham wrote, "Angela and Wilfred were closer than most brothers and sisters. It could almost be said that she was a feminine Wilfrid, he a masculine Angela." If that was true, perhaps Angela was the person who felt the greatest despair and wept most over the premature death in Mexico City. And perhaps this was the first copy the novelist gave away of his literary debut, published seventy-seven years ago this November. The book retains two other traces of its now lengthy past: the program of the funeral or response held for Ewart at Holy Trinity on Sloane Street in London (only hymns and psalms inside, not even a date), and the *ex libris* of some intermediary owner between Angela Ewart (then Farmer, then Waddington) and myself, one B.D. Maurer who marked his books with the figure of soldier with bowed head, leaning on a rifle—perhaps during a truce— probably during the First World War, judging by the uniform, under the motto, in red letters: *Always We Remember*, just what I've been doing for so many pages, if one can remember memories that are not one's own.

There's something a little incongruous and ironic—and perhaps much that is unjust—about the continued existence of this volume or of any of the objects that survive us, that surround and accompany and serve us, feigning insignificance. It is unsettling that today, November 8, 1997, the ink Wilfrid Ewart traced without much thought, or perhaps very solemnly, across an endpaper of the newly printed and bound book he gave his sister on November 15, 1921, is here in Madrid; and it is a bit grotesque and almost an affront that we can read what that ink says without hearing the voice of its master, the voice that hasn't been heard anywhere for almost seventy-five years, not since he almost certainly wished the concierge on night duty at the Hotel Isabel *"Buenas Noches"* or *"Feliz Año,"* before going up to room 53 in Mexico City. Nor does it make much sense that I was able to carry off this book—like a spoil of war—last year for two hundred pounds, when in the ordinary course of things Angela Ewart Farmer Waddington would never have wanted to lose possession of it in her lifetime: "Dedicated by the author to his favorite sister," so it was described in the catalogue of works on the Great War where I saw it, with this further information: "Angela, recently married for the second time but still weeping for her first husband, helped her brother correct the page proofs and took care of him while he worked on *Way of Revelation.*" When Hugh Cecil visited her in the course of his research for *The Flower of Battle*, she was already more than ninety years old and he was moved to hear her "ardent and beautifully enunciated pre-1914 voice," so he says, still ardent in speaking of past and lost time. Yet even more incongruous is the fact that between Angela—who may have died by now—and me there was another owner, this B.D. Maurer whose *ex libris* is not of recent vintage; the volume must have been his already during Angela's lifetime, and he may have been a veteran as well, perhaps of Neuve Chapelle and Ypres and Cambrai and Arras, perhaps she gave it to him herself and it was after the death of Maurer, the soldier, that the copy was placed on sale for me to buy. Objects live on after our deaths, they go on living without yearning for us, and belong to others who treasure them or disdain and sell them, taking up space on their shelves or gleaming on their lapels like the tiepin I acquired at auction not long ago, which belonged to the actor Robert Donat, protagonist of *The 39 Steps* and *Countess Alexandra* and *Goodbye Mr. Chips*, for which he won an Oscar; I got the long silver cigarette case engraved with his initials, too, and these usurpations or false legacies create ghostly linkages I hadn't expected: I can no longer see Donat in the same casual way when he appears in his old movies that are sometimes shown on television—in fact, I stop to watch him as if I were now in his debt: two months ago it was *The Adventures of Tartu*, and the other day *The Citadel*, I saw him moving and speaking in his own voice and alive, despite his death in 1958 at the age of fifty-three, only seven years older than I am now. I watch him as if he had some kinship with me, and when he lights a cigarette on the screen I wonder if he made the identical gesture after taking one out of the silent object now at home in my hand, the same object, carefully preserved all this time in its original pale green box from Asprey in Bond Street, London—or not so silent: "R D" it says, I should give it to Roger Dobson— and whether that wasn't extremely bad for his life-long asthma, which may have had something to do with his death; I also wonder if, after that day's shoot, he wore the tiepin with its enamelled likeness of Shakespeare at dinner, the pin I sometimes wear in my lapel (I rarely wear a tie). Perhaps it's for the best, or the lesser among evils, that I have these relics of the actor Robert Donat, since it is a simple fact that our intentions and traces and exhalations do not disappear at the same time we do; at least I know who he was, and am well provided with videos of his good films. And I can't help knowing that these acquisitions, like all my other objects old and new, will pass on to someone else in the future and pursue their course or go on existing without missing me, and some things will be thrown out because they're useful to no one, tempt no one, and have become encumbrances. The old table on which I'm writing will end up in some other house, and perhaps the pen with which I cross out and make corrections will go to another hand that won't be a left hand or a hand of shadow; the table lamp from the 1920s and my silver match box from 1917, which once belonged to someone else named Muir; my little toy soldiers made of lead, my letter openers, one of which was carved by an anonymous soldier in the Great War who engraved on it "15 Yser 16," the bloody river along which he must have fought and the years he waited, Ewart passed through there, too, and who knows if B.D. Maurer didn't, as well; the books in my library will go back on the market, bearing my name on the first page, and the city and year when I bought them, so that any idiot with money can then buy them again, or a soulless bureaucrat from the Biblioteca Nacional if fortune frowns, and perhaps someone will want to preserve these scribblings of mine on blank pages, traces so remote they'll become like the dedication of the forgotten Ewart and the bantering annotations of his still more forgotten rememberers, Gawsworth and Graham, who tried to rescue the dead young writer from oblivion and leave a record, mementos are fragile and tend to break, the thread of continuity is a slender one that is never pulled taut without some effort, and it must be taut in order to resist and persevere.

What meaning is there in the silent passage through the world of those who don't even have the time to grow used to the air, even Ewart wrote and fought and lived for thirty years, and what would have become of him later? I doubt he would have gone right to the top. What would have become of my friend Aliocha Coll's son, who died as a newborn a few years before Aliocha took his own life, and whom he and his wife Lysiane had given a name, he told me; and what about Juan Benet's first daughter, who died at six months and whose yellowing photo I saw at his house many times, now that her parents have died there must no longer be anyone who remembers her, Eva. What would have become of my

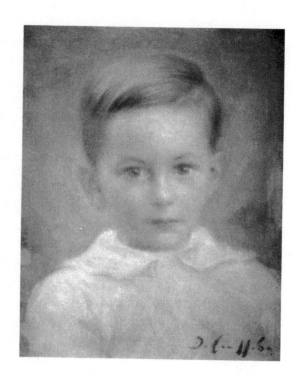

brother who died at the age of three and a half, Julianín was his name, or that was what my parents called him during his brief lifetime; it's understandable that my first thought wasn't to say "his parents" or "our parents" because I never knew him and his reality is not mine, I have only stories of him but no memory, and he never knew anything about me. I think of him at times, always as a child because he could never be anything else, he's remained ensconced at the most advanced age granted him, as he's painted in his portrait, yet he was six years older than me and would have just turned fifty-two now, almost the age that Donat was allotted. It's strange to think that there was someone so close, a brother, whom I never met; if he had lived he would always have been with us during our childhood, he would have been the eldest of us and I wouldn't have been third but fourth, and nothing would mediate my perception of him as nothing mediates between me and my other brothers, Miguel, Fernando and Álvaro, who are just that, Miguel, Fernando and Álvaro, I don't have much opinion or consciousness of them, they are like the air, or were then. I can't know what Julianín would have been like or how I would have gotten along with this unknown brother, prior to my birth, whether he would have protected me or bossed me around from the greater strength and skill of his six-year advantage, and I can't even visualize him because the only image that remains is that of a very small boy who both was and never was older than me and who doesn't appear capable of protecting or bossing around anyone. His portrait has always hung in my father's house, and I realize that my first thought wasn't to say "my parents' house" because my mother, Lolita, died twenty years ago, and so my father, Julián, has lived there much longer, and still does. This portrait was looked upon with a certain reverence, at least by we children, who felt, in its presence, as if we were to some degree usurpers or intruders, and my mother sometimes gazed at the painting, not in pain but as if she were reliving it all and had something to say to him (she must have spoken to him many times in dreams, when both the living and the dead seem so present), it was a natural impulse, and I suppose she took refuge sometimes in that impulse and that memory when she was sad; she was at peace with that little boy who couldn't misbehave or upset her. (Or perhaps she felt unreasonably indebted, because she hadn't been able to save him.) Chin raised, she would look at the portrait for long moments and hum, my mother hummed quite a lot, distractedly, especially when she was preparing to go out. The women I know now dance a little in front of the mirror while they fix themselves up, if I put music on for them from another room. All women dance nowadays, at the least opportunity, as soon as they can, I've verified this.

My brother looks like a thoughtful child in the painting, with serene, wide-open eyes that look out of the picture as if he understood more of the world than his years would warrant. The numbers in the lower right corner are hard to make out, it's possible that the oil painting was done from a photograph when Julianín was no longer alive. I could ask my father, who certainly knows, but I hesitate to call him up and force him to remember and make him sad with all this, he must be serenely occupied with some visitor right now, or typing out an article, or re-reading Simenon or Dumas or Conan Doyle, whom he always re-reads, or Colin Dexter, the detective novelist from Oxford, in fact, the latest one who, with his Inspector Morse, amuses my father. Elderly people shouldn't be made any sadder, they generally are a little sad already, naturally. But I'm also convinced that my father hasn't let a day go by since 1977 without thinking of his lost wife, or, since 1949, of his lost son. Perhaps I've heard him speak more about the child than my mother did, and he wrote something in his memoirs a few years ago, with composure. It may be that the boy did understand more about the world than his years would warrant and perhaps he died for that; he appears to have been a singular boy, though you never know to what extent someone who no longer exists and never did any harm is idealized. And though my parents were careful, we brothers always had the feeling that Julianín would have been better than the four of us were, and we accepted this unproblematically, only the most despicable people are jealous of the dead. In any case, he was not ordinary, to judge by his first comment on seeing our brother Miguel, who had just been born, and over whom he had the benefit of two long years' experience. He leaned over the basket, looked at him, and said with a child's gravity, "He doesn't know how to talk, he has no memory and he has no teeth," and he said it in that order. He appears to have treated Miguel affectionately during the year and a half they shared the world in the house that was later mine; he must have been patient and peaceable because when the littler one took away his toys and broke them, the older brother laughed and said to my mother: "Let him break them. He's a little foolish, but he's good. I love him." That's what they told us.

I remember there were some old-fashioned-looking toys that had belonged to this absent boy, and for that reason we weren't allowed to play with or hardly even to touch them (and here I realize that he is not and cannot be included in this "we," because he never lived to play with us, not even Miguel has his own memory of him). There weren't very many, the only one I can see clearly is a very pretty spinning zoetrope, you could choose the image you wanted among several bands or rolls of painted paper and watch the monotonous movement of the figures through the slits, while the round black cylinder spun in its tall shaft, pushed by your hand: the prehistory of cinema. I remember—how could I forget—a rider and his horse, first trotting, then galloping, then trotting again until he stopped or you gave another spin to the cylinder, which was a bit like an open hatbox. Those few toys, though old-fashioned and a little boring, enjoyed great prestige among us, and had been kept, I imagine, for the reasons I mentioned before, because it is a simple fact that our vestiges and emanations and effects do not disappear at the same time we do, but remain forever stored away as almost untouchable reliquaries, certainly not because it would have bothered that good child for his unknown younger brothers to play with his lost toys, but so that we wouldn't break them and they would last, last, last, when someone isn't there we become aware of the perpetual, silent communion between people and things, and then things take on a vicarious life and become witnesses and metaphors and emblems and often establish themselves along the thread of continuity and seem to enclose imaginary lives, lives that were never lived or were ill-fated, or it may be that objects are the only things that reconcile and balance past and present, and even the future, if they last and are not destroyed. They go on living without missing us and for that very reason they don't change, and in that they are loyal to us.

Julianín was born on November 11, 1945, and died on June 25, 1949; the summer had just begun. My parents stopped going to the place where they'd been spending the summers with him, my mother was pregnant with my brother Fernando and that must have helped her a little, forcing her to look ahead. No one knows what happened, and perhaps it wasn't very important to know, sometimes effects are so annihilating that only a morbid mind can insist on ascertaining their causes, or at least that's how it might have seemed then, in times less inquisitorial than our own. The boy was fine, just a bit of a sore throat was the general opinion; he was seen by the pediatrician and by his grandfather and uncle, both of them doctors, and none of them were worried, though my mother, his mother, was: "only Lolita was oppressed by foreboding, anguished," my father says in his memoirs. The boy was fine and then suddenly he died in the space of two hours. "They spoke to us of meningococcus with a suprarenal location, extremely rare, and for which, then at least, there was no cure. I don't know," my father, his father, says in the first volume of those memoirs, *Una vida presente* (*A Life Borne in Mind*), published almost a decade ago. Three years and seven and a half months was that child's duration in the world, and he is known to have passed through here, though few among the living have seen him. My older brother Miguel, his younger brother, who did live to know him, looked for him everywhere at the foolish little age of a year and a half: "Tintín, Tintín. Tintín?" he called out as he crawled, "and he seemed to be asking for an explanation," that's what my father writes. But Miguel doesn't remember him.

What meaning does this fleeting passage have, this project, someone like me, born of the same father and the same mother, in the same house on calle de Covarrubias where all five of us were born, someone who can be remembered, who was given a name and whose first words were noted down, his face still visible in a painting and in photographs—and perhaps that is something of an affront though it doesn't seem at all grotesque—and my mother, his poor mother, with her black hair and very white skin, the effort made in vain and the diminutive footsteps that left no trace or only in the sharp-edged memory of the person who taught him to take them and made the mistake or had the audacity and

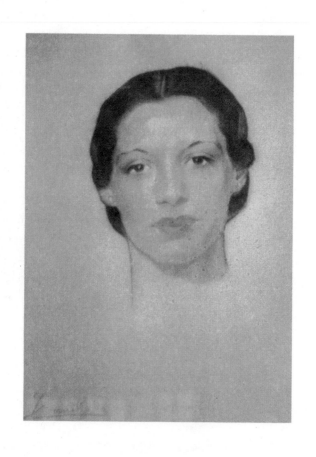

went to the effort to imagine a small, blonde head that had barely began to move when it was captured in a portrait, the child as a costly and superfluous luxury expelled from the earth at once like a breath, not even allowed to be put to the test because neither history nor time claims or seeks him except to leave pain and a few unusable old-fashioned toys in his trailing wake. (I'll have to look for that zoetrope in my father's cellar.) My mother must have thought, as she died, that she was finally going to take care of him again after life and death had separated them for twenty-eight years, and perhaps she felt impatient if she knew he was nearby, being a believer must be a comfort, not because of any mystically divine hope but because of the prospect of reunion. In any case, their bodies, at their different ages, lie in the same tomb and though I don't believe they can know this, I know it and so does my father, and he knows, as well, that there is still room for him and his far more advanced future age there, and that is enough. If the child had lived longer, I might not have been born or might not have been the same person, the two things are identical. And so what, if I hadn't been born, and so what, if my brother faded away and said goodbye so soon, as if the world's weak wheel lacked the strength to include him fully in its revolutions and time lacked the time to take in his enthusiasms and affections and grievances, or rushed to rid itself of his incipient will and forced it to cross over to its opposite side, its dark back, transformed into a ghost. There is time for so many other people, time to take in my life, but not his, it's only an example. I look at a photo of myself at an age close to the final age reached by the brother I have never seen, or else I'm even younger, I must not be more than two—and we don't look much alike, Álvaro looked more like him, perhaps the shape of the face, there might be some family resemblance there, but I don't look thoughtful nor do

I have serene or wide-open eyes, nor do I give the impression of understanding much about the world, even less than my age would have warranted, I'm always slow to catch on. I'm crouching, and laughing, my eyes narrowed, almost winking in great contentment. Maybe Julianín would have thought I was a lunatic, if he'd known me, that is, if I'd been born into a world with him in it, with him on his course. Maybe he would have said about me, to his mother, "Let him do it. He's a little crazy, but he's good."

"It's over now, there, there, it's all over," mothers often say to their children to calm them after a fright or a nightmare or some other woe, lending disproportionate importance to the present, almost as if to declare, "That which is not here now has never been." Perhaps it's understandable, intuition or memory tells us that for children the present is so strong every moment seems eternal and excludes whatever is not there in it, whatever is past or future, which is why children find it so hard to bear even the slightest setback or reversal, they believe them to be definitive; they see no more than the now they live embedded in, so if they're hungry or thirsty or need to pee they cannot wait, they fly into a rage if there's nothing to be done but get to a café or home to solve the enormous disruption, that's how they experience any delay, even if it's only two minutes long, they don't know what a minute is, or an hour or a day, they don't know what time is, they don't understand that in fact it consists in just that, in passing and being lost, in its own passage and loss to the point of sometimes becoming impossible to remember. I've seen the same impatience or incomprehension of the passage of time in certain women, rarely in men, men seem to rely more on the future, and some of them even know that the future exists only to become the past.

When, as a child, I saw a movie that scared me or made me sad, I remember that my mother's way of alleviating my fears also made use of the past if the story was historic, or appealed to fiction if it was invented. Still very young, I was greatly bothered by the film *Lili*, which I saw several times nevertheless, with Leslie Caron and Mel Ferrer, and by its melancholy song, and I was also frightened by one entitled *Safari*, I think, in which the Mau-Mau hordes killed a child, daughter of a none-too-bereaved Victor Mature—his expression was invariably one of disgust, whether during a kiss or at a funeral—nor was I at all entertained by one called *Escape from Zahrain*, with Yul Brynner and a gang of Arab terrorists who committed murder in the streets and marketplaces and made you think there was nowhere you would be safe, which is true enough (with terrorists), and another called *The Secret Line*, which some crazy babysitter took us to under false pretences, telling us it was about the subway; in the opening scene some gangsters threw a man who was pleading for his life out a skyscraper window, and I couldn't get that scene out of my head for the rest of the film, about which I remember no more than that, and for several days more after that, I'm talking about when I was four or five years old. And in those cases of the Mau-Mau or Zahrain, seeing how I worried about what I had seen and how difficult it was to convince me that it was all made up, or out of a desire not to lie to her sons, my mother used to chase the clouds away by saying, "Yes, those things did happen once, but not any more, that was all before." (So as not to lie to us about history, at least, perhaps in the spirit of the free-thinking Institución Libre de Enseñanza. With what scant inner conviction she must have said it, though, when during our war, not long before, she had seen people of all stripes fighting on both sides and her seventeen-year-old brother had been arrested and killed in cold blood in Madrid, and she had gone to all the police stations looking for him without knowing, fearful that he would be a corpse and she would find him like that, but it wasn't even the body she found, only a picture of him, my uncle Emilio, dead, not much time for him either, only half the time there was for Wilfrid Ewart.) Before I was born was what this invariably meant to me, as if I needed to believe that I had arrived in the world just after it had finally calmed down. "Oh good," I thought with practical relief, but that didn't stop me from thinking about what had happened "before," which I had seen with all the force that representations have, what had happened once could happen again, and it also seemed as if the past were still throbbing somewhere, it still seems that way to me, the ever-lengthening past. At other times, as with *Lili* and the other films that made me sad, however fanciful they were and however happily they ended, my mother tried to explain that the actors who suffered and died on the screen hadn't really suffered or died at all; afterward they'd picked themselves up off the bed or the floor, had a good laugh together at what they had all just pretended to do—the living and the dead, good guys and bad guys, enemies and friends, an enviable general reconciliation—and went very happily home to dinner. Which helped us to keep from growing too sad without preventing us from feeling sorry for the characters and their story, it's the fault of the representational dimension: it isn't only that you know what is happening, you are present, so it's hard to forget. That is where I began, I imagine, to differentiate between reality and fiction, and to learn that though they do coexist and are not mutually exclusive, they do not intermix, each travels across its own territory and both have great vitality. "Don't be silly," my mother would say if she saw me looking downcast or troubled by what I had witnessed in a dark theatre. "Don't you see, that can't happen now!" And she must have crossed her fingers as she said it, or silently commended herself to God.

It isn't only that it can all happen now, it's that I don't know if in fact anything is really over or lost, at times I have the feeling that all the yesterdays are throbbing beneath the earth, refusing to disappear entirely, the enormous cumulation of the known and the unknown, stories told and stories silenced, recorded events and events that were never told or had no witnesses or were hidden, a vast mass of words and occurrences, passions, crimes, injustices, fear, laughter, aspirations and raptures, and above all thoughts: thoughts are what is most frequently passed on from one group of intruders and usurpers to another, down across the intruding and usurping generations, they are what survives longest and hardly changes and never concludes, like a permanent tumult beneath the earth's thin crust where the infinite men and women who passed this way are buried or dispersed, most of them having spent much of their time in passive, idle, ordinary thoughts, but also in the more spirited ones that give some impetus to the indolent, weak wheel of the world, the desires and plots, expectations and rancors, beliefs and chimeras, pity and secrets and humiliations and quarrels, the revenges that are schemed, the rejected loves that arrive too late and the loves that never wear out: all are accompanied by their own thoughts which are experienced as unique by each newly-arrived reiterative individual who thinks them. But that is not all. The prestige of the present moment is based on this idea, which mothers hurry to inculcate as a consolation or subterfuge in their offspring:"that which no longer is, has never been." Yet we may wonder whether the opposite isn't the case, whether what has been goes on being indefinitely for the simple reason that it has been, even if it is only as part of the incessant, frenetic sum total of deeds and words whose tally no one takes the trouble to keep, even if it is only more glowing coals or fire for the ever-swelling seethe of thoughts which are thought and then scattered like infectious diseases to further increase the "intolerable woe" of Middleton, the suicide. The fact that something has ceased doesn't seem to be reason or force enough for it to be erased entirely, still less its effects, and least of all its inertia; the black cylinder of the zoetrope that belonged to Julianín, my brother, could be spun in its shaft again and again before it stopped, and even then it could be set back in motion, the horse and its rider galloping, then trotting, galloping, then trotting, watched one more time through the slits. Everything lasts too long, there's no way to finish anything off, each thing that concludes enriches the soil for the following thing or for something else, unexpected and distant, and perhaps that's why we grow so tired as we come to feel that our mothers' precarious response, "It's over now, there, there, it's all over," is by no means true. Nothing is over, nothing is there and nothing is over, and there is nothing that doesn't resemble the slow relay of lights I see from my windows when I'm not sleeping or am already awake and look out at the plaza and the street with its early-rising women and men, their eyes still painted with traces of the dark night, their bodies still imbued with the clean or sweaty sheets that were shared or hogged. Or perhaps the man over there with the loose tie and incipient bluish stubble is heading for those sheets now, more as a matter of convention than out of a genuine desire for sleep, he hasn't been to bed since yesterday. He's waiting for the bus so early or so late, maybe without even enough money for a taxi, and looking at the streetlamps that still belong to the night he's emerging from or hasn't yet left, and in his mind are the many hours during which he had to abandon the bullfighters' serious, ceremonious gambling den, you never know how luck will behave, not even when it gives you signals or resists, and especially when you have to find the money to hold on to the woman who's waiting for you at home, fast asleep and heedless of your efforts and your fears, of which she is the cause. The man watches the streetlamps as the day dawns and gusts of wind blow against the back of his neck and ruffle up his hair, making him looks like a musician, and he has no faith that this relay of lights, when it is finally over, will diminish the night which, for him, is not confined to the sphere of bad dreams; he has forty-eight hours to find the money he owes, and he won't find it, no chance, the worst ones aren't the bullfighters, who can often be magnanimous, but the hangers-on and admirers and managers to whom he is in debt, the exploiters of artists are the least scrupulous of all exploiters because they believe themselves to be justified, perhaps they're recouping their losses. The man looks at the streetlights thinking that maybe a knife thrust to the belly is the easiest way to give up the struggle to keep someone who wants to go but hasn't yet left, maybe out of sorrow or because she hasn't found her next handhold, it's a question of time, sorrow is soon used up and rage takes its place, rage paid out with interest; handholds are everywhere, it's only a matter of time until she sees them and tries one out, or until they catch sight of this woman who has been waving a red flag for some time now, calling out to them, and reaching out her arm to grab hold. It's only a matter of time and the knife thrust secures it, that time, and then silence, and put out the light and then put it out. The woman watches the streetlamps while trying to protect her hair from the wind with a kerchief, an old-fashioned image not often seen any more, maybe that's why she's not very skilled at it and, not managing to tie the kerchief in place, she gives up, her hair flying in the wind like a banner. She has left the night behind, and her bed, and she thinks with some uneasiness about the young man still asleep there, he's spent too many mornings there since he stayed on without ever saying he was staying, coming and going while she's at work, leaving and returning whenever he feels like it with no explanations, as if he'd rented out a room and didn't live with anyone, neither asking nor telling; but at night when he comes to bed in the darkness, far too late, he wakes her up like a hungry animal—like a child who can't bear to wait—and tears off her nightgown and gets her sheets sweaty, taking up her time for rest, robbing her of her sleep to keep it for himself. The woman stays awake almost all night, thinking about what's happened in the darkness and wondering if this was the last time, she leaves in the morning weary of her thoughts, fearful that when she comes back after all the hours in the world outside he'll still be there, and fearful, too, that he'll be gone; she fears both things equally and hasn't even tried to tell him to stay or go because it also frightens her to think that he might listen to her, or that he might not, if she were to say one thing or the other, one thing and the other, if she dared. And she doesn't know what to do so she doesn't do anything, she just waits for the bus, chilled, watching the streetlamps hold out against the rising light of the sun as if it had nothing to do with them, during this time when their two territories coexist and do not exclude each other though they do not intermingle either, just as the real does not mix with the fictitious, and in fiction it can never be said, "It's over now, there, there, it's all over," not even as consolation or subterfuge, because nothing has really happened, silly, and in the territory that is not truth's everything goes on happening forever and ever and there the light is not put out now or later, and perhaps it is never put out.

When a publisher wants to demean or break a writer and is a coward who doesn't dare act openly, the thing is so easy that it's almost shameful that he should set out to do it. The New York publishing house of Harper & Brothers is known to have had an unavowed desire to rid itself of Herman Melville, the author of *Moby-Dick*, after the disappointing early sales of that novel, one of the pinnacles of the genre, and the obtuse, parsimonious reviews it received in most of his country's press (in England it was more favorably received). So when Melville gave them his new book, *Pierre, or the Ambiguities*, the Harper brothers, rather than simply reject the text, resorted to the cowardly technique of offering him an impossible contract; its most humiliating difference from previous contracts (Melville had already published *Omoo, Mardi, Redburn* and *White-Jacket* with them) consisted of giving him less than half of his habitual percentage, that is, twenty cents on the dollar rather than the customary fifty, after the publisher's costs had been earned back, which would happen only after the sale of one thousand one hundred and ninety copies. Melville took a couple of days to think it over and, inexplicably to the Harpers (and no doubt to their disappointment), accepted their paltry offer, for reasons that remain unclear. However, he postponed the final due date for the manuscript, went back to work on it and inserted three somewhat artificial chapters that sketched a bitter satire of the literary world he found himself forced to survive in, fictitiously settling the score with his publishers and detractors, especially one of the latter named Duyckinck. Though these chapters contain brilliant passages, the novel was the worse for them, to the point that in recent years versions of *Pierre* have been published without these additions meant to inflict vengeance or humiliation. The Harpers, finding themselves with a volume considerably more extensive than expected, raised the book's price to $1.25 from the dollar that was initially planned, and Melville's share to 25 cents per book, keeping him in the same contractually agreed upon misery. As was to be expected and feared, the reviews that greeted *Pierre* were even more boorish and contemptuous than those of *Moby-Dick* (Duyckinck aired his wrath but pretended not to have recognized his portrait, an ignoble response, he should have abstained from comment), and the brothers H not only did not support or defend the book after the first attacks but launched unnecessary, underhanded chastisements from *Harper's New Monthly Magazine*, behaving in this respect, as well, like terrible publishers and inscribing themselves in the annals of aberrant conduct, since it was their duty to protect their author and their book. And thus, with the unfortunate *Pierre*, began Melville's decline as a novelist; he never again published anything in the genre that was comparable to his previous achievements, though he did publish some of the best stories in the history of literature, such as *Bartleby* and *Billy Budd*, the latter only posthumously and in an unpolished version he completed not long before his death, which came forty humiliated years after the appearance of *Moby-Dick*.

Except for the infinite difference in merit, I suffered what was, in a way, a disparagement even worse than the one inflicted on the great Herman Melville, for when I gave *Todas las almas* to the publisher who did publish it in its day (and still retains it against my will by means of an advantageous contract that he got because of my naiveté and consideration and the friendship I then had for him), his offer was even more offensive than that made by the brothers H to Mr. M for *Pierre* (dear God, those initials), especially given that my previous novel, *El hombre sentimental* or *The Man of Feeling*, had generally received good reviews in Spain and France and had sold in quantities more than sufficient to cover the advance and yield, as well, no small profit to this publisher, I would prefer that his name not appear in these pages. Despite the healthy balance of my accounts, despite the almost three years that had elapsed since *El hombre sentimental* and the fact that *Todas las almas* was eighty or so pages longer and would therefore be sold at a higher price, the publisher in question offered me an advance 25% lower than the previous one. At the time I chalked it up to his legendary tightfistedness and his feudal concept of publishing, which undoubtedly did have their influence, but now, in light of even stingier and more scandalous later events and with benefit of hindsight, I cannot think that my case was very different from that of Herman Melville or that I was treated any better (which would have been an additional injustice to the creator of the white whale), especially since in addition to making so offensive an offer, the publisher had one of his more capable employees write me a long letter raising all sorts of objections to the novel—generated and inspired by the boss, who had already presented me with some of them over the phone, in vacuous and indecipherable form, eloquent he was not—which, in my view, were every bit as simplistic as they were convoluted. If he didn't write the letter himself it must have been due to his aloof nature and his tendency to open fire unexpectedly while crouching low behind his ramparts, and

236

because, much more of a shopkeeper than an intellectual, despite his efforts to the contrary, he didn't generally feel comfortable reasoning or arguing (he was ill-equipped for those functions) and much preferred obduracy and shamming. With an innocence inappropriate to my age, I listened to his objections as if there were some truth or thought behind them and even took one of them into account; the rest were belabored or misguided and I ignored them, though I was not then or now the right person to refute or deny the undoubted defects of my books. Believing myself to be dealing with a friend and even—good God—a father figure, I wrote to the publisher that "since you are who you are" I was prepared to accept the same advance as I had three years earlier for the novel that was eighty pages shorter, but not a lower one. Feudal as he was, he must have taken this for insubordination and defamation, no doubt thinking I was a seditious ingrate. I didn't realize that what he probably wanted was to stop publishing me altogether or to undermine my confidence, and, like Melville, I finally accepted his unfair and unacceptable terms (it must have been a disappointment to him, and I wasn't getting fifty percent or even the twenty percent that wounded the father of *Moby-Dick* like a harpoon thrust, only the customary, absurd ten percent of our time); and accepted them again several times more for later works, with a good faith so troubling that the only possible conclusion is that I was and may still be— I don't know—a chump or patsy of the first water. Looking back, I must infer, however, that *Todas las almas* was not liked by its publisher, who thought it a desultory piece of work and published it grudgingly and just in case, though now there is no way he will release or free it from the oppression all my titles endure, ground beneath his medieval heel and subjugated by his vinegary editorial imprint (I don't know when that imprint will finally be out of my sight).

Yet whatever fate it deserved, the novel did not meet with bad fortune, though there was at least one person who qualified it as garbage and the worst book of all time, which is surely not without some merit. It has, in any case, been translated into nine languages, and must have sold about 140,000 copies by now, in its various editions and languages, and this publisher has—grudgingly, no doubt, and just in case—collected his very succulent, advantageous percentage on the sale of each one of those copies, with some recent exceptions (the figures are his, of course; what other figures do I have access to?). But one can learn from great masters like Herman Melville even in their darkest, most resentful hours, and it's not worth the risk of further spoiling a text by having someone figure in it at length who doesn't deserve even to have his full name stated here. However greatly my books and I may suffer from his deeds and omissions and wiles, it makes no sense to dedicate any more space to this businessman than to the Harper brothers, who were, when all is said and done, real publishers, capable of literary equanimity. The mere mention of that other H darkens these pages, making them somewhat sordid, while making me somber and rancorous and prone to committing verbal outrages, and, after all, between him and the nineteenth century brothers H there lies at least the same distance as between the poor Mr. M of those days and the other M who speaks here.

Even in sordid matters there is always, despite everything, some comical element that can be put to use, and if I've used the adjective "vinegary" it was purely out of love for precision and strict adherence to the truth. I learned not long ago, from some occasional visitors to the publishing house (but maybe they were joking), that in all of its rooms there was, on at least two successive days, a strong, persistent and extremely unpleasant smell. When the firm's employees were questioned as to its origin, it seems that they, with no apparent embarrassment, told the stunned visitors (one of whom may have been a foreigner, for even greater dumbfoundedness) that the boss and his wife, his chatty wife, had, on the advice of some shaman, unholy madman, or witch doctor, which they followed to the letter, placed, half-hidden beneath the furniture and bookshelves, saucers of salt and vinegar to neutralize and ward off by this mixture the voodoo hexes I'm supposed to have cast on their company—apparently any success or prize I receive is experienced there as a curse, a disaster, and a cause for gnashing of teeth; if they only knew—or perhaps it was my poor dead grandmother from Havana who did it, a goodhearted and cheerful woman such as I've hardly known since. However, if all this really is in earnest, I haven't managed to find out whether the dishes contained a kind of off-white pasty substance or a urine-like liquid with the salt dissolved and invisible, or perhaps, if they used rock salt, with granules floating in it. Be that as it may, and in either case: a stench and a vile thing. Very rational people indeed, healthy and argumentative, in no way primitive or totemic or prone to fits. I don't know whether the witches' brew has been removed by now—to the relief of staff, visitors and authors—in view of its total ineffectiveness in recent times, which have been far more sour and vinegary than piquantly salty, to the point that the company is beginning to be known by a pun that may be too unfortunate. Though to tell the truth, I don't think it is.

Other, more gracious, honorable and mentally stable publishers welcomed the novel hospitably outside of Spain, though there was always some small obstacle or minor change, which was either accepted or avoided by a stroke of luck. Gilles Barbedette, of Rivages, a magnificent and enthusiastic editor who knew everything about Nabokov and whom I miss enormously six years after his death at the unjust age of thirty-six from the slow and murderous virus, felt that the title, translated literally into French—*Toutes les âmes*—did not work well in that language, in which, true enough, there do not exist two different words like the Spanish "*ánima*" and "*alma*," with the worst of the less secular connotations reserved for "*ánima*." Without giving it much thought (finding a new title for a book that already has one involves doing oneself a small violence), I decided it would be called *Le Roman d'Oxford*, which he approved of and which had been my way of referring to the novel while I wrote it, in letters or conversations with Eric Southworth and Daniella Pittarello, the only two people who were abreast of my designs from the beginning (in fact, it was in Daniella P.'s house in Venice, facing the back of the Scuola de San Rocco and the canal or rio delle Muneghette, that I wrote a good part of the book). That was what I was still calling it, "*la novela de Oxford*," when I came down from the second floor and said to Daniella, day after day, in a grave voice and with a half-smile on my lips, "*Non so come contin-*

uare," and she would answer, *"Dai, dai."* And I went on calling it that for a while still, even after it was finished, to the point that when I finally turned the manuscript over to Vinegar & Salt, Inc. for their consideration and final (retrospective) disdain, on the first page, as a working title, was simply *N de O*, and it didn't receive the title it has until the poet Álvaro Pombo informed me one night in an authoritarian manner, and without having read it: "A novel that takes place in Oxford must necessarily be entitled *Todas las almas*, no matter what it's about," and I listened to him. Back then we saw each other often, we almost never do now.

In Germany, as well, the title didn't seem very convincing to Piper, the Munich publishing house that brought it out, and they added an innocent subtitle whose cheapening effect I was unable to gauge at the time since I don't know German. *Alle Seelen oder die Irren von Oxford*, they called it, which apparently means *All Souls or The Madmen of Oxford* (I want to believe that the equivalent word is not even more odious, something abominable like "screwballs" or "nuts"; I was speaking inaccurately when I said I accepted all the changes). Fortunately, in a more recent edition from the Stuttgart-based firm of Klett-Cotta, the book recovered its more sedate and less screwball name.

As for England, the problems there were of another order. After a firm decision to buy the novel was made by the daring and resolute Christopher MacLehose of Harvill—then part of the gigantic Collins group, but now independent again and going by its former name, The Harvill Press—the corresponding contract took far too long, disturbingly long, to arrive. Finally I made so bold as to inquire after it, rather nervously, since it takes no effort to imagine my excitement at the prospect of seeing, for the first time, a book of mine in the language from which I had translated a number of very difficult books since that first rural-descriptive (but fortunately not gallinaceous) one, and I received the odd response that Harvill was awaiting "legal authorization" from the corporation's lawyers, who were studying the text very thoroughly before giving the go-ahead to its definitive acquisition, "since it is a *roman à clef*," and the publishing house could not risk some future lawsuit. In the words of Mac-Lehose himself, whom I hadn't yet met, they had to make certain that my book did not contain any "intentional or involuntary" crime. Once again I watched as reality struggled to incorporate my novel into its sphere, and I felt obliged to communicate to Harvill, in a letter of February 23, 1990, that *All Souls* was not at all a *roman à clef* or an autobiographical account, but simply a novel *tout court*, and a work of fiction; that there was no accurate portrayal in it of any member of the Sub-Faculty of Spanish at Oxford University or of any other real person, living or dead, with the exception of John Gawsworth, who, once again, had been taken for the most fictitious and least worrisome element in the book; that "certain characters have, at most, a mixture of traits taken from more than one real person and—primarily—from my own inventive faculty or imagination"; that "the situations and events described in the novel are not real and, moreover, very few things in it are presented as real. To give an example, the scene in which the character named Alex Dewar questions a Russian ballet dancer is only a product of the narrator's imagination and is presented as such. Much of the book is only supposition or conjecture on the part of the narrator with whom, incidentally, the author cannot possibly be identified, since I am, for example, unwed and childless. Of course," I added, "all of this does not necessarily prevent readers from *believing* that they recognize or can identify some of the book's characters with real people, but I don't see how that can be avoided. As you know, people tend to think there is much more autobiography in novels than there normally is." Then I went so far as to contribute a (weak) argument against the possibility of a lawsuit: "Finally, it is, in my opinion, improbable that any member of the Sub-Faculty of Spanish would attempt to sue me or Collins (Harvill) over this novel. It would be ridiculous, not to say scandalous, for Hispanists (that is, people who have dedicated their lives to the study and promotion of Spanish literature) to attack a Spanish book or prevent its publication in English." And I suggested that they consult with Ian Michael, who in a private letter to me had expressly maintained that there was no reason to speak of it as a *roman à clef*, something that, in his capacity as chair of the department, he was well-positioned to see and know. (I avoided mentioning his little joke, in that same letter, of calling his colleagues by the names of the characters.) Christopher MacLehose responded by thanking me for my explanations and clarifications, which would undoubtedly help to smooth the way, though they did not alter "the legal situation," and therefore he preferred to wait for Ian Michael's response to the inquiry that had indeed been made of him.

It's easy to guess that I immediately phoned Ian to persuade him, if necessary, to take my side, and I must say with gratitude that though he was in an ideal position to demand some compensation or perquisite from me in return for the endorsement that had been requested of him—season tickets for the bullfights at San Isidro, a leading role in a future novel, a guided visit to Madrid's most vice-ridden neighborhoods, the publication of a pitiless attack on some rival professor—he did not. Once again he gave the impression that everything related to this book was, for him, a pleasant detour from his routine and thus a great diversion. But though he didn't ask me for anything in exchange (which attests to his good faith) he did take advantage of the situation to spend a little time frightening and alarming me (which attests to his malice, but almost anyone would have done the same in his place). The British libel or anti-defamation laws, like all British laws, are overly governed by precedent and are therefore too broad and vague to allow anyone ever to feel safe. All it would take was for someone's circle of acquaintances—for example, the students or colleagues of a professor—to believe they recognized that person in a character in a novel "with resultant hatred, disdain, discredit or derision," and the real individual would be able to file suit against the book's author and publishing house and have the suit accepted for consideration. "But how can that be avoided when it depends on the way readers read the book and not on the way the writer wrote it? Any lunatic can believe anything he wants, can't he? Any paranoid could recognize himself, couldn't he?" I was thinking of the woman who had offered to be my cleaning lady in a poetical telegram, had given me orders over the telephone, and had seen herself portrayed in a butler or an elevator. "There's no way around it," Ian Michael answered, well pleased with the peculiarity of his country's laws, "there's nothing to be done." "What then?" I said, seeing my book banned forever in England. "How can it ever be known if the arbitrary identification has caused hatred or derision? I don't see how," I insisted. "It can't be known with any certainty, since that depends, above all, on the perception of the injured party," Ian answered, adding very smugly, "so there's nothing to be done." The term "injured party" was not at all humorous to me. "What then?" I asked again, this time with more curiosity than hope. "Then we must study the real possibility that those colleagues whom Oxford readers might possibly believe they recognize, with resultant hatred, discredit, derision or disdain, may institute litigation against you, their injurer." He paused, to give greater drama to the results of his study, and it bothered me that he had called me their "injurer" on no evidence whatsoever. "I've talked it over with Eric," he said, "and we agree on the main thing: we don't believe any colleague would do any such thing, with one exception," and here he mentioned a name, "who may perhaps believe he sees himself portrayed in the character named Leigh-Peele. It's not that other people won't think they see themselves in other characters, we're all vain; even I think I recognize something of myself in the Irishman Aidan Kavanagh, though I've never displayed my armpits in public the way he does," and here he couldn't help letting out a quick laugh, remembering no doubt the scene in the novel when Aidan Kavanagh, wearing a Nile green vest over a strange sleeveless shirt, is dancing wildly in a discotheque and, throwing up his arms, exposes the two bushy tufts of his hirsute underarms, to the narrator's shock and horror. "None of the others is rich enough to litigate," he went on, "but he's just inherited some money, we don't yet know how much, from some distant, unmarried relatives (maybe church people, we'll soon find out how much it is), and he could be tempted to do so. So you'd best take that character out of the English version, after all he's very incidental, you only spend a paragraph on him, or you could at least change the name to avoid giving rise to a possible false association. And it wouldn't hurt if you included a protectory preface like the one Masterman wrote some time ago." I didn't know who Masterman was, nor did I want to know just then. "I'll send it to you. As far as I'm concerned, I'll write to Harvill with my verdict and then I think they'll consider themselves legally authorized for publication. You needn't worry."

Some time later, in May, Ian kindly sent me a copy of his letter to Mr. Guido Waldman of Harvill. He pointed out that neither the Spanish nor the French edition of the book described it as a *roman à clef*, and that if the English edition did not present or promote it as such he saw no reason for concern. He noted the advantage of eliminating Leigh-Peele and did not refrain from adding that no one could prevent readers in Oxford from making mistaken identifications, "but that is as much a problem for Iris Murdoch, A. N. Wilson, Colin Dexter, Evelyn Waugh, in the past, or any novelist who uses Oxford as a setting, as for Javier Marías." He enclosed for Harvill, and for me as well, Masterman's famous defensive preface, so long that, to tell the truth, I was too lazy to read it and never did. The letter concluded with a decorative phrase which Harvill could, if they liked, cite on the back cover or inside flap of their edition and attribute to David Serafin, which is the pseudonym, no longer at all secret, by which Ian Michael signs his detective novels about Inspector Bernal.

And so *Todas las almas* at last came out in England in 1992, under the natural title of *All Souls* and with the incidental character of Dr. Leigh-Peele transformed into "Dr. Leigh-Justice" in vague memory of the English supporting actor of my childhood, James Robertson Justice; there's been too much deeply resented censorship for a Spanish author to be prepared, today, to eliminate passages from a book, and for the same reason I refused to pay attention to a discreet suggestion about a couple of minimal pontifical wisecracks—it particularly pains me to renounce a joke. As for the protectory preface, I did no more than add, at the beginning, an "Author's Note" similar to the one that appears in the final credits of movies, though I fear that, if read closely, it incorporated an ironic internal contradiction and therefore said something different than what was and is initially understood. It went like

AUTHOR'S NOTE

Given that both the author and narrator of this novel spent two years in the same post at the University of Oxford, some statement may be in order on the part of the former, before he finally yields the floor to the latter, to the effect that any resemblance between any character in the novel (including the narrator, but excluding "John Gawsworth") and any other person living or dead (including the author, but excluding Terence Ian Fytton Armstrong) is purely coincidental as is any resemblance between any event in the story and any historical event past or present.

J.M.

this, "Given that both the author and the narrator of this novel spent two years in the same post at Oxford University, it may not be out of order for the former to take the floor a moment before yielding it, until the end, to the latter, to say that any resemblance between any of the characters in *All Souls* (including the narrator, excluding 'John Gawsworth') and any person living or dead (including the author, excluding Terence Ian Fytton Armstrong) is pure coincidence, and the same can be said with respect to the story, the anecdotes and the action. The Author." The English wording was slightly different, but I believe that neither the translator nor the publishers noticed the contradiction, which went tranquilly to the presses. Amid the growing confusion between reality and invention, the translator, Margaret Jull Costa, to whom I owe so much, noticed the lines from Lawrence Durrell that I cited in *All Souls* and have also cited here, about the dazzling friend of his youth, John Gawsworth, and they struck her as so implausible or overly *ben trovate* that she thought they were apocryphal and coined by me; fortunately a residual trace of doubt led her to consult me, and thus she was able to cite verbatim from Durrell's *Spirit of Place* instead of laboriously translating from Spanish to English the sentences I had previously translated from that language to my own.

It was after the book's publication in England that the tempo of events and coincidences and confirmations I hadn't sought began to accelerate, and it hasn't yet slowed and may never stop, and I sometimes have the feeling that you must be careful about what you make up and write down in books because occasionally it comes true. And if this rhythm never stops, as I foresee, it's very possible that one part of my life—but only one part—will forever be determined and ruled by a fiction, or by what this novel has brought me so far and what it has yet to bring.

Before that, however, something quite remarkable—though more so for the man who wrote to me than for me—had already happened. A few days after November 11, 1991, when it was dated, I received a letter from one Anthony Edkins who lived on Deronda Road in London. The letter said we had seen each other once in Madrid at the home of Álvaro Pombo, but very much in passing and I might not remember it (and indeed, I hardly remembered it, though my memory isn't generally that bad). Now he had read—in Spanish, clearly—*Todas las almas*, and was stunned when he reached the chapter on John Gawsworth. "Gawsworth, whom I never met in person," he wrote, "was the first editor who accepted one of my poems (just, it so happens, as I was about to set out on my first trip to Spain in 1951). At that time, he was editor-in-chief of the *Poetry Review:* he wrote me, by hand, a five-page letter. (I've just located and reread that letter, dated 13–3–51, from Shepperton in Middlesex, and I see that we appear to have had a phone conversation.)" While this was undeniably a great and almost an excessive coincidence, there was really nothing too extraordinary about it up to this point, given that Gawsworth, in the course of the tireless activities he engaged in before becoming vagrant and passive, must have known an infinity of people related to literature, novices and acclaimed authors alike. But the following paragraph of Edkins' letter made his perplexity and even his fear (or mine on reading it) more understandable, that bearable, brief fear that comes over us when we see things fitting together unexpectedly and with too much precision, the fear that the world is more orderly than we like to believe, or that we are better at ordering it. "Subsequently you mention and reproduce," Edkins went on, "Gawsworth's death mask made by Oloff de Wet, someone I met that same summer in the Café Gijón in Madrid. I was having a rough time of it, and he kept me in ham sandwiches and Pernod for a week or more, in exchange for which I had to listen to his fantastical but fascinating stories." And the letter ended amid exclamations: "So, there I was, last week, reading a novel by someone I knew—though very slightly—which presented me with two people who, though I've never in my life run across them again, were of great importance to me forty years ago!"

I had no doubts as to the authenticity of the letter or Edkins' veracity, though anyone who had wanted to play a trick on me couldn't have come up with a better one. In addition to the incredible coincidence, there were certain ironic details that might have induced some suspicion in a less trusting individual: not only had my correspondent had dealings with Gawsworth and with De Wet, but he had known them separately and had never established any link whatsoever between the two men, who were nevertheless united at Gawsworth's death; his contact with both Gawsworth and De Wet had taken place in the same year, 1951, which was also the year when his lasting relationship with Spain began and when, as it happens, I was born in Madrid, not far from the Café Gijón, the place where De Wet protected and fed him for a week or more; finally, Edkins lived on an implausible street named Deronda, and though I know and knew then that *Daniel Deronda* is the title of a famous nineteenth-century English novel, the truth is that the name, in this context, seemed a mocking and facile anagram for Redonda, the Antillean island of which Gawsworth was king.

I answered him immediately, asking for a copy of the letter from the king without a kingdom, if he would be so kind as to send me one; I told him that until then the only thing I had known about Oloff de Wet was his name, which appears as "Hugh Olaff de Wet" in the commemorative pamphlet on Gawsworth's death from which I took the photograph of his plaster death mask. "And if you have the time and don't mind remembering out loud," I added, "I'd like to know more about De Wet, what kind of man he was, what sort of work he did, what type of 'fantastical but fascinating stories' he used to tell, how old he was and what it was that had set him adrift in Madrid at that point." Since the publication of *All Souls*, I told him, a few more diverse facts about Gawsworth had reached me, but this was the first time I had received word from someone who had been in more or less direct contact with him. When I think of that observation, I can't suppress a quick internal laugh, given all the things that have changed in that respect in the little more than six years since I read Edkins' letter, and having in my house, as I now do, what I've grown used to calling "Gawsworth's room."

Edkins' generous response is dated December 8. He sent me the requested photocopy of the letter. "As for Oloff de Wet, well. . . ," he wrote, "I could spend hours talking about him, though I was in contact with him for only a week; later I met two people who had known him: one, a very famous second-hand bookseller here in London, Bernard Stone (perhaps you know him), and the other, like Oloff himself, one of the first mercenary pilots, an American named Jim Tuck, who died a couple of years ago. . . . In 1951, De Wet was about thirty-eight; it was his first visit to Spain since the Civil War, when he had fought on the side of the Republic (having been rejected by Franco's camp, probably because he had previously flown for Haile Selassie against Mussolini in the war of Abyssinia), with which, nevertheless, he was later in conflict; he only escaped being executed in Valencia through the personal intervention of Cisneros." (Edkins was referring to Ignacio Hidalgo de Cisneros, commander of the Republican air force.) "He later worked for the Deuxième Bureau and the Germans arrested him in Prague, so he spent the entire war in a cellblock for men condemned to death . . . He published two books (and some childrens' books as well, I believe). The first, about his aerial escapades during the Spanish Civil War, entitled *Cardboard Crucifix*" (a horrible title if ever one existed), "was published by Blackwood in 1938 and in America by Doubleday as *The Patrol Is Ended*; I've never managed to get my hands on a copy of that book or read it; Bernard Stone promised to loan it to me but never kept his promise. It was from Stone that I learned Oloff had died, in the early 1970s, he thought. The second book is *The Valley of the Shadow*, Blackwood, 1949, with a paperback reprint in 1956, which is the version I have, about his German experience; the promotional copy on the cover indicates that he had appeared on the BBC television program *This Is Your Life*, so he couldn't have been a complete unknown at that point! There was a time when I intended to write a comic novel, with Oloff as protagonist, but reading his book about the cell on death row put me off it. . . ." He then proposed that we see each other the next time he came to Madrid, which would probably be around Easter; he would tell me more then. He also suggested I ask Pombo for the manuscript of another unfinished novel of his which incorporated episodes from the abandoned project inspired by De Wet. He could be recognized beneath the name and mask of the character named Hugo van Renssaler. . . . But Pombo had almost certainly misplaced it, as he had done on other occasions.

My mind can sometimes be of a detectivish and therefore deductive bent, though never scholarly or journalistic, of course. I realize that I don't even do much to track down or seek out the things that arouse my curiosity or interest me, but limit myself to registering them, taking them in; I keep still and wait as if I believed that only what comes to me anyway, without any effort on my part, will be worthwhile or deserved. At times I wonder if this might not be a way of protecting myself or defending my daily life and my few sustaining habits; if so many things, good and strange and bad, come to me anyway with almost no effort on my part, an active approach might deluge my life with good, strange, or bad things, and I'm disinclined to have that happen, even if they were all fantastic. (Or, more likely, then nothing would come to me.) If I were superstitious—I only pretend to be now and then, for fun—I would believe I possessed a strange magnetic force, tangential to my will, that attracts events and coincidences and fulfills many desires that even in thought are unexpressed; the salt and vinegar affair wouldn't be so nonsensical if this ungoverned force were believed to have turned against the vinegar people. Unfortunately for them, the futility of their primitive saline solution has become obvious. Perhaps they should try other remedies, and several occur to me. But it's not up to me to provide them with ideas.

The truth is that I did not call Pombo to ask him to rummage around for the manuscript, undoubtedly lost amid his overflowing morass of papers (so thankless a task would have annoyed him), nor did I shoot off to London to meet Bernard Stone (I already had my own Stones, and my Alabasters, too) or to interview Edkins of Deronda Street without waiting for Easter, and when he at last came to Madrid and we saw each other for a while in my house, it never occurred to me to take notes or record the conversation and the information he was able to give me on De Wet and Gawsworth (what nonsense I'm writing; I don't even possess a tape recorder), most of it concerning De Wet, who, at least, had been his mentor for a week. So I no longer remember much of it, and I'm not writing him back now to put him to the trouble of again composing a few pages for my benefit (this book isn't that important, not even to me). But maybe I don't remember much because there wasn't all that much more to what he finally told me in person, and that, too, is logical: however great an impression the former mercenary pilot had made on him when he was twenty-five, forty years had gone by since that brief encounter or tutelage in Madrid.

Edkins was more than seventy, a bit shy, very affable and discreet, with a guarded way of speaking, a reserved sense of humor, and the vague air of a man with a bohemian past. His eyes were confident and his nose and chin were sharp, which gave him a comical resemblance to his host and friend Pombo, both of them more reminiscent of Dickens' Fagin than of Daniel Deronda, however Jewish Deronda was. He presented me with two booklets containing poems of his and some translations of Cernuda, and out of everything he told me about De Wet I remember only this: the self-assured, jovial De Wet was rather conspicuous in Madrid in 1951 because he sported an earring dangling from one ear, and for all I know he may also have had a blondish and piratical ponytail; he wore a black patch or smoked monocle over one eye, and his face was adorned with a moustache alone or perhaps with a moustache and beard, people's features fade in our undulating visual memory. Though he was well-dressed and wore a tie, it was strange that he wasn't arrested every night by Franco's police, looking like that; being a foreigner must have protected him, or maybe he had some sort of safe-conduct, for of course he had no dearth of criminal and diplomatic contacts. The reason he had returned to Spain, where he had killed and had almost been put to death, was ludicrous, if it really was the reason and not simply a fantasy, a tall tale to entertain the boy while he ate his ham sandwiches washed down with Pernod. De Wet proposed to convince Franco to create and organize groups of partisan guerrillas, based in the Carpathian mountains, which would make raids on the Soviets (from quite a distance away, actually). The reasons he gave for this, however, weren't exactly political, much less ideological; rather, he was convinced that once the Communist regimes had been overthrown, everything confiscated in Russia and the satellite countries after 1917 would be restored to its legitimate owners, among whom was his current wife—or perhaps she was his only wife—a Russian woman whose family had apparently lost, after the October Revolution, the best and most expensive hotel in Moscow: the Metropol, if memory does not fail. As director-general and proprietor-consort of the Metropol, he would often say, he could at last lead, without obstacles, the eventful and effervescent life that he was destined for—and from which, in any case, he was certainly not abstaining, hotel or no hotel. He must have promised himself a long youth and an even longer life if, to arrive at this goal, his first step was to persuade a numskull like Franco to finance a group of impromptu partisans who would then go cavorting around the Carpathians (and without knowing any of the languages, either, if most of them were to be Spaniards). And of course with that earring he wouldn't have gotten very far with the puffy-cheeked, weak-jawed dictator, who would only have looked him up and down and then noted on the corner of a blank card, with petit bourgeois apprehension and preordained disgust: "Effeminate."

I see the scene now, if it ever did take place; I see it even if it didn't, but who knows, maybe De Wet moved heaven and earth through his friends in embassies and underworlds and was granted a very brief audience, ten or twelve minutes to describe his plans to the Soviet Union's greatest enemy, arranging matters so that Franco wouldn't know or remember his henchmen's rejection of this volunteer pilot at the beginning of the war, or the services then provided to the Republic by this *refoulé*, or his years as an inmate condemned to death in the Gestapo's prisons, or his early flights against Mussolini in Abyssinia. I see Franco, disguised as an admiral, sitting with his feet solidly planted, heel to toe flat on the floor, as if they had no joints and lacked all ability to move—the long, white shoes, the white socks that leave his squalid ankles all too visible—and taking a small, provincial satisfaction in the fact of having a foreigner in front of him, and what's more a British subject, there to ask for his help. I see Hugh Oloff de Wet with his imperfect Spanish and contagious joviality running up against the brick wall of this interlocutor incapable of humor or benevolence or enthusiasm, only silent and vegetative, observing the mercenary's far-fetched appearance rather than listening to him, the vehement verbiage merely a distraction, like a murmur that didn't quite reach his ears. And when De Wet had finished explaining his visionary strategy—most assuredly without mentioning the coveted Hotel Metropol or the wife he already had—the dictator probably stared at him with opaque eyes and remained silent a while as if he were unacquainted with the rules of dialogue and the man in front of him had to continue speaking forever, or as if he could never be expected—no more than a totem pole could be, or a suit of armor—to say or answer anything, concrete or abstract. He may have raised a finger to his uninhabited temple, more a sign of vacuity and absence than of calculation or doubt, given a laborious sniff of his anchor-shaped nose which always seemed to be dripping, and cast a sidelong glance at the resplendent gilded buttons on his cuff, and then—perhaps—he spoke, with his long teeth clamped shut and his lips barely moving:

"And tell me, how do you manage to keep that circle of glass you're wearing in your eye from falling off?"

It was the type of thing likely to attract the dictator's attention during that time, which was already beginning to settle down, though death still passed through it, and salt rained down and skulls were scattered: or rather it didn't settle down, it was crushed underfoot, that time. His capacity for comment of any kind was virtually nonexistent; years later, after a series of tempestuous dances was performed for him and his guests by the flamenco dancer Antonio, and the dancer (avid for dictatorial congratulations or accolades) was brought to his box to receive his compliments, the best the usurper managed to say was, "Let's see now. You look as if you're made of rubber."

De Wet knows very well that he must answer the question, though the time allotted for the audience is about to run out and four phrases about his smoked monocle could steer them irretrievably off the subject and use up the two or three minutes still granted.

"Oh, it's a matter of practice, *Excelencia*. Training and discipline, as in all else. After a time the orbital muscles become so strong that in the end one doesn't even remember the lens is there."

"I see: effort," the false admiral answers coldly, and De Wet realizes that the dictator was expecting something more along with the explanation, probably that he would take off and replace the monocle a couple of times without hesitation or error, giving an on-the-spot demonstration of his highly developed orbital muscles, but De Wet has no intention of baring his eye, not even for the Metropol, it's a very intimate thing, nor does he expect the dictator to go so far as to ask him to do so, though he understands clearly now that such would be his desire; this is a man accustomed to being interpreted, unused to asking for or requesting anything; perhaps he is one of those people who only know what would please them once someone else has suggested it, formulating possible ideas for their cruelties or whims, all welcomed. Franco Bahamonde sits in silence again, for too many seconds, and De Wet seizes the opportunity to try to recuperate his partisans.

"So, what do you make of the plan, *mi general?* Does it strike you as feasible? Will you consider it? We could goad them incessantly, we would be a nightmare for the Soviet authorities, whose lives are too calm. They have crushed time itself underfoot, they have crushed those countries."

But the fancy-dress sailor who never sailed except in pleasure boats is interested only in what's in front of his eyes and in that alone, he may not even be aware of the mercenary's puerile and senseless proposal, the moment the usher showed De Wet in he wrote him off as an arrogant European, an outlandish Englishman.

"And tell me," he says at last, after the latest silence and with an absolute minimum of expression in his tiny and faintly grubby-looking eyes, "the earring: does it hurt? Because you're wearing it pierced through the earlobe, aren't you? It's not a clip-on, it goes all the way through like a pin, doesn't it? They're called clip-ons, the kind that don't pierce the ear, according to what I've heard on the radio. I listen to the radio quite a bit, to stay informed."

De Wet instinctively takes his earlobe between thumb and index finger, his earring is a hoop, with no pendant, and indeed it does not clip on. He strokes his earlobe and strokes the hoop, again understanding by some process of infusion or mesmerism that the dictator wants not only a response but to see the ornament up close, as if to admire some minor phenomenon, no doubt it scandalizes and upsets him to see an earring worn by a man, but he also feels a minimal, indolent curiosity towards the thing he disapproves of, he wants to verify with his own eyes the degree of shamelessness attained by this pretentious individual who, on inexplicable recommendations, has wormed his way as far as the dictator's office, heads will roll in the Ministry of the Interior and the embassies, Peman's head will roll and so will Camilo's, Starkie's head will roll and also the heads of some lawyers and a maître d'. And his son-in-law's head, too.

"Yes, *señoría*, I wear it pierced through the lobe, it's an old military badge of my family's," De Wet tries to justify himself. "We are of South African origins, and down in South Africa it isn't viewed as improper. It's a family tradition, as I said, I maintain it out of loyalty. My grandfather used to put it on to win battles."

"But your family are not negros," says the dictator, staring hard at De Wet's blond ponytail. "Not by your skin, you're not negros."

"No, we are not negros, *Excelencia*, as can be seen."

"I've known negros," Franco comments, pensively.

"I don't doubt it, *mi general. Su señoría* must have travelled a great deal," answers De Wet, ever more bewildered as to the direction the conversation is taking. He knows that from one second to the next the door will open and the usher will lead him out to the street, his partisans in limbo, the Hotel Metropol still confiscated.

"Travel, what you'd call travel, not so much," acknowledges the impostor dressed as an admiral. And he adds, laconic, "I'm a man of experience. Negros can be seen from far away." Then he falls silent again, but seems to be searching for words or for their proper order rather than signalling the end of his turn. Or perhaps he is trying to recall something very recent because he then repeats, "So, you say it doesn't hurt, this trinket?"

"No, *mi general*, it doesn't hurt, I've been wearing it since I was very young and again it's a matter of getting used to it, our ears aren't any different from women's, are they?"

"It is true that they are similar. But that depends on how you look at it," says the phony naval officer enigmatically, but there may be no enigma to it at all, just simpleminded-ness, and as he says it he lifts his thumb and index finger to one of his elephantine ears, as instinctively as De Wet just did, and De Wet realizes just how large Franco's ears are— they look like the soles of feet set into his temples—and tries to imagine an earring embellishing one of them but im-mediately suppresses the disrespectful and revolting vision. The dictator keeps his neck stiffly erect, as if he were waiting for something, he's almost seventy, very soon that neck will be wattled. He still has his feet, real feet, and so white, pressed down on the carpet, as if, instead of shoes, he were wearing a pair of steam irons. He gives the impression of not being prepared to stand or even sit up straight in his chair for anything in the world, so De Wet opts to move closer, turn-ing to reveal his profile and inclining his torso slightly the better to show the mechanics of his trinket, which is not as intimate as the eye, it doesn't bother him to give in to Franco on this.

"If *Su Excelencia* would like to see it in greater detail," he said.

"Come closer. Closer," the Chief of State orders in his al-ways uninterested voice, stretching out the neck that will soon look like a turtle's. De Wet turns even more to the side and leans closer, but between them is the large table, almost empty, the administration doesn't spend much on paper.

"Let's see, come over on this side," the dictator dictates, motioning him around the table, "I can't quite make out this badge of war you speak of." De Wet does as he is told and stands to the right of the general's chair, and since the general has no thought of moving and De Wet is a man of some height, he kneels, in an agile motion, to place the ornamented ear at the proper altitude, that is, at the level of the hooded eyes that scrutinize the appendage which is now very close, it looks as if the dictator were whispering into the ear or were about to lick it, De Wet can feel Franco Bahamonde's breath on his face like a steady, sibilant snore. "Let's see now. You pierce your flesh, that must make a pulp of it," says Franco as if he were issuing a decree. "I know negros pierce themselves, too. But not all of them. Moors, no; they don't."

Then the door opened to let the usher in: time's up. The usher stopped short at this unexpected tableau: the fictitious navigator seemed to be whispering a secret to the swaggering Englishman, or else making a confession, a thing unheard of, the trumped-up admiral never confided in anyone. The usher gracefully cleared his throat (certain occupations require this skill) and announced to *Su Excelencia* that his presence was awaited at that afternoon's bullfight, which was to feature yearling bulls. De Wet stood up with a start and immediately retreated to his original position on the other side of the table. Then the tauromachy-loving dictator made an unmistakable gesture of farewell with his hand, a gesture that was mild and almost affable, and said, "*Adiós.* Good luck with your project."

De Wet understood. There was no point in making any further attempt. The gesture had been dubiously affable and the words, though they wished him well, cutting: in a single instant this man was capable of rotting blood and making the somberest shadow flow, Blaw for Blaw, or, for Franco, *golpe por golpe.* Or no: for every blow he got he gave back far too many, which is typical of the insecure. The former pilot stood at attention and expressed his gratitude for the honor done him, the time spent, the ear lent. The dictator did not answer but looked at the usher and said, "Garralde, show Señor de Bet out and then come back here."

De Wet turned on his heel and made his way towards the open door, but before he had gone through it the pinched voice stopped him.

"You haven't told me which battles your grandfather won in Africa."

The mercenary faced him and straightened his shoulders once more.

"With your permission, *señor:* Vechtgeneraal Christiaan Rudolf de Wet. He was at Majuba, Ladysmith, Waterval, Paardeberg, Poplar Grove, Sanna's Post, Bloemfontein, Magersfontein, Roodewal, Koedoesberg, Mafeking, Reddersburg, Tweefontein, Mushroom and River Vet among others, he didn't win them all. He was particularly adept at guerilla warfare, and some of that must have passed down to me."

That last observation was the final attempt he had already decided against. As expected, it was futile. The chimerical commodore made no answer, but only murmured coldly, or his tone may have been disdainful, or surly, or perhaps suspicious, "Those names are not known to me."

"*La Guerra Boer, señor,*" De Wet clarified, in translated English. "It lasted three years." He was about to add, "Like yours, like ours, *señor,*" but forbore.

"Ah, *La Guerra de los Boers,*" said Franco slowly as he began writing something down, also slowly, on the note card where a while before he had written "Effeminate." What he now noted was: "Dandified adventurer. Degeneration of a family." And he then added, speaking out loud: "Your grandfather, then, was a member of the expeditionary forces."

"No *señor*, with your permission, *señor*. I'm British, but my grandfather was Boer. He became commander-in-chief of the Boer army against the English. Later things changed and the family emigrated."

It must have struck Franco Bahamonde as peculiarly contemptible that the commander-in-chief's grandson had the nationality of the enemy, and he lowered his gaze to go on writing, this time noting in more lively fashion, "With that awful ponytail the only place for you is the bullring." He then raised his eyes and covered what he had written with his hand, though there was no chance that De Wet could make it out from the doorway, where he was waiting, turning his hat in his hands, immaculately well dressed. The dictator repeated the gesture of farewell, like someone who is giving his consent, but more distracted, and De Wet heard him mutter: "*La Guerra de los Boers*, and what else. I followed that war in the newspapers when I was a boy. The names would have rung a bell. You don't fool me, ponytail."

De Wet was led out to the street by Garralde, the usher, who had a ruddy face and dense, provincial hair, and as he walked through hallways and down stairs, covertly observed, he thought that at least he had learned a new Spanish word during that audience which had turned out to be such a resounding failure. "*Punzar*, to pierce" he hadn't known it before and now it stayed on his tongue ("*Punzar, punzar*," he repeated to himself), and what was more he had understood it, from the context. And perhaps it was due to the usher, who was quite a gossip, that De Wet managed not to be arrested every night by the police for his adventuresome, dandified look in the Madrid of 1951, not in the Café Gijón with his disciple Edkins or in El Molino Rojo, Pasapoga, El Biombo

Chino or in Conga, El Avión, J'Hay, Tarzán (formerly Satán) or Chicote, and not in House of Ming or even Las Palmeras, if all of them existed already or still, or even in better spots than these and in the best company of bullfighters and actresses: he must have been out all night every night, there's no dictatorship that can put a stop to Madrid's nocturnal ways. Perhaps Garralde, the usher—who may himself have been a little effeminate, though he served the asexual Franco (who would never have suspected it in his life)—couldn't help telling his boyfriend, a policeman, about the incredible sight of the dictator confiding in that tall, blond, kneeling man, with the ponytail, earring and eyepatch, speaking into his ear, so close he could have licked the earlobe. A key figure, that foreigner, what with all the whispered secrets, best to be on good terms and not give him any trouble; on the contrary, best to smooth the way for his escapades during his brief or lengthy stay in Madrid. Or maybe Garralde wasn't gay and had no lover, only a wife who badgered him, but he might have been receiving money from some favored minister who often came to visit, Girón or Solís or Camilo Alonso Vega, Don Camulo they called him (if any of them were around during that period, I no longer remember, nor am I thinking of going and looking it up), so that he would let his tongue run away with him in gratitude; or the bribe may have come from the only son-in-law of the megalomaniac harpooner (hardly anyone remembers this now, but they used to set moribund sperm whales free within firing range to make him believe he was bagging them like some tourist Ahab, poor Melville again), who was reputed to do his utmost to pry into and spy on everything, the better to ingratiate himself with his father-in-law, and there were also rumors that the son-in-law had no objection at all to frequenting the most revelrous and dubious milieux (full of adventurers and even dandies, including Riscal and El

Copacabana), despite the strict asexual who kept him under surveillance. So perhaps, in the end, it was the earring itself, rather than any influence, that served as a safe-conduct here in Spain for the mercenary named Hugh Oloff de Wet, or that may only have been one of his names.

Even though I didn't leap for the telephone to call the untidy Mr. Pombo or race off immediately to Barajas airport to jump on the next flight to London, and failed, as well, to take the precaution of acquiring a device with which to record Edkins' words when I had him in front of me, I wasn't entirely inactive: I did put several British antiquarian or second-hand book dealers (Bertram Rota and Bernard Kaye, the Stones of Titles in Oxford, Ben Bass, who has since disappeared) on the alert so they would keep me in mind if they ever ran across a copy of either of the two rare and inaccessible books De Wet had written.

And in fitting recompense for the many bookish errands Don Juan Benet had sent me on over the years (all of them a mite tricky, as if he were forever putting me to the test), I took the liberty of asking him to hunt down references to the pirate-pilot in his magnificent library on the Spanish Civil War, which was one of his specialties. After a week, no doubt piqued by curiosity and the bibliographic challenge (I had put it to him in the most woundingly effective terms, "So, Don Juan, you who spend your life boasting about your great knowledge of the war: let's see what you can show us"), Benet sent me from his country house in Zarzalejo, where he kept the literature on the war he was so proud of, the following handwritten report, under the mocking title, "Note for Mr.

Javier Marías, B.A.":

As regards Oloff de Wet, I've found some references in the bibliography on the Civil War. Jesús Salas Larrazábal mentions him in two of his books, *La guerra de España desde el aire* (*The Spanish Civil War from the Air*), Barcelona: Ariel, 1972, and *Intervención extranjera en la guerra de España* (*Foreign Intervention in the Spanish Civil War*), Madrid: Editora Nacional, 1974. In the first of these, De Wet is mentioned in relation to the creation, by the new Undersecretary of the Air, of at least fifteen pursuit and bombardment units using imported equipment that went into operation in September, 1936. According to Salas, De Wet was piloting a Nieuport 52 at that time. There are also isolated references to De Wet in Alcofar Nassaes, *La aviación legionaria en la guerra española* (*Legionnaire Aviation in the Spanish Civil War*), Barcelona: Euros, 1975. However, I've found no mention of him in Bill Alexander, *British Volunteers for Liberty*, which claims to provide a very extensive list of the British volunteers, almost all of them posted to the British Battalion in which the author served. Nor does he appear in the documents and memoirs of members of the brigades and British fellow travellers.

In general, these references are due to the publication by Oloff de Wet of *Cardboard Crucifix*, London: Blackwood, 1938, which I've not succeeded in finding and don't believe has been translated or published in Spanish. An excellent angle for further *recherches:* let's see what you can do this time: give us a further display of your skills. From what I can deduce, it's an autobiographical story of his experience as a fighter pilot in Spain, and a well-placed eyewitness account of the birth of the Republican Air Force. A quite extensive excerpt (fourteen pages) from *Cardboard Crucifix* is included in *The Civil War in Spain* by Robert Payne, London: Secker &

Warburg, 1962, who is not to be confused with Stanley G. Payne, the historian of Spanish fascism. The fragment isn't much: a journalistic impression of Madrid in the revolutionary autumn of '36, some impressions of flying in the Nieuport and a few quick sketches of leading figures in the International Brigades.

—Zarzalejo, January 1992

January 1992, only a year before his death. No one could have imagined it then, he himself least of all, no one ever knows the order of these things.

I believe I remember that the next time we saw each other I had the nerve and the ingratitude to belittle his findings and throw back in his face the skimpy, insipid pickings he had served up to me, much of it useless because already known to me (but that was always the style with Benet, those of us who were his friends tended to take our mutual competence for granted and not acknowledge any merit in each other except on very rare occasions, which made it all the more exceptional and unforgettable: my family is of the same school, a prickly, jesting school—a little grace and good humor are required—which I've noticed most other writers won't tolerate, forced as they all too often are into reciprocal cloying adulation and even reverence, constantly addressing each other as Maestro This and Maestro That, as some of them do both in public and in print, to help each other over their complexes, inferiority complexes, that is). In fact, with an eye to my own impending display of prowess, I took care not to applaud him openly, for in his report he had seized the opportunity to issue a challenge, which he then repeated in person and in the presence of witnesses, as I had issued mine: "Look here you great bloodhound of the Baskervilles, you Arsène Lupin of literature, look here, young Marías: is it not your boast that no book, however unattainable, can elude

268

you? I want you back here with that Oloff de Wet, which sounds like the name of a perfume; let's see if you can deliver us a copy of this *Cardboard Crucifix* that you tell us you're so very much in the know about." Thus had Don Juan turned the tables and the investigative challenge on me. "I've done my part. It's your turn now," he said, "and I hope you won't have the shamelessness to appear at the next dinner without that book under your arm." We were always like that, like kids daring each other to do harmless, trivial things (or some things that weren't so harmless), for the fun and excitement of it, and above all for the continuity and deferral, there was always something pending and we'd have to see each other again. Of course I was far from being the only one, he used the same tactic on everyone, Azúa, Molina Foix, Hortelano, Daniella and her famous episteme, Mercedes, the engineers, Peche, any friend who had earned the affection embodied in his irony.

One of those idiotic and dispassionate challenges gave rise to a brief, memorable text he wrote me in a letter dating from my Oxford years, and this book will have been worth the trouble if only to make that text public (though I won't cite all of it verbatim, to avoid ruffling any feathers). He had dared me to guess his new *bête noire* of the moment (November, 1984), and in my answer I got it right on the first try ("Has the same initials as Jaime Salinas," I had said); I also fired off a volley of minor hieroglyphics—a further series of otherwise unidentified initials—and announced that I had an excellent little gift for him that he would find very useful, and that I would present him with on my next trip to Madrid: "an ingenious instrument," I called it, as can be deduced from his answer. Benet had grown a moustache not long before, and though in time we grew so accustomed to it that it isn't easy now to remember what he looked like clean-shaven, at that point his friends were still pondering the daring novelty on his upper lip and hesitating between approval, rejection, condemnation and a forced visit to the barbershop. Meanwhile, what I had bought for him, was a tiny, ridiculous comb glimpsed in a specialty shop in London, designed especially for the grooming and hygiene of such appurtenances, as they used to say in more indirect times.

"It was indeed J S," he acknowledged in the second paragraph of his letter, "a perfect imbecile who mixes piety with arrogance, like Xirinachs. I haven't deciphered a single one of your initials, but to stave off and give the lie to any avowed 'blunting of my intellect,' I've decided to predict that the 'ingenious instrument' you're going to give me is neither more nor less than a small comb. Naturally, you're in the perfect position to deny this and even to acquire a new little gift in order to prove that it wasn't a small comb, but I shall remain persuaded all my life that originally it was a small comb (I give no further details because this alone should suffice to make you blush), and if you conduct yourself ignobly in this grave matter and pull a switch on me, I, for my part, will forever hide the reasons that have led me to unmask the comb. For if you put your mind to it a little, you'll quickly conclude that it couldn't have been anything but a small comb."

Here I was forced to pay tribute to his divinatory gifts or perspicacity, though it irritated me enormously that he had spoiled the mystery of my small, specialized comb, which in due time I gave him, without making a switch, but in a rather peeved, grudging and even spiteful spirit. I often saw him use it in the years that followed, he would take it out during some gathering and, in my presence, delicately preen his moustache for a while with a distracted air, blatantly alluding to his brilliant deductive triumph. (Depending on my mood I either pretended not to notice or gratified him by taking the hint and saying: "Very well, Don Juan, that's fine, yes, I remember, you hit the bull's-eye, you can stop now, there's not a hair out of place.") Very typical of him, that recurrent retrospective delectation.

But let's return to 1992. My self-esteem at stake, I immediately alerted my booksellers, G. Heywood Hill and Bell, Book & Radmall and Veronica Watts certainly, and a few others specializing in military matters, though I didn't know that field very well; I also alerted Eric Southworth and Ian Michael in Oxford, on the unlikely chance that they might run across the damned *Crucifix* in some secondhand bookshop, and I suppose I also said something to Roger Dobson, who is a true, indefatigable bloodhound, but whose streaks of magnificent good fortune alternate with periods of total loss of nose (and consequent bibliographic famine), so everything depended on whether my mission found him in one phase or the other. I told them how much I was willing to spend, which was quite a lot in relation to the probable cost of an utterly forgotten 1938 book on the Spanish Civil War by an author who was known or of interest to almost no one and whose name, like Gawsworth's (but more understandably), did not appear in any encyclopedia, dictionary or literary biography, even if some mention of it was made in certain studies of the Spanish Civil War, according to Benet's information, though not in as many as might have been expected, given his singular, pioneering performance in the airways of the Iberian peninsula—*lutos tras otros lutos y otros lutos*, sorrow after sorrow and more sorrow—or in the wind that sweeps away the weeks, *el viento que se lleva las semanas*.

And it was Ben Bass, whereabouts now unknown but then of Greyne House in Avon, who, not much later, worked the miracle and sent me a note in his flowery handwriting to inquire as to whether I would be interested in one copy each of

Crucifix and *Valley* (the other volume by Oloff de Wet, about his imprisonment by the Gestapo), available to me for thirty-five and thirteen pounds respectively, plus shipping and handling. The *Crucifix* was a little pricey, still I didn't waste a second on the wretched mails but phoned him right away, wondering all the while why on earth he was asking me if I wanted them rather than sending them to me at once, and before the next dinner with Don Juan Benet and friends both titles were in my clutches and I arrived at the restaurant very pleased with myself, carrying them under my arm and ready to settle the score, many years later, for the humiliation endured by my minuscule, absurd and unmasked comb. I remember Benet's feigned disappointment as I tossed the books on the table with a movement of the thumb and index finger as if they were cards ("Who knows what vile acts you've lowered yourself to in order to get your hands on these rarities so fast, young Marías," he said, irked and suspicious), which was immediately replaced by an expression of avid curiosity as he expertly thumbed through the newly bagged specimens. Many months later the great bookhunter Ben Bass (who would have to be hunted down himself now) was able to find me a second copy of *Cardboard Crucifix*, subtitled *The Story of a Pilot in Spain*, which I could then offer as a gift to Don Juan for the enrichment of his collection and in belated thanks and reward for his generous research and his note for the young Bachelor of Arts. (I'm still waiting for someone to come up with a third copy that I can give to Edkins.) He read it, not long before his death—but we didn't know that yet—and, like the excerpt cited by Robert Payne, it didn't strike him as any great thing. I'll never know if this was his true opinion or just an effort to detract literary merit from this figure I had discovered and thereby make light of my irritating prowess as a digger-up of books. In any case, whatever literary interest the work of Hugh Oloff de Wet might have had, it did not by any means match its author's biographical and novelistic interest. But I'll speak of the texts later, perhaps.

Neither of the two copies—mine or Benet's—had kept its jacket, so the books bore no information on their author and no description of his work. But *The Valley of the Shadow* did have its jacket, in good condition, it was published eleven years after *Cardboard Crucifix*—the Civil War well over and the times thoroughly crushed underfoot, even the Second World War was over—and two years prior to the writer-pilot's second strange stay in Madrid in 1951, when, of all possible spots, he frequented the Café Gijón, favored haunt of the leisured Spanish literati—or perhaps no one lacked for time back then, it hardly existed, not even Benet, who must have gone there occasionally at the age of twenty-four—and, of all governments in the world, he sought to persuade the predatory but ultra-tightfisted Franco to finance his partisan project in the Carpathians. On the jacket's front flap were a photograph and a good number of facts, most already reported by Edkins, the protegé. Not all, however.

In the picture, De Wet has the unmistakable look of a British military man, despite his Boer origin—if that was in fact his extraction, and perhaps it wasn't: the moustache is thick and curly and very well groomed, perhaps he kept its tips upturned by means of an indispensable small, special comb. The long tuft on the chin is a bit jarring, giving him the look of a musketeer or an aspiring cardinal—or Buffalo Bill or Custer—inappropriate to a serious soldier of his time; it suggests an extravagant, roguish side to his character that, taken to an extreme in a foreign country, might give rise to an indecent ponytail, of which there isn't a glimpse here. Nor does he sport an eyepatch or smoked monocle, and as for the

Photo by   *Weitzmann Studio, London*

H. OLOFF DE WET

" . . . comes from English military stock
. . . he served nine months as a pilot
and Intelligence officer in the army of the
Negus. Forced to leave Abyssinia on
account of a duel, he offered his services
to General Franco. Not being accepted,
he joined the Reds, and for three months
served as a fighter pilot. During this time
he began his work for the Deuxième
Bureau . . ."

Continued on back flap

9/6

This extract, described by Mr de Wet as "founded on fact," though "in various respects slightly inaccurate," is taken from the *Völkischer Beobachter*'s report of his trial in the People's Court at Berlin, when he was found guilty and condemned to death.

In *The Valley of the Shadow* Mr de Wet gives his own version of his experiences as a secret agent of France in Prague, and of his capture and imprisonment by the Gestapo. It is almost incredible that he should have survived successively the attentions of his gaolers and in-quisitors, his own attempts to escape and suicide, and finally, for four years, a death sentence delivered in the earlier part of the war.

The book is more than an unforget-table record of the horrors of prison life in Nazi Germany. It shows the triumph of the human spirit over brutality, torture and — almost worse — the suspense and deadening routine of captivity. Mr de Wet lost neither his courage nor his sanity in an ordeal which lasted for six years. He has lived to write a terrible but inspiring book.

famous earring, unless it adorned the barely visible right ear which is covered in shadow, he seems not to have dared wear it for the portrait done by the Weitzmann Studio, London. He's dressed as a civilian, which he would have been at that time, and very dapper: the tie is elegant and the jacket's wool fabric is so excellent that its texture is palpable to the eye. He appears somewhat older than thirty-six (his age then, perhaps) but more because of his robust physique and respectably parted hair than because of any noticeable ravages left by his reckless life. Seeing him so imperturbable, no one would ever guess he had been a prisoner for so long or that he'd been tortured. The clear eyes have a penetrating gaze typical of dark eyes, and neither looks sightless, his features are very correct: a fine-looking man easy to imagine in uniform or in some past century, particularly the seventeenth century, as a corsair or noble or both things together in a not infrequent combination, or in the nineteenth century, but farther away, across the ocean in the Wild West. The signature on the photograph is hard to make out against the dark background.

The text on the front flap of the jacket begins and ends with a set of quotation marks and ellipses; the provenance of these citations is then explained on the back flap. "This extract, described by Mr. de Wet as 'founded on fact,' though 'in various respects slightly inaccurate,' is taken from the *Völkischer Beobachter's* report of his trial in the People's Court at Berlin, when he was found guilty and condemned to death." And, in a more overtly promotional tone, it continues, "In *The Valley of the Shadow* Mr de Wet gives his own version of his experiences as a secret agent of France in Prague, and of his capture and imprisonment by the Gestapo. It is almost incredible that he should have survived successively the attentions of his gaolers and inquisitors, his

Norddeutsche Ausgabe

Berlin, Sonnabend, 8 Februar 1941

BEOBACHTER

hen Bewegung Großdeutschlands

Der Fall de Wet

Berlin, Januar 1941.

Das Volksgericht handelte in zweitägiger Sitzung gegen d. 3jährigen britischen Staatsangehörigen ihn und verurteilte ihn zum Tode. De Wet als bezahlter Spion im Dienste des französen Deuxième-Büros und hatte den Auf. Militäranlagen auszuspähen. Er wurde der deutschen Spionageabwehr auf dem Reichsgebiet verhaftet.

Die Verhandlungen Percy William Olaf de Wet fand er Ausschluß der Öffentlichkeit stalinem Vertreter der "Völkischen Beobters" war Gelegenheit gegeben, de Verhandlung beizuwohnen. Aus niegenden militärischen Gründen de allen Verhandlungsteilnehmern Schweigegebot auferlegt. Über diese Schweigepflicht unterliegenden D kann daher hier nicht berichtet wen. Darüber hinaus verdient jedoch die Person des Angeklagten nach d. allgemein menschlichen und politis Seite hin tieferes Interesse.

Die Umstände, ter denen der Verurteilte seine gegde Sicherheit des Reiches gerichte Tätigkeit ausübte, sind kennzeichne für eine gewisse internationale Atsphäre, in die die Grenzen zwische olitik und Abenteuer fallen und d intelligence Service von der Hochstap nicht mehr zu unterscheiden ist. a kann aber kein Zufall sein, daß ch der feindliche Nachrichtendienst r Vorliebe solcher Elemente für se arbeit bedient. Was uns daher bei m Rückblick auf diesen Prozeß vor m bemerkenswert erscheint, ist dies Man scheint in dem unsichtbare ampf gegen das Reich nur Mann zu brauchen

der Spion, der sich seine gefährlichen Geheimnisse nur schwer entreißen läßt. Beide Deutungen sind möglich. De Wet entstammt einer englischen Offiziersfamilie. Sein Vater war Marinekommandant auf einer der Kanalinseln, die sich jetzt in deutschem Besitz befinden. Auch der Sohn wurde für die Soldatenlaufbahn bestimmt und bezog eine Kadettenschule, deren Examen er aber nicht bestand. Er sagt, er wollte dieses Examen nicht bestehen, da es nicht seine Absicht war, in ein Infanterieregiment einzutreten. Man darf ihm das vielleicht glauben, denn er legte bald danach das Pilotenexamen ab und trat als Leutnant in die Royal Air Force ein. Nach kurzer Zeit quittierte er jedoch den Dienst. Die Gründe dafür sind dunkel. De Wet behauptet, ihm seien die vielen ärztlichen Untersuchungen, die er wegen einiger Automobilunfälle über sich ergehen lassen mußte, unangenehm gewesen und er habe darum den Dienst aufgegeben.

In der Folgezeit tauchte de Wet auf allen Kriegsschauplätzen auf. Zunächst war er neun Monate lang als Pilot und Nachrichtenoffizier in der Armee des Negus tätig. Er mußte Abessinien dann wegen eines Duells verlassen und bot General Franco seine Dienste an. Der lehnte sie ab und de Wet stellte sich daraufhin den Roten zur Verfügung. Er war drei Monate Kampfflieger. In dieser Zeit knüpfte er die ersten Beziehungen zum Deuxième-Büro, dem französischen Gegenstück zum englischen Intelligence Service, an. Noch ist er aber kein bezahlter Agent, sondern will, einem der Offiziere des Deuxième-Büros nur aus Freundschaft

---

d Schiffe

ndigkeiten"

nanzminister fordert
en lawinenhaft —
Pfund

allen Erwartung eines schnellen und leichten Sieges vom Zaun brachen, der nun am Mark Englands frißt. Und bald werden sie erkennen müssen, daß alles Bisherige nur ein Vorspiel war im Vergleich zu dem, was Britannien erwartet.

ulgarischer Abgeordneter mahnt:

"Bulgariens Platz ist an der
Seite Deutschlands"

Sofia, 7. Februar.

Der Abgeordnete Deni Kostoff trat vor der Kammer für die Notwendigkeit eines Zusammengehens mit Deutsch-

own attempts to escape and suicide, and finally, for four years, a death sentence delivered in the earlier part of the war." The last paragraph is even more market-minded and not worth bothering with. But it is worth having a look at the article from the *Völkischer Beobachter* of Berlin, dated February 8, 1941, partially reproduced in its original language on pages VI and VII, following the table of contents, the half title, an extremely sinister frontispiece in yellow and black showing a skeletal, chained man seated on the floor of a cell with his eyes shut—a drawing done by De Wet himself— and, filling the entire page that opens the volume, a phrase in quotation marks as if it were a motto or a line of poetry or a Biblical citation that I don't recognize: *"And still death passed me by,"* it says, in other words, "And death continued to pass me by," although, with a bit of a stretch, the word *still* could be understood as an adjective here rather than an adverb, in which case the motto would mean "And silent death passed me by." But I don't think so, because "still" in the first sense has, in Hugh Oloff de Wet's case, all too much significance: the death sentence he received in Berlin was the second of his life, following the one in Valencia five years earlier; he was sentenced to death by the Republicans on whose side he fought in Spain and by the Nazis he fought against in Germany, that is, by both warring parties in the space of a few years. Neither of those two deaths would have been silent. The illustration I described also appears on the jacket and is not the only one in the book, which contains a total of four, all in yellow and black, all sinister, and all done by the volume's imprisoned mercenary author. The graphic ability thus evinced was the first piece of information that could explain or justify the strange task by which I initially learned of his existence—or only of his name, misspelled—as maker of the death mask of Gawsworth, the poet, who was also Juan I, king of Redonda, Armstrong the beggar, and undoubtedly De Wet's contemporary, for he, too, was a pilot during those years, under orders from the Royal Air Force in North Africa and the Middle East.

The article, from the North German edition of the *Vôlkischer Beobachter*, which was kindly loaned by Her Majesty's Foreign Office according to a footnote, is translated into English by De Wet at the beginning of *The Valley of the Shadow* and goes more or less like this:

THE DE WET CASE

Berlin, January 1941

In a two-day sitting, the People's Court proceeded against the 28-year-old Britisher de Wet and condemned him to death. De Wet was a paid spy in the service of the French Deuxième Bureau, his task being the spying out of military installations. He was arrested by the German counter-espionage on German territory.

The trial of Percy William Olaf de Wet [an unusual form of his name, perhaps because he was working as a spy, but then it wouldn't make any sense to keep the family name] was held *in camera*. A representative of the 'Vôlkischer Beobachter' was permitted to be present during the trial. For obvious reasons of military security all participants at the trial were put under an oath of silence. Nothing of such a nature may therefore be reported . . . But quite apart from secret matters, the person of the accused is worthy of attention from the general human and political aspects.

The circumstances under which the condemned

man pursued his activities against the security of the Reich are characteristic of a certain international atmosphere in which the dividing line between politics and adventure vanishes and the Intelligence Service is indistinguishable from swindling. It can, however, be no chance that the enemy Intelligence Service prefer to draw their recruits from such elements. In reviewing this trial, what is most noteworthy is this: in this underground battle against the Reich use appears to be made only of those whose lack of principle and moral instability would seem to fit them for their work. [The edifying commentary is striking, coming as it does from a Nazi publication, but it's even more remarkable in an account of the trial of a spy, as if moral condemnation were optional or subject to subtle distinctions in such a case.]

Those who took part in the trial have had to weigh in their minds whether this de Wet, who stood before them twisting a thin Don Quixote beard [perhaps the comb had been confiscated when he was arrested] was an adventurous fool or a cunning, cold-blooded, calculating spy resolute in concealing his dangerous secrets. Both may be true. De Wet comes from English military stock. [A statement that puts the lie to the famous Boer grandfather.] His father was a naval officer, Commandant on one of the Channel Islands, now in German possession. The son was also destined for a military career and entered a cadet school, for whose examination, however, he did not sit. He says it was because it was not his intention to enter an infantry regiment. It is possible to believe this, for soon afterwards, having got round the examination for pilot, he entered the Royal Air Force. He left that service in a short time and the reasons are obscure. De Wet maintains that the many medical boards he had to attend on account of some motor accidents had been unpleasant, and he had on that account given up the service. [This is all so preposterous that we'd be justified in conjecturing that De Wet was mocking and pulling the legs of his judges and accusers throughout the trial; it's impossible to know whether they were aware of this, though it certainly looks bad for the now defunct Third Reich if they weren't; one person who definitely wasn't aware was our reporter from the *Völkischer Beobachter*, who painstakingly records everything, word for word, and seems perfectly oblivious to the probable detachment or cynicism of the adventurous spy. That must have been it, I thought as I read this drivel.]

Subsequently de Wet appeared in all the theatres of war. First he served nine months as a pilot and Intelligence officer in the army of the Negus. Forced to leave Abyssinia on account of a duel, he offered his services to General Franco. Not being accepted, he joined the Reds and for three months served as a fighter pilot. During this time he began his work for the Deuxième Bureau, the French equivalent of the British Intelligence Service. But not yet as a paid agent, only out of friendship with the officers of the Deuxième Bureau. Is it not possible that de Wet has been for long a member of the British Intelligence Service, entrusted with a mission involving him in the rôle of foreign mercenary? De Wet denies this and says he did once offer his services, which were refused. Is he telling the truth? And if it is the truth, why was he rejected? Did the British consider him vain and stupid and, on account of his drunken bouts, unsuitable for employment? It may be so, and it may be otherwise. In any case de Wet withdraws from his rôle as a Red Spanish pilot to act as arms dealer for a certain Zacharoff. Then he writes two books concerned with his experiences, entitled *Cardboard Crucifix* and *The Patrol is Ended*. [By this point it seems obvious that it was the reporter who was having his own bout of intoxication with adventure and didn't know how to explain this jumble of facts but had fallen under the sway of the foolish or cunning figure of the prisoner, about whom he asks too many useless or overtly ridiculous questions, among which "Is he telling the truth?" takes the prize for mindlessness. Even so, the inference that vanity could be a serious impediment to espionage work isn't bad. At certain moments, he gives the impression that his very fascination with De Wet irritates him and sets him against the former pilot in a way that's quite instructive, but his weakness for the accused shimmers in the air for a second when he takes care to point out that initially the spy spied only out of friendship with the greatest figures in French espionage. Still and all, the most admirable sentence in the paragraph is the one that states with cautious equanimity, "It may be so, and it may be otherwise."]

For a short time de Wet led a quiet life exercising his gifts as a painter. [Here again we catch sight of the mask maker.] When the conflict between Germany and Czechoslovakia broke out, then in his twenty-fifth year, he put aside his palette and hastened to Prague, where he offered his services as pilot to the Benes government. Here he renewed a friendship of

Paris—the friendship with a dancer of southeast Europe, a woman who has left several shattered hearts behind her and of whom little can be discovered. It is not known for certain whether she was an erotic or herself a political adventuress. In any case, when de Wet was arrested she was not only his confidante but also his collaborator. During the course of interrogation she committed suicide, and de Wet, who until the death of his accomplice had confessed to his full responsibility, began to try to defend himself. [Clearly our reporter wasn't entirely indifferent to literary ornament, and while his training in the composition of narrative prose must have been shoddy and generally furnishes him with tired expressions and desiccated lies, the enigmatic felicity of expression he occasionally achieves with his unique euphemisms and unstable syntax must be acknowledged: "It is not known whether she was an erotic or herself a political adventuress." That's hard to match.]

It is firmly established that during his stay in Prague de Wet became closely associated with a certain Czech officer who, when the Protectorate was set up in Bohemia, fled to Alsace and there became a liaison officer of the Deuxième Bureau. De Wet visited this man several times from Prague, smuggling to him gold and information, and it was these and other activities for the Deuxième Bureau that finally landed him in the hands of the German authorities.

At the conclusion of the trial de Wet thanked the President of the High Treason Senate for the correctness of the proceedings, and further for the right of complete freedom to defend himself. He heard the sentence of death with indifference, and with a polite bow left the court, whose tribunal included as lay judges three officers of high military and party rank. [We can imagine that the Gestapo wasn't taking any chances, and sent over three bigwigs to guarantee and underscore the sentence.]

Everything possible has been done to elucidate the actions and character of the accused. His crime is evident. His character, however, still remains enveloped in mystery. Brought up in two cultures (de Wet attended a French school and speaks French in preference to his own mother-tongue), this descendant of an interesting family—he is related to the Boer General de Wet—is now destined to be a wanderer into nothingness. [And here, giving rise to the frivolous and accusatory adjective "interesting," appears the Boer grandfather who may not have been all a lie after all. I've also found a portrait of him and a book he wrote, but we'd best conclude first with the tale of the Berlin death sentence, the ending of which strays very far from what a journalist's account of a trial should be, to venture unequivocally onto the terrain of meditation and lament.]

He is intelligent and gifted with several talents, he is fearless and capable of noble feelings, yet he ends his life in a chaos of uncertainty and in the society of dubious men and woman, who all, though patriotic phrases are upon their lips, are themselves without a country and live on foreign money. The ideal of this society is the legendary Colonel Lawrence, but none of them achieves his ideal. Life does not want them and spews them forth [as if they were a costly and superfluous luxury that life expels at once like a breath]:

uprooted limbs of a tree that once flourished fruit-fully; scattered members of a race whose way of life has become infamous.

Up to this point the speaker has been the journalist from the *Völkischer Beobachter*, who, curiously enough, mentions Lawrence of Arabia as the unattainable ideal of the disastrous De Wet and others of his ilk, though Lawrence himself had died in 1935 in an obscure motorcycle accident or suicide, at the age of 46, my present age.

The translation of the German article complete, De Wet himself begins to speak, as he prepares to embark on his tale:

Thus ran their story of "a wanderer into nothing-ness." Though founded on fact, in various respects it was slightly inaccurate, and some of their deductions were wide of the mark. And, obscure though these errors may have been, they still offended the truth; they offended something else, something deeper and more enduring than that—something for which I did not then propose to find a name—could not, perhaps.

The following is my version of the story of myself—and of one other, she who bore me company "on the shores of Avernus" for a little while. . . .

With the passage or loss of time, old books are no longer text and binding alone but also what their former readers have left in them over the years, marks, comments, exclamations, profanities, photographs, dedications or *ex libris*, a letter, sheet of paper or signature, a waterspot, burn or stain or simply their names, as the books' owners. Just as the books by Ewart and Graham and Gawsworth spoke of their own short history, one of the two copies of *Cardboard Crucifix* that were obtained had something between its pages, two or three old newspaper clippings. It must have been Benet's copy, since I have only photocopies and not the yellow and crumbling newsprint itself. So not only did I conduct myself honorably in the grave matter of the intercepted comb, but I also resisted the understandable temptation to keep what belonged to the second copy which was intended for him, and was not found in my own, more silent copy. I almost always behave well and sometimes I'm even taken advantage of, it can happen. But I'm no saint.

Someone had kept the clippings since 1941—the advertisement even before that—though none of them includes a date or the name of the publication it appeared in. But the size of the largest of them indicates that the De Wet case was in its day and its protagonist's country as widely known and written about as Wilfrid Ewart's famous novel had been twenty years earlier. And likewise forgotten shortly there-after, even more quickly, I imagine, if that's possible: De Wet was sentenced to death in the middle of a World War, when any news had to be ephemeral, one moment's news drowned out by the next moment's, that from one part of the globe by that from another, the same thing happens in our own day, lived as fleetingly as if each second were wartime, I don't know if this book has a place in its time, it may require patience and slowness; or perhaps it does have a place and belongs to its time alone, for everything in it also passes fleetingly by as it's told, and if the reader should wonder what on earth is being recounted here or where this text is head-ing, the only proper answer, I fear, would be that it is simply running its course and heading toward its ending, just like anything else that passes through or happens in the world. But I don't believe anyone who has reached this point would still ask such a question.

The first and principal clipping was less a news article than a profile signed by one Graham Stanford who, to judge from his comments, had known De Wet personally, though he doesn't seem any too pained or enraged by his impending appointment with the guillotine. The two headlines are: "MAD DEVIL DE WET" and "Gestapo Thought He Was 'Crazy'." And the rest of the evocation or portrait goes on to say:

> They called Percy William Olaf de Wet [again the new name, or perhaps it was the name he was using at that time] a brave and curious man before they sentenced him to death in the German People's Court for spying for the French Secret Service.
>
> Percy de Wet would enjoy that description. I can imagine his lips curling sardonically as he heard the words. For no soldier of fortune that ever left England

'MAD DEVIL DE WET'

Gestapo Thought
He Was 'Crazy'

By GRAHAM STANFORD

THEY called Percy William Olaf de Wet "a brave and curious man" before they sentenced him to death in the German People's Court for spying for the French Secret Service.

Percy de Wet would enjoy that description. I can imagine his lips curling sardonically as he heard the words. For no soldier of fortune that ever left England lived a more lurid, fantastic life than this tall, handsome "devil-may-care."

He was known in the hotels and bars of every capital in Europe. He was known in the world's strange places and among the world's strange people. He sought adventure and he always found it.

Now his latest and greatest adventure has ended in disaster. But I doubt whether de Wet cares much, for he had the fatalism of all soldiers of fortune. It is reported that he accepted the verdict calmly, and de Wet's strange friends will be glad of that.

I do not know much about the boyhood of de Wet. His mother, Mrs. P. W. de Wet, who lives in St. Albans, would not talk about it when I spoke to her last night.

This restlessness sent him chasing across the European and Eastern stage in later years—Abyssinia, Spain, and Europe when it became the seething melting-pot for the present war.

★

WHERE all the trouble was, there was de Wet—a rather swaggering figure with a flowing moustache and a black shade over one eye. No one ever knew quite what he was doing. But he always lived well, was always giving parties, and telling the most extraordinary stories of his adventures.

Just after the Munich Agreement in 1938 de Wet was in Prague. Those were feverish days in Central Europe. Spies clustered around every bar, and no one knew whether to trust his neighbour.

Prague quickly learned of de Wet's presence. He took a suite of rooms gave champagne parties which were attended by beautiful women and a strange group of men.

Some say that the Gestapo investigated the activities of de Wet, but came to the conclusion that he was just another "crazy Englishman."

He got to know a beautiful Russian woman. It is reported that he married her, and that she was arrested, as his accomplice when the Gestapo got on his trail. It is also reported that she afterwards committed suicide.

★

HE was familiar to newspaper men. To some of us he offered information—"inside information."

He was proud to say that he was "on the inside." But you could not always take this man too seriously.

He had a fine time in Abyssinia.

He went to Addis to fly for the Emperor—he and that 'world-famous figure Herbert Fauntleroy Julian ("The Black Eagle of Harlem"), who was a strapping African Negro who enjoyed putting seven sorts of fear into the hearts of the natives.

My colleague Noel Monks met him at the Hotel Imperial—surely the most cosmopolitan war hotel of all time. Then de Wet and "The Black Eagle of Harlem" were apparently rivals for the favours of the Emperor. Both of them had gone there to fly. But apparently the Emperor had only one communicating plane and most of their time was spent on the ground.

★

YES—de Wet enjoyed the Abyssinian scene. It had all the things he loved—colour, adventure, uncertainty.

The Germans say that he had to leave Abyssinia because he fought a duel. I cannot substantiate that story, but I can well imagine that it is true, for de Wet ran into "scrapes" wherever he went.

He was in Spain, too, along with the rest of that brave and laughing crowd of men who will follow a fight to the ends of the earth. He flew against Franco. He used to say that he lost an eye in an air fight.

Later he wrote a book about his adventures, called "Cardboard Crucifix."

But . . . no one quite knew de Wet. Perhaps no one will ever know until this war is over and the full story comes to be written. Some thought him a pleasure-seeking fool. He certainly played the part.

It is possible that this was merely a mask, that behind that swaggering demeanour was a keen, agile brain working for the cause that he thought right.

The Germans described de Wet as 'intelligent, unafraid, and talented."

He was all of those things. He was, in fact, one of the old-time soldiers of fortune who, throughout history, have left Britain to seek adventure.

BLACKWOOD

The Imprint of a Good Book

CARDBOARD CRUCIFIX

The Story of a Pilot in Spain.   By OLOFF de WET.

8/6 net.

A *remarkable book; live, absorbing, entertaining.* The author is an artist in human motives, emotions, and most vigorous action. Horrors tread delicately, almost casually, among feats of unstudied heroism.

THE BLIND ROAD
By FOREPOINT SEVERN,
author of "The Garden of the

A SAIL TO LAPLAND
By DOUGLAS DIXON, author of
"Seagull and Sea Power," 10/6

NO KNOWLEDGE OF SPY

LONDON, Feb. 7— (Æ) —British officials asserted tonight they had no knowledge of the activites of Percy Williams Olaf De Wet, 28-year-old Englishman sentenced to death in Germany as a spy.

The case recalled here his book "Cardboard Crucifix," which was published in 1939 and dealt with the Spanish civil war.

lived a more lurid, fantastic life than this tall, handsome devil-may-care.

He was known in the hotels and bars of every capital in Europe. He was known in the world's strange places and among the world's strange people. He sought adventure and he always found it.

Now his latest and greatest adventure has ended in disaster. But I doubt whether De Wet cares much, for he had the fatalism of all soldiers of fortune. It is reported that he accepted the verdict calmly, and De Wet's strange friends will be glad of that.

I do not know much about the boyhood of De Wet. His mother, Mrs. P.W. de Wet, who lives in St. Albans, would not talk about it when I spoke to her last night.

This restlessness sent him chasing across the European and Eastern stage in later years—Abyssinia, Spain and Europe when it became the seething melting-pot for the present war.

Where all the trouble was, there was De Wet—a rather swaggering figure with a flowing moustache and a black shade over one eye. No one ever knew quite what he was doing. But he always lived well, was always giving parties, and telling the most extraordinary stories of his adventures.

Just after the Munich Agreement in 1938 De Wet was in Prague. Those were feverish days in Central Europe. Spies clustered around every bar, and no one knew whether to trust his neighbour. [This paragraph seems to imply that perhaps De Wet's much-rebuked "bouts of drunkenness" merely resulted from the uncompromising fulfilment of certain indispensable prerequisites of his profession as a spy, since his profiler Stanford could have said "around every hotel" or "every café" or "every nightclub" or even "every brothel," but he says clearly "around every bar."]

Prague quickly learned of De Wet's presence. He took a suite of rooms and gave champagne parties which were attended by beautiful women and a strange group of men.

Some say that the Gestapo investigated the activities of De Wet, but came to the conclusion that he was just another "crazy Englishman."

He got to know a beautiful Russian woman. It is reported that he married her, and that she was arrested as his accomplice when the Gestapo got on his trail. It is also reported that she afterwards committed suicide. [Here we have a Russian woman with whom he may have contracted matrimony; this may have been the legitimate proprietress of the Hotel Metropol in Moscow, but if she "committed suicide" during the Gestapo's interrogation, then there are two possibilities: either she didn't commit suicide and hadn't died and was still alive in 1951, or else De Wet was married twice, both times to Russian women. Neither of these two things seems at all likely, and still less likely is the possibility that he aspired to possess and preside over the Moscow Metropol in his capacity as bona fide heir and widower.]

He was familiar to newspaper men. To some of us he offered information—"inside information."

He was proud to say that he was "on the inside." But you could not always take this man too seriously.

He had a fine time in Abyssinia.

He went to Addis to fly for the Emperor—he and that world-famous figure Herbert Fauntleroy Julian ("The Black Eagle of Harlem") who was a strapping African Negro who enjoyed putting seven sorts of fear into the hearts of the natives. [To tell the truth, the absurdities assembled by the German reporter from the *Völkischer Beobachter* seem like the height of good sense next to this English portrayal, especially after the stellar and aerial appearance of the Black Eagle of Harlem, whose true name could not possibly sound any more false or novelistic, so much so that it was undoubtedly authentic; keep in mind that in 1941 there weren't yet many movies about the war to cause dementia in tabloid newsmen. But Herbert Fauntleroy Julian: who could dream that up?]

My colleague Noel Monks met him at the Hotel Imperial—surely the most cosmopolitan war hotel of all time. Then De Wet and "The Black Eagle of Harlem" were apparently rivals for the favours of the Emperor. Both of them had gone there to fly. But apparently the Emperor had only one communicating plane and most of their time was spent on the ground.

Yes—De Wet enjoyed the Abyssinian scene. It had all the things he loved—colour, adventure, uncertainty.

The Germans say that he had to leave Abyssinia because he fought a duel. I cannot substantiate that story, but I can well imagine that it is true, for De Wet ran into "scrapes" wherever he went.

He was in Spain, too, along with the rest of that brave and laughing crowd of men who will follow a fight to the ends of the earth. He flew against Franco. He used to say that he lost an eye in an air fight.

Later he wrote a book about his adventures, called *Cardboard Crucifix*.

But . . . no one quite knew De Wet. Perhaps no one will ever know until this war is over and the full story comes to be written. Some thought him a pleasure-seeking fool. He certainly played the part.

It is possible that this was merely a mask, that behind that swaggering demeanour was a keen, agile brain working for the cause that he thought right.

The Germans described de Wet as "intelligent, unafraid, and talented."

He was all of those things. He was, in fact, one of the old-time soldiers of fortune who, throughout history, have left Britain to seek adventure.

That was Graham Stanford, writing in his unknown newspaper. As for the other two clippings, the shorter one is curious, and it is also curious that anyone would have kept it:

NO KNOWLEDGE OF SPY

LONDON, Feb. 7 (AP)—British officials asserted tonight they had no knowledge of the activities of Percy Williams Olaf De Wet, 28-year-old Englishman sentenced to death in Germany as a spy.

The case recalled here his book *Cardboard Crucifix*, which was published in 1939 and dealt with the Spanish civil war.

The third clipping is an advertisement for *Crucifix* placed by its publisher, Blackwood. The only odd thing about it is something that doesn't really belong to it: the note written by hand, vertically, on the left. It isn't entirely legible, at least not to me, but from what I understand of it, the handwriting must be that of someone who knew de Wet personally, someone close to him or his family, since it refers to him as "Hugh," the first of his Christian names, apparently not often used, even Edkins called him "Oloff" both in person and in his letters. Looked at long and hard, the first line says: "Hugh has just written. I thought it might" (though I wouldn't swear to the "just"). The sentence does not go on in what's left of the second line; the clipping was probably larger and the note began and continued further below, in the part later cut off and lost. In that second line—darker, the penstrokes thicker—I can only manage to read, I think, the last four words: ". . . daughter are quite well." I can't make out anything in the third line, that of the farewell and signature. Someone sent this advertisement to someone else, saying something like "So you can see what Hugh has just written. I thought it might interest you. I hope your wife and daughter are quite well." Impossible to know who this copy belonged to before briefly passing through Ben Bass's hands, then into mine, and then belonging to Benet, and after January 5, 1993, who knows.

In the first clipping, the rather jovial and not very mournful profile done by the reporter named Stanford, there is something remarkable, over and above the string of storybook elements, the suites, champagne, beautiful women and boozing spies in and around the bars of Prague, the vain, hedonistic, enigmatic and belligerent character of the man portrayed (a combination of Beau Brummell, Blackbeard Teach and the Scarlet Pimpernell—he would have been right at home in the *General History of the Pyrates*), not to mention his Russian wife and accomplice and of course the spectacularly flashy figure of the very fabulous, fearsome and fatuous Herbert Fauntleroy Julian or Terror of the Air of Addis Ababa. I mean the tense in which the sketch or article is written—the past tense, as if De Wet had already been executed, were already dead. Though the date is missing, it must be close to that of the trial in Berlin, yet Stanford, perhaps involuntarily but certainly without great sorrow, uses a tense that makes a death sentence the same thing as an execution. Perhaps he knew that for the accusers and judges, there can be no difference between the two. (There was a difference once in 1939, against all the odds, and that's why I'm here to make trouble.) But still death passed De Wet by, as it had passed Ewart by precisely when it was most likely to notice him, flung into the mud of the front with his lone, defective eye, and pause.

Whether it was true in the mercenary's case, or a sham adornment, both men appear to have been one-eyed, Ewart by maternal inheritance as I said, but De Wet from a Spanish war wound, according to Stanford. But as I mentioned a few pages back, a book came into my possession by his presumed grandfather or perhaps great-uncle, the Vechtgeneraal Christiaan Rudolf de Wet, which is, naturally, about the war in which he played such a significant part, titled *Three Years War* (three years, like our war, when the wind swept away the weeks and death did not know how to walk slowly, *No sabe andar despacio* is what Miguel Hernández said, and it almost never passed by), the English edition dating from 1902. That book's portrait of the Vechtgeneraal, while not bearing a striking resemblance to his degenerate descendent, does allow for a certain shared family air, or let's say that no one would doubt their possible kinship on seeing them; there is some similarity in the shape of the eyes and nose, the old man older, of course, with a profuse beard rather than a mannered goatee, his gaze softer or more defeated, he could be a tranquilized Redbeard (he, too, would have had his place in the *General History of the Pyrates*, which I still read sometimes when I'm under attack by the pirates of contemporary culture who are more like petty thieves disguised as patrons); he can't yet be fifty in the picture, and who knows if he and his guerrillas had fought some skirmish against Wilfrid Ewart's great-uncle, Sir John Spencer Ewart his name, who went on to fight in the South African war after having fought at Khartoum, as if he hadn't had his fill; it's more than probable that the two great-uncles saw each others' faces or rather the distant forms that are to be feared, advancing fiercely with their imagined faces and taking aim at each other to fire off a hot or cold bullet that did not in any case find its billet in either; it wouldn't be strange at all, because on the elder Ewart's service record appear the places that the younger, more pretentious De Wet reeled off

to impress and earn some respect from the fisher of ceta-ceans, but without taking the trouble to make his pronuncia-tion conform to the Spanish diction he and the dictator had been using until that Anglo-Dutch torrent erupted: Magers-fontein, Koedoesberg, Paardeberg, Poplar Grove, Bloem-fontein, Waterval Drift, River Vet. And also Driefontein, Blaauwberg, Roodepoort, Wittebergen, Slaapkranz, Retief's Nek.

Conan Doyle also speaks of all those battles or skirmishes in one of his "serious" books which he so stupidly preferred to the ones about Sherlock Holmes: *The Great Boer War* (1900), partially based on his own experience during his five months as a volunteer field doctor (at first he wanted to en-list, but all the corps told him he was too old for military service; he hadn't yet turned forty-one), though neither as se-rious nor as long as the book in six volumes he later wrote, under the title *The British Campaign in France and Flanders*, about the First World War of Stephen Graham, the orderly, and Wilfrid Ewart, his captain. In *The Great Boer War*, Conan Doyle makes only one reference to Major Ewart, who as at Khartoum, accompanied Lord Kitchener, but devotes numerous pages to the stratagems and feats of the two De Wets, for there was a second general of the same name, though of lesser rank, Christiaan's brother Piet de Wet; and a bullet did find its billet in another person of that name, for this De Wet's son, Johannes de Wet, fell at one of those sonorous sites and did not rise again, and a son of the Vecht-generaal, Jacopus de Wet, was taken prisoner. Conan Doyle, by the way, returned to the subject again in 1902, with his shortest book, *The War in South Africa: Its Cause and Conduct*, to refute the many lies about the British troops' supposed brutality that were being published everywhere, particularly in England itself. That didn't keep him from admiring the strategically astute and audacious tactics of the great De Wet; according to Conan Doyle's memoirs, the worst reproach that could be levelled at him from the perspective of military ethics—"one of his least sporting actions, or the only one," he wrote—was his incineration of the sacks of mail on a British mail train he attacked and looted at Roodewal Station, which darkened the air with thousands of floating cinders. None too grave an iniquity, really, for a guerrilla leader, who, in addition, was immortalized by the creator of Holmes in a brief description at the beginning of Chapter XXVII of *The Great Boer War:*

"Christian de Wet, the elder of two brothers of that name, was at this time in the prime of life, a little over forty years of age. He was a burly middle-sized bearded man, poorly educated but endowed with much energy and common sense. His military experience dated back to Majuba Hill and he had a large share of that curious race hatred which is intelligible in the case of the Transvaal, but inexplicable in a Freestater who has received no injury from the British Empire." And then comes the most arresting detail: "Some weakness of his sight compels the use of tinted spectacles, and he had now turned these, with a pair of particularly observant eyes behind them, upon the scattered British forces and the long exposed line of railway." And a little further along he insists on this detail, which it's impossible not to associate with the eyepatch or smoked glass monocle worn by his mercenary descendant who was most assuredly deceptive but perhaps not so fraudulent as all that, "The tinted spectacles" he says "were turned first upon the isolated town of Lindley."

Ewart's sightless eye was undoubtedly hereditary and perhaps De Wet's was, as well, despite his fascinating and fantastical stories, as Anthony Edkins described them, so both were one-eyed soldiers—Ewart in the trenches and the De Wet in the air—very ill-equipped to keep death from passing through space with its single eye and time with its rusting lances. My father hasn't seen through one of his eyes for years now, either; when he's not wearing his glasses his eyes look even bluer, which is why my mother would say, whenever he took them off, "You've put on your German face." But he doesn't wear any sort of patch or monocle, nor has he ever in his life worn dark or tinted or smoked glasses, though I do from time to time. My eyesight, too, has a certain weakness (which is of no importance to me because I may not have it any more these days), though in the past it was a slow but certain cause of ultimate pain and blindness, and perhaps death, too, I don't know. To mention only men of letters, a weakness of the eyes embittered James Joyce's existence; operated on eleven times with hardly any improvement, he appears in many of his photographs with a bulky black patch over his left eye, though there are those who say he wore it less out of necessity than out of affectation, to make himself more original. I know what it is to have one eye covered: as a child of eight or nine I had to wear a patch over my left eye for several months when the right one was diagnosed as "lazy," thus forcing it to work and strive to make up for lost ground, while my better eye, which tended to take the whole task of looking and seeing upon itself, was covered up. I remember detesting that piece of gauze or bandage or patch over my good eye, and I think I cheated and took the dressing off during recesses at school and then stuck it back on carelessly; fortunately the torture didn't last long but perhaps it's because of that long-ago impatient disobedience that today my bad eye continues to be lazy, I think, or in any case, less active and perspicacious than the other one, whose superiority I always attributed to the fact of its being on the left, just as my left hand was stronger and more skillful than the right one, I found nothing strange in observing this ascendancy throughout the body. I was lucky that no attempt was ever made to correct my lefthandedness during a period when it was almost mandatory to do so, I wouldn't have been able to stand having my left arm tied in a sling, and to have felt one-armed and one-eyed: the school I went to, the Estudio, was liberal and secular and clandestinely co-educational, a disguised appendix or remainder of the Institución Libre de Enseñanza from the time of the Republic, before the wind swept away the weeks; and my parents were also liberal and would have had their work cut out for them, since my unknown brother Julianín was also left-handed as is my brother Álvaro, three out of five. When I learned to write names, among them my own, I wrote the letters from right to left, as Arabs do, and though I read "XAVIER"—that was what they named me, Xavier with an X, and that's how I wrote it as a child and how my mother always wrote it—what was really written or what everyone but me read was "REIVAX," and when she, laughing, wouldn't give me her approval, I didn't understand why and protested, since it looked to me as though I had written all the letters in the right order, without leaving any out or making any mistake; I still read "XAVIER" where apparently, by other peoples' standards, I had written "REIVAX," and when my mother said I had at last written "XAVIER," I read "REIVAX."

I sometimes think that time must be different for someone who began writing and reading in reverse—a tendancy that naturally corrected itself—than it is for most people, who have never tried to go from back to front but have always progressed from front to back, never trying to begin at the end but only to adjust to it, to the expectation and fear of it and to its arrival; and I sometimes think that might be why

I often move through what I've called in several books "the other side of time, its dark back," taking the mysterious expression from Shakespeare to give a name to the kind of time that has not existed, the time that awaits us and also the time that does not await us and therefore does not happen, or happens only in a sphere that isn't precisely temporal, a sphere in which writing, or perhaps only fiction, may—who knows—be found. That might be why I often see the past as future—I see it when it was only that: future—and the future as past, what must come as if it had already arrived and happened and, what's more, as if it no longer had much importance since even its vanishing or oblivion has already begun, so far gone, so lost is everything, with time. Or perhaps only what has occurred and can be told is lost and gone, or so it may appear, and therefore it is the only ambiguous thing or the only thing that permits of ambiguity, as Don Juan Benet wrote thirty years ago. And he also made another enigmatic statement at that time which I hadn't read until thirty months ago in the old article that contains it, and about which I can no longer ask him anything: ". . . it seems to me that time is the only dimension in which the living and the dead can speak to each other and communicate, the only one they have in common," that's what he said. I don't understand it, I don't understand it at all, but I know he did not write gratuitously, though like all good writers he did sometimes write arbitrarily. I don't understand it unless I think instead of that other side, that dark back through which the fickle and unpredictable voice we all know nevertheless passes, the voice of time when it has not yet gone by or been lost and perhaps for that reason is not even time, the voice that is permanently in our ears and that is always fictitious, I believe, as perhaps is and has been and will be until its end the voice that is speaking here.

Perhaps in that time, which has so often invaded my own time, I mean, the time assigned to me by other peoples' standards, fiction is compounded with reality, or with realities that are not only improbable and implausible but incompatible. Perhaps in that time a novel can interfere in real life, and it would not be strange that Sir John Spencer Ewart had aimed his rifle at the tinted lenses of Christaan Rudolf de Wet at Paardeberg or River Vet, or perhaps it was George Steabben who drew a bead on him at Magersfontein or Retief's Nek, centuries before dying in Mexico of a gunshot to the forehead during the famous shootout between Constantino and Leovigildo at the doors of the Salón Phalerno; it would not be strange that the letter opener with the inscription of the years and the bloody river, "15 Yser 16," had been carved by Stephen Graham or Wilfrid Ewart in their muddy trenches without truce, or that Hugh Oloff de Wet had sculpted the death mask of the poet monarch John Gawsworth, beggar, or that the spent New Year's Day or New Year's Eve bullet didn't spend itself quickly enough to initiate its downward curve and miss the target, or that the porter Tom and the porter Will of the Taylorian are one and the same traveling back and forth through their eternal territory, "Good luck, professor," with a festive, obliging hand raised high. It's possible that in that dimension or time my friend Eric Southworth died seven years ago at the hands of the Galdosistas (truly a sad fate) and my friend Aliocha Coll is still finishing his last glass of wine, and that the patriotic doctor Conan Doyle, the model of all recruits, and Lawrence of Arabia, the unattainable ideal of all adventurers, were the very men who happen to have bestowed the highest praise on the ill-fated talent of the war veteran novelist who didn't see the bullet his blind eye was to billet in the pandemonium of Mexico City; it may be that the balcony which does not exist on the fifth floor of the Hotel Isabel has always moved through that time, and always, too, the Austrian Ödön von Horváth's German girlfriend, who saw the same impossible accidental death happen to her father and her lover in the course of a single lifetime, her life, both struck by lightning and the younger man on New Year's Day; and that this is where Toby Rylands enjoyed his binges with a witty prince of Haiti or Honduras, Antigua or Barbuda or Belize or volcanic Montserrat, or perhaps of Redonda, which is uninhabited; it may be that the entire kingdom, which sometimes appears on maps and sometimes does not, lies and resides within that dimension or time, as befits a place that simultaneously exists and is imaginary, the Realm of Redonda, the Kingdom of Redonda with its intellectual aristocracy of fake Spanish names and its four kings, and it may be that following the abdication of the third one in my favor, since July 6, 1997 I have been the fourth of those kings, King Xavier or still King X as I write this, and also the literary executor and legal heir of my predecessors Shiel and Gawsworth, or Felipe I and Juan I: it's hard to resist the chance to perpetuate a legend, it would be mean-spirited to refuse to play along; in that nebula must float my alternating memory and non-memory of a scar on a thigh like a smooth, scorched crater that I saw and kissed every day for three distant years, and certainly also the occasional thought or the now almost fictitious memory of the person who bore it ("Oh yes, a young man used to live here with me, he was from Madrid, I wonder what's become of him, that was so long ago") and in that penumbra must invisibly smolder the kinship I've acquired with the actor Robert Donat through the objects of his that are mine now, the cigarette case in our pockets and the pin in our ties or on my lapel; and maybe De Wet is still piloting his Nieuport through that domain or in that wind, who knows if it isn't

that very airplane which is moving off, high and alive, while the enemy falls into an inferno (but it may be a Polikarpov and not a Nieuport, and then it would not be De Wet who pursued and brought down); and it may be that that adventurer coincided in Spain with another one whose escapades were of longer standing, the Red Dean, the bandit Dean of Canterbury, for whose cause and involuntary trumped-up accompaniment death was on the point of not passing my father by, and of leaving me without existence. Perhaps the unlived and truncated life of my small elder brother Julianín also moves through the other side of time, along with the person I would have been, or the one I would not have been if I hadn't been born. And so what, if I hadn't been born.

One person who was not born, for example, was a first-born son of my family who was under a curse, and was therefore expected in order to see the curse fulfilled in its entirety. And though I've already told the story twice—once as fiction, in a short story with false names, "El viaje de Isaac" or "Isaac's Journey" its title, and again as fact in an article on real names, soberly called "Una maldición" or "A Curse"—not many people will remember it or will have read it, and its most fitting place is here, or so I believe, as if for once, and without my foreseeing it in 1978 or in 1995, I had followed the precept of the eminent short-story writer Isak Dinesen, whom I translated during my time at Oxford and according to whom "only if you are able to imagine what has happened, to repeat it in your imagination, will you see stories, and only if you have the patience to carry them within you for a long, long time, and to tell them to yourself and retell them again and again, will you be capable of telling them well."

One of my grandmothers came from the very Caribbean Sea where Redonda lies when it does appear on maps or in photographs. She was Cuban, born in Havana; she was

The Realm
of
Redonda

H. M. FELIPE I
(M. P. Shiel, 1865-1947)

H. M. JUAN I
(John Gawsworth, 1912-1970)

H. M. JUAN II
(Jon Wynne-Tyson, 1924-   )
(abdicated 1997)

H. M. XAVIER I
(Javier Marías 1951-   )

. . . .

named Lola Manera and she was the mother of my mother Lolita. In reality, both she and her father, my great-grandfather, were less Cubans than Spaniards of Cuba, to put it in an understandable and inoffensive way. My great-grandfather was named Enrique Manera and I believe his second surname was Cao ("from Cao the Indian, Montezuma's lieutenant," my grandmother's youngest sister, our Tita María, used to proclaim with *folies de grandeur*, holding up her index finger); he was a soldier and owned land in Havana.

While still young and unmarried, he was going home on horseback one morning when a mulatto mendicant crossed his path and asked him for alms. He refused and spurred his mount onward, but the beggar managed to stop him by grabbing the bridle, and then pronounced his somewhat baroque and unusually precise curse: "You, your eldest son and the eldest son of your eldest son will all three die when journeying far from your homeland, none of you will reach the age of fifty and none of you will ever have a grave." My great-grandfather, who paid no attention and shoved the beggar out of the way, told the story at home over lunch and then forgot it (but someone remembered and that's why it has reached me: perhaps a black nanny or an apprehensive mother, women who are no longer young are always the repositories, and the transmitters). That happened in 1873 when Enrique Manera was twenty-four or twenty-five, two years younger than when he published a little novel I found not long ago—books are always travelling toward me, not sparing me their acquaintance—*El coracero de Froeswiller* (*Froeswiller's Cuirassier*), subtitled *Recuerdos de la Guerra Franco-Prusiana* (*Memories of the Franco-Prussian War*), and printed at number 4 calle del Rosario in Seville, by the press and lithographic studio of Ariza y Ruiz, according to the half title page. Its first lines are very much in the old style: "It was the 15th of July, 1870, and the nocturnal hour of eleven o'clock had just sounded on every church clock in Paris. The capital of the French empire had, at the moment our story begins, a highly strange and exceptional appearance." And this, apparently, was not the only novel of his to reach the presses, there's a novelistic family antecedent for me here, an Antillean antecedent. Much later, in 1898, by which time he had been married for half his life to a woman of the Custardoy family with whom he had produced seven offspring (which is why the false name in the story was "Isaac Custardoy"), my great-grandfather Manera decided he would rather not see the Stars and Stripes waving over his island, so he hastily sold off his lands and embarked for Spain—his country, which he may have known only as a name—with his entire family, including my cheerful grandmother Lola who was seven or eight years old at the time, my grandiloquent Tita María, even younger, and the first-born son, considerably older, and also named Enrique. The doctors had advised against this radical measure since my great-grandfather suffered from Ménière's vertigo and the crossing posed a grave risk to his health. But the soldierly Manera was not inclined to dance attendance on Commodore Schley's victory over and occupation of the island, so he paid no attention, as he had paid none to the mulatto beggar twenty-five years earlier. Halfway across the Atlantic he suffered a mortal attack of his illness, which struck while he was on deck. He was about to turn fifty and was already far from his homeland— and from the other homeland which he had never seen— when he died, and his body was thrown into the ocean, weighted down with a cannonball.

Twenty-three years later, in 1921, his oldest son Enrique Manera Custardoy, my grandmother's brother and therefore my great-uncle (so I, too, have a military great-uncle, like

Ewart and De Wet) participated in the War of Morroco at the rank of colonel and as adjutant to General Fernández Silvestre, who commanded the Spanish troops in their great humiliation. It is is known, but almost no one still remembers, that the Spaniards fled in disarray at what has become known as "the Disaster of Annual." Amid the mad, scattered rout by Abd-el-Krim's Kabyles, Fernández Silvestre, his son and Colonel Manera were isolated from the main body of the troops, completely helpless but with a small truck at their disposal. The general, in an old-fashioned gesture, refused to abandon the field of his defeat, and my great-uncle, in a still more old-fashioned gesture, refused to abandon his superior officer and defeated friend. Between the two of them, they convinced the young Silvestre to try to flee for his life with the vehicle, and there they stayed, waiting for slow death and long fire, *muerte larga, fuego largo*. Nothing more was learned. Their bodies were never found, and the only thing of Manera's that was retrieved were his field glasses and his leather gear, which I saw in my grandfather's house on calle de Cea Bermúdez (and in Spanish field glasses and cufflinks are both called *gemelos*, so here again only the *gemelos* could be identified). It's feared that the two were drawn and quartered. Manera was forty-six years old, my age now, and was far from both his homelands, the colonial Havana of his birth and the Madrid that saw him depart for that colonial war to fall victim, in Africa, to the curse he had inherited. He had no grave, nor will he ever have one. He left only a widow, that is, a wife.

The first two threats of the elaborate curse had been fulfilled so fully and exactly that it seemed impossible it wouldn't continue on to the third generation as well. So, after the premature, remote, and unmarked death of Manera Custardoy in Annual, some family member—perhaps a superstitious nanny or an apprehensive mother, perhaps my own grandmother, the doomed man's sister—predicted, with a mingling of consolation and fear, that the dead man must have left his spouse pregnant at his loyal departure on the fatal expedition with Fernández Silvestre. The wait lasted a month or two, but there was nothing. The oldest son never had an oldest son, and the thought of an illegitimate child is too facile and trivial. What if none of it had come true? What if all of it had come true? There was another Enrique Manera, whom I've met, but he descended not from the colonel who died in Morocco but from one of his younger brothers. He attained the rank of admiral—not a phony one like Franco the whaler, a real admiral—and he used to talk about his feats during the Civil War: he sank a Russian submarine with his bare hands and was put to death by the Reds, a sobering fate from which, as he told it, he emerged un-scathed thanks to his short stature. The firing squad or mili-tia had taken aim at a group of condemned men, most of whom were much taller than he was, and the bullets passed over his head, ruffling his hair. Like all the others, he fell when he heard the shots, and he pretended to be dead for hours, making use of his companions' blood, which he was drenched in, until night fell and he saw that the field was clear—they did not bury, they did not bury, they denied him a tomb—and then he emerged from beneath the corpses and joined the living once more and managed to escape. If all this is true, perhaps the curse did try to fulfill itself to the end, despite being deprived of its final object: if not the third first-born son in direct lineage (who never existed), then at least the man of the same blood who bore the same name that would have been given to the one who never had a name because he never came into being, though he was announced and foreseen by a mulatto mendicant in the city of Havana in

1873: the admiral was, in any case a grandson of the impru-
dent and guilty Manera Cao. But the veracity of this third
and final attempt must be questioned, given that another of
the heroic feats the admiral described involved sinking a Bol-
shevik submarine by hammering at it with his fists. It is certain, in any case, that there was no one to suffer the foreor-
dained third death, before the age of fifty and far from his
own land and without ever deserving a tomb.

In that short story written in 1979, a friend of the Custardoy family pondered the question in these or similar words:
the oldest son of the oldest son had been prophesied, as had
the form of his demise, but he had never been born, he had
not reached the point of being engendered or born, yet the
mulatto beggar and the unfortunate Manera who crossed
paths in 1873 had already conceived of his existence and
knew of him. Where had that being or concept been since
then, and where was he after the death of the man who would
have been his father according to the prophecy, that bellicose
death with its old-fashioned gesture, in Morroco, ruled out
the possibility of his birth for all the centuries of centuries
and forever more? He had to be somewhere. The friend tried
to solve the enigma, and in the end, "when he was about to
die," the story says, "he wrote his thoughts on a sheet of
paper: 'I foresee that I am about to die, I shall undertake the
final journey. What is to become of me? Where will I go?
Will I go somewhere? Where will I go? I glimpse my death
because I have been alive and was engendered and born, because I am still alive, and therefore death is imperfect and
does not encompass everything, it can't keep something else
from existing, something that is different from it, and which
awaits it from here, thinks of it from here: it isn't only a subject as it would like to be, but also the object of thought and
expectation, and it must yield. Only the one who has never

been born belongs to it wholly, or rather the one who has never been engendered or conceived, and therefore has never entered into time or passed through it for a single second and will never have to disrupt it by leaving it. The one who is not conceived is the one who dies most. He has travelled endlessly by the most circuitous, the most intricate and invisible and silenced route: the route of possibility. He is the only one who will never live out any year or any day and will never have a homeland or a grave. He is Enrique Manera, the missing one. I am not."

No, he was never born, the Manera who was prophesied and expected in order to conclude the curse which his nonexistence left incomplete, and perhaps pending (and has there ever been anything that was not unfinished); and maybe his absent being still moves through the other side and dark back and abysm of time, together with all that has not happened and all that has happened but without leaving a trail or a trace, neither smoke nor breath, and all that has happened but cannot be reproduced and is no longer possible and is therefore ruled out, and all that is still torn between sharp-edged memory and half-blind forgetting, like that scar on a thigh that fades away and returns and comes into focus and vanishes, as if it were trying to spare me its acquaintance ("Listen, come here, look, there is this thing on me and maybe you'd rather not see it. You still have time not to, and if you don't then you won't ever have to.") Maybe everything moves through that other side of time, all that lies within our known time and all that it does not know, all that it does not register or take into account. Through that dark back may also pass the facts which, in the telling and narration and memory of them, are transformed into fictions, maybe the maritime crossing of my grandmother Lola is wandering there now, the crossing she undertook a century ago at the merry age of seven or eight, from Havana to Madrid, so that my mother Lolita could be born here and later me, from her, and maybe the girl is also roaming that abysm, the girl my mother was expecting and hoping for in that room where she gave birth to us, and who was not born because I was born in her place, though a name was already waiting for the girl, thought up and selected, Constanza, and undoubtedly her imagined face, as well. And maybe, in that case, Spain had to lose Cuba so that the journey could take place in the boat from which my island-dwelling great-grandfather was thrown to the bottom of the ocean, wrapped in a flag and with a cannonball on his chest to help him sink ("Let me sit heavy on thy soul tomorrow, let me be lead within thy bosom and in a bloody battle end thy days: fall thy lance"). And who knows if the island wasn't lost in order to satisfy a beggar's private, passing curse, and for a hundred thousand other reasons of that nature which affect only individuals.

Everything is so random and absurd, it's incomprehensible that we can grant any transcendence whatsoever to our birth or our existence or our death, determined by chance combinations as fickle and unpredictable as the voice of time when it has not yet gone by or been lost, when it is not yet ambiguous, when it is not yet even time, that voice we all know and hear murmuring as we move forward, or that is what we believe, because really it is the voice that moves forward; how can any importance be conceded to our fragile and insignificant passage which could so easily not have occurred because of a lie or some false testimony, or could indeed occur because of the excessive fancifulness and hatred of two of Franco's informers—two future professors, both made so in recompense, though one may already have been a professor—who fabricated accusations that were finally too improbable and novelistic about the man who couldn't yet even dream of being my father, or anyone's; how can we even take our own breathing seriously, this breathing that we owe to an attack of an antiquated illness or vertigo on the deck of a ship travelling into exile, or to the capricious, baroque curse a mulatto beggar hurled at a contemptuous horseman one hundred and twenty-five years ago, across the ocean, on an island off the coast of another continent; or that we lose this breathing because of a bullet that goes astray on that same continent, in the enthusiasm of a Mexican New Year's Eve, or because a tree struck by lightning falls on the head of a foreigner waiting to go into a theater shortly before emigrating to be safe on that other continent; or more simply because one page has been brought to a close and there is no desire to write the next; or, even more innocuously, because one December evening the only son who was missing, the fourth one, comes home; or, still more painfully, because the treacherous onset of a sudden fatal illness leaves a zoetrope ownerless, bringing it to a stop and laying it aside until the end of time or of the world that the toy imitated and represented, the toy with its flimsy wheel that no longer spins. Put out the light and then put out the light. And put it out.

Yet all we can do is grant ridiculous importance to the products of these inchoate combinations, to each one and to our own—or rather, the one that we are—to those already obliterated and to those that are present, and even to those that are fictitious, if we don't want our passage through time to be entirely idiotic as well as fragile and insignificant. So we spend our lives pretending to be unique and chosen when in fact we're interchangeable, each the random outcome of a spin of the wheel of fortune at a dank, decrepit carnival. The pretence is necessary, but what's bad about it is that our actions or misfortunes or good luck make most of us forget, in the end, that that was all we were doing, just pretending.

There are people who become convinced they were destined for what they attain or endure, as if the enduring or the attainment explained their history and the reason or cause for their birth, it is the cause, it is the cause. I've said what I'm saying here before, in a novel, but that doesn't matter: everything has to be said again and again so it won't be lost, until nothing is said any longer and there is no longer: the shortcuts and twisting paths taken by our efforts are what make us vary though we end up believing it was destiny, we end up seeing our whole lives in light of the last or most recent thing, as if the past had been only preparation, as if we were gradually coming to understand it as it withdraws from us and will understand it entirely in the end. And therefore the mother believes she had to be a mother, the spinster that she had to remain unmarried, the murderer a murderer and the victim a victim, the ruler believes that from the beginning his steps were leading him to command other people, and the genius's childhood is dredged up when his or her genius becomes known; the king convinces himself that it was his lot to be king, if he reigns, and that it was his lot to become the martyr of his lineage if he does not; and the person who lives into old age finally remembers the whole of his life as a slow arrangement for elderliness: the life that has passed is seen as a story or merely a sign and thus it is twisted and distorted. And the man who dies young will always be seen as a man who died young, even in the portraits made when he was alive, which are now contaminated.

In fact, it wasn't me who said this (except for the last phrase); it was a character in a novel named the Only One or Solus, a real king, even if he was fictitious, and not the literary king of a fantastic realm that even so sometimes appears on maps, and when it does it is a harsh blackened rock, uninhabited or inhabited only by boobies, a diminutive island not far from Cuba that takes its name from a church in Cádiz and is only the territory, the superfluous vessel of the imaginary. Who knows whether it hasn't disappeared into the depths of the sea like my great-grandfather Manera, after the tremendous eruptions of the Soufrière volcano last year on the larger, neighboring island of Montserrat, where Shiel, or Felipe I, the first monarch, was born, Montserrat now almost reduced to ashes in an urn, like Shiel, and perhaps scattered (there's no one on Redonda to send any news). It's a realm inherited through irony and writing, never through solemnity or blood, the realm of Shiel's successor Juan II, who chose me when he reached the age of seventy-three, and of Juan I , the beggar poet, who became a kind of anachronism, living on handouts and sleeping on park benches in the final days of his long death, and who certainly must have hurled more than one curse against someone, there on his native island, our continent's largest, unleashing by those curses who knows what combinations or pandemoniums, then dying in a hospital, forgotten and penniless, under his true, recovered name of Terence Ian Fytton Armstrong, "a poet" according to Vinten the civil servant, and Lewis the informant, who certified his death. This cursing or poetic voice is nevertheless not entirely silent and now murmurs in my house, in what for some time I've been calling "Gawsworth's room," as if it were a butler's room, or a ghost's.

But nothing will ever make me believe that this was my destiny or that anything else will be, or that there was a reason for my birth.

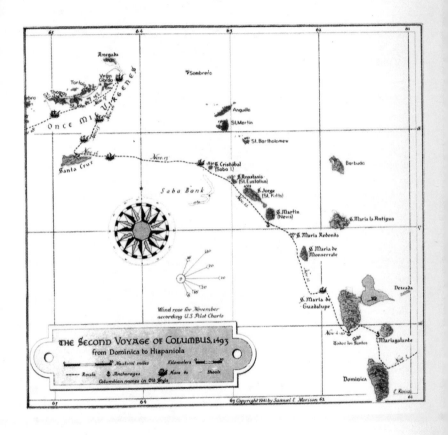

65   64   63   62   61

Anegada

Sombrero

Virgin
Tortola Gorda

St.Thomas

Culebra

Once Mil VIRGENES

Anguilla

St.Martin

St. Bartholomew

Nov. 14

Nov. 15

S. Cristóbal
(Saba I.)

Barbuda

Santa Cruz

Saba Bank

S. Anastasia
(St. Eustatius)

S. Jorge
(St. Kitts)

Nov. 12

S. Martin
(Nevis)

S. Maria la Antigua

S. Maria Redonda

S. Maria de
Monserrate

Deseada

S. Maria de
Guadalupe

Nov. 4-10

Todos los Santos

Mariagalante

Nov. 3

Wind rose for November
according U.S. Pilot Charts

Dominica

The Second Voyage of Columbus, 1493
from Dominica to Hispaniola

Nautical miles   Kilometers

- - - - Route   Anchorages   Move to   Shoals
Columbian names in Old Style

E. Raisz

65   64   63 Copyright 1941 by Samuel E. Morison 62   61

A Chart of the Antilles, or Charibbee, or Caribs Islands by L. S. De la Rochette, MDCCLXXXIV (1784).

Note the view of Montserrat from the southeast in the upper right which clearly shows Redonda, "Called by the Sailors Rock Dunder" as indicted on the map below.

Some time will have to pass before this voice or writing speaks more clearly and I can tell what it tells, I have to take a certain distance from recent events; I prefer to pause here and wait a while, everything is still changing. It isn't only that I have yet to tell of all the short-cuts and twisted paths along which this fantasmal literary title came to attach itself to my name (and I don't know whether it transposes me into what, for me, was fiction only fourteen or even nine years ago, or whether, instead, fiction is embedding itself in my life and making it even more unreal and chimerical, as well as absurd, indicisive and somewhat calamitous). It isn't only the accession that remains to be told; the whole story is intricate and possibly picturesque and also comical, of course. And neither is it only the ludicrous characteristics and vicissitudes of this kingdom, which, though imaginary—and it is that, above all—is not free from what all kingdoms have known throughout history: usurpers, imposters, intrigues, lunatics, betrayals, "subjects," patrons, rebellions, chroniclers, false favorites, "dynastic" disputes—in which I shall certainly not be participating, all I need right now is to engage in heated epistolary arguments over "legitimacy" or "lineages" that are no such thing, for kinship matters not at all here—and I believe there's also been a bloody deed. And a modest legend, which I'm told I now incarnate. I'll have to name my own peers, since I must play along with the game. Perhaps there will soon be a Duke of Svolta, a Duke of Norte, a Duke of Caronte, a Duke of Babel, or a Duke of Tigres, possibly. A Duke of Región is no longer possible.

When from time to time I've hinted at what was happening or revealed some isolated fact, making tentative probes among those of my friends who wouldn't make fun of me or disapprove, I've seen them all react with an incredulity that's never entirely left them; they, better than anyone, know of my inclination towards fabulation and levity, and they can't be sure that I'm not making up stories. I doubt this skeptical reaction will ever disappear, even after they've read these pages and seen the images I've placed in them, though each one's incredulity had its own character and stance: Eric Southworth's combined mirth with ingenious ideas and glosses; Mercedes López-Ballesteros' concern over the more somber aspects of the invading fiction was infused with a childlike enchantment, the sheer pleasure of an arbitrary tale; Daniella Pittarello's fragile irony, overcoming her theoretical perplexities, let her youthful spirit embrace the coincidences; Anna Sala's, or just "Anna's," apprehensive anticipation, as if she feared these adventures might change my life or do me harm, was also tinged with the bewildered contentment of being present at the unfolding of a fable; in Ruibérriz de Torres, whose surname I bear as I do Custardoy and Manera and Cao, the incredulity was mingled with a sarcasm that couldn't quite banish his curiosity, at least not to the point of telling me to be quiet and stop bothering him with this foolishness; Manolo Rodríguez Rivero's critical distance ultimately concealed a perfect understanding of this type of deliberately provoked, hilarious English extravagance and of the temptation writers sometimes feel to dilute themselves in their own pages; and Julia Altares' incredulity was, how shall I put it, seasoned with revelry and fantastical plans and the maximum degree of encouragement, or rather, more precisely, with binges. All of them are good at playing along, and all are a little worried and don't know whether to believe me, but at least they listen and ask for more information, which until now I've strictly rationed and parcelled out among them. My agent Mercedes Casanovas, to whom I was forced—red-faced and worried that she might take me for a madman—to spill the story several months ago, in order to find out if she would agree to handle the rights to Shiel and Gawsworth in my name, can't, I believe, quite get used to the idea that she's now part of what was for her, less than a year ago, only the vague memory of a novel, though she conducts herself with cheerful professionalism and has already negotiated our first Shiel contract, for an edition of the novel *The Yellow Danger*, from 1898, a century ago. Only my brother Miguel, after raising an eyebrow and taking his pipe from his mouth for a moment, immediately banished all doubt and listened to my news as if it were perfectly natural, he's known me since I was a child, and not in vain, and he does have a memory now. It's curious that I find myself enveloped in all of this without having sought it out or tried to attain it—or only with my writing—when at heart I'm a republican and islands make me nervous. But the same things exist in republics as in kingdoms: imposters and intrigues, lunatics and rebellions, and bloody deeds. And legends. Maybe I'm the lunatic.

I'll hazard a guess that the reason for all the quarreling over something that is imaginary is not the dream or symbol of a literary realm made of paper and ink (no usurper or pretender to the throne has been a real writer, the primary, implicit requirement), but the geographical location and material existence of the territory that accompanies it, the Leeward Isle; for it seems that when Queen Victoria annexed

Redonda in 1872, through the government of Gladstone, in order to thwart the United States which was trying to do the same in order to exploit the phosphate of alumina in its poor, rocky soil, the British Colonial Office, in response to the protests first of Shiel's father and then, later, of Shiel himself, made no objection to the latter's title ("King of Redonda"), assuring him he could use it as long as his kingdom were devoid of substance and he refrained from rebelling against the colonial power. Besides, it's debatable whether Shiel's sovereignty fell under the jurisdiction of British law, and even the Colonial Office harbored some doubts as to the validity of his claim and right to an uninhabited island.

Redonda was discovered by Columbus during his second voyage, on the 10th, 11th, 12th or 13th of November, depending on the source. His illegitimate son Hernando Colón has this to say about the discovery in his biography of his father, *Vida del Almirante:* "Sunday, November 10th the Admiral weighed anchor and took the fleet northwest along the coast of the island of Guadalupe in the direction of Hispaniola [Haiti]. He reached the island of Montserrat, to which he gave that name because of its height; and he learned from the Indians he was carrying with him that the Caribs had unpeopled it by eating all its inhabitants. From there he proceeded to Santa María la Redonda, so named because it is so round and smooth that it seemed impossible to climb its sides without a ladder; the Indians called this island Ocamaniro," a name which, incidentally, is almost an anagram of Manera Cao, or at least has all the same consonants, which are the substance of words.

It was also mentioned by the famous historian and humanist Pietro Martire d'Anghiera or Peter Martyr of Angleria, an official chronicler of the Indies, in his *De Orbe Novo or The Decades of the new world*, written in Latin after the manner of Titus Livius, beginning in 1511. From what he says in his lengthy description of the neighboring island of Madanino, it can be surmised that Columbus did not disembark at Redonda, though, as with everything else he caught sight of, he made note of it, christened it and claimed it for the Crown of Spain: "The Prefect," (this was the classical term Peter Martyr used to designate the Admiral) "for the desire he had to see his companions, which at his first voyage he left the year before in Hispaniola to search the country, let pass many islands both on his right hand and left hand and sailed directly thither. By the way there appeared from the North a great Island which the captives that were taken in Hispaniola called Madanino, affirming it to be inhabited only with women to whom the Cannibals have access at certain times of the year, as in old time the Thracians had to the Amazons in the Island of Lesbos. The men children they send to their fathers. But the women they keep with themselves. They have great and strong caves or dens in the ground, to the which they fly for safeguard if any men resort unto them at any other time than is appointed, and there defend themselves with bows and arrows against the violence of such as attempt to invade them. They could not at this time approach to this Island, by reason of the Northnortheast wind which blew so vehemently from the same, whereas they now followed the East southeast." This island, which also appears as "Matinina" and "Matinino" is believed to be the eastern side of Guadalupe. And Peter Martyr goes on: "After they departed from Madanino and sailed the space of forty miles, they passed not far from another Island which the captives said to be very populous and replenished with all things necessary for the life of man. This they called Mons Serratus [Montserrat], because it was full of mountains. The captives further declared that the Cannibals are wont at some time to go from their own coasts above a thousand miles to hunt for men. The day following, they saw another Island the which, because it was round, they called Sancta Maria Rotunda. . . . They affirm all these islands to be marvelous fair and fruitful." *De Orbe Novo* was first translated into English by Richard Eden, in 1555, and into German in 1582.

And there is even a first-hand description by Doctor Diego Álvarez Chanca of Seville, physician to the King and Queen and to the Princess, Doña Juana la Loca, who at his own request went "as doctor on the second fleet Columbus prepared for the Indies." Prose was not his strong point, but he says in a letter to the Cabildo of Seville: "We went along the coast of this island and the Indian women we were carrying said it was not inhabited, that those of Caribe had unpeopled it and so we did not stop there." That was Montserrat; then comes Redonda: "Later that afternoon we saw another, night by then, near that island we missed some shoals for fear of which we lay at anchor, for we didn't dare go unless it was day." It would appear from all of this that though they never set foot on the island, probably because access to Redonda was so difficult, they did spend a night near it, because of some shoals.

A much more recent mention, and in another language, is that of the historian and professor, first at Oxford—where else?—then at Harvard, Samuel Eliot Morison, who, in addition to writing an important biography of the Admiral in 1942 for which he won a Pulitzer Prize, led the Harvard Columbus Expedition, which in the autumn of 1939 and winter of 1940 followed the Navigator's routes in two schooners, in order to describe in detail all that Columbus found, saw and did in his journeys, point by point and step by step. In the biography he said, "Proceeding in a general northwesterly direction, the fleet passed along a small, steep and rounded but inaccessible rock less than a mile long which Columbus named *Santa María la Redonda*, 'St. Mary the Rotund.' Redonda retains her name and her importance as a sea mark to this day; but she has never been worth inhabiting." His mention of it in a later book, dating from 1974, is less reserved: "Then came a minuscule, round island, *Santa María la Redonda*: it has never been inhabited, though a crazy American once declared himself its king." Of course the word had to be "crazy," the same word that, according to the British press, the Gestapo used, in its day, to describe Hugh Oloff de Wet. If only Professor Morison were still alive, and knew.

Accustomed to the robbery, looting, plagiarism and endless espionage of the contemporary university, which leads professors to avoid breathing a word about any project-they're working on until it is no longer at the research stage but is safely entombed in shelvable print, my friend Eric Southworth sometimes asks if, since I'm dividing these pages into two volumes, I'm not worried that someone will "appropriate" the "real characters" while I write or think about or await the second volume, and, for example, recount all that I have yet to tell or still don't know about Ewart or De Wet or Gawsworth or the bandit Red Dean or the Maneras.

That might not be very pleasant, but I don't fear it, and anyway, these "characters" don't really belong to anyone, they are real, and if I feel that they are in some way mine it's only because I happened to notice them while I was writing novels or plotting stories and they were hardly remembered by a living soul: perhaps only by Hugh Cecil, Anthony Edkins, Steve Eng, Roger Dobson, Jon Wynne-Tyson, my estimable father and myself—I mean until recently. Or it may be that it was these characters who crossed paths with me. Nor would I want to know everything, about them or about anyone, least of all about myself. And if I did know everything I don't believe I would ever tell it, we're always selecting and discarding, knowing or not knowing often doesn't matter much. Or sometimes true knowledge turns out to make no difference, and then invention can begin.

Anyway, as I've already said, I'm devoid of scholarly or journalistic inclinations and would never dive into libraries and collections of periodicals or the Internet, which I don't use, I write on a typewriter and go over the pages by hand; I would never dash off to interview witnesses or heirs or survivors, recording their scraps of memory in order to find out things that don't come to find me spontaneously and of their own accord, without any effort on my part, without my moving from here, from my place, from where I can send requests to the booksellers of Oxford and York and London or challenge Don Juan Benet to demonstrate his sagacity. It's as if I scorned any knowledge that is achieved by force or seized, that is active and anxious and dependent upon the will, my own will, of course: any knowledge I don't deserve. This attitude would be unforgivably incompetent in a scholar, reporter or scientist, but I am none of those things nor am I thinking of becoming any of them in order to speak of things that have happened to me or interest me or affect me, or of things that have not happened to me but that I have slowly learned of and therefore remember.

It wouldn't be particularly unlikely or strange were some thief or looter or plagiarist or opportunist, who also abound, silent and masked amid the tempest of literature, to speed-read all of *Cardboard Crucifix*, if it can be found (but Ben Bass has disappeared), and all of whatever Wilfrid Ewart and James Denham published in their short lives and Stephen Graham in his long one, and a biography of the bandit Dean of Canterbury, if any such thing exists, and all the unknown short novels of Enrique Manera, my Antillean great-grandfather. Or were they to dredge up the living relatives or resentful ex-lovers or the silent papers, waiting without impatience. That is not my work. The most such a person could ever tell would be the facts, and facts in themselves are nothing, language cannot reproduce them just as any number of repetitions, with their sharp edges, cannot reproduce the time that is past or gone, or revive the dead who have already gone past us and been lost in that time. And at this point who knows what has become real and what has become fictitious.

Who can say if the unlikely news I'm now pondering is real or fictitious, about a Spanish daughter of Matthew Phipps Shiel, native of Montserrat with its high mountains and first king of Redonda (but perhaps it's no more incredible than the fact that his royalties now belong to me): a child born on July 16, 1900, in London, to his ephemeral wife Carolina or Lina, inscribed in the register of births on August 30 as Dolores Katherine Shiel, the only known legitimate descendent of Felipe I, whose parents called her Lola like my grandmother or Lolita like my mother, as women named Dolores are always called. Shiel and Lina were married in the Italian church of St Peter in the London district of Holborn on November 3, 1898, soon it will be a century ago, in the presence of their respective mother-in-law and mother, another Lola, and a friend, Arthur Machen, Archduke of Redonda. Shiel was thirty-three years old; Lina was only eighteen.

It isn't necessarily texts that make things most real, but it's worth listening to Shiel's voice for a moment as he speaks of himself when he was still young and in Paris, it isn't hard to imagine that voice, looking at his brilliant, magnetic, disturbing eyes, his gleaming black hair and smooth skin, he may have been a touch mulatto on his mother's side: "In the

thick of [this]," he says, "my fate takes me one afternoon into the Palais de Glace in the rue de Madrid" (what other street could it have been) "where I see a girl of sixteen skating, a Parisian Spaniard. Of course, I had seen lovely girls—in Cuba—in Andalusia—in Martinique—but never before seen *a beauty*; and she resembled a girl I had loved at seven, another girl whom I had loved at thirteen, and my mother. Now, I had long ceased 'to pray' like my parents, considering that improper; but that afternoon I dashed in a cab to my chamber, and, prostrating myself, I prayed, 'God! give her to me!' And the good God did. I did not know her name to begin, but out of the grasp and drag of some twenty I grabbed her, got her. It was natural, after this, for me to pray for girls; and I can say that, if ever I have prayed for a girl, I have got her from God. She—Lina—was the 'Laura' of my *Cold Steel*" (one of his best novels) "at least her face and manner; in the streets of London every creature turned the head to look back at her, and observe the handicraft of her Father. But she did not think London 'pretty' (*'Londres n'est pas jolie'*), and it was thus that I got the habit of living long in Paris. However, she was not strong—died after five years, leaving me and a daughter; and it was some fifteen years before I married again, when I met at a lecture Lydia, who resembles Lina and my mother."

"Leaving me and a daughter." So the news I received some time ago but am only now pondering must be true, despite everything. Shiel may not have been entirely sincere, however, because he also reports that before Lina's death he had rejected her in a letter of June 12 1903, returning to London shortly thereafter and abandoning her in Paris with her daughter. Apparently Carolina died at the end of that year at the age of only twenty-three, who knows how much the rejection and abandonment of the man who had prayed to get her had to do with it. An older sister, Salva, and perhaps a younger one, Micaela, the two aunts, took little Lola to Madrid, she was a three-year-old then who may not have remembered her father if she never saw him again, a little Madrileña who must be dead by now, or no less than ninety-seven years of age, and the bearer of these distant tidings—arrived from Dayton, Ohio—asks me about her and her Spanish history, asks that I apply myself and track her down and find out about her life and learn about her descendents, if she had any. Perhaps I should try it this time, despite my disinclination toward journalism, not to mention biography, which all too frequently has become among the most vile and defamatory activities of our time. Or else, as always, I'll have to wait for Lola Shiel or her ghost or offspring to come to me and tell me.

This girl or old woman or dead woman must also have moved, from the age of three, through the other side or dark back of time, among the things that are both real and fictitious, that disappear or never appear and yet are known because they have been spoken of. I don't know, anything is possible. It may be that the girl, though decrepit, is still alive, or that she died long ago, perhaps during the war, gunned down by Hugh Oloff de Wet's Nieuport or bombarded by a Junker of the Condor Legion in the service of the fake admiral; put to death by the militia like my mother's younger brother, my uncle Emilio, or, as my father could have been and so many others were, by the triumphant Franquistas with their informers and henchmen, still unpunished, their names concealed. Or she may not have been, she may have been granted more than enough time to watch a daughter grow, a daughter who would now be a venerable matron, one of the many we see at mid-afternoon, taking over our streets. And since Shiel's lineage was primarily female (perhaps he was from Madaninó, he was his parents' first son, born after his eight or nine sisters), it may be that the daughter had, in turn, a daughter of her own, in which case Shiel's Irish surname, borne by little Lola, would have fallen farther and farther behind, and would only be the fourth surname of that possible granddaughter of thirty-odd possible years, as Manera is my fourth. It may be that I've walked past that granddaughter during my rambles across Madrid, because if she exists she could be anyone, and whoever she is she probably doesn't even know she had an Antillean great-grandfather who was a real monarch of the imaginary, and whose novels are now under my care and management, as his unlikely successor.

She may be the woman I see from my window now, as dawn finds me awake, the woman who is no longer young and waits for the bus with her early-morning weariness, and I can see her smiling slightly today, as if she were daydreaming or couldn't forget the person she left between the sheets, she's getting used to him now without realizing it, and that's what is dangerous, when the departure starts to be feared more than the continued presence of the object of our habit and constancy. She raises one well-shod foot, with a high heel to heighten the silhouette effect of her black stockings, then raises the other, like a wading bird, as she waits for the bus which is not in view, even in the distance, I know because I'm watching from the height of my upper-storey window, I don't have to stand on tiptoe as she must, enveloped in the advancing light of day that blinds or half-blinds the thirteen streetlamps that are still lit as a testament or reminder of the night that is already past and lost: though the night still impregnates us and isn't always easy to shake off, just as it isn't easy to shake off the time that has disappeared, our time or other people's time or a time that has never come.

Or it may be that the granddaughter of Lolita Shiel is the woman who waits in bed with no impatience, only boredom, for the man with the receding hairline, whose hair looks like a musician's when the wind ruffles it, the man with the incipient, bluish beard and the loosened necktie who is trying to settle his debts and hasn't yet been given the knifing he thought he was certain to get, sooner or later. He's on tiptoe, as well, anxiously calling in a low voice ("Come, come") to the bus that doesn't come and that I know isn't even close to arriving, maybe he's thinking that the later he gets home the more time she'll have had to think up and prepare her story, or to move out in his absence, leaving only a note of rejection on a piece of yellow paper taped to the mirror. The wind sends his tie dancing, he's wearing an antique enamelled pin in it that he hasn't lost in his gamblings only by a miracle, only because he refused to wager it in spite of the bullfighters' insistence, they're greedy at first, they only become magnanimous later. His eyes look almost Oriental and his lips as if sketched on with a pencil—"beaky lips, beaky lips"—the chin is almost cleft, the hands broad, a cigarette in the left one. But everything is still a question of time and time is what the knifing makes fast.

A great deal has yet to be told, some of it recent and some still to come, and I need time. But even not knowing what is to come, I do know that whenever the moment arrives I will go on telling it as I have until now, for no reason and in no particular order, without making an outline or seeking coherence; what I tell will not be guided by any author, fundamentally, though I am the person who tells it; it will not correspond to any plan or be ruled by any compass, or have any reason to make sense or add up to an argument or plot, or answer to some hidden harmony, or even be a story with its beginning and its expectation and its final silence. I don't think this is going to be a story, though I may be mistaken since I don't know its ending which may never be put into writing because it will coincide with my own, some years from now, or so I hope. Or it may also survive me. I'm going to stop now and say no more for a while; I remember what I said long ago, in speaking of the narrator and the author who have the same name here: I said I no longer know if there is one of us or two, at least while I am writing. Now I know that of those two possible figures, one would have to be fictitious.

I raise my eyes above the balcony for a moment to shake off the long night and the doubt and perhaps to be only one person again, and when I look back down the bus has come and carried off its passengers. I look at the incongruent lights still lit beneath the sun that is making them insignificant as it rises, and they are time, respectful, benign time that wants to leave some record of what has now ceased, until the sleepy hand of some civil servant takes note of the waste and puts out the light and then puts it out. And even then the passengers are still there, and even then the light has not been put out.

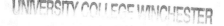